Seas

Also by Sadie Matthews

The *Seasons* Trilogy
Season of Desire
Season of Passion

The *After Dark* Series
Fire After Dark
Secrets After Dark
Promises After Dark

Sadie Matthews is the author of provocative, romantic novels that explore an intense and intimate side of life and relationships. The *After Dark* series was her first trilogy, and entranced readers with its sensual, engrossing story and unforgettable characters. The *Seasons* trilogy is her latest series, telling the story of the Hammond sisters.

Sadie Matthews is married and lives in the south-west of England.

Find Sadie Matthews on Twitter
@sadie_matthews.

Season of Longing

SADIE MATTHEWS

HODDER

First published in Great Britain in 2015 by Hodder & Stoughton
An Hachette UK company

1

A CIP catalogue record for this title is available from the British Library

Paperback ISBN 978 1 444 78122 9
Ebook ISBN 978 1 444 78123 6

Typeset in Sabon by Hewer Text UK Ltd, Edinburgh
Printed and bound by Clays Ltd, St Ives plc

Hodder & Stoughton policy is to use papers that are natural, renewable
and recyclable products and made from wood grown in sustainable
forests. The logging and manufacturing processes are expected to
conform to the environmental regulations of the country of origin.

Hodder & Stoughton Ltd
338 Euston Road
London NW1 3BH

www.hodder.co.uk

To C.B.

PROLOGUE

He's out there, just beyond this room. I imagine him, standing at the open doors, gazing out to sea. One arm is raised against the doorframe, and a gentle breeze plays through his hair. In my imagination I can walk out of here and there he is, his back turned to me, broad and muscular under his white T-shirt. I can see his dark hair ruffling slightly in the breeze and the soft dark fuzz at the top of his neck that I long to run my fingertips through.

What is he thinking as he stares out over the great stretch of the ocean to where it disappears into the horizon? The sun sinks into its navy depths, leaving streams of pink-gold light flaring out over the grey-blue clouds. It's peaceful and beautiful, the kind of scene that makes you believe, even for just a second, that everything is going to be all right.

Is he thinking about me? Perhaps he's picturing me, right now, just as I am imagining him. He knows I'm here, lying on this bed, thinking only of him.

But in my mind, I'm looking at him, drinking in the sight of his tanned skin, so smooth and warm, and the way his jeans fall over his taut muscles. I guess that beneath his T-shirt is a ripple of abdominal muscle, a broad ribcage and strong, powerful shoulders. I can even smell the musky sweetness of his scent, letting it climb into my nostrils and feed my senses with pleasure. The thought makes my mouth water. My imagination lets me walk silently towards him

1

and put my hands on the hard heat of his back. He jumps and turns round, his eyes startled.

'Hey!' he says. 'What are you doing?'

'I can't resist it,' I whisper. 'I can't resist this need. Can you?'

The dark brown eyes soften, then drop down, taking me in. His gaze wraps around me and makes my skin prickle in response. Just the way he looks at the curve of my form, the swell of my breasts, and way my lips are parted, already thirsty for him – just that sets me on fire.

'You know we can't,' he murmurs, but he's turned to face me completely. The way he stands there – his head to one side, his skin darkly shadowed with stubble, his muscular form so powerful but graceful – makes my nerves sing with desire. 'It's not allowed.'

'What's stopping us?' I breathe and take another step towards him. Now the evening breeze catches my hair, lifting a strand or two to float in the air. He puts out a hand and brushes them down. 'We're alone. What can stop us?'

His velvet-brown eyes harden with desire as we stand so close to one another. I gaze at the prickles of dark stubble scattered over his skin, and the curve of his lips, and the way his dark lashes frame his eyes under those black eyebrows.

He's the most beautiful man I've ever seen.

We move imperceptibly closer. His breath is on my cheek now and his hand is almost touching mine. My lips are ready for his touch, tingling and alive with the anticipation of it. My stomach twists with desire and I can feel the hot swelling of desire.

God, I want him. I long for him.

I can read the same thing in his face and in the way his breathing is coming faster now. The tension building between us is almost unbearable. It's been this way since the first moment we laid eyes on one another: his presence was like a punch to my gut, like running into a wall. I let my gaze travel slowly over the expanse of his chest, to his narrow waist and the black leather belt he wears. My fingers itch to unbuckle it, slip my hands inside and discover every last secret about him. My own body yearns for the touch of his fingers, the scraping of his rough stubble over my soft skin, the bite of his teeth on my most tender places, the wetness of his mouth where our juices mingle.

I'm breathing hard now as well, my pulse racing. I don't know how I'll ever resist this, when I feel pulled towards him with a force I cannot fight. I don't think I'll ever be complete if I don't press myself against him, take possession of his mouth with mine, let him wrap his arm round me and plunder my body with his.

Our gazes are locked, our lips almost touching, our fingertips buzzing with the urge to meet, stroke, caress.

'Don't fight it,' I whisper. 'Let it happen.'

A gasp of need escapes him, the brown eyes soft as molasses. 'Christ, the things you do to me,' he murmurs in a voice that sounds almost desperate. 'You know why it's not allowed. You know why it can't happen.'

'So we won't tell.' My cheek is almost against his. I feel the hot rush of his breath on my skin. *How much longer till I can have you? This is sweet agony.*

'Yeah. We won't tell. We'll never tell.'

'We'll never, never tell,' I repeat, in a low, hypnotic tone. Maybe if I say it often enough, we'll both believe that what we want is possible.

Our mouths are about to touch. My tongue is at my lips, moistening them, ready. I'm so hungry for him and I know he feels the same.

'Now,' I say, half-pleading, half-commanding. 'Please. I can't stand this. Now.'

And his eyes close, his arms wrap round me and he pulls me against him with the barely restrained strength of his desire. 'Oh my God,' he moans, 'you feel so good. I need you so badly . . .'

My eyes close too. I want only to lose myself in the dark velvet of his kiss, the warm, wet embrace of his tongue, the sweet taste of his mouth, the touch of his hands on my skin . . .

My eyes snap open. I'm staring at the wall, my heart pounding, blood racing hot through my veins. He's not here. He's out there. I can't reach him and I don't know if I ever will.

But he's right. It's not allowed. It's forbidden.

I can't ever be his.

PART ONE

CHAPTER ONE

'I'm cutting all three of you off. No more money. And I want all of you out of here too. You have to make it on your own. You've been spoiled and pampered for too long and it's going to change – as of now.'

We stare at our father in shock, unable to speak for a moment. Flora looks over at me, her eyes wide and frightened. I know what she's thinking; I always do. Perhaps it's because we're twins or perhaps it's because she shows her emotions so easily on her face, even when she's not aware of it.

It's not the money.

I know that's what is going through her mind. It's going through my mind too. I look over at my elder sister, Freya. I haven't seen her in such a long time but the joy of being reunited has been soured by this terrible confrontation. Freya is pale and bites her lower lip hard as she struggles to keep her composure. Perhaps this is hardest for her. She always seemed to suffer most during our childhood. I'm sure that, just like Flora and me, Freya doesn't care about the money either. When she walked out of here three months ago, she risked being cast out of our father's life. But none of us expected it to go this far.

I look over at my father. He's standing near the wall of glass that looks out over the stunning Alpine view. This time of year, as spring reclaims the mountains from winter's bare grandeur, the house comes into its own. Beyond my father's short stout frame, I can see the carpet of green that now covers the rocky slopes, and the patches of colour that are bright spring flowers. Out there, things are coming back to life, renewing themselves. In here, it feels as though something is dying.

I glance at Flora again. I can tell she wants to leap to her feet and let loose a fierce defence but she's restraining herself. No one wants to make this situation worse. Freya, I think, just wants to escape. I don't know how my father managed to persuade her to return, but somehow he has. Her longing to get away and back to the arms of the man she loves is written all over her face. Flora, too, has the air of someone who has left half her soul in the care of someone else. I know she's in deep, and that knowledge both frightens me and makes me feel bereft. I'm the only one alone now.

My father clears his throat and speaks again, breaking the frozen silence that fell once he made his announcement. He says, 'This doesn't change how I feel about you all. You know I love you. I'm only doing this because I think it's best for you.'

I can't help looking over at Estella. A ghost of a smile flits across her face. I bet she's loving this. It's what she's been working towards for a long time now, and she's finally succeeded in driving us and our father apart. I know she'll be triumphant because my father will be keeping more of his money for her to spend. But she doesn't realise that what breaks our hearts is the way she's taken him away from us.

Freya speaks up. 'You have a funny way of showing it, Dad.' She gets up from her place on the sofa. I've always looked up to my big sister and now she looks more impressive than ever, solemn in her black clothes, beautiful and more mature than before. 'I don't know how things ever came to this,' she says simply.

My father isn't about to back down, or consider that he might be in the wrong. 'I think you do, Freya,' he snaps back. 'Your behaviour has been little short of scandalous.'

'I fell in love,' Freya says firmly, her dark eyes fixed on our father's face. 'When did that become scandalous?'

Dad splutters a bit and then says, 'You got yourself all over the papers! You let yourself become tabloid fodder, the thing I've spent a fortune trying to prevent. And you very possibly fell for a man who is out to get his hands on your money!'

Freya's gaze slides over towards Estella, who is sitting in a chair near my father, poised and Barbie-doll perfect. 'Really?' she says softly. 'What would you know about that?'

Luckily my father doesn't hear her barbed remark. He's rattling on. 'You disobeyed me, Freya! I told you not to have anything more to do with Murray while we investigated him, and you threw that back in my face. You proved to me that you need a dose of reality, young woman. We'll see how long your love affair lasts when the money tap is turned off!'

Freya raises her eyebrows very faintly at Estella and murmurs, 'Yes. That would be interesting, wouldn't it?'

I don't know how she is restraining herself. The old Freya would have shouted and yelled and stormed off. Miles Murray must have done something extraordinary to change her into this controlled, self-possessed woman.

Is that what falling in love does to you? I wonder, and then I look over at Flora whose eyes are blazing and who is evidently agitated. *Maybe not.*

I know what she's about to do. She can't hold it in any longer, and before I can reach out a hand to stop her, she's leapt to her feet – passionate Flora, who has to say what she feels and can't hide her emotions. 'That's not fair!' she bursts out. 'Do you want to know why Freya ended up all over the papers? Didn't you ever wonder how the photographers knew exactly where she was, when she'd told nobody, not even us, where she was going? Who leaked the details of her break-up with Jacob? How did all that happen?'

I admire her spirit but I want to tell her she's wasting her time. Dad doesn't want to know and he won't believe her anyway. 'Flora,' I say, cutting in when I see her pause for breath, 'don't. It'll only make things worse.'

She looks at me, her eyes burning. 'How can it be worse? He has to know the truth about all of this!'

Dad is staring at Flora and I've never seen his expression so cold. It makes my insides tumble with nausea. *How did this happen? Why? Is it really all Estella's doing? How can one woman drive a wedge between a man and his daughters like this? Why doesn't he care enough to stop her?*

'I don't know how you dare, young lady,' Dad said in a freezing voice. 'Not after what you've done. I thought that Freya selling herself cheap to a gigolo was bad enough. But you . . .'

Flora's cheeks are staining red. With her fall of russet curls against the pink of her complexion, she looks stunning. I can tell she's mortified at the way Dad's talking to her, what he's implying. She's already told me that Estella surprised her one afternoon in Paris and made it clear she had compromising photos of Flora and intended to use them if she had to. For the first time, according to Flora,

Estella spelled out her agenda: she would protect her position at my father's side by turning him against us with whatever means necessary.

Flora is trying to control herself but her voice is tremulous and shaky. 'I don't know why you think you have the right to tell us who we can or can't see,' she begins, but Dad cuts her off with a snort.

'You're mixed up with a gangster, Flora! I stopped doing business with Dubrovski when I discovered some of what he gets up to. No doubt he's hoping to worm his way back into my good books by using your influence. Well, it's not going to work. We'll see how long he stays interested when he finds out that you don't have any influence with me at all.' Dad gives us all a sweeping look, his expression stern. 'You girls might think I'm being cruel, but you'll understand one day that I'm protecting your best interests. You'll thank me for it when you see that.'

'Andrei is not a gangster,' Flora protests, her cheeks scarlet. 'He's kind and decent and—'

Dad makes a mocking face as he shakes his head. 'You're blinded by whatever passion he's managed to inspire in you. You can't see it how it is.'

Flora almost gasps with indignation, and Freya shakes her head slowly. I want to laugh when I think about how Dad can't see the parallels with his own situation. Here he is, suspecting every man in the world of being after us for his money, while right there on a chair just a few feet away sits a woman who as good as told Flora that she gave our father a good time in return for financial security.

That's what hurts. We'd love him no matter what. But if he lost everything, Estella would drop him so quickly he wouldn't know what had hit him.

11

I suddenly find my own voice. 'What about me, Dad?' I ask quietly. 'Is there anything you want to say to me?'

He looks at me almost as though he'd forgotten about me altogether, and then his expression softens. I haven't offended him yet. And besides, he's always had a soft spot for me, maybe because I, out of all of us, look most like our mother. 'Summer,' he says, and for a moment I hear in his voice what I've always longed for: tenderness and concern. Then Estella shifts subtly in her seat and his eyes harden a little, as though he's recalling a lesson that she's taught him. 'I'm sorry, but that goes for you too. You've got used to being bankrolled. All you do is flit around the world going to parties. Well, it's going to stop from now. You have to learn to look after yourselves, and that's that.' He stares around at us one more time. 'You'll thank me one day,' he says in a tone that tells me that he's thoroughly convinced that he's acting in our best interests. 'Now, girls. You'd better go and think over what I've said.'

We meet in our sitting room, a snug place where we've always found a little warmth and privacy in the coldness of this mountain mansion of steel and glass. As we sit down, the door opens and Jane-Elizabeth comes in, her face strained and unhappy.

'Oh girls,' she says as she goes to each of us for a hug and a kiss. 'I can't believe what's going on!' She sits down on the sofa next to Flora and takes her hand. 'If you'd told me a year ago that this would happen, I would never have believed it.'

'That's because a year ago Estella didn't have the power she has now!' exclaims Flora, pink-cheeked again.

'And she didn't want to destroy us then,' Freya adds, her

expression solemn. 'But now she's made it clear that this is war.'

'Don't say that, girls,' Jane-Elizabeth says with a groan, and she goes whiter than ever. 'It shouldn't be like this.' She looks so agonised. I've never seen Jane-Elizabeth in this state: she's less plump and round than she used to be, and her face looks hollow. The grey streak at the front of her dark hair is thicker than it was last time I saw her, I'm sure. She's been like a mother to us all these years, ever since our own mother died, and my father's right-hand woman for as long as we can remember. We love her dearly. It's awful to see her so upset.

'But it is like this, no matter what we want.' Freya gets up and walks over to the fireplace, staring into the empty grate. I can tell from the whiteness of her knuckles and the clenched fist resting on the chimney piece that she feels as agitated as Flora. She's just hiding it better. 'Estella is succeeding in driving us apart from Dad.'

'Do you remember what was like when she first came here?' I ask.

Flora laughs mirthlessly. 'I certainly do – we couldn't have guessed how things would turn out.'

I picture her now: Estella, with her hourglass figure, glossy caramel hair and the big doe eyes she emphasises with lashings of mascara and eyeliner. That's not the way it was when she arrived. Then she was unremarkable, pretty when you looked hard but not in any way that drew the eye. She wore sensible navy suits, tied her mousy hair back in a ponytail and padded around in her flat shoes, deftly taking care of all our problems and never too busy to help. Estella was our personal assistant, hired when our busy lives began to take up too much of Jane-Elizabeth's time. Estella – quiet, efficient, intelligent and eager to please – was hired to help manage our hectic diaries, and for a while, everything was fine. We liked her. After all, she wasn't that much older than us and she was fantastic at organising our lives. Her ability to magic away problems was so impressive that Flora and I joked that she was some kind of witch. Flights fully booked? Not any more – Estella managed to get a seat or two. A dress sold out? She could find it in the right size and have it delivered within the day. Diary clashes were smoothed away, arguments were settled, appointments were made and in the schedule weeks in advance. She was good at her job, but maybe she got bored of looking after three spoiled rich girls and wondered why she shouldn't have a little bit of the high life too.

Along with the rest of the world, Estella knew perfectly well that our father was a billionaire, with a fortune built up from a lifetime of hard work and astute business decisions. And gradually, very gradually, she began to show her hand. It was the flirting we noticed first. The way she acted with our father changed subtly from a businesslike politeness to a playful, rather intimate style. She started to tease him, make jokes, light up when he came into the room and show a deep interest in every facet of his life. Then she started to be concerned for him. 'Are you tired, Mr Hammond? You could do with a rest, you've been working so hard! Here, come and sit down and let me get you a drink . . .' or 'Mr Hammond, you need to look after yourself or you'll wear yourself out. Here, I've brought you this wonderful tea that will settle you and calm you and give you the best night's sleep in the world . . .'

Our dad had been alone since our mother died, or if he

hadn't, we didn't know about it. We'd always secretly hoped that he and Jane-Elizabeth would get together. After all, we could see that Jane-Elizabeth genuinely adored him, even with his paunch and his bald spot and his controlling streak. It had never happened and now here was Estella, cooing and fluttering over him in a way that, frankly, looked fake. But Dad never saw it that way. He blossomed under the attention, and as he began to look at Estella differently – not just as that useful girl with the notepad and the good attitude – sure enough, she began to change. Her hair bounced around her shoulders, longer and with honey highlights that glinted in the sun. Her clothes got tighter and her heels higher, and she wore a face-full of make-up every day. I have to admit, at first we thought she looked good. I hadn't realised how pretty she was until she began to make the most of her features. But soon it was too much. She wriggled around the house in figure-hugging dresses and high heels, and it was obvious to all of us that she had an agenda. But by the time we realised that Estella was serious in her full-on flirtation with our father, it was too late. He was already hooked and didn't want to hear a word we said to warn him about her. All we girls knew was that our relationship with our father was changing in ways we didn't understand. Dad was as controlling and paranoid about our safety as ever, but the easy affection and open communication we'd had before disappeared. Estella seemed to possess him, heart and mind.

'Girls, do you really think that Estella is behind this?' Jane-Elizabeth asks, her eyes anxious.

Freya snorts. 'Of course she is. We know she has access to your email, Jane-Elizabeth. When she sent the paparazzi to spy on me with Miles, and to the hotel that I'd only told you about, it was obvious. But she's also got access to Dad's files – that was how she knew the story about my break-up with Jacob, and leaked it to the press. She was doing all she could to cause trouble between Dad and me.'

Flora pipes up. 'She tailed me in Paris too. That's how she got the photographs she threatened me with.'

Freya turns to her. 'Did she show them to Dad?'

Flora shakes her head. 'Andrei arranged to get them back.'

There's a strange moment between my sisters as they look at each other. There's something like accusation in Freya's eyes as she says, 'Did he, now? How did he do that?'

Flora looks defiant as she retorts, 'He didn't hurt anyone, if that's what you're implying.'

They stare at each other. I know that there's trouble between them, and that it's something to do with Flora's lover, Andrei Dubrovski. My heart sinks. As soon as I found out that Flora was involved with a man like him, I'd been frightened for her. But it's even more complicated than that, it seems. He has some kind of power over Freya as well, but I don't yet know what.

I get up, filled suddenly with panic. 'Please . . .' My voice is shaky. 'We mustn't fight, we have to stay together and be united. I can't bear it if we're not . . .'

They both look over at me, and the tension subsides a little. Jane-Elizabeth gets up and comes over to hug me. I take comfort from the scent of irises that she always uses and the familiar warmth of her body.

'Summer,' she murmurs. 'Don't worry, it's going to be all right. I promise.' Turning to the other two, she says, 'Summer's right, though. You mustn't let anything come between you now. If you're right about Estella – and I think you are – then there's no knowing how long this situation with your father will go on.'

Flora goes pale suddenly. 'What if . . . he marries her?'

'I bet he does,' Freya says brusquely. Then she shrugs. 'Let him. I don't want him, or his money if that's the way he's going to treat us. I don't care if I never come back here. All I want to do is get back to Miles as soon as possible.' Her eyes soften suddenly as she thinks about him. I know that she's loving her life with him in Scotland, far from everything and everybody.

'I agree,' Flora says, lifting her chin into the air. 'I intend to get back to Paris. I have to continue with my training. I still have another year at the Academie.'

I stare at her, knowing that she means it. She loves the Academie where she is training to be an actress. But she also has Andrei to return to, and the life he can offer her there. I've never felt so alone. My sisters have love in their lives, a whole other meaning to their existence. And I have no one.

Flora shakes her head. 'I just can't understand how one minute we're wrapped so tightly in cotton wool we can hardly move without Dad knowing about it, and the next, he couldn't give a damn what happens!'

Freya says darkly, 'It just shows the extent of Estella's power over him. Besides, I wouldn't put it past Dad to keep tabs on us anyway.'

Flora considers this. 'I'm not so sure. Maybe he thinks we'll be looked after by Miles and Andrei.'

There's a slightly awkward pause as it occurs to us all that there's no one to look after me, but I'm still being cut off with the others.

'There's something we've not mentioned,' I say, trying not to show I care as I go back to sit down.

Jane-Elizabeth regards me with a worried frown as she sits down in an armchair. She seems to know that I'm a mess inside, even though I'm hiding it as well as I can. I blink hard and avoid her gaze.

'What's that?' Freya asks.

'Money. Dad's cutting us off. That means no more cash on tap. Nothing to live on. Unless you girls have been more careful than me and built up a pot of savings.' I'm already wondering if Dad intends to cut off the credit cards I use without even thinking about it. I live from moment to moment, without planning for the future or questioning how the money is found to pay for things. I send bills to Jane-Elizabeth, and book hotel rooms, order food, pay for meals, and I never even think about it. A world without that security seems huge, dark and frightening.

There's a pause as my sisters stare at me, and I know what they're thinking. They both have a partner in their lives, someone to share their troubles with, and someone to turn to while they work out how to get through this. The icy coldness of isolation crawls over my skin.

I have no one.

Jane-Elizabeth says suddenly, 'I'm not sure that he can do that. Cut you off entirely, I mean.'

We all turn to look at her. 'Really?' Flora asks. I can see that she's thinking of the fees at the Academie and the cost of her life in Paris. She lives in a beautiful flat in the Marais and, like me, she's used to living a life without having to count the pennies.

Jane-Elizabeth nods. 'You've all got trust funds that your father can't touch for tax reasons. I suspect he could make arrangements to prevent you being paid anything from the funds for a while, but he'd have to get the trustees to agree.'

'I'm sure he could do that,' remarks Freya drily, 'considering they are all friends of his.'

Jane-Elizabeth thinks for a moment. 'There's something else,' she says. 'You three are on the board of the Hammond Foundation.'

We stare at her, none of us comprehending. We know about the charitable foundation our father set up but we haven't had anything to do with it so far.

'What does that mean?' asks Flora, frowning.

'You are paid a salary by the foundation,' Jane-Elizabeth says. 'It's a small one, but it's something. It will give you enough to live on while this is sorted out.' She looks solemn. 'But I'm afraid it won't go as far you're used to.'

'We'll get through . . .' Freya smiles ironically. 'Until we find proper jobs.' She laughs. 'Maybe Dad is right and we will all thank him one day.'

'None of us cares about the money,' Flora declares fervently. 'But it wasn't his idea. It was Estella's. So she could get more for herself. That's what I object to.'

'I think we're all agreed on that,' Freya replies softly.

Jane-Elizabeth looks at us, her hands clasped tightly in her lap. 'If I can do anything to help you girls, you know I will. But I don't know how long I'll be here. If Estella has her way, I think your father will be suggesting that I move on.'

I gasp and the other two look just as shocked. *Lose Jane-Elizabeth? No! Surely not . . . it would be like losing our mother all over again!* For the first time, I feel the sting of hot tears behind my eyes. 'Would she do that? Why is she threatened by you?' I ask, choked.

'Because she knows I love the three of you,' Jane-Elizabeth says simply, and none of us can reply. It's all I can do not to break down.

'We won't let it happen!' declares Freya, banging her fist down on the chimney piece.

I look up, squaring my shoulders. I muster my strength and say in a loud voice, 'You don't understand.'

They look at me. I'm usually the quiet one, the peace-maker, the listener. No one is used to me taking centre stage.

I take a deep breath. 'We don't have any power, don't you see? We have to let it go, we have to let Dad go. All we can do is make sure he knows we love him and that we'll be there for him if he needs us. From now on, we're on our own.' I gaze at my sisters and at Jane-Elizabeth. 'And I don't know about you, but I, for one, am getting out of this place as fast as I can.'

CHAPTER TWO

'Would you care for some champagne, ma'am?'

I open one eye and see the glistening white teeth and sticky red gloss of the stewardess's smile, next to the proffered bottle.

'Oh. Thanks, but . . . it's still a no.' I smile politely back, trying to hide my irritation. This is the fourth time she's been round and the fact I'm trying to sleep doesn't seem to put her off. I'll have to put on my sleep mask next, drape a blanket over myself and hope that deters her.

I want to rest. I was exhausted even before I arrived home for the awful meeting with Dad, and now I'm completely shattered. I've been partying too hard lately and it's taken a toll on me. Despite the hope that my riotous social life can give me what I'm looking for, nothing seems to shift the sadness that lives at my core.

And it's a hundred times worse now.

The chill I've felt since arriving home won't leave me. I'm always shivering and I can't seem to get warm. It's the cold I felt when the blast of loneliness blew round me as I realised that my sisters both have their lovers but I have no one to protect me as my family shatters and disappears around me. When my mother died, I was afraid that the others would be taken away too, and I clung to them. Gradually I began to trust that Dad and my sisters weren't about to leave me. But now . . . it's as though my

21

childhood nightmare is coming true. Dad has thrown us out and cut us off. He's chosen Estella over us. Somewhere deep inside me I want to scream and cry but I can't. Instead I have only this frozen feeling of cold abandonment.

But I've always had Flora. We've always had each other. Until now.

After our mother died, Freya, the oldest of us, was the most outwardly affected by the loss; she became angry and distant and tried to shut us out of her life. Flora was always more self-reliant than I was – she had her vivid imaginative world to retreat into, the place that feeds her creativity and makes her the wonderful actress she is. I became clingy, trailing around after one or another of my sisters as though I was afraid of ever being left alone again. As I grew up, I began to travel all over the world – it was easy enough with my father's money at my disposal and my social circle of international jet-setting friends. I was always looking for somewhere that would give me the feeling of belonging.

But I'm twenty-two now and I've never found it.

As we approach LAX, I get myself ready for landing, handing back my blanket and putting on my jacket. I hope that the sunny weather here can shift the cold that still prickles my skin. It was a horrible moment when we left home, all three of us taking separate paths. Freya was clearly desperate to get back to Scotland and Miles, and Flora was taking a flight back to the life she's made herself in Paris and, no doubt, Andrei Dubrovski, though she never mentioned his name. She knows how worried we all are about her relationship with a man like that: tough, self-made and perhaps not always on the right side of the law. But her affair with him is so new and fresh that she only sees the side of him he wants her to see. I hope with all my heart that she's not in for a nasty surprise.

'Please, Summer, come with me to Paris,' begs Flora, taking my hand as we prepare to go our separate ways. 'You can stay with me for as long as you want, you know that! I'd love it so much – and you'd get to know Andrei and find out what he's really like. Please?'

I gaze at her. I adore her, my crazy, talented, gorgeous twin sister, the person who knows me best in the world. It's tearing me apart that she now has someone else to share her soul with. But I'm so happy for her too. 'No,' I say softly. 'I'll come soon. But not right now.'

How can I tell her that it's too painful to see her happiness when I feel so alone? I don't have anyone to reassure me that I'm loved and it's tearing me up. And there's no way I can spoil her joy with Andrei.

I'm scared for her too. I'm scared of what Andrei really is, and of what he might do to Flora.

Her fingers tighten around mine. 'But where are you going, Summer? What will you do?'

I smile at her, wanting to reassure her that I'll be all right. I don't want her to worry about me. 'I'm going to be just fine. I'll go and see Jimmy, of course.'

Los Angeles. Heat. Light. Blue skies. Palm trees. If I can't shake off my chill here, where can I?

'Summer! Summer, honey, over here!'

I turn to see Jimmy leaping up and down, waving wildly. I laugh at his antics, just as I'm supposed to, and the next minute he's beside me, enveloping me in a huge hug and kissing my cheeks. I notice a couple of women looking at me enviously, and I can't blame them. Jimmy is

23

model-handsome, with tanned caffè-latte skin, white teeth and dark hair, and built like the champion polo player he was, not so long ago.

But you don't need to be jealous, ladies. He's not in the market for a girlfriend.

I kiss him back, relaxing into his familiar embrace. I knew that if anyone could comfort me, it would be Jimmy. He stands back and looks at me.

'You're as hot as ever, Summer Hammond! I can't believe you haven't been snapped up by now.'

I shrug. 'Straight men have no taste, I guess.'

He rolls his eyes. 'And *how*. C'mon, I've got the car out-side. Not as glamorous as you're used to, but it'll get us where we need to go.'

I shoot him a meaningful look as he starts to push my luggage trolley and he picks up on it at once.

'Uh uh. You've got news, young lady. Save it for the ride into town. You can tell me all about it.'

It's hard not to feel younger and more carefree as the car cuts through the morning sunshine, racing back to the city. The top is down on the convertible and the wind picks up my long fair hair and flicks it about. I'm wearing sunglasses and marvelling at the china-blue sky as I feel some of my troubles melt away.

I catch a glimpse of Jimmy and me in the rear-view mirror, and think how we must look like some young Hollywood couple as we fly along the highway. It's not quite like that. Sure, Jimmy is a wannabe actor who goes to as many auditions as he can, tiding himself over between acting jobs with modelling work and photo shoots, like so many of the guys in LA waiting for their big break. But when I first met him, he was our riding and polo instructor, and on the polo team of some Argentinian magnate, winning trophies for his boss all over the world. We loved Jimmy, and he became our dear friend. What made life difficult was that Flora fell deeply in love with him, to the point where Jimmy felt he had to leave and pursue the dream he'd always had of making it as an actor. It helped that he had recently acquired a boyfriend just as gorgeous, glamorous and set on LA as he was. When he broke the news to us, we were all devastated, but no one as much as Flora, who fainted dead away when she realised that not only was Jimmy leaving us, but he was gay. It was only her relationship with Andrei that finally released her from the heartbreak of knowing that the man she loved would never love her back in the same way.

'So,' shouts Jimmy over the roar of the engine and the whipping of the wind, 'what's been happening in the Hammond world? Tell me all the news.'

'We're all fine.'

'Hmm – okay. But something's up. How is the wicked step-girlfriend? Is she still up to her usual tricks?'

Jimmy's perception is pretty good. He could be a spy if he doesn't make it as an actor. 'How did you guess? She's the cat with the cream,' I call back. 'She's finally got what she always wanted.'

'She has?' Jimmy shoots me a glance and I can sense the apprehension behind his dark glasses. 'What's happened?'

'She's persuaded Dad to kick us all out. And cut off our money too. Everything she's done for the last few months has finally borne fruit. He thinks we're all spoiled and likely to fall into bed with the first gigolo who comes along. So he's decided to make sure we learn some hard lessons.'

Jimmy whistles. 'Holy crap. I can't believe it. That's not like him! He worships you girls.'

'Not any more,' I say drily.

'When I remember what he used to be like about you . . . he was terrified about a hair on your heads being hurt. I mean, I've seen some security but never like the kind your family had. I thought I was going to be microchipped, for Christ's sake.'

'If he could have, he would have!' I say brightly. 'If he could have locked us away from the world entirely, he'd have done that too.'

'He didn't want you girls to grow up,' Jimmy says sombrely.

'Well, we have, and he can't handle it. He can't handle not being able to control us like he used to.'

'He sure as hell doesn't like other men taking the number one position in your lives.' Jimmy shakes his head. 'It's textbook, man. Textbook.'

'You're right.' I sigh, and prop my chin against my fist, staring out at the approaching city. 'But I guess what happened to make him that way is not so textbook.'

Jimmy nods. 'Yeah. That's true. Not every man has to deal with what your family went through.'

We say nothing more for a while. Jimmy knows the story of what happened to us when my mother died. He's one of the few who does. It's helped him to understand my father's paranoia about our security and his need to control us.

Jimmy bursts out, 'It's crazy that he would cut you off! I just can't see it, not after the way he's been all these years.'

I look over at him, smiling sadly. 'You haven't met Estella, Jimmy. Maybe if you had, you'd understand.'

'She's gotta be some kind of hottie, that's for sure. What is she? Mata Hari, Cleopatra and Marilyn Monroe, rolled into one?'

'You're giving her a bit too much class, but you're kind of on the right lines. She's unscrupulous, smart and looking out for her own interests with a sort of paranoid mania, like we're living in Ancient Rome and the only way to deal with her enemies is to dispose of them. She wants us out of our father's life because we threaten her position – we can see right through her and we don't like the view.'

'Boy, Mary Poppins, she ain't.' Jimmy shoots me a sympathetic look. 'It's the last thing you girls need. If only your dad had found someone who could heal the rifts and the pain and make the family whole again. It's crappy that he got together with someone who's just made everything a lot worse.'

I sigh and close my eyes, relishing the way the wind buffets me as we drive. 'You can say that again, Jimmy.'

Jimmy's apartment is on Sunset Boulevard, which sounds very glamorous and as though he's in the heart of Hollywood, until you realise the Boulevard is miles long and Jimmy's place is on a ramshackle stretch, tucked behind and above a florist's shop called Gail's Petals & Blooms. Usually when I come to LA, we rent a bungalow at the Chateau Marmont and stay there together, going out on the town and living it up. I like showing Jimmy a good time, and he enjoys the high life that he knows well but can't afford on his part-time acting salary. And we always say that it's good for his career for him to be seen in the best restaurants. Because of what Jimmy calls my fame (but I

27

think of as my notoriety) as one of the Hammond heiresses, we sometimes get snapped for the gossip sites or the celeb mags, and Jimmy thinks that might help get his name out there. I'm not sure how much good it really does, but he loves it, and I love making him happy.

'I'm sorry it's not the Marmont or the Beverly Wilshire this time,' I say apologetically as he carries my bags in through the front door to the passage that leads past the shop to the apartment. 'I guess it's going to be strange getting used to the fact that my credit cards aren't going to take the strain the way they used to.'

'Are you crazy? I don't mind a bit,' Jimmy says, grinning. 'I love having you here, and it gives me the opportunity to repay a little of your hospitality. Charlie is going to love it too – he always gets so jealous when we go off together.'

'He's always welcome, you did tell him that, didn't you?' I say hastily.

'Sure, but I discouraged it!' Jimmy replies with a laugh. 'I don't want him getting too accustomed to a life we can't afford. Besides, I like keeping you to myself.'

'Well, I'm looking forward to getting to know him a bit better.' I realise with a pang that I've not really taken the trouble to become familiar with Jimmy's life in LA. I've always swooped in, whisked him off to the coolest hotel in town and done the whole thing on my terms. Maybe an upside to this whole mess is learning more about how Jimmy and Charlie really live.

Jimmy takes my bags to his tiny spare room and sets about making me tea, while I look around the apartment. It's very chic and carefully put together in a way that has obviously been done with love, patience and a limited budget. I like the way everything has a story to tell, and a reason to be there. Our homes have nearly always been decorated by interior designers, people who are wonderful at fabricating a look and providing a setting that makes the owners seem cultured, well read and with impeccable taste. None of it means anything to us, though. The pictures are from auction houses, the ornaments from department stores, the furniture carefully selected for us. We just inhabit someone else's vision of how we should live.

'So,' Jimmy says, coming back from the bright kitchen that overlooks their little courtyard garden with our tea, 'exactly how much money have you girls got? Don't tell me you're destitute. Your father wouldn't do that, would he?' He shakes his head as he sits down. 'I mean, when I think about the way you three have always lived . . . like little princesses.'

I laugh with a touch of embarrassment. 'Come on, that's overstating it a touch. And besides, it seemed normal to us. We didn't have a sense that we were anything unusual. After all, most of our friends lived in the same way.'

Jimmy nods. 'The clique of the rich. Hey, I'm not criticising you. No kid chooses its parents or its place in life. You end up where you end up, and it's up to everyone to make the best of what they get. Life ain't fair.'

'No,' I say, suddenly sombre. 'I do what I can to count my blessings.'

Is that really true? Do I count my blessings? Have I been guilty of taking everything too much for granted?

'So . . . what's the situation? What have you got?' Jimmy isn't going to let it lie.

I pick up my teacup and take a sip. It's hot and comforting, the way only tea made at home can be. Hotel tea never tastes the same, and I wonder why that is. Then I sit back on Jimmy's squashy couch and say, 'I don't really know. Jane-Elizabeth is going to write and clarify the situation for us. The credit cards will be stopped, I know that. I managed to book my flight on mine just in time. But apparently we girls are on the board of the Hammond Foundation and for that we're paid a salary.'

Jimmy looks amused. 'You're paid for doing nothing?'

I nod. 'Looks like it. Tax reasons, or something. I don't know. But it's enough that we won't starve.'

'And you're not exactly short of possessions either.'

'No ... but they're mostly in Dad's house and for the time being, we're not welcome there. So I'm going to have to find somewhere else to live.'

Jimmy frowns and sits forward in his chair as if he wants to hear better. 'Wait, let me get this straight. Your father – who hardly let you out of his sight without a bodyguard and a full itinerary – has cast you girls off, just like that. You're banned from his houses?'

'I don't know if he'd describe it like that. I don't think we're banned – but we're supposed to go out and make it on our own somehow. He's had enough of us living off his money and doing nothing to earn it.' I laugh ironically. 'I mean, it's a healthy idea. I just wish he'd given us a bit of notice of his intentions.'

'So what are you going to do?' Jimmy looks like he's finally realising that my gilded life has come to an end. 'You've got a college degree, right? You can get a job.'

I nod. I went to Brown University here in the States, which is why I've always felt so at home in America, and why I slip into an American accent almost as soon as I land. My sisters are more British than anything else, but I've always felt American. We spent a lot of our childhood in Connecticut when our father was building up his business here. Flora always hankered for Europe but I loved America, and came back as soon as I could after we moved to Switzerland. 'I don't know what kind of a job a degree in literature will equip me for, but I'm going to do my best to find one. I guess I'll have to.'

'But you've got a job,' Jimmy says with a grin. 'For the Hammond Foundation, right?'

'Yeah.' I laugh. 'If I had a clue what the Foundation does. It's in Paris, anyway. Or at least, the headquarters are.'

'You better investigate it. It could be interesting.'

'Maybe.'

'But I want you to get a job here,' Jimmy says, looking excited. 'It'll be such fun, hanging out together. It'll be great.'

'Live here?' I hadn't really thought of that. LA is a place where I come to relax and party. I've never imagined I could stay and make a life in this city.

'Why not? Where were you thinking of going?'

'I . . . I don't know . . . I guess somewhere in Europe. I mean, Flora is in Paris. That's so far away from here . . .'

Jimmy gives me a look and says, 'I know you guys are twins and you need each other but you've not had a problem with flitting around the world without her before.'

'That's different. I wasn't settled somewhere so far away,' I say. A feeling of bleakness overcomes me.

'Hey.' Jimmy has seen the look on my face and picks up on it instantly. 'What's wrong? You looked so tragic just now that it nearly broke my heart. Is there something up with Flora? Is she okay?'

'She's fine. But . . .' I look away. I feel like a heel for not being overjoyed at my sister's happiness.

'Her love life is coming between you.' Jimmy knows. He always does. It's one of the reasons I love him.

'I'm happy for her, but I can't help feeling that it's taken her away from me. I know that's selfish. I feel dreadful. But once we were always there for each other. We spoke every day. Now . . . I don't hear from her for days at a time and I know it's because she's with him and that she's forgotten about me completely.'

'It's tough,' Jimmy says, sympathetically. 'You're not selfish. It's normal to feel that way when you've been so close.'

I manage a smile. 'I still feel like a lowlife. Believe me.'

Just then the door to the street slams and there are footsteps in the hall. Jimmy looks up towards the passage with a smile. 'Oh great,' he says, 'Charlie's back from the market. I hope he remembered the coffee, we're completely out.'

A second later, a well-built man in a white T-shirt and jeans saunters through the door, a paper bag full of groceries in his arms. He's got short sandy-blond hair and a tan, his eyes concealed behind aviator shades. 'Well, hey!' he says as he sees me. 'Our visitor is here! Hi, Summer, how are you?'

'Hi, Charlie. I'm great, thanks.' I stand up to greet him, and he puts down the groceries and holds out his arms. I've always liked Charlie, though I don't know him very well. He and Jimmy haven't been together all that long. He's certainly in good shape – his biceps look like they've been inflated with a bicycle pump. He must put in some hours in the gym, that's for sure.

'I was just talking about you,' Charlie says, kissing me on both cheeks. He turns to look over his shoulder into the passage. 'Hey, Jack, don't be shy! C'mon in!'

I follow his gaze and a second later, another man walks into the room. I catch my breath. I can't help it. He's the most gorgeous guy I've ever seen in my life.

CHAPTER THREE

'Hi Jack,' says Jimmy, and I catch a certain something in his voice – a kind of reservation – but I'm too busy staring to take much notice.

This guy is younger than Jimmy and Charlie – he's about my age, I guess, in his early twenties – and there's something heart-stopping about him. His eyes are chocolate-brown and as soft as velvet. His straight thick eyebrows match the dark hair above. His skin is an olive-brown, dotted with dark stubble around his jaw, and his face almost too beautiful. Even though we're in a town where there are scores of handsome men, he's stand-out gorgeous. I catch myself staring at him – I know it's rude, but I can't help it. What is it that makes him so attractive? Is it the regularity of his features? He's got the nose and chin of a perfect Renaissance statue, and a bone structure that mixes strength with delicacy. Is it the almost black hair and the impossibly brown eyes, the colour of a cup of coffee with just a splash of milk in it? Is it the way his lips, unsmiling, have a brooding cast, and the way he stands with a faintly defiant turn to his shoulders? He's not tall or built like a muscle man, but he's got incredible presence. Whatever it is, I can't stop looking at him, and then I realise that I'm gazing right into those mesmerising eyes with a stupid expression on my face, and I instantly look away, embarrassed.

Get a grip, Summer, you're making a fool of yourself.

Charlie hasn't noticed; he's unloading the groceries while he talks on. 'Jack, this is our friend Summer, who I was telling you about. Summer, Jack is a friend of mine. We met in the gym a while back and got talking, the way you do around here.'

'Oh, right. That's interesting,' I say, and risk looking back at him. He's still looking straight at me and at once, my insides do a kind of upward leap followed by a somersault. *Oh my goodness, I've never responded to anyone like this before. Not before we've even exchanged a word.* I can hardly look at him and I can hardly bear not to. It's a curious position to be in. I must look an idiot. I force myself to take his gaze and return it. 'Nice to meet you, Jack,' I say, trying to sound as normal as possible.

At last he speaks, but, I notice, still doesn't smile. Just carries on staring at me in that intense way that's setting my insides on a slow burn. 'Hello,' he says. 'Good to meet you too.'

He has an accent: American mixed with something else I can't identify. I drop my gaze to the floor and sit back on the couch. When I glance up, it's to find Jimmy looking at me hard, one eyebrow slightly lifted. At once I feel my colour rise. Jimmy always knows exactly what I'm thinking, which means he'll be under no illusion that the presence of the guy who walked through the door has hit me with the force of a truck.

'Are you an actor?' I ask in a sudden breathless rush. Surely he is. He's got heart-throb written all over him, with the kind of face that would gaze moodily out of posters on thousands of teenage bedroom walls.

'No,' Jack replies. 'I'm not an actor.'

I'm confused and don't know what to say. I thought that

with looks like his, he must be an actor – just about every-body in this town is, after all. I want to ask if he's a model but that makes it so obvious I think he's gorgeous that I don't. 'Okay,' I say lamely.

'Jack's a designer,' Charlie supplies. Jimmy is still watching the exchange without saying anything. I wish he would help me out somehow.

'Oh right,' I say, and of course it all becomes clear. He's a designer, he hangs out with Charlie and Jimmy, and they met in the gym, probably while bodybuilding. *You idiot. He's gay, of course. No man is that beautiful and straight.* As soon as I think it, something almost like relief washes over me. I don't have to worry about the mad attraction that's just possessed me. It will fade and disappear and I'll be able to appreciate his looks without feeling this burn of breathless desire. *He designs dresses, I expect, for skinny girls with no tits or ass. So that's me out.* I'm about to ask if he's designed for anyone I'd have heard of, when Jimmy speaks up.

'Jack, it's great to see you but we're taking Summer out for lunch in a while. We have so much to catch up on. We'll see you around, maybe?'

Jack still has that dark-brown, utterly seductive gaze resting on me, as though he's drinking in the sight of me. It makes my skin prickle and burn where he looks. *I guess my body is having a hard time catching up with the knowledge that he's not interested in me. But why is he staring like that?*

'Jack?' repeats Jimmy more loudly, and Jack seems to jump a little. He blinks hard and looks over at Jimmy. 'We're going out now, so we'll catch you later. Okay?'

'Yeah. Sure.' Jack looks over at me again. 'Nice to meet you.' His voice is interesting – not deep, but with a low rasp in it, and I still can't work out what that accent is. It's really sexy though.

Summer – he's gay! Get over it.

Still, I can't ignore the waves of attraction crashing through me. It's been a while since I've had a boyfriend; maybe my body is telling me I need to find someone sooner rather than later. My social circle is not that wide in many ways, and a lot of the boys I see at various parties are too spoiled and immature for my tastes. When I look at some of them, I get my father's point about being given too much. They are such kids and I don't know how they're ever going to grow up when they've got no responsibilities and everything in life is just handed to them on a plate.

'Nice to meet you too,' I say and smile awkwardly.

Jack turns and heads out down the passage, Charlie going after him to let him out.

I try to avoid Jimmy's piercing gaze but he isn't about to keep quiet. 'So,' he says wryly. 'Looks like Jack had quite an effect on you.'

I make a face at him. 'C'mon, Jimmy. He's pretty amazing-looking, you have to give me that. I was a bit overwhelmed by it.'

'Right,' says Jimmy, still scrutinising me, a slight frown across his brow. 'Just be careful, that's all.'

'You really don't have to worry,' I return, smiling. 'Do you have a problem with him?'

Jimmy's frown deepens. 'I don't know. I shouldn't – I don't even know the guy. But there's something about him . . . something I don't trust. I just can't quite see why he and Charlie are friends, is all. I mean, I can see why Charlie likes Jack – you're right, he's a complete knockout – but it's the other way round I can't fathom.'

'Nice!' I say with a laugh. 'I won't tell Charlie you said that!'

Just then, Charlie comes back into the room, a cross look on his face. 'Jimmy, that was so rude! You practically asked him to leave the premises!'

'No I didn't,' Jimmy says calmly.

'Yes, you did. You could have asked him to join us for lunch,' Charlie retorts.

'That's the point. I don't want him to join us for lunch. Summer's only just arrived. I'm not going to share her yet.'

Charlie harrumphs a bit, but he seems to see Jimmy's point. 'I guess we can see Jack anytime,' he concedes. 'So – where are we going for lunch? Are you hungry, Summer?'

I smile at him, feeling on a more even keel now that Jack has left. I'm happier too – here in this sunny apartment with my two friends, and time with them stretching out in front of me. 'Starving,' I say firmly. 'Let's eat.'

Not surprisingly, Charlie and Jimmy know all the best places to go in LA – the restaurants that have just opened, the old classics and the ones worth trying because they're kooky and different. Today, we're at one of Charlie and Jimmy's favourites, where the chef's salad has a near mythic status. We sit in a pretty courtyard at the back of the restaurant at a wrought-iron table and we all order the legendary salad, which comes in huge bowls and includes smoked chicken, snippets of anchovy and tiny soft-boiled salted quail's eggs. Just as I was promised, it's delicious. The boys amuse me with their gossip and easy repartee, as they wind each other up for my entertainment, parrying and returning each other's barbed remarks. I can feel the weight of misery I've been carrying around with me beginning to lift a little.

'So Summer, Jimmy tells me you've been having a bad time of it lately,' Charlie says, chasing a stray romaine lettuce leaf around his bowl. 'I'm sorry to hear that.'

I shrug. I don't mind confiding in Jimmy, but I find it hard to open my heart to anyone I don't know really well. Perhaps the years of my father's paranoia about strangers and keeping out the big bad world has had an effect on me; perhaps it's soaked into my DNA, and has left me incapable of trusting anyone. 'You know,' I say cheerfully. 'A lot of people have it harder.'

'True.' Charlie spears the lettuce leaf and lifts it up on his fork, examining it thoughtfully. 'Life could be a lot worse than this, right?'

'Here's to that,' rejoins Jimmy, lifting his glass of coconut water. He smiles over at me. 'You could be happy here, Summer. I hope we're going to persuade you to stay.'

I think suddenly of Flora in Paris, and wonder what she's doing and if she's thinking about me. *I'll call her later.* I get a flash of her walking hand in hand with Andrei Dubrovski, the man who's stolen her heart in such a spectacular fashion. I've seen him only a couple of times in my life, and of course I was struck by his huge magnetism, but I was wary of the cold cast of his blue eyes and the way he seemed to hold his aggression only just at bay, letting it simmer somewhere deep inside him. Is this really the man that Flora loves? But more than that, is he capable of loving her back? He looks as though tenderness and sweetness are entirely alien concepts. My sister needs all those things; she has a hungry soul.

But Flora's no fool. She wouldn't give herself to a man who would hurt her. Would she?

'Hello?' Jimmy waves at me across the table. 'Paging Summer Hammond. Are you there?'

I smile back. 'Sorry ... sorry ... I was suddenly miles away.'

'You weren't thinking about our visitor this morning, were you?' Jimmy asks with a look that has the tiniest quality of slyness about it. 'The way you looked at Jack ... I've seen looks like that on rabbits when they see snakes.'

Charlie nudges him. 'Hey. That's not very nice. Jack isn't a snake.'

Jimmy munches on his salad and says, 'Maybe.'

'I don't know what you've got against him,' Charlie says in an exasperated tone. 'He's done nothing to offend you, as far as I know.'

I relinquish thoughts of Flora and listen to them, my interest spiked. I've been wondering what place Jack has in their world and why Jimmy has reservations about him.

'I don't have anything against him as such,' Jimmy says. 'I just find him kind of weird, that's all. Why does he hang out with us? He doesn't seem to enjoy himself all that much, but he's always about. At least, he is lately.'

'He's shy.' Charlie looks obstinate. 'You haven't spent the time I have with him. He's really sweet. Once he comes out of his shell and starts to smile ... well, you'll understand when you see it.'

'Have you got a crush on him?' demands Jimmy, putting his fork down and fixing his partner with a look. 'I bet you have!'

'Jimmy, honey ...' Charlie smiles patiently. 'He's a beautiful specimen, we can all admit that, and when beautiful specimens fix you with their heartbreaking brown eyes and smile at you like you've just made their day, I'd defy anyone not to have a little heart judder. But ... I have my very own brown-eyed boy right here, and he's all I want in the world. You're just as gorgeous and a hundred times more my type of guy.'

It looks as though calm has returned to the world as Jimmy smiles and blows him a kiss. 'Thanks. Ditto.'

I'm glad that Jimmy has been diverted from my reaction to Jack but none of my curiosity about him has been satisfied. I have no idea why I should want to know more about him, but I do.

'I just hope you'll be nice to Jack tomorrow at the party, that's all,' Charlie continues, as he leans back in his seat and waves to the waitress for more ice water.

'Is he coming to Sasha's?' asks Jimmy.

'Sure he is. I asked Sasha if he could come, and she said yes. So I'll expect he'll be there.'

Jimmy makes a face. 'I'll be nice, sure, but I just don't get it. He hardly says a word. How come he wants to come to all these parties? I mean, our friends tend to be pretty loud and keen for airspace. What does he get out of it?'

'Relax. I thought you liked an audience. Maybe he enjoys all the witticisms and hilarity.'

'Yeah, I noticed that.' Jimmy shakes his head and laughs. 'Are you coming to Sasha's, Summer? It's a pool party out in Laurel Canyon.'

'Yes. Yes, of course,' I say. 'I wouldn't miss it for anything.'

It's strange to be someone's guest in such a small apartment. The guest room is also the study and I'll be sleeping on a fold-out bed surrounded by bookshelves and a desk. I'm used to bigger spaces than this, houses with guest wings or bungalows in the grounds for visitors, or huge hotel suites with plenty of room to spread out, and people on hand to clean, cook, serve and hold open doors.

'Well, I guess you've fallen out of your gilded nest with a bump,' I say to myself, catching sight of my reflection in the mirror on the wall. *Do I look different? Does suddenly being demoted from an heiress show on my face?* So far I look the same, a heart-shaped face with a chin my father always described as obstinate; blue eyes, the lightest in the family – although I always think there's more than a hint of the greenish tinge that Flora has; long fair hair that gets a helping hand from the hairdresser to keep it glinting honey-gold. *Oh my goodness – will the hairdresser have to go? How much does it cost to get it done?* I'm vague about things like this – I usually just hand over a card and wait for the machine to churn out the little ticket that says I've paid. How much I've paid has never mattered before. But twice a week I have my hair blow-dried into golden billows that float around my shoulders, and every six weeks, highlights are applied. *I'll email Jane-Elizabeth,* I think, seeing the spark of anxiety in my own eyes. *She'll know what to do.*

Or – says a little voice in my head – *you could learn how to stand on your own two feet and work out how you're going to afford the things in life you're used to. And how many of them really matter.*

Instantly, I feel better. So I won't be going to Rodeo Drive to shop on this trip. So what? At home, I have closets of clothes and shoes and bags, and yet I always seem to travel with the same things in my suitcase. *We'll see how much I miss them.*

I get into my pyjamas and climb on the rickety fold-out bed. I'm exhausted, I realise. I travel so frequently that I don't give jet lag time to catch up with me, and I'm lucky that usually I can sleep anywhere. But tonight, I feel as though I'm weighted down with concrete blocks on me. So much has happened in the last few days, and the emotions have taken their toll. Despite my bravado and determination to make it on my own, I still feel a huge and miserable darkness inside. Except that a small light flickers inside me, like a lone candle in a dungeon.

I'm going to see Jack at the pool party.

What – the gay guy? I say to myself sternly. *Summer, you do not want to get into the same situation that Flora was in! She wasted years on an empty passion for a man who could never love her back. You know how that ends.*

I lie back on the pillows, staring at the books on the shelves opposite me. Jimmy has eclectic tastes: biographies of Hollywood greats sit next to tomes on Renaissance art and heavyweight history and philosophy. I know it's hopeless but nevertheless I can't help the surge of excitement I feel when I recall Jack's face. His presence affected me so strongly and I can still feel the ripples of it.

I've liked people from afar but I've never let anyone get close enough to find out if it was the real thing or not. My father's paranoia bred in me a wariness of other people's motives. If I suspected a guy was cheating on me, or flirting with other girls, that was it. I saw the way some girls gave themselves away easily, and how they were taken advantage of. Maybe they had a good time and didn't mind the way they were treated, but I never wanted that for myself. As a result, my relationships were few and far between. Too many guys gave up on me when I didn't sleep with them right away. There were a couple I adored from afar, but when I got to know them, my idols turned out to have feet of clay. There were guys that I considered sleeping with, just so I could find out what all the fuss was about, but in the end, it didn't happen. I didn't want my first time to be at some drunken party on a yacht, or on some strange bed in a place I barely knew.

Well, it's not going to happen with Jack either. You can be sure of that.

CHAPTER FOUR

The next morning, a message is waiting for me from Jane-Elizabeth.

Hello, Summer darling
I hope you're all right. I'm worried about you. You looked so miserable when you left here. If it's any consolation, the house is empty and bleak without you all and I think your father will soon regret what he's done. However, in the meantime, we have to keep on as best we can. Your credit cards have now been stopped, I'm afraid. But you're to let me know if you're in serious need. You'll be receiving a small salary from the Foundation, and your father considers this enough to live on while you look for a job. I'll send the details in an attachment.

Please keep in touch. I can still arrange travel for you if you need it and you know I'll do anything I can to help. If you need your things, let me know and I'll send them. I've sent the same information to Flora and Freya.
Lots of love
Jane-Elizabeth

My eyes fill with tears as I read the message. I can feel her affection in every word. It amazes me that my father can't see that Jane-Elizabeth is worth her weight in gold – she's the woman who has anchored our family over the years since we lost our mother. He doesn't even know how much he needs and relies on her. One day she won't be there and then he'll find out. The thought causes me actual physical pain as I imagine Jane-Elizabeth not being a part of our lives, and I send her back a quick message thanking her and promising to keep in touch.

I wonder how much my salary is. Even though I'm grateful to have it, I feel guilty that I'm doing nothing to earn it. My father wants us to support ourselves and yet here we are, still getting money for nothing.

I'll give mine up as soon as I start earning. Though what I'm actually going to do, I have no idea . . .

'Summer! Coffee's ready!'

Jimmy's voice comes up the stairs to the guest room, and I jump out of bed. 'Coming!' I shout. 'Give me a moment!'

Five minutes later, I'm in the kitchen sipping on fresh coffee and watching motes of dust dance in the sunbeams falling in through the window. The sunlight cheers me up and makes me feel hopeful again.

'Did you sleep okay?' Jimmy asks. He looks like he's just come back from a modelling shoot, he's so handsome in a dazzling white T-shirt and baggy cotton trousers, his dark hair tousled.

'Yes, thanks, perfectly,' I say brightly. I did, too. Ten hours of absolute blankness. 'I needed it.' I look around the kitchen. 'Where's Charlie?'

'He's gone out early. It's his morning for working at the Hall.'

'The Hall?'

'Yeah. It's a community programme downtown. The Hall

46

is for kids who've been mixed up in gangs and crime and drugs. The usual stuff. It's an outreach scheme to help them change their lives. Charlie goes down once a week to serve breakfast and do what he can.'

'Wow.' I look at Jimmy over the top of my coffee cup. 'That's very good of him.'

Jimmy nods. 'He has his reasons – he was in trouble himself when he was younger, but he managed to get through it. Now he gives a little back to help other kids like him.'

I blink, thinking about how you can't know anything about people just from looking at them. Charlie never seemed to me like the kind of person who might have been into crime or drugs when he was younger. 'He's a good man.'

Jimmy's expression softens. 'The best. I'm really happy.' Then he shoots me a meaningful look. 'But what are we going to do about you?'

'What do you mean?' I'm wary at once. I don't like talking about my personal life, even to Jimmy.

'Freya is loved up with her bodyguard; Flora's in the grip of her Russian passion. But how about you?'

'I'm fine,' I say a little gruffly. 'There's no need to worry about me.'

'Really?' Jimmy eyes me quizzically. 'You don't seem fine.'

'Is that surprising?' I roll my eyes. 'You know what's going on with my family. I don't need a relationship to complicate everything even more.'

'Maybe it would make things easier.'

'Yeah, right. Of course. That's what they say about relationships. They're easy.'

'Summer . . .' Jimmy's so gentle all at once. 'You don't need to be so defensive. It's okay. What are you scared of?'

'I'm not scared of anything,' I shoot back, still sounding defiant even though I don't want to act this way with Jimmy.

'It seems a little like it.' He puts his hand out and rests it on my arm in a comforting gesture. 'I'm worried about you. You act like falling in love is something to be afraid of.'

'I guess I haven't been very lucky in love so far, that's all.' I shrug lightly, wondering why I find this so hard to talk about. 'The guys I've liked have turned out to be jerks. You can't blame me for being a little cynical.'

'So you haven't met the right guy yet.' He smiles. 'That can happen. But someone is out there for you. You can find him if you want to.'

'Maybe.' I drop my gaze and sip my coffee. I don't want him to see that I am afraid. I've learned to trust no one from outside our circle and I don't know how I'll ever overcome that.

'There's Sasha's party tonight,' Jimmy goes on. 'Maybe you'll meet someone there.' He grins at me. 'Then there'll be all the more reason for you to stay here with us.'

I laugh. 'Keep hoping, Jimmy! You never know.'

But the little voice in my head tells me that it will never happen.

To my surprise, another message arrives from Jane-Elizabeth that afternoon and I read it on my phone as I sit in the cosy armchair in Jimmy's sitting room.

Summer, dear,
I'm having trouble getting hold of Flora. Do you know
where she might be? She's not answering my emails.
Let me know if you've heard from her.
J-E x

At once, I'm filled with panic. A flood of fear washes over me, and my hands begin to shake. I gasp and my breath starts to come in short, frightened bursts. Jimmy looks up from the sofa where he's reading his iPad.

'Are you okay?'

'It's Flora,' I say, my voice coming out high-pitched and scared. 'Jane-Elizabeth can't get hold of her.'

Already various scenarios are dashing through my mind, and I start imagining the worst.

'Okay . . .' Jimmy's voice is calm and soothing. 'I'm sure it's nothing to worry about. Have you been in touch with her lately?'

'No!' I start flicking through my other messages, looking to see when I last heard from Flora. There was one message to say she was back in Paris, and another with a photo attached of her in costume for a play at the Academie, taken as she posed in front of the dressing-room mirror. That was yesterday. I haven't spoken to her since we parted at home. I have a sudden flash of the way she and Freya looked at one another, and remember the sense I had of something going on between them that I didn't know about.

'So call her,' suggests Jimmy. 'Before you start to worry. It's only about ten o'clock at night in Europe.'

'Yes . . .' I say breathlessly. 'Good idea.' I speed dial her number. It takes ages to connect, and then it rings. I'm sure her voicemail is about to click in when at last she picks up.

'Summer?' Her voice is muted, as though she's trying to talk quietly.

I'm so relieved, releasing a long breath and running my hand through my hair. 'Flora! Are you okay?'

'Yes. Why shouldn't I be?'

'Jane-Elizabeth said she couldn't get hold of you. I was worried.'

'Oh. Yes. I should have got back to her. The thing is . . . I'm not in Paris at the moment.'

'Really?' I blink with surprise. Jimmy is watching me, and he raises his eyebrows, evidently curious about what Flora is saying. 'You were there yesterday, weren't you?'

'Yes.' She sounds evasive.

'So where are you now?'

'We're on our way to England. On Andrei's plane.'

'England? Why?'

'I . . . I can't really explain right now,' she says. 'Can we talk later?'

'But you're all right?' I ask, feeling anxious again. *Why can't she talk freely? Is she in danger?* 'If you're not and you need help, say "I love London town".'

For a reply, she starts to laugh quietly. I feel a little hurt as she says, 'Oh, Summer, I'm fine. But Andrei's asleep in the seat opposite and I don't want to wake him. You're as paranoid as Dad.'

'Maybe,' I say with a bit more force. 'But Dad was right to be paranoid – wasn't he?' She says nothing and I carry on. 'So, is there something going on between you and Freya? Are you two quarrelling about something?'

There's another pause, and an unaccustomed feeling of anger rushes through me. Flora and I never used to have secrets from one another but ever since Andrei Dubrovski came into our lives, I've felt her pull away from me, and known there are things going on she's not explaining. I hate the way that makes me feel. 'Flora? Are you there?'

'Summer, I really can't talk right now.' There's a slight impatience in her voice that cuts me to the quick. 'I'll call you later. When I can. Tomorrow probably.' She pauses and adds, 'Please don't worry about what's happening with Freya. I'm sorting it all out and I'll explain when I see you. Bye, hon.'

With that, she disconnects the call. I hold the phone to my ear, frozen. Jimmy notices my aghast expression, comes over and puts his arm around me. 'Hey – are you all right?'

'She . . . she rang off. She's in the air.'

'Oh. Well, she'll call back, won't she? You don't have to look so tragic, Summer. Nothing bad has happened.'

I shake my head. 'I can't get rid of this feeling, though. I'm sure something is up, and I don't like whatever it is.'

'Honey, you have enough going on in reality to worry too much about something imaginary.' Jimmy smiles comfortingly. 'Now, how about catching a movie before the party tonight?'

It's a balmy Hollywood evening, with a navy sky darkening towards midnight velvet and the lights beginning to sparkle all over the city. It's only just after seven and we're already on our way to Laurel Canyon in Jimmy's car.

'It's so early,' I say. Charlie's given me the front seat so my hair doesn't get too mussed up by the wind. 'I wouldn't usually think of arriving at a party till nine.'

'It's Hollywood, baby,' Jimmy says with a grin. 'We start early because everyone pretends they have to be up at four for their make-up call on set. You'll see who's really working

51

– they won't drink and they'll leave at ten to get to bed. Everyone else is faking!'

We cruise through downtown LA and towards the hills in the north-east. It's a glamorous city, that can't be denied, and it throbs with youth and ambition and money and business, and the great cycle of making and fulfilling dreams and desires. Anyone you pass on the pavement could be the next movie legend or the surprise winner at the Academy Awards. It might be some struggling writer just putting the finishing touches to his screenplay, or an agent about to get his chance at a major agency. Then there are all the others, who don't get the glory but who are needed in the huge industry that is motion pictures: make-up artists, dressers, runners, electricians, cameramen, scene dressers, sound men, editors, carpenters, photographers, builders, costume makers, designers, animators, special effects, lighting . . . it makes me dizzy just to think about it. No wonder this city is so huge, so busy, so awake.

Out in the hills the scenery changes; below us LA stretches out vast and twinkling, and above, lights shine between trees, showing where massive mansions are spread out, shielded by foliage. The road snakes upwards past one huge set of gates after another.

'How was the Hall?' I ask Charlie, turning to look at him.

'Yeah, very good,' he replies. 'There're a couple of kids there I keep an eye out for. They've got hard lives, you know. Take Jackson. He's one of eight kids, and his dad is nowhere to be seen. His mom scrapes by on welfare and they live in a tiny apartment. Jackson has done badly at school and got in with a bad crowd, which in turn got him into trouble with the law. He's one offence away from prison, and that would be a disaster for him. I don't think there'd be any coming back from that for him. That's why I'm working so hard to keep him focused on what life can give him if he gets away from all that shit. But it's not easy when crime seems to offer a quick route to what hard work will take years to achieve.'

The other side of life here, away from the dream factory. Kids in a city with no prospects, surrounded by what they can't have.

'I admire what you do, Charlie,' I say fervently.

'Don't,' he says with a shrug. 'Anyone can do what I do. And I know how lucky I am.'

I feel guilty suddenly. I was born to the kind of material security most people can only dream of. I'm the luckiest girl in the world, right? *It doesn't work like that . . . and anyway, I'm not rich any more.* But in my heart I know that I'm still a million miles from the kind of poverty that the kids at the Hall live with.

Jimmy breaks the slightly uncomfortable pause. 'Hey, here we are!' As we pull in through the gates towards the house, Jimmy says, 'Sasha's a pretty successful underwear designer and ex-model. You'll love her. You'll know people here, too.'

Jimmy pulls up on the paved circle in front of the house and we get out of the car. I straighten my dress and make sure my hair isn't too wild. Only a week ago, I would have arrived here eager to see my friends and ready to party. Now I feel different, as though I've come in disguise as my old self when in reality everything has changed. *Now that I'm not an heiress, do I deserve to be here?*

The thought won't leave me as we enter the large, Spanish-style house. It's already packed and Jimmy is in full sparkle mode, greeting people effusively with kisses and exclamations. He introduces me to lots of people and most of them instantly recognise my name, lighting up with interest and looking at me curiously.

I feel a fraud. If they knew what's happened to me, would they be so interested? Now I'm just an ordinary girl with a living to earn, will they care? Without Dad's money, will the paps take my picture, or the magazines want to feature me? Will all those invitations keep flooding in? I don't have to search very hard for the answer. Of course they won't.

Then something else occurs to me.

And without that money, no one is going to want to threaten us, or hurt us.

As I wander through the party, with its crowds of glamorous partygoers, I start to feel the strangest emotion: freedom. Can the loss of my inheritance liberate me from the fear that's dogged me since I was a girl?

How great would that be? Imagine – I could learn to trust people and maybe this gnawing anxiety I've had for so long would finally leave me …

I'm smiling, though I hardly realise it. I've left Jimmy and Charlie behind, chatting happily with their many friends, and wandered out of the house to the pool area, on to one of the terracotta-paved terraces, my slender heels a little unsteady on the uneven surface. There are people standing around the bar area, or sitting on loungers that have been draped in throws. Lanterns glow around the edge of the pool area, and the water shines an undulating luminous turquoise.

'You look happy.'

I jump and turn to see who has spoken, but the voice sends a ripple of recognition across my shoulder blades. It's deep and raw-sounding, with a kind of crack in the higher notes. I respond to that voice in a way that's almost elemental: even though it's new to me, it feels as though I've always known it. I blink. The light from the pool's translucence has made the darkness even blacker, and all I can make out is a shape emerging from it. Then my vision begins to adjust and I can see who it is.

Jack.

My insides do the kind of somersault I haven't experienced since one of our nannies took us to the funfair and let us ride on the giant roller coaster. She wasn't supposed to and when news of the trip leaked out, she vanished. Another of the disappeared in my life. Right now I feel that strange, exhilarating mixture of excitement and fear, that sense of being out of control as the summit approaches and with it the inexorable plummet into the unknown. My knees feel weak and I fight to regain control of myself. 'Oh,' I say, trying to sound natural. 'Hi. How are you?'

He's taking shape, and now that I see him again, he's twice as gorgeous as I remembered. The velvet-brown eyes glimmer in the darkness, and the lantern light gives him black hollows below his cheekbones and under the curve of his lip.

'I'm fine. How are you?'

I nod stupidly. The sight of him is making my brain whirl and I can't process my thoughts properly. 'Good. Thanks.'

We stand there, looking at each other in the warm darkness. Reflections from the pool flicker over his face, illuminating his eyes for an instant. He says nothing, just stares at me in that curious way of his. Usually people look at me with interest – who is she, this Hammond heiress?

55

– and I know they're sizing me up. But this man is both more detached and more intense. I can't make him out.

'Are you having a good time?' I ask, feeling the need to fill the silence between us.

'Sure. Are you?'

'Yes,' I reply. But I can't help thinking, *we look like the loneliest people here. Both of us.* And all at once I'm filled with the sense that I'm more like this man, this complete stranger, than I am like any of the other guests. A feeling of kinship rises up in me and without thinking, I smile at him, a proper, warm, friendly smile. Flora always says my smile is my best feature. Like the sun coming out, she says. Maybe she's right because as I smile I see something in his face change. He looks surprised, almost perplexed, and then he smiles back, as though he can't help but respond. Watching his mouth move is a delicious experience, and as I notice the way his whole face softens, something melts inside me. Then I see that he's holding two bottles of beer, and he's handing one to me.

'You haven't got a drink,' he says. 'Would you like one of these?'

'Thanks.' I take it, the bottle cold and wet in my fingers.

'Would you like to sit down somewhere?'

'Yes . . . let's do that.' I've recovered enough of my equilibrium to be able to walk fairly easily. We go to the loungers and sit down. Mine is covered in a white fur throw, and I relish the softness against my bare legs; I'm wearing one of my short white party dresses, the kind that can be scrunched up into my handbag and then still look great when I've unrolled it and put it on. A burst of laughter from the group on the other side of the pool makes us both look over.

'Do you know many people here?' I ask.

Jack shrugs and takes a swig from his beer bottle. 'A few,' he says. 'Jimmy and Charlie, of course. One or two others. How about you?'

'The same. I know a few faces. I come to LA quite a lot to visit Jimmy and he always brings me to a few of his parties. His friends seem very welcoming.'

Jack stares at me and then says, 'Yeah. I guess.'

Wow. You're a man of few words, aren't you? I'm a little surprised at how quiet he is. I had the distinct feeling that he'd come to find me. The disturbing quality of his nearness has worn off a little now and I'm able to talk to him more normally. 'So, you haven't known Charlie and Jimmy long, have you?'

'No,' he says. 'They're good guys.' A little smile plays on his lips.

'What's funny?'

'Oh. Nothing.' The smile fades away, leaving him looking as moody as ever. It must be something about the way his mouth is in repose. Whatever, he looks just as gorgeous whether he's smiling or not. I prefer the smile, but there's something intriguing about the air of sadness I can sense around him.

'What's your accent?' I ask.

Jack looks surprised. 'You can hear an accent?'

'Just faintly. Something in your voice . . .' I feel awkward now, and shift uncomfortably on the fur throw. 'Sorry . . . am I wrong? I didn't mean to be rude.'

'You're not rude,' he reassures me, but he's still frowning. 'It's just that people don't usually hear it.'

'So where are you from?'

There's a pause before he says, 'I was born in Italy. My

family came over here about nine years ago when I was thirteen. I thought I'd lost my accent.'

'Oh no. It's there. It's faint but it's there.' I smile again and take a drink from my beer bottle. *Is he lightening up a little? Or am I imagining it?*

'You're very perceptive,' he says, gazing at me.

'Well . . . I don't know about that.'

'I'd like to know a little more about you,' he says in a low voice, with a look almost of vulnerability on his face.

I stare back, my mouth going dry suddenly. I'm clutching the cold hardness of my beer bottle even more tightly. *It's hard to believe this guy is gay. I could swear he's looking at me like . . . the way a guy looks at a girl.* 'That would be nice,' I reply, and a question hovers at the edge of my mind. *Why is that?* Before I can consider it, a voice interrupts us.

'Summer, there you are!' It's Jimmy, coming across the pool area towards us. When he clocks Jack, he pauses just for an instant, then smiles broadly. 'Well, hello, Jack. I wondered where you were. Does Sasha know you're here?'

'Er . . . no. I haven't spoken to her.' Jack's brooding look is back, his expression closed and his dark brows almost stern.

'Well, you should. I'm sure she'd love to know you're here.' Jimmy sits down next to me. 'Go on. It'd be rude not to.'

'Okay.' Jack gets up slowly and looks at me. 'Catch you later, maybe.'

'Yes.' I try to sound bright but I'm strangely disappointed that we've been interrupted like this. I watch Jack stride away towards the house and turn to Jimmy. 'Why did you do that? I can see Charlie's point! You virtually sent him away.'

Jimmy adopts an innocent expression. 'I don't know what you're talking about. He ought to say hello to Sasha, seeing as he's at her house and drinking her beer.'

'Well, I haven't said anything to her yet, come to that!'

'That's different – you're my guest and I've just spent twenty minutes talking to her.' Jimmy sips his drink, some kind of clear cocktail, and says, 'Don't tell me you're falling under his spell as well. Charlie's the same. He can't get enough of our friend Jack. I seem to be the only one immune to it.'

'You positively don't like him.'

'No . . . it's not that. I just don't care to have him around all that much.' Jimmy frowns. 'I don't know why.' He gives me a strict look. 'And I think you should keep away from him too.'

'I don't see what the harm is . . . considering,' I say.

'Considering what?'

'Well, considering that's he's gay.'

Jimmy bursts out laughing. 'Your gaydar needs retuning, honey! He's not gay.'

'He isn't?' I blink in astonishment.

'Not as far as I know. That's kind of what mystifies me about him. He wants to hang out with us, come to parties, be our friend . . . but he's really not a part of our world. Not at all. And he doesn't seem all that comfortable in it.'

'I thought you said he was a designer.'

Jimmy gives me a reproachful look. 'So he has to be gay, right? Some straight men work in fashion, you know! Anyway, he doesn't design dresses. He designs cars.'

'Oh.' I absorb this news. *He's not gay* . . . A thrill of dark excitement folds over in my stomach and gives me something like a pain there. *Of course he's not. I knew that.*

Maybe I didn't want him to be straight. Maybe I'm afraid of what might happen if he is.

'But honey, do me a favour? Please?' continues Jimmy. 'Will you stay away from him?'

'Sure,' I say carelessly. I don't want Jimmy to guess the whirlwind passing through my mind. 'You're making something out of nothing. I've hardly exchanged more than a few words with him.'

'Okay . . . good.' Jimmy stands up. 'So let's go inside. I've got some amazing people for you to meet. And Sasha's set up a dance space you're going to love.' He offers me his arm. 'Shall we?'

I stand up and put my hand on his arm. 'Sure. Let's.'

We head inside. And despite keeping my eyes peeled, I don't see Jack again for the rest of the night.

CHAPTER FIVE

I lie awake in Jimmy's spare room, staring at the ceiling and wondering what I'm going to do with my life. Up until now, I've always had the vague sense that it hasn't really begun. I loved college and the social spree I've been on since I was old enough to get on a plane on my own, but it was always as though this was just filling time until the real business of living began. I mean, it couldn't all be about parties and clothes and money – could it? I remember one drunken boy on board a yacht in the Med, all suntanned chest and white linen trousers, drawling to me: 'Baby, we've got what everyone else spends their life trying to get their hands on. Why do you think anyone works? So they can try and live like this, of course.' He'd leaned in to me and said quietly, 'All those little worker ants, slaving away, and here we are – completely free to do what we like and have exactly what we want.'

I'd smiled and turned back to the azure sky blazing above me, feeling uncomfortable. Really? This is the best it could get? Despite the expensive surroundings and the luxury I enjoyed, I felt hollow inside and I knew it and didn't want to know it at the same time.

Well, now life is beginning. Now you have to go out there and grab it. So . . . what are you going to do?

The thought of the Hammond Foundation floats into my mind. It's the charitable organisation my father set up ostensibly in my mother's memory, but apparently it had sizeable tax implications to my father's advantage, though I've never understood what they might be.

A sudden idea seizes me and I sit up on the bed, clutching myself with glee. 'It's certainly a thought,' I say to myself out loud, and laugh. 'It's really quite a thought.'

Filled with sudden energy, I climb out of bed and get ready for the day. When I get to the kitchen, Charlie is there, sitting at the table, wearing dark glasses and holding a cup of black coffee in one hand. 'Feeling the after-effects?' I tease as I go to fill a cup from the pot.

He groans. 'You'd better believe it. Jimmy's still sleeping it off. My head is killing me. I drank about a dozen of those cocktails. What a disaster!'

'Still, it did mean you performed some interesting dance moves.' I laugh.

He winces. 'Don't remind me! I really went for it last night.' He peers at me over the top of his glasses. 'You were very restrained, Summer. I didn't see you going crazy on the dance floor.'

'I never go too wild,' I reply with a smile. 'Too boring, sorry.'

Charlie sighs. 'Well, I'm glad you were there to order a cab to bring us back. No point in Jimmy getting a DUI on his licence.'

'Someone has to stay sensible round here.' I take a sip of my coffee. It's mellow and bitter at the same time, and I can feel the caffeine zing into my bloodstream almost immediately. 'Charlie, I wanted to ask you something about the Hall. How is it funded?'

Charlie looks a little surprised at the change of subject. 'Er . . . well, it's run by a charity. I guess they raise funds.

I've not been involved for long but I do know it's not the kind of charity that puts on big glitzy parties and balls. People aren't that interested in kids who've already been in trouble – some of them think of it as rewarding bad behaviour.'

'So you're short of funds?'

Charlie laughs. 'Always! It's pretty rough down there. But have you ever heard of a charity that says they have enough money and don't need any more funds, thank you very much?'

'No, I guess not.' I lean towards him eagerly. 'Would you take me down there, Charlie? To the Hall? I'd like to see it.'

'Okay. Sure.' He shrugs lightly. 'Whenever you like. Anyone can go. It's just that not many do, I suppose.'

'Thanks,' I say, leaning back in my chair, satisfied. My plan has taken its first step. I'm not going to let this opportunity go by.

Charlie goes off to work in the smart designer boutique he manages, and Jimmy doesn't surface. He was really tanked last night, and had to be dragged off the dance floor to go home. Even then, he wanted to drive and we had to force him into a cab. I haven't seen Jimmy like that before; he's usually a little calmer when he's with me. I never get too out of it because I'm afraid of becoming vulnerable. What to, I'm not entirely sure. All I know is that I have to stay on guard all the time and drinking so much that I lose control is not something I've ever been able to do.

I decide to go out for a walk, grab my bag and head out. Within a few minutes I realise that I'm crazy to go for a walk in this town. It's all about the car here. I consider asking Jimmy if I can take a cab up to Sasha's and collect his car, pull out my phone to call him and see that I've got a text from a number I don't recognise. I open it.

Hey, Summer. It was good to talk to you last night. I'd like to spend more time with you. Are you free for lunch today? Jack

A tingle of delicious excitement prickles over my skin. *How did he get my number?* I wonder. He's been on my mind ever since last night, floating into and out of my consciousness, always setting off those strange tingles, even more now I know he's not gay. I try to push him out of my mind, remembering my half-promise to Jimmy that I would stay away from him. But . . . I think of Jimmy last night, letting his hair down, going wild on the dance floor with Charlie. *It's all right for him. He's settled and happy. Jack doesn't know who I am, he just wants to have lunch. How dangerous can that be? Maybe it's my turn to go a little wild.*

Pushing away thoughts of Jimmy, I text back that I'd love to, and the reply appears almost at once.

Great. Let's meet at Lazlo's in half an hour.

I hail a cab and set off to meet him, feeling a thrill of naughtiness and very pleasant bubbling excitement in my belly.

Summer Hammond, I can't believe it. This isn't like you!

But there's something about Jack that makes me throw caution to the winds.

The restaurant is one of those very quiet, expensive ones where the staff act like they're all titled Europeans who are too good for this place and its clientele. Jack's already there when I arrive, even though I'm early. As the haughty waiter leads me through the restaurant to our table, I get to see him sitting there, gazing moodily at the screen of his phone, scrolling through something or other. The sight of him sets my insides on fire and I can't help gasping at the intensity of the heat that whooshes through me. I can hardly believe that other people are sitting around him, seemingly unaffected by the gorgeous man at the table by the Picasso print. But as I approach, I'm sure I can see women nearby steal glimpses of him from under their eyelashes, taking covert glances at his incredible male beauty.

He looks up as we approach and his expression changes: not to joy exactly but to that bewilderment I've seen before in his eyes when he looks at me. As though there's something he can't quite believe. But it's gone in a moment and a smile lights up his face. 'Summer.' He stands up and leans over to kiss my cheek. 'I'm so happy you're here.'

My skin burns where his lips touch it, and I flush lightly, talking quickly to hide my reaction to him. 'Thank you for asking me. I'm afraid I'm not looking very smart for this place, I didn't realise I was coming somewhere so grand for lunch when I left home.'

'You look beautiful. Really. Please don't worry about it.' He waits for me to sit and then takes his own chair. 'I'm just really glad you could join me.' He glances around the room, full of tables dressed in white linen, silver and sparkling glass, peopled with rich business types and Chanel-jacketed LA ladies. A worried look crosses his face.

'I hope you're comfortable here. We can go somewhere else if you like . . . I didn't think . . .'

I feel a surge of tenderness towards him. *He thinks I'm not used to places like this.* 'It's fine – really, it's not a problem.'

Jack looks apologetic. 'This place is near my office. I was looking for something special.'

'Really – it's okay.' I smile at him. 'I'm fine. I like it.'

He leans forward, and grins at me. 'Well, you know what, I'm not sure that I do. It's kind of stuffy. We bring clients here, and they love it but you can guess what kind of people they are – more money than sense. Why don't we go and get a burger somewhere instead? I know a really good place, with the most delicious fries you've ever had.'

I lean in towards him too. 'You know what? That sounds wonderful. Let's do it.'

The haughty waiter returns with a tray of ice water and menus, but Jack is already standing up.

'Sorry,' he says in that broken, cracking voice of his. 'We've decided we're not hungry after all.'

'Oh?' The waiter raises his eyebrows. He has a comical accent, like someone pretending to be a butler. 'I hope there was no problem, sir.'

'None at all. Charge my drink to the company account.'

'Yes, sir. Very well.' He looks momentarily discomfited, as though he's completely unused to people walking out of his restaurant. 'Remind me, sir . . . your company . . .'

'Mondriano,' Jack says patiently.

'Of course. I trust we will see you again, sir.'

'I'm sure you will.'

'Thank you,' I say, grabbing my bag. 'It was really very nice. All three minutes.'

Giggling, we stride out through the restaurant, ignoring the curious glances of the diners, and heading for the bright sunshine outside.

'I'm so glad you did that,' I say sincerely as we emerge on the pavement outside.

He looks at me and smiles. 'I am too. I don't know what I was thinking of. I wanted to impress you, I guess.'

'There's no need for that.' I smile back. 'I'm still starving though. Didn't you say something about a burger?'

The burger joint is close enough for us to walk, and by the time we arrive there fifteen minutes later, I'm breathless and happy in a way I haven't been for ages. Jack has taken off his smart jacket and tossed it over one shoulder, and we're laughing at the sight of a guy in the street performing magic tricks that went wrong.

'Do you think he meant that to happen?' I ask, still laughing.

'I think it's part of the act,' Jack says. His face looks quite different when he laughs; he loses that moody expression he usually has and his looks take off into the stratosphere to such an extent that I'm finding it hard to meet his eye.

'He's too convincing, he'll have to watch out, or everyone will just think he's rubbish.' I look around the restaurant. It's all bare wood tables and benches, and American flags are strung up around the place. 'This is cool.'

'It's a new place. I like it a lot. Come on, let's sit down.'

We take a table and Jack orders us a grand feast. There's a burger with beer-cheddar, smoked onion strings and a glorious chopped gherkin and tomato relish, arriving in a shiny glazed bun that yawns open over the oozy patty within. Another comes in a double stack with bacon and blue cheese on one patty, and a sticky spare rib on the other.

'I hope that's for you,' I say, my eyes wide. 'How do you even eat that thing?'

'You'd be surprised,' he says, and his dark eyes sparkle. 'Oh wow, look at that. This is the part I love. The fries are in a truffle cheese sauce.'

I eye them up, golden sticks of fried potato drenched in a wicked-looking pool of goo, little bowls of ketchup and mayonnaise nestling beside them. 'I'm going to need a salad after this.'

'You won't be able to eat after this, trust me.'

We dig in and the activity of eating our lunch breaks down all sorts of barriers, as Jack points out the blobs of sauce on my chin and I watch him gnawing a rib, sending a trail of grease down his fingers and over his lips. He's right, it's delicious, but I don't focus all that much on the food. I can't stop thinking about the man opposite me, his brooding quality gone as he talks and smiles easily. I ask him about his work, and he tells me about designing cars. The company is very small and designs exactly to each customer's specifications, creating one-off bespoke cars that cost huge amounts.

'These people have fucking crazy money,' he says frankly, 'and they're looking for something to spend it on that will make them look great among their equally loaded friends. It's all kinds of stupid, but at least it provides work and a living for the rest of us. And the designs we make can be patented and sold on to the big companies so they can copy them – in a year or two, when the rich guys have moved on to something else.'

'Golly,' I say. 'Imagine.' I try not to think about friends of mine who've spent that kind of crazy money without thinking twice.

After we've talked about his job, he turns the subject back to me. 'So, Summer – you're English, aren't you? I think Charlie said your mom was from England.'

'Well . . .' My natural evasiveness kicks in. I don't like giving out information about myself. And, more than ever, I'm reluctant for this guy to know who I am. I don't want the burden of my family and all its complications to come between us. But I don't want to lie either. 'That's right, I'm half-English through my mother. I studied here in the States but I also live in Europe with my father.' I quickly change the subject back to him. 'You're from Italy originally, you said. Do you still have family there?'

Apparently diverted from the subject of my background, he nods. 'Yeah. My grandparents. I haven't seen them for years, not in the flesh. It's pricy to go back to Italy and there's no question of them coming here. They're too old for that. Besides . . .' His face takes on a closed expression for a moment.

'Besides what?' I ask, worried that he's going to change on me, and become that inscrutable, moody man I first met.

'Well . . .' He stares hard at the remains of his burger and then says, 'My mom has never wanted me to go back there.'

'Really? Why not?'

He thinks for a moment, his lids fluttering slightly. Then he sighs. 'My dad died there and my grandparents have never got over it. My mother can't stand it. I mean, she was upset about my dad and all that, but she needed to move on and raise us. My grandparents just couldn't stop mourning. That's why we left.'

'I'm sorry to hear that,' I say quietly. The atmosphere is

69

suddenly sombre. 'It must have been hard losing your dad like that. How old were you?'

After a pause, he says, 'Nine.'

My heart goes out to him. 'I know how you feel. Honestly I do.'

He flicks a quick look at me, his dark eyes hooded. 'I don't think so.'

'I do. My mother died when I was nine. The exact same age as you. I know how terrible it feels.'

He nods slowly. 'Okay. I see.'

There's a long silence and I feel suddenly close to him. It's broken by the waiter coming up to our table and saying jauntily, 'Can I get you lovely people anything else?'

'No thanks,' Jack says brusquely, pushing away his plate. 'Check please.'

'Sure,' says the waiter, and he loads a tray with our dishes and heads away. Jack is staring at the table, his forefinger tracing a pattern on the bare wood, seemingly completely absorbed in it.

'Are you okay?' I venture. I want to put a hand on his, to comfort him, but I don't dare. We know each other better now, but in reality we're still almost strangers.

He looks up and gives me a half smile that's full of sadness and makes me want to throw my arms around him. 'Yeah. I'm fine. Really.'

The waiter brings the bill and Jack tosses down a pile of notes. I reach for my bag but he shakes his head. 'My treat.' His expression lightens. 'It's a hell of a lot cheaper coming here than staying in Lazlo's. I ought to be paying you.'

'Don't be silly.' I laugh lightly. 'It was completely my pleasure.'

He frowns. It's not the reaction I expected. He has that same look of faint bewilderment that I can't quite make out. Then he gazes over at me again, pressing his fingertips together so hard that his nail tips turn white. 'I've enjoyed today, Summer. I mean it. Have you?'

I nod, feeling colour stain my cheeks. 'Yes. I have.'

'Can I . . . would you . . . I wondered if you'd like to go out one evening.'

A thrust of excitement goes through me. 'Oh . . . yes, I would. Very much.'

'I'm testing a prototype of one of our cars tomorrow night. It's all mine for the evening. What do you say we take it for a ride up the coast and stop somewhere for some dinner?'

I beam at him. 'That sounds wonderful. I'd love to.'

'Great. I'll pick you up from Jimmy's house at seven, okay?'

I nod. 'Okay.'

The waiter comes to take the money and a few minutes later we're standing outside on the pavement, looking at each other with a slight awkwardness. I realise he's looking at my mouth and I know with absolute certainty that I want him to kiss me. The knowledge of his gaze on my lips sets me tingling all over with an almost painful intensity.

'See you tomorrow, Summer,' he says softly, his voice even raspier at such a low volume.

'Bye,' I say. 'See you tomorrow.'

For a moment, I think he's going to lean over and press his lips on mine. The possibility of a kiss hangs in the air between us, almost vibrating with the power our nearness creates. But I'm afraid that if he did, we'd lose all control right here outside the restaurant. Perhaps he thinks the same, because a moment later he says, 'Goodbye,' turns as he slings his jacket over his shoulder and strides off down the sidewalk.

It's the weirdest feeling, but watching him go, I feel like someone is tearing a piece of me away.

CHAPTER SIX

It's the day after my lunch with Jack. Jimmy, Charlie and I are in the kitchen, the midday sunshine streaming in. Despite the beautiful weather, the atmosphere is distinctly cool.

'Jimmy, be reasonable. Only a couple of days ago, you wanted me to find someone in LA and stay here for ever.' I gaze over at Jimmy who has an uncharacteristically sulky look on his face. 'And anyway, it's only one date! I'm not getting married to the guy. He's not even my boyfriend. We haven't even kissed! For all I know, he just wants to be friends.'

Jimmy snorts. 'Yeah, sure.'

Charlie puts in his contribution from the sink, where he is washing up. 'Jimmy, honey – are you sure you're not jealous?'

'Of course I'm not,' snaps back Jimmy. I can see that he feels mixed up about all of this, and the fact that Charlie and I seem united against him isn't helping. 'Why should I be?'

'I don't mean romantically,' Charlie says, obviously trying to sound balanced. 'I mean – Summer is your best friend. It's no wonder you don't want to lose her to someone else.'

'That's fucking ridiculous,' snaps Jimmy. He bites down viciously on his sandwich.

'Please don't get upset,' I say, my voice a little shaky. 'I

73

don't want to cause any problems here. Listen, I'll call Jack and tell him I don't want to go with him tonight.'

Jimmy sighs and finishes his mouthful. Then he says in a calmer, kinder voice, 'No, Summer, don't do that. Charlie's right. I'm being an idiot. I just honestly don't think it's because I'm jealous. I mean, I really want you to be happy! It's just that Jack doesn't seem right for you.'

'You don't know him!' calls Charlie from the sink. 'You should give him a chance. I've told you, he's a perfectly nice guy.'

I lean towards Jimmy, putting out a hand towards him. 'He's got reasons for being a little distant. He lost his dad when he was just a boy. He moved here from Italy when he was just a kid. He obviously feels like an outsider.'

'Maybe.' Jimmy shakes his head. 'I'm just surprised, Summer. It's not like you to rush into something like this. Especially with a stranger. I mean, we don't know very much about Jack.'

'I know.' I shrug with a helpless smile. 'I'm surprised, too, believe me. But there's something about him. I like him.'

Jimmy stares at me for a moment with an unreadable expression. Then he says gruffly, 'I'm sorry. I shouldn't interfere. I really want you to be happy, you know that. You deserve it after all the shit that's happened lately. I won't stand in your way.'

'It's just a date!' I laugh. 'We're going for a ride up the coast and then coming back. Maybe I'll decide he's a jerk and not for me at all.'

Jimmy makes a face. 'Hmm. That would certainly surprise me. But okay. One date can't hurt, I guess.'

*   *   *

Jimmy's right, I think, as I get ready for my date. I don't usually go off with guys I hardly know. Every instinct in me normally tells me to be ultra-cautious. But this morning I went with Charlie to the Hall and I asked him to tell me everything he could about Jack. What I really wanted to know was what Charlie had told him about me. We spent the morning working the small kitchen area, making drinks and snacks for the kids who were spending the day at the centre.

'Summer, you're not used to this kind of thing, are you?' Charlie said, watching with amusement as I attempted to make a sandwich.

'Er . . . not really. But I can learn – I'll get better!' We both laughed as I tried to cut the sandwich so that it didn't look like someone had hacked it with a machete. 'So, Charlie, I need to ask you something . . .'

'Uh huh?' Charlie glanced over. He has such a friendly face, I thought, with those warm blue eyes and tanned skin.

'Did you by any chance give Jack my number?'

He paused for a moment in mid-buttering of a slice of bread and then gave me a guilty look. 'Yes, I did. He told me he wanted to get in touch with you. I knew Jimmy never would and I thought it would be nice for you to have a message from Jack.'

'Yes – I'm not angry or anything,' I reassured him. 'I wondered if you had. But – what did you tell him about me?'

'About you? Nothing much. Just that you're a friend of Jimmy's from way back and you're staying with us for a while.'

'He knew my mother was English.'

'Did he?' Charlie frowned. 'I don't remember saying that, but maybe I did. He asked a couple of things about you, but nothing unusual. He didn't seem all that interested. He only came in to meet you that day because I asked him to. Otherwise he would have gone home.'

'So . . .' I concentrated hard on putting the filling on my next slices of bread but my mind was also whirring over what this meant. 'He doesn't know I'm . . . about my family . . .'

Charlie shook his head. 'I never mentioned that, Summer. I know how you feel about people knowing about it. And anyway, you've got so much crazy stuff going on that I hardly know how to describe your family at the moment!'

I laughed wryly. 'Very true. So you're sure Jack doesn't know about my background?'

'I didn't tell him if he does,' Charlie declared. 'I don't think he has a clue.' He turns to face me, looking me straight in the eye. 'You need to stop worrying, Summer, and enjoy yourself. Have some fun. I know some bad shit happened in the past and it's no wonder you've found it hard to get over it. But you've got to remember that you're a beautiful young girl who doesn't need to be so scared. Go out. Meet people. Trust people. It will be okay.'

I felt as though as weight had been lifted off my shoulders and began to butter the bread at twice the speed, excitement tingling all over my skin. 'Maybe I will, Charlie! Maybe I will . . .'

Even now, standing in front of the mirror, putting on my make-up – very light, just a touch of sparkle here and there – I still have that sense of freedom. The knowledge that Charlie has said nothing to Jack about my background has put so many of my fears to rest. I feel as though I can enjoy tonight without the usual nagging worries about whether I can trust the guy I'm with.

Now all I have to find out is whether he's a good guy or the kind who expects the world on a plate, and a girl to give herself to him because he's been nice enough to deign to like her.

I can't suppress the hope that bubbles inside me.

He's a good one. I'm sure of it.

A text pops through to my phone.

Hey. Bring your swimming stuff and a change of clothes in case we go to the beach. See you at 7. Jack.

I pick up a bag and put a few things in it in case I get wet later: a change of underwear, shorts and a T-shirt and some sandals. My swimsuit. A comb. A cardigan in case I'm cold after a dip in the sea. Then I check out how I look: I'm in a vintage-style tea dress and wedge espadrilles, my long fair hair spilling out over my shoulders, and a light silk scarf over my shoulders. I hope it's suitable for wherever Jack is taking me.

There's also a sparkle in my eyes that hasn't been there for a long time now. I look happy and excited.

Well, I am!

That's it. I'm ready.

Now all he has to do is turn up.

Jack does not disappoint. He arrives on the stroke of seven, and after a slightly uncomfortable encounter with Jimmy and Charlie – with Jimmy being cold and Charlie too effusive – we head out of the apartment to the bright warm evening outside. The car waits for us at the roadside – a truly beautiful specimen of motor engineering. It's a glorious satin silver colour, low and sleek with a black canvas roof that's folded back, leaving the white leather interior open to the air.

'Your ride. Like it?' he asks, with a grin.

'I love it. Did you design it?'

'Yep. But the outside is just the beginning. It's what's under the bonnet that matters, right?' He's staring at me, those dark eyes of his more velvety than ever. His gaze moves over me and fixes on my mouth, then at last, he's looking into my eyes. 'You look beautiful tonight, Summer.'

'Thank you.' I smile back, feeling as though I've just plummeted fifty floors in a lift, leaving my insides somewhere near the top. 'You don't look too bad yourself.'

It's an understatement. He looks gorgeous in indigo jeans, an olive-green shirt and a black jacket. His dark hair is artfully mussy – I love that he's made an effort – and I can smell the vetiver cologne he's wearing, a scent that's musky and rich. 'Thanks.' He opens the door of the little silver bullet of a car and bows theatrically as he gestures to my seat. 'Please – it's all yours.'

I get in, stooping down to drop into the low-slung seat. Once I'm in, it's very comfortable. I look around and notice a wicker box on the backseat. 'What's in there? Are we having a picnic?'

'No. But . . . you know, just some things we might need. A blanket in case we want to sit on the beach. A lantern for when it gets dark.' Jack walks round the bonnet and gets into the driver's seat. He looks at me and smiles. 'Best to be prepared.'

A pleasant shiver ripples down my spine. I imagine all sorts of lovely outcomes that involve the two of us, the soft starry night, the sound of waves breaking on the shore. *Maybe this is it. Maybe this is my time. Is it so crazy that romance might come my way now?* I push the thoughts out of my mind. I don't want to ruin it all by thinking ahead too much. That's always been my problem, after all. I've over-thought everything, analysed things so much, that I've ended up not doing anything. Tonight is the night to throw caution to the winds and follow my heart.

Jack presses the ignition button and the car engine purrs into life. 'Come on then. Let's go.'

At first we don't talk. I'm enjoying the sudden sense of complete freedom I have with Jack. He's focused on the road, the snaking LA traffic, the constant stop–start of the wide lanes with their winking lights hanging above them. I'm seized by a sudden feeling of being young, as my hair is wafted by the breeze and the evening sun warms my face. Even in world-weary LA, people stare at our car, their expressions admiring. Maybe they even like the sight of Jack and me, him so dark and me fair, young and full of life, heading out for the night. None of them know our story, though. And nor do we.

'Where are we going?' I ask Jack.

'A little way up the coast. There's a fantastic place in Malibu, I really want to show it to you. Do you like seafood?'

'I adore it.'

'Then you'll love this place.'

Soon we're leaving the boulevards and their long-trunked palm trees behind, taking the road to Malibu. Jack picks up a bit of speed and turns on the stereo, which blasts out some vintage rock that I don't recognise but which lifts my spirits even further. The car is amazing: smooth, quiet but vibrating with the possibility of immense power. I enjoy the view as the azure ocean spreads out beside us, white-tipped waves curling into shore. Beautiful houses nestle by the beach, their jetties stretching out into the water.

'We're not far now!' Jack says, speaking loudly over the sound of the engine and the wind that's beating round our ears. 'I hope you're hungry.'

'I am.' *For everything. For life. For . . . for you . . .* I hardly dare to say it, even to myself.

'Good. Ten more minutes.'

Jack is spot on. We stop exactly ten minutes later in front of a long low restaurant, light-blue clapboard New England style, with lights strung around the wooden veranda that surrounds the whole building. At the side that looks over the sea, there are tables, each with a candle burning on it.

'Randy's Seafood Shack,' Jack says. 'Though it isn't really a shack. Come on, let's go in.'

We're shown to a table in the best position, right in the middle of the veranda, with a wonderful view of the ocean. Jack orders us a drink each and I scan the menu, which is full of my favourite seafood.

'I recommend the platter,' Jack says, 'it's for two.'

I close my menu, beaming at him. 'Then that's what we'll have.'

'So,' Jack says, when the food is ordered and we're settled with our drinks. 'Why don't you tell me a little bit more about you?'

'What do you want to know?' I say, sounding coquettish. I can't break the habit of a lifetime and open up just like that. Just being with someone who doesn't know who I am is a novelty.

'How do you know Charlie and Jimmy?' he asks.

'I've known Jimmy for years – he's an old family friend. And Charlie's been part of his life for a while now. They're both lovely people.'

Jack nods. 'Yeah. Charlie seems like a very sound guy. But I've picked up that Jimmy doesn't like me much.'

'You mustn't take him too seriously,' I say. 'He's protective. And maybe you remind him of himself a little too much. I mean, when Jimmy was younger, he was seriously hot.' Instantly I realise what I've said and blush violently. To distract Jack from the fact that I've just pointed out how hot he is, I start to gabble. 'Did Jimmy mention I have a twin? We're not identical but she's my soulmate just the same. She's abroad right now, studying drama in Paris. Have you ever been to Paris?'

'Er . . .' Jack looks surprised but amused. 'No. I haven't. Have you?'

'Yes. I highly recommend it.'

'Good, that's good. So, you have a twin. That's really interesting. Tell me more about her.'

I start to talk, and to my astonishment the words come pouring out. I haven't entirely lost my inhibitions: I don't mention her name, or that our surname is Hammond. I keep things vague and don't go into specifics but, even so, there's a lot to tell, and Jack listens intently, asking questions, drinking it all in.

'And do you have any other brothers and sisters?' he says after a while.

'I have an older sister. She's travelling at the moment.'

'What's she like?'

I shrug. Our second round of drinks is here now, as is the huge platter piled up with seafood: lobster, crab, oysters, langoustines, scallops, mussels and much more vie for space on the ice chips, spilling over the edge of the plate. Right away, we dig in, cracking shells, ferreting out morsels and dipping the juicy flesh into mayonnaise or chilli vinegar. 'You know – she was my big sister. I thought she was amazing but when we were growing up, she was often cross with us, or in a temper about something or other. For a while my twin and I had a league against her, so we could drive her mad with teasing or practical jokes. But then you grow up. You realise everyone has their problems and we've all suffered. I still think she's amazing, but now I know she's had a hard time too.'

'Really? Anything in particular?'

I look away, sweeping my gaze over the large blue ocean. I can't even begin to go there. 'Just . . . the usual teenage problems. She took the loss of our mother hard. She was the oldest, she had the most on her shoulders. You know the kind of thing.'

Jack nods, his expression solemn. 'Sure. And do they have names, these sisters of yours?'

I glance back at him and then look down at the tablecloth. I don't want to lie to him but I don't want to say their names. How many sisters are there called Freya, Flora and Summer? He'd have to have lived on Mars not to have heard of us. It's not that I don't trust him, it's that I don't want the vibe between us to change. We're just two ordinary people on a date. If he finds out he's accidentally dated a minor celebrity, he'll either want to run for the hills, or he'll change – subtly maybe, but even so, he'll change. They always do. 'Well . . .'

'Sorry – am I being nosy?' Jack leans back, his face closed again. 'I apologise. I've overstepped the mark.'

'No. You're not nosy. I'm sorry.' I lean forward to re-establish the bond we've had up until now. 'My twin is called . . . Florence. And my older sister is Frances.'

He stares at me, nodding. And then smiles. 'Those are pretty names. Now that wasn't so hard, was it?'

'No.' I smile, even though I feel a pang of something in my heart. Guilt? Sadness that I feel compelled to lie about who I really am? I'm not sure. 'But what about you? Do you have brothers and sisters?'

Jack tells me about an older brother still in Italy, and a younger sister who came to America and is now training to be a nurse. 'She's out such long hours, I worry about her. You should see how hard she works.' He shakes his head, tapping his fingers on the tabletop. 'She's still so young. Sometimes I go down to the hospital to get her, when I can't bear the thought of her taking the bus home so late and so tired.'

'Do you all live together?' I ask softly.

He nods. 'Yeah. I'm the man of the house now. I'm not going to leave them until I know they're okay.'

Jack's world is fleshing out for me. I can see them, his small family, living together in a cramped apartment or a small condo somewhere. His mother makes traditional Italian meals and nurtures her two grown-up children, doing her best to put them on the right path as they both set out to make their way in the world, trying to be a mother and father to them.

'Why did your brother stay in Italy?' I ask.

There's a pause while Jack takes a drink, then he shrugs and says, 'Oh, he wanted to stay with my grandparents. He kicked up such a fuss that my mother let him.' He laughs suddenly. The cracked nature of his voice makes his laughter sound harsh.

'What is it?' I ask, unsure of what's so funny.

'Nothing. I can see how hard it is, that's all. Talking about your family to a stranger. Trying to describe who they are and what they're like without giving them away somehow.'

'Yes. I know what you mean.' I smile at him. The bond is restored.

It's late when we get up to leave. The tables around have filled, emptied, filled again and are now cleared away, with a few staff waiting to do the same to ours. The lights along the veranda have been turned off and we're almost in darkness.

'Come on,' Jack says as we stand. He takes my hand. 'Let's go.'

'Yes.' I stare at him, entranced. His face is familiar to me now that I've had so long to look at it, the cheekbones, the straight nose – almost absurdly perfect – and the mouth that moves from moodiness to laughter in an instant, and then back. Tonight has been so wonderful. I don't want it to end.

As we walk to the car, my hand in his warm, smooth one, his voice comes to me through the darkness. 'Shall we go on somewhere?'

My stomach twists with excitement. 'You mean, to the beach?' I look over my shoulder to the where the waves are whispering down on to the shore.

'Or someplace else. A friend of mine has a place not too far from here. What do you say? Shall we go there?'

In the dim glow of the last light from the restaurant, his

face is full of strange hollows. I can't see his eyes, just two black sockets. There are cavernous black shadows under each cheekbone.

I barely hesitate. 'Yes please,' I whisper, and his grip tightens around mine.

CHAPTER SEVEN

We're back on the coast road, cruising along by the Pacific. It's late and it feels strange to be heading away from the city and everything I'm familiar with. I've never been this far out of town before. The beach houses of Malibu are as far as I usually go. Jack has put some music on the sound system: a harsher seventies rock that beats hard around us as the wind whips up my hair. He's going faster now.

'How far is it?' I call to Jack above the noise of the engine. He's staring straight ahead at the dark road snaking away, his hands gripping the steering wheel with a kind of fierce determination.

'Not too far,' he calls back.

It's not easy to talk over the noise now that Jack is putting his foot down. The great power inside this sleek little car starts to emerge as it picks up speed with ease, powering us along the road. It's exciting but I'm naturally cautious and I realise I'm gripping my seat as if to keep myself in it.

'Wow, we're going fast!' I shout over to Jack, lifting one hand to push tendrils of hair away from my face. They whip back behind me, carried by the thrust of the wind. 'Aren't you worried about the speed limit?'

Jack doesn't reply, but continues staring straight ahead at the road. Lights in the distance show some traffic ahead and I sigh with relief. He'll have to slow down now. But as we approach the red brake lights of the cars ahead, he doesn't slow but instead accelerates with another burst of speed and swings us out into the oncoming lane. I gasp and clutch my seat even harder.

'What are you doing?' I cry, turning to look at him. He is seriously worrying me now.

In the shadows, his expression is strangely blank, as though he's not really there, and he doesn't reply, just presses his foot down even harder. Now we're flying past the slower traffic, leaving cars behind as if they were stationary, still on the wrong side of the road. Then I see it: the glare of the approaching lights of a huge truck. It's powering towards us and we're racing to it. I can't believe what I'm seeing – there is no room for us to pull into the right side of the road, and Jack isn't slowing down.

'Jack, Jack, what the hell . . .!' I scream. 'We're going to crash!'

The truck is bearing down on us. I can't imagine what the driver is thinking as he sees us speeding towards him, with no time to slow and prevent the collision. The great beast blasts out a roar on its horn. I look over at Jack again, and that strange expression is still there – as though he isn't in the car with me but somewhere else entirely. Why isn't he responding? Can't he see what's going to happen to us?

This is it. We're going to die here on the road. I brace myself for an impact, and close my eyes, unable to do anything now but surrender to whatever is about to happen to me. The one word exploding in my mind is *Why?* Then I feel myself being thrust violently to the side. I open my eyes to see that Jack is swinging us out of harm's way, back into the traffic on the right side. There's a cacophony of noise from the horns of the other drivers as they angrily rebuke Jack for his stupid driving. It took some violent braking from the cars travelling beside us to create a gap for our car to slip into. Thank God they did.

I'm gasping for breath, adrenalin coursing through me and making me shake all over. I twist in my seat to face Jack. 'What the hell were you doing? How could you risk our lives like that? Don't you know how fucking dangerous that was? We were nearly killed!'

Jack is pale-faced, his hands gripping the wheel so hard his knuckles are white. 'Shit,' he says, and I can hear the fear in his voice.

'What were you thinking?' I demand, my whole body shaking. 'Couldn't you see that truck?'

'I was overtaking,' he says, sounding dazed. 'I . . . I didn't notice the truck.'

'What? How could you not see it?'

'I don't know,' Jack says grimly. 'But I didn't.' There's a pause. He lets out a long breath and shakes his head rapidly, as though bringing himself back to the moment. 'It's okay. We're all right.' He shoots me a sideways look. 'I'm sorry I frightened you. I didn't mean to.'

'Well, it was fucking stupid.'

'I know. I said I'm sorry.'

In the moonlight, I can see that his expression is set like stone now, his eyes on the road ahead.

I sit back in my seat, my trembling hands clutching my seat belt. The starry night which had looked so benign now seems full of dangers; the romance of the road has disappeared completely. 'Take me home, please.' My voice is high and shaky. 'I don't think I want to go on after all.'

Jack doesn't respond. The car continues to speed along the coast road, taking the bends easily.

'Jack, did you hear me?' My fear is turning into anger

now. I'm furious at what he's just put me through. 'Take me home!'

Then he glances at me, his expression unreadable, his eyes glimmering in the darkness.

'I can't do that, Summer,' he says, his tone almost apologetic. 'We're not going back.'

'What? I told you, I don't want to go to wherever you're taking me.' I'm indignant. Does he really think that we're going to have some cosy romantic evening after this? He must be crazy. 'Turn the car round, Jack. I want to go home.'

He says nothing for a moment, and then he sighs. The sadness in that sigh frightens me. 'You heard me. We're not going back. Neither of us.'

My mouth goes dry and my heart starts to thud. 'What are you talking about?' I swallow but there's nothing there. My throat is raspy and I can hardly speak. 'Jack, tell me what you mean!'

'I'm sorry,' he says again.

The terror I felt as we faced down that truck at speed is nothing to what jolts through me now. This is something I recall from my worst nightmares, the ones where the bad people come and take me away. My head whirls and a bitter sickness swirls around my stomach.

I can't believe this is happening. Where is he taking me? Does he want to hurt me . . .? I close my eyes. I just want to wake up from all of this, safe at home, with Jimmy and Charlie. *They don't know where I am.*

No one does.

We drive on through the night. The moon is obscured by clouds and when we turn off the coast road for a while, I have no idea where we are. I'm frozen with fear, my mind racing as I try to work out why Jack is doing this and how I can make him stop it. Images flash into my mind of what might be about to happen when we reach our destination: gruesome, terrifying pictures like something from a horror movie. I push them away as hard as I can.

Stay calm, Summer. Don't let your fear get the better of you.

I need help but my phone is in my bag on the back seat and there's no way to call anyone. I visualise my sister, and concentrate on conjuring her up until I feel as though she's beside me. When we were younger, we tried to work on our twin telepathy, but whenever we wanted it to, it never worked. It sprung surprises on us instead, like the time I was playing with my dolls and suddenly had the strongest sense I needed to find Flora. She was in the bathroom and had accidentally broken a glass bottle. The cut on her wrist was letting blood flow out, scarlet and gushing, and she was watching it entranced as it poured down the sides of the white porcelain basin.

Flora! I call in my mind. *Are you there? I need you.*

Summer. It's her voice. She has a sweet, melodic tone, perfect for an actress because it's capable of incredibly rich beauty. Hearing it, even just in my mind, comforts me profoundly. *You're in trouble.*

I know. What shall I do?

You're doing the right thing, honey. Stay calm. Keep in control. Be ready to seize any opportunity you have to get away.

How did I get into this situation?

It's not your fault. I'm with you. Don't be afraid.

I'm calmer. I steal a look at Jack. He's still gazing implacably ahead, his skull just a black shadow in the darkness.

He's a stranger to me and I was a fool to think he was anything else. But the sense of Flora's presence has given me a new strength. I might not know what's about to happen but I'm ready for anything. I'm not surrendering without a fight.

I don't know how long we've been driving when Jack takes several turns into tree-lined blackness that finally bring us out into a clearing by a house. It's in darkness but I think I can make out a square white-painted clapboard structure.

The car comes to a halt and Jack turns off the engine. The sudden silence is almost a shock, and we sit there for a moment, the reality of our situation sinking in. I turn towards him, even though I can hardly make him out in the dark.

'What are we doing here, Jack?' I ask softly. I don't want to antagonise him, and I'm trying to stay very calm and reasonable. 'I'd like you to take me home.'

He says nothing but runs his fingertips along the steering wheel in little arpeggios.

'Bringing me here against my will is a mistake,' I continue, still gentle. 'You know that. Why don't you start the car and take me back to the city, and we'll forget all about this? There's still time to put this right.'

I let my words hang in the air and hold my breath, hoping that I've said enough to pull him out of whatever madness has possessed him. I don't know why he's taken it in his head to bring me here, but maybe I can talk him out of it. He must understand that nothing good can come of doing this.

Unless he's insane.

91

I push that thought out of my mind. I hear Flora's voice again and she's saying, *We are not at home to Mr Fear!* I have a sudden irrational impulse to laugh. Flora says *Don't do that, honey. You don't know what might press his buttons.*

At last Jack turns to me. He reaches up and I suppress a gasp of fear, my ribcage shrinking back towards my spine, as I imagine him reaching for a gun, but he only switches on the inside light. His skin is greenish in the yellow glare, and for a moment it all seems incredibly normal and I half expect him to say, 'Hey, I'm only kidding. Let's have coffee and then head home. Did I really scare you? Sorry . . .' but then I notice that he looks afraid.

And that frightens me more than anything.

At last he speaks, his voice raspier and more broken than ever. 'Get out of the car, Summer.'

'And if I don't?' I return smartly, before I've had time to think.

'Just get out,' he says a little more loudly. His expression is even more unhappy now. 'Come on. Do as I ask.'

I unbuckle and go to open my door, thinking that I've got more chance of making a break for it if I get out quickly, but he moves faster. He's out and round to me in a second, taking my arm in a strong grip as I climb out of the car.

'Don't have any silly ideas about running,' he says. 'There's no one around for miles. You'd be lost in five minutes.'

But at least I'd be away from you, I think. I gauge the strength of his grip and guess that I have no chance of breaking free from it. *Okay. So not yet.*

'Are you taking me inside?' I ask.

He nods and we start walking towards the dark house.

Fear spirals through me again. What will happen in there? Will he attack me? I can't believe that Jack would do anything like this.

But it's happening, so you'd better start believing it.

I've never felt so helpless in my life.

Jack unlocks the door of the house and leads me inside. When he switches on the light, I see the kind of old-fashioned beach house I've always dreamed of owning. It's rustic but still chic, with polished floorboards and old painted furniture. There is a small wood-burning stove in a cast-iron fireplace, and cosy armchairs piled with cushions in front of it. Near us is a scrubbed wooden table with antique church pews on either side and Jack leads me over, switching on another light as we go. He guides me down to the seat and then sits opposite me.

I stare at him. He's pale and there's a thin film of sweat across his brow. A thought strikes me.

He's more frightened than I am.

That one thought fills me with such surprise that there's no room for my own fear. Instead I gaze at him, taking in the way there's a slight tremor in his fingertips, and I wonder what has brought us both to this place in the middle of the night.

'Jack,' I whisper softly. 'What's happening? Why are you doing this?'

His fists clench. 'Don't ask questions,' he growls. 'I can't explain.'

'At least tell me what's going on.' I lean over the table towards him, trying to keep my voice calm. 'Come on, this is serious. You must understand that.'

Jack's dark eyes seem to flare up and burn, as though I've

just set light to something inside him. He gets up and starts pacing about. I watch him.

He's very tense. This isn't right. He isn't sure about this.

I'd worried that he was going to force me into this place and then attack me, make me succumb to him physically. But now I sense that he doesn't have that on his mind. There's no sexual aggression in the air at all. It's something else entirely.

But what?

When he starts to talk, his words come rapidly, and his voice is low and intense. 'Summer, don't ask me questions, I can't explain. I'm not going to. You're gonna try and make me change my mind, and I can't do that. It's too late. It's already too late. Besides . . . I promised . . .' His voice trails off and he seems lost in thought for a moment. Then he turns back to me, his eyes still lit with that intense glow, and says, 'You've just got to accept this, that's all. Please don't make it more difficult than it has to be.'

At once, anger ignites in me and I hit my fist on the table. My resolution to stay calm deserts me. 'What the hell? Jack, how dare you? You almost kill us on the road, you bring me to this weird place in the middle of the night when I've expressly asked you to take me home, and you scare me witless with your crazy behaviour. Now you're asking me not to make this difficult for you! For *you*? I mean – what the fuck?' All my fear and anxiety is bubbling up inside me, boiling over, and I jump to my feet. 'Jack, what is going on? You'd better tell me right now!'

He's been staring at me while I shout, his jaw clenched and his shoulders set. The dark brows are knitted into a frown, the lips tight. Even through my anger, I can't help admiring his beauty.

'Well?' I demand.

His eyes narrow and then he glances to the floor before looking up to stare me straight in the eye.

'It's best you understand now, I guess. I've taken you hostage. You're my prisoner for as long as it takes for me to get what I want.'

CHAPTER EIGHT

I stare at Jack, dumbfounded, and sink back into my seat.
I can't seem to get what he's just said through my head. At
last I find my voice.

'What?' I say, almost laughing in disbelief. 'You mean –
you've kidnapped me?'

Jack gives a sharp nod, his lips tight.

'But ... how on earth are you going to get away with
this?' I'm struggling to take it in. 'Jimmy and Charlie know
I'm with you. They know who you are.'

'Do they?' The words rap out and strike me with a force
that makes me blink.

Do they? I feel like I've plunged over the edge of a cliff.
*They don't know where we are. I don't know where I am.
Oh my God – no one has a clue.*

'But you're Charlie's friend,' I say lamely.

'Charlie has no idea,' Jack says. He walks into a small
galley kitchen that leads off the dining area and gets two
glasses of water from the tap. My mind races as I watch
him.

'They know your name and where you work!' I call
through the open door.

'No they don't.' He returns and puts a glass down in front
of me, then sits and gulps his while I stare into the ripples in
the water, a cold horror filling me. I look up at him.

'You're not ... who you said you are,' I whisper.

He shakes his head. 'Nope.'

'You don't design cars.'

He shakes his head again.

'Then what about the one outside?'

'That's nothing for you to worry about. Let's just say a friend lent it to me.'

'Then . . .' I'm putting pieces together. It's a puzzle that I seem to have been doing all my life, afraid of seeing what it will finally reveal. And now the pieces have slotted together and it's finished. The picture on it is my worst nightmare. The words come out shaky. 'Then you know who I am.'

Jack gulps more water and gives a short, mirthless laugh as he slams the glass back down. 'It was kinda cute, the way you tried to put me off the scent.' He does an imitation of my voice. '"Oh yes, my sisters are called Florence and Frances."'

I wince. I feel heavy, sick and dazed, as though someone has put stones in my stomach. 'But you already knew.'

'Of course I did.' He won't look at me. Instead he's pushing a droplet of water around the tabletop.

'How? Charlie says he didn't tell you.'

'He didn't. I've known a long time.' Then he looks up at me, the expression in his dark eyes unreadable. 'I've always known.'

A cold shiver runs down my back. I'm suddenly freezing in my thin dress. There's more here, much more than I understand. I manage to speak, though it's barely more than a whisper. 'You want money.'

Jack's fists clench and a look of fury crosses his face. 'I don't want your money,' he spits.

'But then ... why?' For the first time, I feel a rush of misery and tears spring to my eyes. 'Why, Jack?' A tear spills over and runs down my cheek. 'Why are you doing this?'

He sees and looks away. 'I told you, I'm not going to explain. No more questions.' His voice is rough, as though he can't bear to see my sadness. When I sniff, he strides towards the door. 'I'm getting some things from the car.' Then he stops and turns back towards me, breathing hard. 'But before I do ... I'm sorry, Summer, but you can't stay there.'

I look about me at the blameless dining area, wiping away my tears and sniffing. 'Why not?'

He comes over and takes my arm again, lifting me up although not roughly. 'Follow me.'

Jack leads me to a door that opens off the living area. Inside is a small room with one window, tiny and set high up in the wall so that it's more like a skylight. It's impossible to reach without standing on something. There's some sparse furnishing, including a single bed covered in a patch-work quilt. 'Wait in here,' he instructs.

I look around the bedroom. 'Oh – I see. Is this my cell? Is this where you're going to keep me?' I turn on him, my eyes flashing. My tears are gone. And I'm not going to let him see me cry again. 'Are you one of those crazies who takes girls and keeps them prisoner for decades? Have you been building some kind of dungeon for me, like those evil losers in the news? Maybe you've seen my picture in magazines and decided that you're going to adopt me as your own little pet, is it that?' I laugh bitterly. 'You're pathetic!'

His own eyes darken in response. 'Shut up! Don't say that.'

'Well, it *is* pathetic!'

'You don't know the first fucking thing about this,' he shoots back, his expression fierce. 'And I'm putting you here so you don't do something stupid like run off and get lost where nobody can fucking find you. So shut up and stay here till I get back.'

He steps out of the room and slams the door. The key turns in the lock and I'm left staring at the white-painted wood of the door, wondering how on earth I got here, and how I'm going to get out.

I walk to the bed and sit down on it, staring at the pretty squares of patchwork.

Flora, are you there? Can you believe this asshole?

Summer . . . you flew close to the wind talking to him like that. You need to be more careful.

I'm not going to let him treat me like this without putting up a fight! Besides, what if I'm right? What if he's decided to keep me for the foreseeable, like those poor girls I've read about?

Your safety is paramount. Don't do anything foolish until you understand more about what's going on here.

I close my eyes and realise my fists are clenched hard. *But this is my worst nightmare! What am I going to do? What if he wants to hurt me, or kill me? What if I never see you again?*

Stay strong. I'm with you. I'll find you, wherever you are.

I'm shaking. The shock is hitting me now. I hunch over to keep warm, my body beginning to shiver violently. I hope to God my twin telepathy is real. I pray that Flora, wherever she is, can hear me or at least sense that I'm reaching out to her. All my life, I've feared this very thing. And now it's happened and I have the horrible feeling that this has always been my fate and there was nothing I could do to avoid it. I've been walking towards Jack without knowing it. I had to meet him. And now, here I am, alone and completely at his mercy.

I'm afraid.

I don't know how long it is before Jack returns but when the door opens, I don't open my eyes. I stay where I am, hunched and shivering on the bed.

'Summer?' he says roughly as he throws a bag on the floor. 'Are you okay?'

I don't answer. I can't. My teeth are chattering and I'm shaking so hard, I must look like I'm wired to the mains or something. He's beside me in two strides.

'What's wrong? Are you cold? Here, I'll get a blanket.' I hear him go to the closet and open it. He rummages about and a moment later he's back, and a blanket is draped around my shoulders. 'It's not so cold here but your dress is thin. What did you bring with you . . .?' He leaves me again and I hear him unzip something. I open my eyes to see him squatting by my bag, frowning at the contents. The sight is enough to enable me to speak through my chattering teeth.

'Not much, I'm afraid. I guess I would have brought more if you'd told me I was going to be kidnapped!'

Jack says nothing but pulls out the cardigan I packed in case of a midnight swim. He tosses it over towards me. 'Put it on if you're still cold.'

I take it and pull it under the blanket. Instead of putting it on, I clutch it to me like it's a comforter, hugging it as though it were my favourite teddy. Jack is watching and when I glance up, I can see that same look of bewilderment in his face.

He doesn't know why he's doing this.

That thought comes unbidden into my mind, a little spark of revelation. But when I look again, his face has taken on the closed-off look I already feel I know so well. That glimpse of his humanity helps me calm down and take control. I force myself to breathe regularly, and attempt to stop shaking. As Jack stands up and looks down at me on the bed, I manage to control myself enough to bring the trembling down to a minimum.

'What's going to happen now?' I ask.

Jack paces about again, his agitation returning. 'We're going to stay here for a while. I'm not sure how long. Please don't think about calling anyone – I've got your phone and there's no landline here. And if you've got any crazy ideas about trying to escape, then forget it. All the doors and windows are locked, and even if you did get out, there are miles between us and anyone else. You'd never find your way.'

There's always a way, I think, but I don't say anything. I need to listen to what he's saying.

'Your family will see sense pretty soon,' he continues. He stops pacing and turns to look at me. His eyes are glowing with a fierce intensity. 'They won't want to risk anything happening to you. Not after last time.'

'So you know about that, do you?' A bitter depression swamps me. 'You know what we've been through in the past and yet you're still able to inflict that kind of pain on my family again?' A mirthless laugh escapes my lips. 'Well, congratulations. I think you've just won the Fucking Shit of the Year competition.'

His expression changes in front of my eyes, his face contorting with fury. 'You don't know what you're fucking talking about!' he roars. 'You have no idea!' He seems to want to burst out with something more, but stops himself, turns on his heel and storms out, slamming the door behind him. The lock shoots back into place. He's left me on my own.

I don't know how much later it is when the door opens again. I've been lying here, staring into the darkness, my thoughts whirling round and round until, without realising it, I'm trembling on the edge of sleep. It's only when I start up at the sound of the door that I guess how close I was to unconsciousness. I can't believe I could relax so far as to sleep.

'Summer?' Jack's voice comes softly from the doorway. 'Are you okay?'

'What do you care?' I retort, pulling the blanket tighter around me. I'm warm now but I still need its comfort.

'The light was still on. I wondered if maybe you can't sleep.'

'You expect me to sleep?' I demand, not admitting I was about to sink into slumber despite the light blazing out. 'After what you've done?'

He stands there silently for a moment. I won't look at him so I have no idea of his expression. After a while he says, 'I haven't done anything to you.'

I can't let that go. I wrench myself round to stare at him furiously. 'Then take me home! Right now.'

He looks tired and there's a shadow of dark stubble on his chin. His hair is mussed as though he's been running his hands through it. He sighs, his shoulders hunching slightly, and then says quietly, 'I can't do that. Not now.'

102

'Why not?'

'It's . . . it's too late for that.'

I sense something wavering in him, and push on. 'Why is it? It's not too late! Please, Jack . . .' My voice is filled with all the beseeching I can put into it. 'Please, take me home. We can put this behind us, I promise.'

He looks down, and puts his hands in his pockets. He's like a boy whose been caught out doing something wrong and now wants to admit it and makes amends, but is too proud to stoop to it.

I speak in a soft, cajoling voice. 'Please take me home, Jack. You know it's the best thing you can do.'

His face twists and he bursts out, 'I can't do that, Summer! I told you, it's too late now. I've got you here, and I have to keep you here.'

'Why? For how long?'

'Until your family does the right thing!'

'My family? So this *is* about money!' I can't hide the scorn that I feel from showing in my face. 'All along you've planned this abduction so you can ransom me for cash . . .' I shake my head. 'And I trusted you. Jimmy said not to, but I didn't listen. I thought he was being unkind not giving you a chance. I should have paid attention to him – after all, I know for sure that he's a genuine friend. Not someone who wants to make a buck out of me.'

'It's not that simple,' Jack says shortly. 'You don't understand.'

'So tell me.' I stare at him furiously. 'Make me understand.'

He returns my stare mutely, his eyes narrowing.

'So here's something *you* don't understand,' I snap. 'If you think you're going to make money out of my family, you're wrong. For your information, my father has just decided to cut me off. I'm not the rich little girl you think I am. I've probably got less money than you.'

Jack's complexion visibly pales. 'What?' he stammers.

I feel something like a surge of disappointment. So it was all just for cash. He's done this for the money. He is no different to all the rest of the gold-diggers and gigolos. No, wait, he's worse. After all, none of them tried to kidnap me.

'Your father has cut you off? He doesn't care about you?' He looks almost agonised.

'I can see you're clearly sympathetic to my plight,' I say sarcastically. 'But yes. He doesn't give a shit about me any more. So if you're after money, you've made a big mistake. You may as well let me go right now!'

Jack hardly seems to hear me. He's staring at me, flabbergasted. I expect him to say something, but he says nothing, just turns on his heel and walks out. As he goes, he flips the light switch and slams the door to behind him.

I'm left in total darkness, staring at the unseeable walls of the strange room I'm in.

Flora's voice seems to whisper in my ear. *That was dangerous, Summer. Maybe he thinks you have no value if there's no money to be had.*

I don't care! I sound defiant but I'm scared. *He may as well know right now that my father isn't going to pay any ransom.*

With that thought, I lie back on the pillows and curl up under my blanket. When two hot tears break out from under my lids and flow down my cheeks, I wipe them angrily away.

'Fuck it, I'm not going to cry,' I say through clenched teeth.

But the fear that my father won't care when he learns what's happened makes my heart want to break.

CHAPTER NINE

Jack is in my dreams all night, finding me wherever I am. Sometimes I'm scared of him, sometimes, strangely, I'm happy to see him. Once, we are on the verge of kissing when I realise he's grown the face of a snake and has venomous fangs dripping poison as he prepares to bite. I'm pulling away in panic when suddenly I'm home again – not in the Alpine mountain retreat but in a home from my childhood. My mother is there, smiling and holding out her arms to me. 'Summer,' she says, 'we've been worried about you! But you've come home.'

I run to her and she envelops me in an embrace of such comfort I want to sink into it and never come back. 'Oh, Mama – where have you been? I've missed you!'

She croons as she hugs me and then says, 'But honey, I've been with you all the time. Didn't you know?'

I start to cry with relief and happiness that my mother is back, and wonder at myself that I didn't realise she'd never left. Then gradually I wake. Hot sunshine is pouring through the thin blinds at the window and I blink in the brightness. Tears are damp on my lashes. I was crying in my sleep.

Then the memory hits me.

Holy shit. I've been kidnapped.

I'm off the bed in a second and turning the handles of every door I can see – one is the closet, another leads into a tiny bathroom with a skylight that's also locked and impossible to reach anyway, and the last is the door back into the main room. That is also locked. The little window is too high up to reach and doesn't look as though it opens anyway.

It's no good. I can't get out. I'm a prisoner.

I shake my head in sheer disbelief. I remember how Jack stormed out last night, and I wonder what he's thinking as he wakes up to the first day of being an official abductor.

Sitting back down on the bed with its homely-looking quilt, more mussed now I've spent the night on it, I wonder how long he intends to keep me here. I'm pretty sure now that he's in it for money, so I don't have to worry that he wants to put me away for years on end. But on the other hand, if he can't get the money, what's he going to do? Say 'Sorry for the error, I didn't realise you were no longer an heiress. Off you go and please don't tell anyone'? Somehow I don't think that's very likely.

But he must have started all this with a plan. What was he going to do if my family actually paid up? He must have some kind of escape strategy, surely.

I think back to the last time this happened in our family. No ransom was paid. And as a result . . . I shiver, and push that thought out of my mind. I don't want to think about it. I can't. But the horrible notion won't be silenced. It hisses through my head: *Dad didn't pay for her. He won't pay for you either . . .*

I clamp my hands over my ears and screw up my face. 'Shut up!' I whisper. 'Flora, are you there? Please . . . speak to me . . .'

I concentrate as hard as I can, trying to hear the voice that came to me last night. But there's nothing.

I get up and go to the bathroom. It's tiny but well equipped: in the tooth mug is a new toothbrush still in its wrapping and a tube of toothpaste. There's soap, face wash and a towel. Heck, there's even a nail file and loofah brush. What next? Some relaxing bath oil and a candle? I laugh to myself, even though the sight of these careful preparations makes me feel rather sick. How long has he been planning this? God, I've been so stupid, I should never have trusted him. Jimmy said all along, he warned me . . .

Jimmy!

Of course, he's going to wonder where I am. I haven't come home or called him – that's not like me. He's going to try to get in touch and when I don't reply, he'll know something's wrong and then the search will begin. Jack might be clever, but he's not so clever that he can't be tracked down. Plenty of people saw us last night; we left the kind of trail we all leave wherever we go: caught on traffic cameras, car park CCTV, credit card payments . . . We'll be traced.

Then I have a flashback to the end of our evening the night before. Jack asked for the bill. He paid it. In cash.

There's no credit card payment to discover.

My breathing starts to quicken, my heart pounding as panic starts to shimmer through me. I make an effort to calm down.

That doesn't mean you won't be traced. A thought bursts into my mind. *My phone! My phone will have something in it that can be traced . . . a location service or something.* Then my heart sinks. Jack has already told me that he has my phone. He must have done something to disable it so we can't be found. Relying on the possibility that he might be too stupid to have thought of it seems a forlorn hope.

I use the toilet and take a shower in the tiny cubicle. The water is hot and pumps hard through the shower head, washing away the grime of sleeping fully dressed. As I clean myself with the small bar of soap left out for me, I remember that I have a change of clothes. I brought fresh underwear, shorts and a T-shirt with me.

At Jack's instigation.

The way it all falls into place makes me feel sick to the stomach. There I was, thinking I was getting set for a romantic evening on the beach, when all along I was aiding the kidnapper by helpfully packing a bag for him.

What an idiot.

But there was no way I could have known.

When I'm dressed, I pace about my little room, wondering what will happen next. Five days ago I felt powerless because I no longer had a bulging bank account at my disposal and the world as my playground. Boy, I didn't even have the faintest inkling of what powerlessness was. I could go where I pleased, do what I wanted . . .

Get a cup of coffee when I wanted one.

Just then, the door opens and Jack is standing there in the doorway.

My stomach twists at the sight of him, a feeling so intense I can't tell whether it's pleasure or pain but considering that he's abducted me, it must be pain. He's dressed in loose linen pants and a white T-shirt, his feet bare. His hair is damp and he looks freshly showered. Last night's shadow has gone from his chin.

'Hey,' he says, not exactly chirpily, but with a certain friendliness, 'do you want some breakfast?'

I have the sudden urge to pick up any moveable object within reach and throw it at him as hard as I can while screaming, 'Why don't you take your fucking breakfast and cram it up your ass!' But then I remember that I need coffee and that perhaps it would be better if I lull Jack into a sense of security so I can find out as much I can about what's going on.

And anyway . . . at least he's offering me breakfast and not coming in to finish me off.

I sniff the air, and there it is. The deal-breaker. *Mmm. Fresh coffee.*

'Sure,' I say, and force a smile. 'I'd love some.'

A moment later, I'm following him out into the main room of the beach house. Now that it's day, I can see that the whole of the front is a glass wall that opens out on to a wooden balcony, and ahead of us is the glittering blue of the Pacific Ocean, stretching away into the distance until it fades into the soft sky at the horizon. There are the white sails of boats against the water and further out, the dark shapes of ships. A few clouds are scudding across the deep blue sky. The view is intoxicatingly beautiful but I can't afford to spend too much time admiring it. I need to stay alert.

I take in the room as fast as I can. It's small and as cosy and pretty as I remember it from the night before. A door leads off on the opposite side to mine – that must be the room where Jack stayed last night. Apart from that, there seems to be this one room, divided into a kitchen and dining space, and the living area by the glass wall. I spot my purse on the couch, its flap open. Jack has obviously been investigating the contents. A hot stream of anger flows through me at this invasion of my privacy but I try to stem it. There's no point in getting worked up about that when there is so much more at stake.

Jack is already in the kitchen, pouring out two cups of coffee from an espresso maker. I can forgive a lot for a decent cup of well-brewed coffee.

'Milk?' he asks. He's so casual, this could be just any sunny morning in any beach house.

I reply, trying to sound nonchalant. 'Yes please.'

He pours hot frothy milk into my cup and passes it to me. 'Do you want something to eat?'

The thought of food makes me feel nauseous. 'No. I'm good, thanks.'

'Okay.'

I take my cup and go back to the couch, sitting down so I can see the beautiful view of the ocean as well as what Jack is up to. Something about this weird normality is setting my teeth on edge. 'So,' I say brightly, 'what are we going to do today, Mr Kidnapper?'

He says nothing but shoots me a dark look as he takes his own cup and pads through to the living room. The floorboards are honey-coloured oak, well worn and warm in the morning sunshine. 'Please don't call me that,' he mutters.

'What am I supposed to call you?' I retort. 'After all, I don't really know who you are right now.'

Jack sits down in an armchair opposite me. He stares into his coffee for a moment, then flicks his dark gaze up to me. 'I'm sorry, Summer.'

He's sorry. A little bud of hope opens inside me. 'So you're going to take me back?'

He shakes his head. 'No. I can't.'

A now-familiar swirl of emotion engulfs me: anger, confusion, fear. I'm completely bewildered about how this happened at all. More than that, I'm finding it hard to grasp the fact that I have no control over my surroundings. I've lost my liberty and I can't get used to it. I try to stay calm despite the hot fury building inside me.

'I hoped you might have seen sense overnight,' I say, trying to keep my tone gentle. 'After all, if I go back now, I can just tell them we spent the night together. I would do that if you wanted me to.' I let that comment hang in the air for a while but he doesn't respond. I've offered that bait a few times but he won't bite. I try again. 'No one will be worried about me yet. But give it a few more hours and it will be too late.'

Jack gets to his feet and goes to stand by the glass doors. He stares out over the sea, leaning on one tanned arm. I can see the bulge of muscle below the T-shirt sleeve. He sips at his coffee, looking for all the world like an advert for some coffee brand in his linen pants, that perfect profile touched by sunlight that finds mahogany glints in his dark hair. But he says nothing.

I try another tack. 'Remember what I said last night? About my father cutting me off? It's true. He's decided to make all us girls live on our own wits. He won't pay a penny. I promise, you have nothing to gain by keeping me here.'

Jack turns to look at me, an impatient look on his face. 'You don't expect me to believe that, do you?' he says roughly.

I stare back in surprise. He seemed to believe it last night. I recall his face when I told him – the startled, almost horrified expression that confirmed to me that he was in this for the money he could squeeze out of my father. 'It's true,' I say vehemently. 'That's why I was staying with Jimmy instead of in a hotel. I don't have any money now.'

Jack narrows his eyes. 'Sure. Your billionaire father has cut you off without a penny, after treating you like a princess all these years. I'm sorry. It doesn't convince me. I've seen all the pictures of you and your sisters jetting around the world, doing nothing but indulging yourselves. You've never worked a day in your life, have you? Because your daddy keeps you in as much as cash as you could ever need.' He looks like he wants to spit on the floor in disgust, but he doesn't.

'I'm sorry you don't approve,' I say. 'Really. I have a lot of sympathy with your point of view – but I never asked to be born to a rich father. It just happened.'

He snorts. 'Sure. But after that, you have a choice about what you do with your life. Everyone does. And you're an adult.'

'Okay. You're right. Maybe I could have spent my time more productively. I'm going to have to, now that I don't have my father's money to rely on. But . . .' I put my coffee cup down and lean forward in my desire to convince him of what I'm saying. 'But it all makes no difference, because he wouldn't pay a ransom anyway. He didn't last time and he won't this time either.'

'Oh, I think he will.' Jack turns back to the ocean view, then says idly, 'It doesn't matter anyway. This isn't about money.'

'Then what is it about?' I ask helplessly.

He turns to me, his dark-brown eyes glittering suddenly, and he says one word in that cracked voice of his. It chills me to the bone.

'Revenge.'

PART TWO

PART TWO

CHAPTER TEN

Flora wakes suddenly in the night. Something has jerked her out of sleep and her eyes are wide against the darkness. She's pulling in a breath fast, her chest rising hard, as though she's just had a nightmare. But she is certain that whatever has woken her has come from outside her consciousness.

Is there someone in the apartment? she wonders. She half turns to make sure that Andrei is beside her, but she can feel the heat radiating from his body. He never seems to feel the cold; perhaps over many generations Russians like him have grown accustomed to the chill of Slavic winters. She feels an instant sense of comfort to know that he is close. Ever since they arrived in London, she's felt displaced somehow. She's used to Paris, where she has an apartment in the Marais district. Here, she is on Andrei's territory.

The sensation that wakened her comes again: an unpleasant tingle over her skin, a bad taste in her mouth. *What is it? I'm afraid but I don't know why.*

Rationally she knows there should be nothing to fear. They are in a building that's closed to the public; no one can enter without a specially assigned key. There are porters at the front gate at all hours. Not only that, but Andrei's bodyguard is asleep in a tiny bedroom at the back of the apartment. He's trained to wake up at the squeak of a mouse and there is only silence, no matter how much she strains to hear something. It's hard to believe they are in central London, surrounded by all the bustle and traffic of the capital city even in the darkest hours.

Then it comes to her, in a wash of cold realisation. *Summer. It's Summer. Something's wrong.*

Quickly she runs over what she knows about Summer's whereabouts. Her twin is in Los Angeles with Jimmy. Apart from the obvious fallout from the breach with Dad, everything is fine.

A pang of guilt strikes her. She knows that she hasn't been there for Summer lately. She's been too absorbed by her intoxicating relationship with Andrei. The early days of their affair were mysterious, exciting and more erotic than anything she'd ever known. Even now, it's a young relationship, just a few months old. They still hunger for each other and hate to be apart for more than a couple of hours. But that has made her selfish, only able to think about the joy she feels in Andrei's company, about the delight of his flesh under her touch, the feeling of him moving inside her, pushing her towards the peak of pleasure and the ecstasy he can create for her.

I've left Summer by herself for too long.

An image flashes into her mind: Summer at the airport, her expression wan, looking too small and slight somehow. *No, not too small. Too alone.*

Flora had wanted to be there for her; but she had also been in a hurry to rejoin Andrei, to taste his kisses, to revel in the delight of being close to him. And there had been the small matter of what was unfolding in Andrei's business life, things that were affecting Freya too. Summer had been pushed to one side in the absorption of all that.

Flora looks at her watch, its luminous hands glowing in the darkness, and does a quick calculation. It's afternoon in LA. Summer will be out shopping, or having tea some-where. Now is a good time to reach her. Flora slides out of bed and pads lightly from the bedroom and into the pan-elled sitting room dominated by a huge portrait of Napoleon. The apartment is beautiful and around two hundred years old, but if she ever gets the chance, she'd relish redecorating it. It's so male, with its neoclassical inlay and paintings that glorify military endeavour. It needs some soft touches to ameliorate the macho atmosphere.

Her phone has Summer's on speed dial, and soon she is listening to the tone that tells her she is connected. She waits, hoping to hear the moment of silence followed by that beloved voice saying 'Hi! What's up?'

But there is no answer. After a dozen rings, the phone clicks to voicemail and she hears the message she knows so well but that now sounds faintly chilling.

'Hi! It's Summer. I'm busy so leave me a message. You know what to do. Bye.'

'Summer? It's me. Call me back, hon. I'm awake.'

She clicks the call off and sits in the semi-darkness of the sitting room, that cold feeling of panic growing in her chest.

On the west coast of Scotland, Freya lies wrapped in her lover's arms. They sleep like this all the time, locked together like two halves of a whole. In the night, they change about, taking turns to take the other's head on their chests, to spoon into each other's backs, to press close, one above and the other below. But all the time, they're intertwined, taking comfort from the other's nearness.

She wakes hearing her phone chime with an incoming text. There aren't so many texts these days, not since she ran away and left her old life behind her. Looking back, she can't imagine how she tolerated it for so long: the emptiness, the misery, the endless, pointless socialising. Everyone told her how lucky she was, how full of joy her life must be because she had money. And, no doubt, behind her back they were bitching about how spoiled and unpleasant she could be, how she took everything for granted and thought only of herself. No one ever sat her down, looked her in the eye and asked her why she was so unhappy. It was only when Miles came into her life that she saw herself for what she was: the cross, difficult, uptight girl who felt that she wasn't allowed to be sad, or even to talk about what had happened to her.

But Miles did come along. He was a bodyguard and at first she couldn't stand him, though she didn't know why. Then the car he was driving took that skid on the icy mountain road and flew her out of one life and into another. Remembering it, she thinks that it was as though she was killed in the plunge down that mountain, and was brought back to life by Miles as someone else. It wasn't immediate. It took time for her to relinquish the self that issued orders, gave commands and expected to be obeyed. It took lessons from her master to show her that there was a joy to be had in surrender that she had never dreamed of. He took his time over her education, teaching her how to find bliss in the beauty of being alive; he made her understand that she was a feeling human being, capable of heights of delight she had only imagined, able to pull another body into hers, both equally hungry for one another.

An addiction to that pleasure and her love for Miles led her away from everything she'd ever known and brought her to this place: a thick-stone-walled cottage in the middle of a stretch of land encompassing forests, lochs and mountains. It was here that Miles wanted to create his dream business: teaching people to understand nature and survive outdoors. He himself had trained as an SAS commando and had learned to master his environment and push his body to the limits. It was those skills that had saved him and Freya when they'd plummeted down the mountainside in a snowstorm.

Freya blinks and reaches for her phone. The message is from Flora.

Have you heard from Summer? I'm worried about her. She isn't answering my calls.

Freya stares at it for a moment, then sighs lightly. Flora is a drama queen, there's no doubt about it. When she announced her decision to train as an actress, it made complete sense. Her whole life is a drama, Freya thinks, forgetting that she has had her fair share of adventure too. But Flora's overreacting – there's no need to worry. Summer is in LA with Jimmy. She'll be safe enough with him. Freya thinks that Flora and Summer have made too much of their twin communication thing. They're close, of course, but she's never seen any evidence of their being able to talk telepathically. She considers leaving the text until the morning but Flora's probably working herself up into a state, so she quickly dashes off a reply.

I'm sure she's fine. Why don't you call Jimmy and check if there's no reply from her phone?

She puts the cellphone back on the nightstand and lies back on the pillows but she's not sleepy now. Instead, she thinks

121

about the distance that's come between her and Flora since she found out that her sister is seeing Andrei Dubrovski. She'd heard of Dubrovski, of course, but only to the extent that she knew he was an absurdly rich tycoon who did a lot for charity. When she told Miles, though, he filled her in on the truth about the Russian businessman and all his various dealings.

'He's a gangster,' Miles had said, his expression grave, 'and an evil bastard too. He doesn't like anyone to cross him, and he never forgives a slight. Even years later, he'll do all in his power to destroy whoever he thinks has wronged him.'

'Really?' Freya gazed at him in astonishment. 'I thought he was devoted to helping Russian orphans!'

'I expect he's made a few in his time.' Miles shook his head. 'He might do his bit for charity but he's vengeful and unscrupulous.'

'Oh my God!' Freya felt a surge of anxiety wash through her. 'I've got to tell Flora. She can't possibly know what he's like!'

'You can try,' Miles said ruefully, 'but I have a feeling she won't listen. She's probably crazy about him.'

'I've got to give it a go,' Freya retorted. 'I can't let my little sister get involved with a man like that without saying anything! She's always listened to me in the past, I'm sure she will now.'

'Good luck with that,' Miles said with a shrug. 'Just prepare yourself for the possibility that she completely ignores you, that's all. You know what people are like when they're infatuated.' He dropped a kiss on her forehead. 'I don't think you paid much attention when you were told you'd be better off without me.'

'True.' She smiled despite herself and leaned in against the soft lambswool of Miles's jumper. This was her favourite place to be: cosied up in front of the huge fireplace with Miles, watching the pine logs burn. 'How do you know so much about Dubrovski?'

'Dominic told me,' Miles replied.

Freya turned her face up to him. 'Dominic? As in Dominic and Beth?'

Miles nodded. 'He used to work for Dubrovski. He knows all about his methods. At one point, Dominic thought he'd seen Dubrovski off for good when he found out that he was using his purchases of artworks to launder money from dealings with criminal gangs. But Andrei managed to wriggle out of that one and come back stronger than ever.'

'Oh my God!' Freya sat up in panic. 'I really do have to tell Flora! I'll send her a message in Paris.'

'I expect Dubrovski will hear of it if you do.'

'Then I'll go and see her in person. And I'll ask Beth to warn her. She's in Paris right now, I'm sure she'll do it if I ask.'

'Beth certainly knows all about Dubrovski,' Miles said drily.

'Really?'

He nodded. 'It was because of Beth that Andrei really took against Dominic. He wanted her for himself but Beth was true to Dom. Andrei has never forgiven Dominic for that.'

'This is awful,' Freya said, grabbing his arm. 'What is my sister doing with a man like that – a man who can't get over the fact that a woman didn't fall at his feet but wanted to marry someone else? I've got to stop it.'

123

Miles frowned and pulled her to him. 'I don't want you getting mixed up in this. It's bad enough that Flora is in a relationship with Dubrovski, but you can't do anything about it now.'

'I can warn her,' Freya replied obstinately. 'I can tell her what he's like. And I'll get Beth to tell her too.'

'You can try, but my instinct is that Flora won't listen,' Miles said. 'And maybe it would be worse for her if she did. At least Andrei is in love with her right now. Whatever happens, she doesn't want to get on his bad side.'

Freya bit her lip, worried, then said, 'I can't stand by and do nothing. I'm going to ask Beth to see her right away. I'll pretend I need help – that will put Dubrovski off the scent if he sees the message. We'll work out a way to get her out of this.'

Miles shook his head. 'I'm not sure involving Beth in this is a good idea.'

'I can't ignore the situation. I'll send an email to Beth. She'll know how to handle things. She'll be able to tell me if Flora needs me.' She got up, determined to send the message at once.

But things hadn't worked out as she'd hoped. Just as Miles had predicted, Flora had not taken kindly to being warned off. Beth had called Freya right after her meeting with Flora.

'It did not go well,' she said in her soft voice, her tone rueful. 'She didn't like what I had to say.'

Freya stood at the cottage window, looking out over the majestic Scottish landscape: the pine forests and the purple and white mountains. The season was changing and the colours were deepening to green and dark lavender over the heather-covered hills. The phone was clamped to her ear. 'But did you tell her the whole story – how far Andrei was prepared to go to get you? Didn't he threaten you if you wouldn't cooperate?'

'Of course I told her. But I could tell it wasn't having any effect. If anything, she became more mistrustful of me.' Beth sighed. 'And that's difficult, because I also had to ask her for her help.'

'Really?'

'Andrei has discovered that one of Dominic's major investors is also a business partner of his in a Chinese commodity company. He's prepared to blackmail this partner of his into removing all his investment in Dominic's business, and bring it crashing down. I asked Flora if she could do anything to change Andrei's mind.'

'And?'

There was a pause, then Beth said quietly, 'She asked me why on earth she should help me after everything I'd just accused Andrei of. She said that maybe I was jealous of her – and that I wanted to keep Andrei's passion focused on me.'

Freya gasped. 'That doesn't sound like Flora!'

'I know. She's in a mixed-up place. She's in love with Andrei but she knows how we all feel about him. She's defensive on his behalf – but my guess is, she's also a little frightened about what she's got herself into.'

'I'll come to Paris,' Freya declared. 'I'll see her myself. She'll listen to me.'

'You can try, Freya. I just don't know if you should expect results, that's all.'

Freya had booked her trip to Paris, leaving Scotland that afternoon. But things had been no different for her than they had been for Beth. If anything, Flora was angrier and more resentful.

'So it's all right for you to choose the man you love, but not for me!' she said hotly, standing by the fireplace in her Marais apartment. She looked magnificent, her eyes flashing, her auburn curls falling around her face. 'You all think you know everything about Andrei, but you don't.'

'I think Beth probably knows quite a lot,' returned Freya. She was used to her sisters respecting her opinion and listening to what she had to say. It was strange to see Flora facing off with her, prepared to stand her ground. 'If anyone knows about Dubrovski, it's her.'

'I think you'll have to agree that situation was complicated. No one is exactly objective. Andrei had feelings for Beth, I know that. If he hadn't, we probably would never have met. But those feelings are gone. Maybe Beth is having a hard time accepting that.'

Freya narrowed her eyes at her sister. 'We both know that's not true.'

'Maybe,' retorted Flora. 'But I think she's got a nerve to tell me to dump Andrei in one breath, and then ask for my help influencing him in the next!'

'Beth's been a friend to both of us,' Freya said quietly. 'Why wouldn't you want to help her and Dominic if you could?'

Pink circles appeared on Flora's cheeks. 'I just want everyone to leave us alone, that's all! We only want to be happy! Why do I have to get pulled into all these difficult situations?'

'That's life,' Freya replied. 'Nothing is easy. And you have to be a part of the world, you can't cut yourself off from everyone and everybody.'

Flora spun to face her sister full on and put her hands on her hips. 'Then what the hell are you doing? You vanished! You left all of us to cope without you when you ran off with Miles! You're the reason Dad is so angry with all of us – and why Estella is having more and more influence over him. Can't you see that? You running away to Scotland or wherever you and Miles have holed up has caused trouble for all of us! So excuse me if I don't do exactly what you want, and finish with the only man who's ever really loved me. Excuse me if I don't threaten what I have for the sake of Beth and Dominic. Excuse me if I don't jump to everyone else's orders. Because those days are over.'

'I see.' Freya had stood up tall, tossing her dark fringe out of her eyes. 'Fine. I'm only trying to help you, Flora. I'm doing this for you, not me. But if you really think you can tame Dubrovski, then good luck.'

She marched out of the apartment and caught the next flight home. They hadn't spoken again until the three of them were summoned to the Alpine house to receive the bombshell news that they were about to be disinherited and cut off without a cent. The undercurrent of hostility between them had been hard to conceal but they had tried. And Freya had hoped that their shared difficulties might bring them back together. But this text about Summer is the first she has heard from her sister since Switzerland.

Freya turns over and tries to get back to sleep.

Summer will be fine. She's far too sensible to get into trouble.

Jimmy checks his phone for the third time in less than five minutes. There's still nothing there.

'I'm worried,' he says to Charlie. 'Why hasn't she called to say where she is?'

Charlie looks up from the magazine he's reading and

grins. 'I think she's probably got better things to do than worry about us!' He's supremely unconcerned despite Jimmy's evident discomfort.

'It's not like Summer,' Jimmy says, frowning. He refreshes the screen again, as though that will make a message pop up. 'I don't think she would stay out the whole night either. Not without telling me.'

Charlie flicks another page and says without looking up, 'Baby, she's a grown-up. She doesn't have to check in. And anyway, I expect she's rolling around in bed with Jack right now. Lucky girl, I say!'

'It's just not like her.' Jimmy stares at his phone and then says decidedly, 'I'm going to text her. Just so I know. Then I can stop worrying.'

'Great. But if she's listening out for her phone, I'd be surprised.' Charlie smiles again. 'We should be happy for her. She needs something like this.'

'Mmm.' Jimmy's not listening. He's tapping out a text.

Hey! Did you have a good time? You've been out the whole night, so I guess so! When will you be home? x J x

Then he sits back to wait, relieved that he's done something. Almost immediately his phone rings, and he snatches it up. But it's not Summer. It's Flora.

CHAPTER ELEVEN

I've been on my own in this room for so many hours now, sometimes sitting on the bed and sometimes lying on it, staring up at the ceiling and wondering how my life has shrunk down to these four walls.

Jack must have seen the expression of horror on my face when he told me that this was about revenge, because he hustled me quickly back in to my tiny bedroom as though he couldn't stand the sight of me. Since then he's knocked at the door and offered me food, but I refused to answer and eventually he gave up and went away. I spent a whole day in here and fell asleep crying. Now I'm awake again, wishing it wasn't to find I'm still in this nightmare. My stomach feels so empty and the hopeful gurgles it gives out from time to time tell me I'm hungry, but I have no appetite at all. I'm afraid, and that seems to have quelled my ability to feel hunger.

Why am I here?

I always thought that it was my father's money that was the risk factor in my life. It was the motivating force for people who wanted to harm us. It was the reason we lived in fortresses with guards, watched over by ever-observant cameras and security screens, why our homes had panic rooms and electric fences. As long as money was the motive, then there was also a way to buy safety – a ransom could always be paid. Even if my father didn't choose to pay, he had the means to.

But Jack doesn't want money . . . his motive is something else entirely. What could he want revenge for? What have I ever done to him?

I lie, staring up unseeingly at the white-painted ceiling, feeling almost frozen by the emotions swirling through me, wondering what on earth I can do now and what Jack intends to do with me. I know nothing about him and yet I can't believe he truly intends to hurt me. I think back to the way he talked to me about his family, his sister, his mother. I think of the expressions on his face – the bewilderment, the concern, the happiness and laughter. Either he is the greatest actor the world has ever known, or he has at times been honest with me, and been himself. I'm sure I've seen the real Jack – and that's why I can't understand how he can be capable of a ruthless kidnap.

But if he can do that, what's to stop him doing something worse?

It's early evening when there is another knock at the door.

'Summer? C'mon, you must be hungry by now. Do you want something to eat?'

His voice comes through the door a little muffled, but I can still hear the beseeching note in it. I can tell he's worried about me.

Good. He should be.

I don't reply but carry on staring upwards. I'm wondering what Jimmy is thinking right now. Surely he must be getting worried, without any word from me for two days and nights. He'll be doing something to find me now, I'm certain of it.

Jack knocks again. 'Summer? Are you okay in there? Please say something.'

130

No. *You might be able to control where I am, but you can't control what I think or say.* I stay silent.

He waits a little longer and eventually says, 'I'm going to open the door, okay? I need to make sure you're all right.'

Do what you want. See if I care.

A moment later, I hear the key turn in the lock and the door opens. He's there. I don't look but I can sense his presence in the doorway. He doesn't come in, as though he's hesitant about invading my territory. It's strange how the ownership of a place can change: when I got here, this room was his place but now that I've inhabited it for almost two days, it's become my space. Even Jack senses that, which is why he doesn't barge right in.

'Are you all right?' He takes a step over the threshold and I can tell he's looking over at me. 'You're so quiet in here.'

I won't look at him. What does he expect? That I'll be singing to myself? Chatting away happily? Doesn't he understand that when you do something bad to a person, it changes them and how they relate to you? We can't be what we were.

'Can I get you something to eat?'

My silence is so intense it can almost be heard. The stubbornness of my refusal to look at him or speak to him is practically vibrating in the air.

'Please, Summer . . .' He takes another step towards me, his voice full of pleading. 'I don't want to hurt you. You've got to understand that.'

Don't do this. Don't ask for my pity. I'm the one who's suffering here. Not you.

He sinks down into the small rattan armchair by the closet. I can hear it creak under his weight. It's ornamental, really, not made for sitting in. He's silent too and after a while, I slide my gaze over to see what he's doing. He's not looking at me any more – he's hunched over with his head in his hands. I stare at him, wondering why he's looking so defeated. Then at last he speaks, his cracked voice low and husky.

'Shit, I'm not cut out for this,' he mumbles to the floor. 'I thought I could do it easily. But it's not as simple as I imagined.' He looks up at me, his dark-brown eyes agonised, his expression almost pleading. 'You think I'm a pretty evil guy, don't you? Well, I'm not. But I thought I'd be able to see this through all right and that I was tough enough to do it without getting affected by it. I told myself that all I had to do was think about why I was doing it, and that would be enough to keep me strong. And – if I'm honest with you – I thought you'd be a bitch. That would make it easy, you know? Because you'd be a haughty mean girl with your nose in the air, someone who needed a fucking good lesson. But you're not like that at all.'

I stare back at him, hoping my gaze is an eloquent one. I'm thinking that even a spoiled little rich girl doesn't deserve to be frightened like this, no matter how irritating she might be.

Jack gazes back at the floor as though he can't take the look in my eyes. Despite everything I can't help admiring him: the taut muscles under his T-shirt, the width of his shoulders and the depth at his ribcage. His dark hair gleams in the late afternoon light coming through the small window, and his skin looks warm and smooth.

He speaks again. 'But I've done it now. It's done. It had to be done. I've got to see it through.'

I can't stop myself. 'But *why*?' I ask, my voice full of

despair. 'Why? I thought we were friends. I thought we were becoming more than friends.'

He winces. 'I ... That wasn't supposed to happen. I mean, it was the way I was going to get close to you – pretending I wanted to date you and stuff. But I honestly imagined I was going to have to steel myself to bear your presence. I told myself I could do it, even if it repelled me. I wasn't supposed to enjoy it but then I did. As for actually liking you – I would never have believed it was possible.'

His words make my mouth go dry. 'Why do you hate me so much?' I whisper. 'What have I done to you?'

'It isn't you.' He sits up, straightening his body, looking me full in the face. 'It's your tribe, the people you belong to.'

'My family? But why?' I crease my brow, trying to think of what my father might have done to hurt Jack. 'Is it business?'

He shakes his head. 'Nothing like that. No.'

'Then I don't understand.'

'Your family hurt my family. We were both kids at the time, so I guess neither of us were to blame for what happened, and sure, it wasn't just your family's fault. But we've suffered ever since, every day. We lost so much and I've never forgotten it. I can't. My grandparents ... they've suffered too. My brother. He told me that one day it would be my destiny to redress the balance, and make sure that your family pays its dues. That's what I've been planning for and working towards. I'm halfway there. I've got to keep going.' His eyes take on that agonised look again. 'I can't let them all down.'

'How can your family possibly want you to do this?' I ask. I push myself up on an elbow so I can look at him properly, then sit up completely, tucking my legs up under myself. 'This is a criminal act, Jack! You can go to prison for it. Your own life could be ruined. Why would they want that?'

'They want justice!' he says, his voice rougher all of a sudden. 'And so do I. We want recompense for everything we've gone through. Your family has money to cushion itself against life, and we have nothing. It's not fair, Summer. I have to make it right for all of us, and if that means I sacrifice my future, then that's the way it has to be.'

We're back at the money.

'You need to explain,' I say. 'I want to help you if I can. If my family really has caused yours pain and distress, then I want to make it right. But unless you tell me what we're supposed to have done, I can't do that. Will you tell me what we did to you?'

'Yes.' He closes his eyes and seems to think for a moment. When he opens them, the soft brown velvet is smouldering with intensity. 'You killed my father. You condemned my family to a life without him, and to poverty. You condemned my grandparents to unending grief in their old age. You made my brother rot away his life in prison. That's what your family did to mine.' He stands up, his face twisting with the emotion that's clearly surging through him. 'That's why you're here. I need something the Hammonds really care about, to make them listen to me and to make them understand what it feels like to have someone take away a person you care about.' He looks at me. 'You're that person.'

I'm aghast. 'How did we do those things to you?' I demand.

'Did they never tell you about us?'

I shake my head. 'No, not a thing.'

He laughs bitterly. 'I guess no one gave us another thought.' Then his lips tighten. 'Well, they're going to think about it now, I can promise you that.' He sits down again and looks over at me. 'I wasn't going to move so fast, but I don't think I can wait this out as long as I'd expected. They were going to sweat for a good long time, but I can't do it.' He pulls something out of his pocket. I realise it's my phone. 'Soon I'm going to send a message.'

'Who to?'

'To your family.'

'What's the message?' As I stare at the phone, I feel a surge of energy. This is a lifeline. Surely if I move quickly, I could snatch it from him. Maybe run to the little bathroom and lock myself in – I'll be able to call the police, find my location with the maps app, alert them to what's happened . . .

Jack gets up and comes to sit beside me on the bed. 'Tell me your code.'

'Tell me the message,' I say, turning my head to look at him. His nearness is disturbing. I can smell that delicious cologne he wears coming warm from his skin. I can see the dark shadow of stubble sweeping up his jaw and the soft hair at the nape of his neck.

'I have something to ask you first.' He fixes me with a piercing look. 'Do you believe those things I told you – about how your family has hurt mine?'

I gaze back. I can't doubt his sincerity – he clearly thinks he has a good cause to hate the Hammonds. But I've never heard of the things he's told me, and I can't imagine my father actively doing the things Jack's described. It has to be some kind of misunderstanding. Doesn't it? Then I think of my father's ruthlessness and his drive to succeed. I know he delights in flattening the competition and trampling over others in his quest for victory. But killing someone? Putting innocent people in prison? Really?

If he's not capable of it, then the people who work for him might be. There's Pierre, his horrible head of security – I can imagine him wiping people out with no qualms at all. I can picture him ordering that sort of thing. Anything to stay in my father's good books.

'Yes,' I say slowly. 'I think I do.'

'Then will you help me? Please?' Jack looks as though he's holding his breath.

I gaze down at the phone in my hand. It's strange that this small rectangle is capable of so much, if I should choose to use it. It could liberate me, it could help Jack, it could change lives in an instant. It's also dependent on being charged and I don't have my charger with me. I wonder how much power is left in the battery and if Jack has a charger for it.

I look over at him. 'I want to help both of us to get out of this as quickly as possible,' I say frankly. 'But I need to know more, Jack. I need to know exactly how my family hurt yours. Right from the start.'

He stares back at me. 'Okay,' he says. 'I'll tell you everything.'

CHAPTER TWELVE

Flora's plane is approaching Los Angeles airport. The flight has taken the usual time, but it has felt like a lifetime. Yesterday's conversation with Jimmy seems an eternity ago. She was almost hysterical when she put the phone down. 'Flora, you need to stay calm.' Andrei regarded her with his piercing blue gaze across the breakfast table. He'd eaten his way through a bowl of porridge and was sipping at a cup of steaming black coffee, dressed for a meeting he'd be having in about half an hour.

'Haven't you just heard what I said?' Flora couldn't sit still, she was so on edge. She pushed her own bowl away from her and then pulled it back. 'Jimmy says he hasn't heard from Summer!'

She'd received Freya's text in the night and while she lay agonising about what to do, she fell back into a fevered sleep, the kind in which dreams are as vivid as real life. She was with Summer in a small room and they were both looking for a way out. But while Flora easily found the door and opened it, no matter how hard she tried to show the way to Summer, her sister couldn't see the door or go through it. Flora woke with nausea rolling around in her stomach, and got instantly out of bed so that she could call Jimmy from the kitchen phone. He answered almost as soon as the call connected.

'Flora?' Jimmy's voice was tentative, hopeful. 'Has she called?'

At once Flora felt a cold rush of panic. She knew in that moment that things were bad. 'You mean Summer, don't you? I can't reach her. She's not picking up. I thought she was with you.'

'Oh God,' Jimmy groaned. 'I knew it. I just knew something wasn't right.'

'Tell me what's going on, Jimmy – tell me right now!' Flora tried not to let the fear sound in her voice but she knew it was there, high and tremulous.

'Summer went on a date last night – more than twenty-four hours ago now – and she hasn't come back.'

'Who is she with?'

'A friend of Charlie's – his name's Jack. Believe me, he seemed okay. I would never have let her go if I hadn't thought that. I mean, I didn't exactly like the guy but—'

Flora interrupted. 'Have you called this Jack guy?'

'Charlie has. But there's no answer. It goes right to his voicemail.'

Images flew through her mind. A car accident – the vehicle off the road somewhere, Summer trapped, needing help. 'We've got to find her.'

'I know.' The helplessness in Jimmy's voice frightened her even more. 'I just don't know what to do.'

Flora couldn't stop the stream of ideas flooding through her mind and hardly knew which one to get out first. She said, 'Get Charlie to find out if anyone else has heard from Jack – his family or friends. And Jimmy, you'd better start phoning the police and the hospitals, to see if anyone has come in answering to Summer's description.'

'Oh God. Flora – you don't think we could be over-reacting, do you? I mean, Charlie thinks we're insane. He thinks there was so much chemistry between Summer and

Jack that they've lost track of time. You know – that over-whelming first attraction and everything it brings with it – like the inability to remember that other people might be worrying about you.'

Flora shut her eyes and took a couple of deep breaths, trying to calm her panic. 'What do you think?' she asked at last. 'Does that seem likely to you?'

Jimmy's voice when he spoke again was low. 'I saw how she reacted to him, and yes, she was clearly blown away by him. He's got that dark, brooding look, like an Italian James Dean, and Summer couldn't take her eyes off him. But we both know what she's like. She's careful.'

'She's more than that,' Flora said wretchedly. 'She's terrified.'

'Yeah. She's never trusted any man. That's why I was so surprised that she seemed to throw caution to the wind and go off on a date with Jack, just like that. But even so, I don't think she would have stayed the night with him on the first date. And she would have called before now, I'm sure of it. I mean, it's getting late here.'

'So you think it's him,' whispered Flora, a dagger of ice twisting in her stomach. 'You think he's done something to her?'

'I can't believe that either. I mean, I didn't warm to him, but he didn't seem *bad*.' There was a pause, then Jimmy said, 'But I keep going round in circles, you know? If she's okay, why hasn't she called? She must know we're getting worried by now.'

'Call the hospitals, Jimmy, like I said,' Flora commanded, desperate to start something happening that might give her some answers.

'And what are you going to do?'

139

'I'll be there as soon as I can.'

When she'd told Andrei that she'd made the arrangements and was leaving for the airport in an hour, he'd been puzzled.

'What?' Andrei frowned across at her. 'Why on earth are you doing that?'

'I can't stay here and do nothing.'

Andrei shrugged. 'And what can you do over there? You'd be better off finding a detective or someone, and put them on the case. But really, Flora . . .' He shot her a bemused look. 'Your sister has barely been away for a day. I don't understand the panic.'

She gazed at him, impatient. How could he understand? *Andrei is such a loner, so independent. He has no family and he's always relied on himself for everything.* Getting past that cordon of self-reliance was part of the challenge of loving a man like him, but Flora knew he loved her, and that passion and need for love burned as brightly in him as in anyone else. 'We're twins,' she said simply. 'I know she needs me.'

He gazed at her thoughtfully, then nodded slowly. He understood that there was a bond between her and Summer that would always be beyond his comprehension. He took another sip of coffee, then said, 'Okay. But how will it help her for you to be in LA? Take my advice: get a private investigator on the case if you're that worried. But to be honest, I think any PI will tell you to give it another day. She's an adult. She doesn't have to call in every few hours to reassure everyone she's fine.'

'Maybe that's a good idea,' Flora said, standing up. She'd already scooped up her phone to start a search for a likely agency. 'But I'm still going.'

'I'm going to miss you,' Andrei said, fixing her with a look in his blue eyes that she knew only too well. A pleasurable tremor shook out over her skin, pricking between her shoulder blades and down her spine. She found the idea of being apart from him horrible – only something like this could have the power to make her desert the hot pleasures of their bed.

'I'll miss you too,' she said softly.

He reached out and took her hand, pressing it to his lips and pulling her round the table to him, still keeping his gaze upon her. 'Stay,' he muttered. 'Let me make some calls. I'll get some of my best people on to it. Right away. Then you can stay here with me. I hate being away from you.'

'So do I.' A rush of liquid desire flooded through her, heating her from within. A quiver between her thighs told her where her body wanted him most. She clutched his other hand. 'But will you call your people anyway, Andrei? Please?'

He frowned. 'So you're going.'

'I have to.' She lifted her beseeching gaze to him. 'Please understand. I'll be no good to you until I know what's happened to Summer.'

Andrei released her hand and turned back to his coffee. 'You'll be halfway across the Atlantic when Jimmy calls to tell you it's all a waste of time and she's home safe and sound. You'll have to turn right round and come back.' But he smiled at her. 'You go. I'll get my people on it. Spend whatever you need. And hurry back.'

She flung her arms around him and covered his face with kisses. 'Thank you, darling Andrei. Thank you.'

He laughed. 'You're welcome, my little firework. Just don't forget where you belong.'

'I won't. I won't . . .' She brushed his lips with hers, then returned to them, unable to resist another kiss. They pressed together harder, then their mouths opened to each other and she felt his arm pull her closer. His cup clattered down and his other hand was at her head, pressing her to him so that he could possess her mouth.

'I think we have time,' he growled, one hand stroking up her leg and under her skirt, 'to say a proper goodbye. Don't you?'

Miles comes striding into the kitchen still wearing his walking boots, looking for coffee after his early morning excursion. Freya looks up from the kitchen table, where she's scrolling through news sites on her iPad.

'Hi,' she says absent-mindedly. 'The coffee's on the stove.'

'Hmm.' Miles goes to the range and picks up the pot warming on the hotplate. 'This looks a little old. I'll make some fresh.'

'Uh huh.' She flicks to another page.

'Are you okay?' Miles starts to make another pot of coffee, tipping the old dregs down the copper sink.

'Yeah.' She looks up. He's busy packing ground coffee into the pot, frowning as he makes sure not to spill it. The sight of him, so handsome, standing there in his khaki shorts, blue T-shirt and hiking boots, doing something so ordinary, fills her with happiness. Their lives are bound together now, from the mundanity of everyday tasks to the excitement of the bedroom, the place where she still has so much to learn from him and where the lessons he gives her never fail to fill her with joy. 'Did I wake you in the night?'

He shakes his head. 'No. I slept like a baby. Getting the

forest ready for the course is wearing me out. But I've taken a good look at the arrangement this morning and it should all be fine.' He grins at her. 'I'm ready to put them through their paces.'

'I feel sorry for them.' She smiles back. 'I know what you can be like when you decide to push someone to the limit.'

He gives her a knowing look and laughs. 'Everyone is capable of more than they think. You know that.'

'I do now.'

A crackle of something intense and elemental passes between them. Then Miles turns back to the coffee pot and says, 'I really want this to go well. This client could become the mainstay of my business, if they like the results.'

'Corporate team bonding,' she teases. 'Paint guns and giant Jenga!'

'Hey!' He looks wounded as he puts the coffee pot on the hotplate. 'Confidence-building. The journey of self-discovery. The realisation that anyone can do anything if they put their minds to it.'

'I know. You're going to be amazing and inspirational. I just hope they realise how lucky they are.' Freya swipes the tablet and brings up another page. It's a glimpse of her old life: some LA party with the girls in couture frocks, all perfectly groomed, hiding all their fears and insecurities behind glossy smiles and hoping designer bags will make people like them. She doesn't miss it. But Summer is out there somewhere. Freya imagines the businessmen and -women coming here this weekend to live in the log cabins that Miles has had built and go on the gruelling survival course he's designed. They'll have to learn endurance in miserable conditions, to draw on reserves of strength they never knew they had, to use skill, stamina and quick thinking to get themselves through it. Somehow, she feels as though Summer is in the same kind of situation.

Although LA never really involved as much mud as Miles is going to provide.

Miles is getting milk from the fridge. This cottage kitchen is a rough old place: he has to kick the door hard to make it shut. But she loves its worn cosiness, the rag rugs over the slate floor, the heat emanating from the ancient range. 'So why were you awake in the night?' he asks.

'Oh . . . nothing really. You remember the text I had from Flora? I just got another.'

'She's still worried about her?' Miles brings the milk to the table and plonks it down. 'Why?'

'Well . . . Summer hasn't been in touch so she thinks she's gone off somewhere.' Freya sighs shortly. 'You know what a drama she makes out of everything.'

Miles frowns. 'And has she heard from her now?'

She gives him a look. 'Once a bodyguard, always a bodyguard . . .'

'I know Flora can be a little over the top, but she doesn't usually cause a fuss about nothing, does she?'

'Well . . .' Freya looks away. She's still angry with her younger sister over the confrontation in Paris. Flora as good as refused to help Beth and Dominic, despite the friendship they'd shown to both Hammond sisters. After all, Flora wouldn't even have met Andrei if Beth hadn't invited her to their wedding. 'The thing is, Jimmy says he hasn't heard from her. He doesn't know where she is either. I wonder . . . I mean, I'm starting to feel worried myself. Flora says she's on her way to LA.'

Miles is still frowning, a thoughtful look on his face. 'I remember Summer as a very cautious girl. Not the type to cause any trouble. Flora, on the other hand, liked to give her guards the slip, which is why she always requested the laziest.'

'And me?' Freya asks, putting her head on one side in a questioning attitude.

'You . . .' Miles's eyes grow tender. 'Everyone knew you were a handful. No one wanted your detail, least of all me.'

'Until . . .' She still loves to recall the way the chemistry between them sparked into life as they holed up in the hut on the mountainside, the attraction growing more fierce and irresistible until she needed him to touch her so badly that she virtually ordered him to. Although, as she quickly learned, Miles did not respond well to orders.

Miles leans towards her and puts his hand over hers. 'Until I learned that under that prickly, spoiled exterior was a beautiful, tender, loving girl who wanted to be loved in return.'

Her heart melts pleasurably in her chest and she beams at him. Her love for Miles feels like a prize that she earned through all the suffering that went before. She never wants to go back to that cold, miserable time before there was him.

The coffee pot begins to bubble on the stove. Miles gets up, saying casually, 'Why don't you call Flora? Leave a message and ask her to call you when she's landed. Just so you can find out the latest.'

'All right then.' Freya's secretly relieved to be told to reach out to Flora. She picks up her phone. 'I'm sure there's nothing to worry about.' She calls up her sister's number as Miles pours steaming, fragrant coffee into a mug. The phone tries to connect but there's no signal. 'Oh, damn it, the signal's gone again.'

'So email her.'

'I guess that's all I can do right now.' She goes to her email screen. 'And I'll send one to Jimmy too, asking for an update.'

'Good idea.' Miles comes back to the table, still thoughtful. 'I think we'll all feel better when we know that Flora's fears are just a storm in a teacup. Don't you?'

CHAPTER THIRTEEN

We're sitting out on the balcony of the beach shack. It's built right on the edge of the shore, and when the tide comes in, the water reaches up and under the balcony itself. This little house must get battered in the storms, I think. It means the balcony is too high to jump off, and Jack blocks the way to the little gate at the side that leads to a staircase down to the sand. He's sitting in a low deckchair, gazing out to see where the dark shape of a liner or a tanker or something drifts past in the distance. He's lit a cigarette and is taking long drags on it, releasing a plume of curling smoke into the late afternoon air.

I don't usually like smoking but the smell is somehow comforting. It reminds me of summer evenings on yachts in the south of France or off the coast of Italy, with loud English boys who smoke and drink like there's no tomorrow.

Jack turns to see me watching him. 'You want one?' he asks, lifting up the smouldering cigarette.

I shake my head. 'No, thanks. So you smoke, huh?'

'I gave up a while back. But somehow I want one right now.' He takes another drag, holds the smoke in his mouth while he flicks the butt out over the beach towards the sea, then exhales the soft cloud. 'Shit,' he says forcefully. 'Fucking . . . fucking shit.'

'What's wrong?'

He looks at me with a look of ironic amusement. 'Oh

nothing. Nothing at all! I guess it's most days that I abduct a wealthy heiress in order to get my revenge on her family, only to find that I'm a fucking pathetic kidnapper.'

'What do you mean?' I ask. 'You seem fairly effective so far. I mean . . .' I spread out my hands and smile at him. 'Here I am!'

He looks at me, and then starts to laugh. 'Yeah. I guess so. Well, thanks for those supportive words. Maybe I'm not as bad as I think.'

I see the ridiculous side of it and say, 'You're a great kidnapper, Jack. Maybe a little more practice though, and you'll really crack it.' I giggle as well. Suddenly, the situation seems hilarious and both of us are laughing so hard that it seems like we'll never stop. Tears squeeze out from my eyelids and then they're pouring down my cheeks. I clutch my stomach, which aches from laughing mixed with hunger. Jack has thrown back his head and can't stop either. The laughter breaks out of us, a release valve after all the horrible tension of the last two days. But when it eventually eases off, we're left feeling empty and suddenly nothing is funny after all.

'I can't change it, Summer,' he says softly. In the distance, the waves are breaking rhythmically on the shore. 'It's too late. I can't go back.'

'My family will be worried about me,' I say in a half whisper. 'My sisters. Jimmy and Charlie. They'll be frantic. Maybe even my father.'

'That's kind of the point,' Jack says wryly.

'You were going to tell me why this is happening,' I say. The fear that possessed me in the first few hours here has changed into something else. I'm not so afraid of Jack now – but I'm frightened of why is he is doing this, and what the power is that has moved him to take this drastic step. In my heart, I believe he's not a bad person. Something has so much influence over him, it's made him do this terrible thing. What else can it make him do? And what is it exactly?

Jack is staring out over the sea. The sky is turning that delicate shade of smoke-blue, the west touched by gilded lilac and rose as the sun prepares to set. When he speaks, his voice is low, the cracked tone almost gentle in that register. 'You know what happened to your family in Italy all those years ago?'

I nod slowly. I do . . . but in a half-remembered way, like a story someone told me once a long time ago that I understood was important but was never allowed to ask about again. Because of that, I told the story to myself over and over until it changed into something I'd invented and then I could no longer distinguish between what was real and what I'd made up. All I knew was that bad men could come and take you away, and when they did, you might never come back. Like my mama.

'My mother . . . and my sister . . .' I say. The words come out strangled. I used to talk about it with Flora as we lay in our beds side by side at night, working ourselves up into such pitches of fear that we would scream at a squeak in the floorboards or the wind at the window. We would end up in one small bed, wrapped around each other and getting what comfort we could from being close to one another. The trouble was that we couldn't pretend that the bad men didn't exist when we knew they did, and when our father did his best to barricade us all into the safety of our homes, protecting us with gun-toting guards and armoured cars.

Once we went to Freya and asked her what had

happened and what it had been like. She went white as the lacy canopy hanging over her bed. 'It was terrible,' she whispered.

'Did they hurt you?'

'No . . .' She looked sick. 'And yet, they hurt us all the time. But not with their hands or anything. Just by frightening us.'

We asked her more but she refused to answer. We heard whispers from our maids and nannies and that's how we knew that Freya and Mama had been taken by bad men, and when they came back, Mama was too ill to live any more.

Jack is looking at me. I can see something in his eyes at the sight of my face. I think it's compassion.

'I'm not pretending it was a good thing to do,' he said, 'what happened. But it was supposed to be straightforward. No one hurt them. No one wanted to. They just wanted the ransom, and your father wouldn't pay it. You gotta understand that the men who planned the whole thing, the ones who wanted the loot, they weren't the guys who actually did it. Life in Italy was hard. The Mafia – they controlled the city – the families, the gangs. It was all about survival, you see, and when my dad was ordered to take part, he didn't have a choice. Mom always said he didn't want to do it, but that was the kind of stuff that happened then. If you knew how poor they all were, you'd understand why they couldn't resist it when there was a chance to get their hands on some of the money your family had.'

I listen to him, appalled. 'By kidnapping a helpless child and her sick mother?'

'They didn't know how sick she was. The men who had

to keep them, they didn't speak English, they didn't understand.'

'Oh right. They couldn't see what was in front of their eyes. Until it was too late,' I say, sarcasm heavy in my voice.

'I don't know,' Jack says, almost wearily. 'I wasn't there. But that's what Fredo told me.'

'Fredo?'

'My brother. In Italy.'

'In prison,' I supply.

Jack nods. 'Yes.' He turns dark-brown eyes on me that are suddenly alight with intensity. 'Suffering for the whole goddamned mess.'

'Wait!' I hold up a hand. 'Tell me what happened.'

He sighs. 'I know the story from Fredo and from my mom. It was never in the papers, you know why.'

'No, I don't!' I say helplessly. 'Don't you understand? I don't know anything about all of this!'

'But you know your mom and sister were taken while on holiday in a villa outside Naples.'

I nod. 'And your father was involved.'

'Yes – not in the kidnap. He didn't take them, and he was glad he didn't. He never wanted to. But he had to be on duty at the caves where they were hidden. That was his job – to guard them. He didn't like it. He was as kind as he could be . . . but it was more than his life was worth to cross the bosses, so he did as he was told. He kept them comfortable, fed, treated okay . . . but he had to keep them prisoner. But then your dad wouldn't pay up. They'd counted on him giving them the ransom in a matter of days and there was nothing. He didn't go to the press or the police, as far as we could tell. He just . . . did nothing.'

151

I think of my father: so successful and yet so pig-headed in so many ways. I could just see him, desperate about his wife and daughter but too proud to give in to a bunch of Italian hoodlums and pay up, even if the money was a drop in the ocean to him. 'What happened next?' I ask, my voice coming out raspy and dry. I'm almost afraid to hear the answer.

Jack's lips tighten and he turns back to stare moodily over the sea stretching out in front of us. It's dark grey now, touched with pale crests of surf. 'Dad could see that your mother wasn't well. He understood enough to know she was asking for a doctor, and he could see how frightened your sister was. So he went to the boss and said they would have to let the woman and the girl go – it wasn't right to let them die. But the boss wasn't having any of that. He was all for chopping off bits of them and sending them to your father to show that they meant business. Dad didn't like that at all, and so when he was approached by someone working for your father, someone who'd infiltrated the gang, he decided that he would cooperate. He turned on his people and he gave away the information they needed for your mother and sister to be rescued. But he did it on one condition: he would need enough money to get away from there for good so that he could move here to America with his family, where we'd be safe.'

My heart is pounding. I can see everything he describes: the hillside cave, my mother getting weaker without her medication but trying to hide it from Freya, my sister as a child frozen by fear, wondering if she'll ever go home again. No wonder Jack's father couldn't bring himself to be a part of it. It must have taken courage to do what he did and risk his safety for the sake of strangers. But I have a terrible feeling about what's coming next.

'And?'

Jack pulls another cigarette from the packet on the table between us and lights it. The end flares gold and orange as he inhales, his feet tapping on the wooden boards of the balcony with the agitation he's evidently feeling. He lets out a column of smoke on a sigh. 'I suppose you can guess the rest. Your mother and sister were rescued, but the police managed to shoot a couple of the guys dead. My dad got away, but when he requested the money he needed to get out of town, there was nothing. Your family left immediately, and not surprisingly they never came back. Dad was abandoned, even though he'd been the one to get your mother and sister out. And then, somehow, the information got out that he'd been the one behind the rescue.' Jack takes another toke on his cigarette. He looks strained, almost despairing.

Nerves flutter inside me and I say, 'Oh my God.'

He turns to look me, his eyes dark and intense. 'Yep. Oh my God. I guess I don't have to go in to details about what happened next. Let's just say that your mom died a kind and peaceful death compared to what my dad went through. His boss had some refined techniques for squeezing the life from a man, and he made sure that his victim knew about every second of the long hours it took to die.'

I shudder. 'Jack – I'm so sorry.'

'Me too, babe.'

There's a long silence. A breeze dances across us, lifting my hair and ruffling Jack's short dark spikes. I shiver lightly as it plays over my bare skin. The story has chilled me. Who is at fault in the whole sorry mess? The man caught up in

153

a kidnap who does his best to sort it out? The man who refuses to hand money over to criminals? Or . . . I hate to think about it . . . *the man who reneges on his word, and leaves someone to be tortured and killed in return for helping his family.*

I can see it now, suddenly. Why Jack hates us. Why he felt he had to get revenge for the way his father was treated. I say again, 'I'm so sorry.' It doesn't seem enough somehow. 'Tell me what I can do – what we can do – to make it right.'

'It's way too late.' He takes another puff on the cigarette, then drops it to the deck and grinds it underfoot. 'My dad is long dead. My brother is supposed to get out of prison next year. He got caught up in a stupid cycle of revenge and ended up being on the spot when a rival gang member was stabbed. He got locked away for eight years.' Jack looks over at me with a wry smile. 'Believe me, there's not much you can do.'

'So . . . what do you want from kidnapping me?'

Jack looks darkly out to sea again. 'I want your father to experience pain and loss, the way my mother has. I want him to feel out of control, and to realise that his money can't buy it back again. I told you . . . I want *revenge.*'

'Not money,' I say weakly.

He shakes his head. 'It was never about that. Of course I'd love to buy my mother and sister an easy life. Just a tiny slice of what you've got could make a world of difference. But that wasn't my motivation.'

'Then . . . what were you going to do with me?' I'm pulled back into the present with a jerk. None of this changes what is happening right now: I'm still a prisoner. It's still a terrible situation to be in, even if I can now understand it a little better.

154

Jack stands up, lifts his chin and looks up into the sky, as though seeking inspiration from the pinpoints of light where the stars are beginning to emerge. The wind makes his T-shirt ripple. He looks beautiful. Something in me creases up with emotion at the sight of his pride. It's wrong but he's done what he can to redress the balance somehow, and to seek justice the only way he could think of. Should I really be afraid of him?

He takes a deep breath and looks at me, blinking in the breeze. 'I'm telling you the truth – I have no idea. All I thought was that I would get you here, and somehow it would all become clear.' He smiles a half smile, one corner of his mouth sloping up. 'I thought I would hate you, I guess. I thought that would make it easy.'

'Make what easy?' I ask, a chill prickling over my skin that has nothing to do with the wind.

'Whatever I had to do,' he says with a shrug. 'Come on. Let's go inside.'

I stand up, a heavy weight of fear inside me. For the first time, I wonder if Jack intended to kill me.

And if maybe he still does.

CHAPTER FOURTEEN

Flora gets off the flight at LAX in the brightness of the afternoon, but for her it's the early hours of the morning. She hardly slept during the eleven-hour flight from Heathrow, and she feels terrible: groggy and dry-eyed, dehydrated from the air in the first-class cabin.

Jimmy is waiting for her, his expression strained as he searches the crowd for her face. Once he's spotted her, he manages a smile but he still looks anxious.

'Flora!' He waves, and when she reaches him, tucks her into a tight embrace. 'You're here. It's lovely to see you.'

'Any news?' she asks breathlessly, even though she's just checked her phone and there was nothing on it.

Jimmy shakes his head. 'No. Not a thing.'

'That's two days,' Flora says miserably. Jimmy takes her suitcase and they head for the door. 'You have to tell me everything, Jimmy, right from the start. You need to tell me about the guy she went off with.'

Just then a man in a black suit and dark glasses blocks their path. 'Miss Hammond?'

'Yes?' Flora gazes up at him, her eyes frightened.

'Your limo is this way.'

'Limo?' she echoes, and looks at Jimmy. He shrugs and she turns back to the man. 'I don't know about any limo.'

'Mr Dubrovski arranged it.'

'Oh, I see . . .' She shakes her head as if to clear the cobwebs inside. 'Of course. Um . . .'

'I have my car,' Jimmy says.

She looks at him swiftly, knowing she needs to talk to him, and turns back to the driver. 'I won't need you, thanks.'

'I've got my orders,' he replies gruffly. 'Mr Dubrovski says you're to ride with me.'

'He's worried about you, I guess,' Jimmy says smoothly. 'Listen, it's no problem. I'll meet you at your hotel. Where are you staying?'

'I thought I could stay with you,' Flora begins but the driver interrupts again.

'My orders are to take you to the Ritz-Carlton, ma'am.'

Flora raises her eyebrows. 'Are they really? It seems everything's been sorted out on my behalf.' She is half tempted to tell this goon to get lost and that she'll arrange her own life, thank you very much. But Jimmy puts his hand on her arm before she can.

'Flora, it's fine. You should take it easy on yourself. I'll meet you at the Ritz-Carlton – it's not so far. You'll be much more comfortable there than on our spare fold-out.'

She smiles at him. 'Okay. If you're sure.'

'Of course.'

A moment later, she's being led to a waiting limousine, her case stowed in the trunk by the driver, and then, when she's ensconced on the back seat, they're driving smoothly out on to the highway. Her eyelids flicker against the bright sunshine and the next minute she's asleep on the warm leather, a cool breeze playing over her hair. Less than half an hour later, she jerks awake, blinking with confusion as the car comes to a halt outside the hotel and the door is opened by a uniformed attendant.

'Ma'am?' he says, peering in at her.

She gathers her wits and reaches for her handbag, which has slid on to the floor. 'Oh . . . yes, thanks . . .'

The heels of her boots clack on the polished marble floor of the foyer and, almost on autopilot, she checks in, following a bellboy to the lifts and up to the floor where her room is situated. It's a vast suite, decorated in muted tones of peach and pale grey, and a huge bouquet dominates the table in the sitting room.

'Thank you,' she says to the bellboy as he puts down her bags. 'No need to show me the room – it's fine, thank you. Here.' She tips him ten dollars and watches with relief as he lets himself out and leaves her alone. She goes over to the table and looks at the lavish bouquet of white blooms: lilies, hydrangeas and roses set against silver-grey leaves and dark-green ferns. There's a card. She opens it.

My darling
I miss you already. Hurry back to me as soon as you
can. Everything you need is at your disposal.
Andrei

She smiles. She might have known that Andrei would be thinking about her and ensuring she had every comfort. She misses him too – the huge hotel bed, perfectly made, looks cold and lonely, and for a moment she longs for the warmth of his arms and his body pressed against hers. Then she remembers why she's here.

Nothing is more important than finding Summer. Nothing.

The cool air in the hotel room and a drink of water from the fridge revives her. When there is a knock on the door, she rushes to it, opening it with an effusive, 'Jimmy! You made it!'

But the man outside is not Jimmy. He's a tall, gangly figure with shoulders hunched, as though he's spent too long poring over a computer screen. His battered complexion shows he's in middle-age, though his hair is a bright chestnut-brown, suspiciously even and without a trace of grey. He wears a leather jacket and jeans with a pair of elaborately patterned cowboy boots.

'Helloooo,' he drawls. 'Do I have the pleasure of addressing Miss Flora Hammond?'

'Yes.' She blinks, suddenly nervous, aware of colour rushing to her cheeks. 'Who are you?'

The man tips his fingers to his forehead in a polite salute. 'Well now, it's a pleasure to make your acquaintance. My name is Calvin McManus. You can call me Mac. I'm a private investigator, and I believe you have a matter you wish to be looked into.' He smiles, showing a row of even white teeth, a little too broad and perfectly shaped to be real. She notices that his lips don't quite close over them and wonders if they're inexpertly done veneers. Then she remembers herself and puts out her hand.

'How do you do. I suppose Andrei Dubrovski recruited you . . .?'

'I believe that was the name mentioned by the man I spoke to. But it wasn't Mr Dubrovski himself.' Calvin McManus carries on smiling, his large white teeth moving up and down as he chews a piece of gum. 'I have been apprised of your little matter, though. And I'm here to start work right away.'

'That's great. Please come in, Mr McManus.' She stands back to let him in.

'I told you – Mac is just fine.' He saunters past her and looks around the palatial suite. 'Nice. Very nice. I'm fond of peach for decor myself.'

'Would you like a drink, Mr . . . Mac?' She goes to the well-stocked mini-fridge. 'I have just about everything here.'

'Just water for me, thank you, ma'am.' Mac is inspecting the view, lifting the gauzy curtain that keeps out the blazing sun. 'I only drink water now. Ever since I gave up living on vodka.' He turns to flash another smile at her. 'Now. We oughta get down to business. Why don't we sit down and you can tell me everything from the start?'

She has almost finished explaining her side of the story when Jimmy arrives, apologising for his late arrival.

'I stopped to pick up Charlie,' he explains, gesturing to his partner who stands behind him in the corridor. 'So he could give you his side of the story too . . .' He catches sight of Mac regarding him with interest from his armchair. 'Who's this?'

Flora beckons him in. 'Jimmy, this is Mac. He's a private investigator Andrei has put on the case.'

'Okay . . .' Jimmy comes in, looking suspicious. 'Does this mean we're not going to the police?'

'It doesn't mean that at all, my friend,' drawls Mac. 'Although, to be honest, I wouldn't advise it.' He's crossed his legs, and one huge cowboy boot sways up and down as he jiggles a foot. 'But it doesn't hurt to have someone like me on the side looking into what's happening here. Especially if the police are of a mind that a grown-up woman is at liberty to go off on her own for a few days if she so desires. But . . .' He looks over at Flora. 'I understand from Miss Hammond here that this behaviour is extremely out of the ordinary. And I don't have to tell you people that a woman with the Hammond name and fortune can be very vulnerable to a certain type of . . . adventurer.'

Flora has returned to the sofa and at Mac's words, she sinks down, feeling sick. 'Guys . . . please . . . tell Mac anything you know. Has anything more come to light since I left London?'

Jimmy and Charlie exchange looks as they sit down themselves, Jimmy pouring out glasses of water from the large bottle on the table and handing one to Charlie.

'Tell them, Charlie,' he says.

Charlie puts up a hand to take off the mirrored aviator sunglasses he's wearing, and once they're off, his bloodshot eyes show the strain he's under. He looks five years older, pale under his tan and tense. 'God, this is so awful,' he says in a shaky voice. 'I feel so guilty.'

Jimmy puts out a hand to comfort him, rubbing his arm gently. 'Hey – you weren't to know.'

'But you knew there was something wrong,' Charlie replies, rubbing his forehead. 'You didn't trust him.'

'I trusted him enough to let Summer go off with him.'

'We're talking about this fellow Miss Hammond here mentioned . . .?' puts in Mac, who's watching them both carefully.

'Yeah.' Charlie turns his head to look at him. 'Jack. Jack Fuoco.'

'Jack Fuoco, huh?' Mac nods his head, his rich chestnut hair glinting in the sunlight. 'Jack *Fire*. Interesting.'

Charlie looks unhappy. 'Yeah. Well . . . it seems there isn't a Jack Fuoco, at least not the one he told me he was. He doesn't appear to live in the apartment building he told me was his address. The car design company he said he worked for haven't heard of him either. He's not answering the cellphone number he gave me – although it's always worked in the past. I've texted and called dozens of times but it goes to a standard voicemail reply.'

'I expect that phone is at the bottom of the ocean,' drawls Mac, with a smile. 'You might get an answer from a crab or something, but I doubt you'll be hearing from Mr Fire.'

Flora turns to look at him with frightened eyes. 'So you think it's definitely something to do with him?'

Mac nods, his cowboy boot moving in time with his head. 'I should say so. You'd have heard by now if your sister was in an accident – barring the possibility that she and her friend have not been discovered, but that's pretty unlikely. The fact that her date hasn't left a trace of himself that you can find makes him look like what I would call a suspicious character. It's got all my antennae tingling, and I've learned to trust them over the years.'

'Oh my God,' Jimmy says, his fingers clenching. 'I didn't want to believe it. I really didn't.' He closes his eyes. 'I let her go off with that guy. I can't believe it. I actually thought it would be good for her, considering her issues with trust.' He laughs bitterly. 'Can you fuckin' credit it . . .'

'Jesus, Jimmy!' cries Charlie, agonised. 'I gave him her goddamned number! I'm the one to blame here. God, he sweet-talked me all right. But I had no idea – no idea that he knew who she was. I never told him she was Summer Hammond.'

'My guess is that he already knew before he got friendly with you fellas,' Mac says. 'If he had his eye on her, he would have known that you were pals with her. I've seen the Hammond sisters plenty on those gossip sites and newspaper pages. There'll be reams of stuff out there, and dozens of ways to piece together a picture of Miss Hammond's life. He was sitting waiting for her like a spider on his web, I've no doubt about that.'

Flora can't speak, she's so knotted inside with horror and fear. She can only concentrate on keeping as calm as possible so that she can understand everything that's going on. Her tiredness has vanished, to be replaced by fluttering panic and surges of adrenalin. She manages to get out a few words. 'So what now? Do we go to the police?'

Mac stands up and wanders back to the window, lifting the gauze curtain again and peering out as though he expects to see something of interest there. 'My advice would be no. Because they'll be able to do no more than we can right now. And the news will also hit the headlines quicker than you can say "police sources selling juicy titbits about missing heiresses". No. We'll lose control of the situation if we do that.'

'Then what do we do instead? What do you think has happened to Summer?' Flora is not even sure she wants to hear the answer.

Mac turns back to the three anxious faces in the suite. 'There are two possibilities in my mind right now,' he says. 'And we'd better hope we hear from this guy Mr Fire soon, cos otherwise the other possibility looks more likely.' His battered face grows grave. 'And I don't think any of us wants that.'

In bed, Freya is sleeping lightly, coming to the surface of wakefulness occasionally, and then trying to sink back into slumber. Miles is curled up against her, a rattling snore coming from his throat every now and then.

That's why I can't sleep. He keeps snoring and waking me up.

Miles only snores when he's exhausted and the preparations for the weekend course have been draining. He's had to go through what he'll be asking his clients to do several times over to test equipment and safety standards.

When Freya wakes again, floating back to consciousness, she picks up her phone from the bedside table on reflex and checks it. Her email to Flora has gone unanswered up to now, and she can't help feeling uneasy. But a new message has just come in. She scrolls to it swiftly.

> *Hi*
> *I've got some bad news – it looks as though Summer*
> *has been kidnapped. We don't have any more informa-*
> *tion right now but we're on it. The police do not yet*
> *know for reasons I'll explain when we speak. I'm in*
> *LA with Jimmy. Call me when you can.*
> *Fx*

Freya sits bolt upright in bed and reads the message again. Then she switches on the light.

Miles stirs and says sleepily, 'What is it? Are you okay?'

She looks down at him and for a second she envies the fact that he is still in happy ignorance. 'No. I'm going to LA right away. Summer's been kidnapped.'

CHAPTER FIFTEEN

I'm back in my small room, alone in the dark.

Jack led me inside after our talk, his mood sombre. He seemed to be sinking away somewhere into a kind of bleak weariness. My fear wavered again. Whenever I thought the worst and wondered what he was capable of, I felt sure he wasn't the man he was trying to be. I was convinced that he was forcing himself to be a ruthless revenger but that his nature went against it.

Nevertheless, he took me to my room and opened the door.

'I thought I was going to send a message to my family,' I ventured, not wanting to go back into that tiny bedroom. I don't want to be alone. I want to be with Jack.

He sighed. 'Not tonight. And anyway, we'll probably use another phone. Do you know your father's contact number off by heart?'

I thought, and shook my head. 'No. I keep it in my contacts. But I know Jane-Elizabeth's.'

He nodded. A nasty shiver crawled across my skin as I realised that he knows exactly who Jane-Elizabeth is. I can't close my mind to the fact that he has been researching me and my family for some time. 'Okay,' he said. His low voice rasped and I couldn't help the tremor of response in my belly. He stood close to me, setting my skin alight with tingling awareness. I felt as though I needed him near me, and an intense longing for him cut through me – a deep desire for him to fold me in his arms and hold me close.

That's ridiculous. He's my captor. How can I feel like that about him?

But I remembered how I felt at the pool party when he emerged out of the shadows to talk to me. We were the two loneliest people in the whole place. And now, here we are. We have only each other. If only it wasn't in this awful way. We're together but there's a gulf between us that seems unbridgeable. A wave of sadness washed through me at the mess we're in.

He was looking at me, watching my face intently with those dark velvet eyes of his. I wondered if he could read what I was thinking. He murmured, 'I'm going to sleep now. Can I get you anything?'

I shook my head. We'd eaten a simple supper earlier and my appetite is minuscule anyway.

'Okay. Then I'll see you in the morning.'

'All right. Goodnight, Jack.'

'Goodnight, Summer.' He held the door so I could enter my tiny bedroom, then he pulled the door shut behind him. I had nothing else to do, so I curled up on the quilt on my bed to think.

I must have slept but I'm awake now, watching light play on the walls of my room. As I watch it, I realise I can also hear a sound. A kind of snapping and cracking. The light on my walls is yellow and orange. Then I smell it: the acrid scent of wood smoke.

All at once I'm on my feet. I know that these things together mean one thing: fire.

Is someone having a bonfire on the beach? I remember

parties late at night on warm shores under starlight, the golden warmth of a flickering fire, its salty smoke fed by driftwood. *Maybe I can call out to them – get some help!*

I'm at the window, the tiny opening high in the wall that only opens on one side, making it impossible to climb out of. I pull my bed so that it's under the window but I need the small cane chair by the wardrobe to stand on as well so that I can peer out. Even then, the chair sinks into the mattress and wobbles precariously as I climb on to it. I haul myself upwards, putting my weight on the sill so that the cane of the chair doesn't crack and bend quite so alarmingly. Now I can look outside and see what's going on. I gasp.

Oh shit. Oh my God.

The wooden balcony where we were sitting just a short while ago is ablaze, huge tongues of red flame shooting up into the night air and releasing a dark cloud of thick smoke. I can feel the heat of it, intense even from the distance I'm at. It only takes a second for me to understand the extent of the danger.

The cabin will catch light soon if we can't douse the flames. Then there'll be no stopping it.

Cold panic drenches me as I grasp what this means. I will burn to death in here. I can't escape.

But I have to get out.

I slither down off the chair, and from the bed to the floor. I'm at the door in an instant, wrenching at the handle and screaming.

'Jack! Jack! Wake up, for God's sake! We're on fire! Please wake up!'

I shake the door, panting, close to hysteria. He's on the other side of the cabin but surely he can hear me . . . Unless

167

his room is already on fire. I couldn't see the whole balcony. Maybe the blaze has taken hold of the other side of the building.

Panic builds in my chest, threatening to choke me. I can feel the oxygen fighting its way into my lungs as I gasp against the tightness in my throat. Is this what it will be like when the room fills with smoke and I can't get the air I need?

Okay, Summer. Calm down. You need to think. If Jack can't let you out, you need to get out yourself.

I try to remember what I know about fire safety. The smoke will rise, so if it comes into the room I should stay close to the floor. I have to beware of windows heating up and exploding.

Come on. I need to do something fast. The fire could be spreading very quickly. If only the door wasn't locked.

A thought springs into my mind. When I wrenched the handle of the door, it rattled. It hasn't done that before. I'm back there in two steps, on my knees and squinting into the key hole. There it is. The key in the lock. Jack hasn't taken it out like he did before.

That's my only hope.

Years ago when we were children, Flora and I were put in separate rooms by a nanny who told us it was time we were big girls and didn't sleep in the same room any more. We hated it and always crept to one or the other, so that we could fall asleep whispering our secrets. So she started locking the doors of our rooms. But she always left the key in the locks and once we figured out how to do it, we easily escaped. She was baffled for weeks by the way we were always in one unlocked room – but the other room was locked with the key still in the door. In the end, she gave up and let us go back to sharing. At least that way we stayed in our own beds.

I look about for what I need, but I can see nothing at all. Then I remember my bag, the one that had my beach clothes in it. At the bottom is a thin magazine left over from some trip somewhere, the kind that is mostly advertising and made from thin, slippery paper.

It's not ideal. But it will do.

I take it to the door. There is a decent gap between the floor and the bottom of the door and, thank goodness, there are smooth wooden floorboards. I push the magazine under the door, but it's too thick, so I pull it back, open it and detach some of the centre pages. My hands are shaking and my fingers are clumsy but I try not to let panic overcome me.

Come on, Summer. You've got to do this. Come on . . .

Split in half, the magazine works better now, and I slide it under the door until only a strip of it is showing on my side. Now I need something small enough to slip into the lock. I don't have any of those useful hairpins I had when I was eight. I rush around the room, throwing things about in my quest to find what I need. I dash into the bathroom but it's as bare as I remembered. I can't see anything that will help me. Back in the bedroom, gazing frantically around, I feel my breathing start to race. I'm going to hyperventilate in a moment. I can hear the fierce crackling of the fire and the heat seems closer now. I imagine the flames licking at the balcony door, then catching the curtains and racing up them to engulf the ceiling. I've probably got only minutes.

I glance down and see my sandals on the floor. They have strips of leather that buckle at the ankle. I snatch one up and stare at it. The leather is thin and supple but still strong. I stride to the door and poke the ankle strap into the keyhole. It hits an obstacle at once, but I wiggle it gently, sure that it's just slim enough to do the job. It moves past the first obstacle with a gentle jerk and then hits another.

Calm. Stay calm . . . Just a little bit more . . .

My tongue is clenched between my teeth as I try to manipulate the little piece of leather into the keyhole. I'm holding my breath and every muscle is tight with strain. Then I slip and the whole strap comes out. I have to start again.

'Oh shit!' I say, my voice high and tremulous with panic. 'Fucking hell. This has to work. It has to!'

I start again, sliding the leather gently into the keyhole. It goes past the first and then the second obstacle. Now it hits a hard wall. I hope it's the key itself. I start to push, wiggling the leather as hard as I can. It bends and gives. It won't push the key out at this rate. I try to hold the sandal in such a way that it gives the leather more rigidity and wiggle it again. I don't want to panic and find that I'm wasting my time.

'Come *on*,' I beg it, as I shove it forward. 'Come on, please, please, please . . .'

Then, suddenly, the wall is moving, the leather slides forward rapidly and I hear the clunk of the key hitting the floor.

Elation rushes through me as I drop the sandal to the floor. *I did it! Now, please let it have fallen on the paper . . .*

Carefully I pull at the edge of paper showing under the door, and obediently it slides towards me, bringing its treasure with it: the heaviness of the key to my room.

It's there in my hand. I can hardly believe my eyes. With

shaking fingers, I slide it into the keyhole and turn it. The door is unlocked. I can get out. The next moment, I'm standing in the main area of the house and looking out aghast at the balcony. It's alight, the flames reaching up into the night sky. Thank goodness it hasn't yet reached the house, but it's feeding heartily on the wooden veranda, and the thick smoke is filling the room, hovering in dense layers. I realise with a start that I'm free now. I can go. The car key is on the counter in the kitchen area. The door is easy to unlock. In a moment, I can escape entirely and I can leave Jack to his fate. Let him take his chances, the way he left me to take mine.

Go, says a little voice in my head. *No one knows about this. Go, and you can leave it all behind you. Your family will be safe from his dream of revenge. You'll be safe too. The fire will destroy him if he doesn't wake up. Even if he does, it might be too late . . .*

I know I can leave, but behind that closed door opposite mine, Jack is asleep. He has no idea what's happening. I can't abandon him to such an awful fate.

But he was prepared to hurt you. He's taken you away from your life against your will. He doesn't deserve your compassion.

I stand there, the crackling of the fire growing more intense in my ears as thoughts whirl around my head. The heat from the balcony is fierce on my bare skin. I know I could walk away and leave Jack to die. But I'm not that person. I'm not, and I won't let anyone make me into that person, no matter what they choose to do to me.

I run to his bedroom door and fling it open. Instantly I start to choke and my eyes sting. The smoke has been coming in through the open window and now hangs thick and dense in the air, grey ribbons floating through the room. Jack is asleep on the bed, still fully dressed, one arm flung up on the pillow. How can he sleep in this horrible fug? Unless . . .

A terrible thought strikes me: *unless he's already dead from smoke inhalation.*

I rush to him and touch him – he's breathing but very deeply and he's closer to unconscious than asleep. I shake him. 'Jack! Jack – wake up.'

He's a heavy weight under my hand and barely moves. I use both hands to push his shoulder back and forth, shouting his name, but he still doesn't wake up.

'Fuck it! Will you wake the fuck up, Jack!' I turn and see the bathroom door open. Dashing in, I turn on the light and see a bucket on the floor by the bath, with a sponge and a back scrubber sticking out of it. I toss them out into the tub and run the bucket as full of cold water as I can, the water hitting the tin with a loud ringing sound. When it's nearly full, I lug it back into the bedroom and with a huge effort, I toss the lot over Jack's prone body.

The icy drenching has the effect I want. He moans and turns over, opening his eyes.

'What the fuck . . .?'

'Wake up, Jack, we have to get out! The balcony is on fire.' I grab his arm and put it round my neck, and help him off the bed. He moves in a daze as if he's hardly heard what I said, but at least he's moving, taking some of his own weight and the load off me.

'Summer?' He's blinking at me, his eyes streaming under the acridity of the smoke. I can hardly see myself with the tears starting under my lids in reaction to it. Then he starts to cough.

'We've got to get you out of here,' I say, taking as much of his weight as I can. He's heavy and I stagger under him until he regains some strength and stands more upright. 'C'mon!'

It's only a few steps to the doorway, but the view in the main room is even more terrifying: the fire is bigger and closer than ever, the flames crackling and the smoke pouring into the shack. Jack and I struggle over to the front door, him choking with the smoke and me coughing too, our eyes streaming. Then the door is open and we're out in the fresh night air.

'Oh shit!' groans Jack, shaking his head in the cooler night air. 'What the hell is happening?'

'We're on fire, we've got to call the fire department right now. Where's my phone?' I'm still coughing but at least I can speak. 'Where is it?'

He points back in the shack. 'In there. But they'll never get here in time.'

I stare at him for a moment. 'Fuck,' I say emphatically. 'I'm not letting this happen.' Then I turn on my heel and head back into the smoky interior, keeping as low as I can, hearing Jack shout at me to stop and what the hell am I thinking.

Inside, I assess the situation quickly. The fire is still on the balcony – thank God the breeze has changed, taking the flames with it away from the shack. The smoke has made the whole thing seem worse than it is, but we still have a chance.

My eyes are stinging again, and everything in me is shouting that I need to be back in the fresh clean air and away from this choking, stifling smoke. But I force myself back into Jack's room where the bucket lies abandoned on the floor by the bed. I pick it up and run back to the kitchen, filling it as fast as I can from the tap, and collecting saucepans and any other container I can see as the water gushes out.

Jack is by my side. 'You think we can fight this thing?' He's still coughing and wiping his eyes.

'We can try.'

'Okay.' He opens a cupboard by the door and pulls out another bucket, and a hosepipe. 'Let's do it.'

My bucket is almost full and I haul it out of the sink, while Jack quickly attaches the hosepipe to the tap. For a moment, we stare at one another though the smoky haze, then we turn towards the flames outside.

Jack goes first. The door frame is hot, the handle too burning to touch, so he wraps his hand in a blanket from the couch to pull open the door. At once, the heat ratchets up a notch and I can't help turning my face away from the blast of hot air. Jack yells, 'Turn on the tap!'

Obediently, I twist the handle on, and the limp hose stiffens as the water flows through it. The next moment a spray of water flies out of the end Jack is holding and he directs it into the heart of the flames. There's a loud sizzle and a cloud of steam but otherwise, there's not much difference. I grab my bucket and run out to join him, nearly beaten back by the heat. I throw the water as hard as I can, a fountain of water that spatters into the fire, steams and is gone. Then I head back to refill the bucket.

From my position at the sink, there doesn't seem to be any change. I can hear an ominous creaking of wood, as though the balcony is on the brink of collapse. The far rail is a mass of flames and then, suddenly, it's gone, crashing down to the beach below in a shower of red-gold sparks and flying embers. 'It's not working!' I yell. 'It's too strong!'

'No, we've got to keep going,' shouts Jack. He's sweating and rubbing at his eyes to get rid of tears while he directs the stream of water into the fire. It looks far too paltry to affect the roaring flames. We need the solid gush of a proper fire hose. 'We can do this.'

I come back with another bucket of water, leaving the other bucket filling, and throw it as fast as I can, unable to bear the heat for long. No wonder Jack is drenched with sweat. Then I return for the other bucket. On and on we go, dousing the heart of the fire and killing any flames we see spreading out towards the shack. Then, when I'm wondering how long we can go on like this, I realise it's working. The heat is diminishing, the heart of the fire is reduced to a smaller core and the flames are no longer encroaching hungrily on the rest of the balcony, which isn't a balcony any more but a charred skeleton of one. At last, with the hissing of steam and the acrid smell of burnt wood, the fire seems to be out.

'Turn off the tap,' Jack says to me, his face smeared with black streaks.

Exhausted, I nod and go back to the sink, dropping my bucket on the floor. The hose goes limp again as the water flow is turned off. It's strangely cold without the rampaging heat of the fire.

Jack drops the hose and comes back inside, coughing and shaking his head. 'I can't believe it.'

'We did it!' I say, filled with sudden jubilation as he comes up to me. 'We put it out!'

We're close now, looking into one another's eyes, grinning like idiots.

'Hey,' he says softly, '*you* put it out. You're responsible. You saved our lives.' His eyes are tender and his expression almost bewildered. 'I don't how you got out of a locked room but you did. And then you saved me when you could have run for it.'

'I wasn't going to leave you to die, no matter what,' I say, a strange feeling brewing inside me. It's probably the result of shock, I think. *Yeah, that's it.*

'You're amazing,' he says in a tone that's almost helpless. 'I don't know how to thank you.'

'I can think of one thing,' I return with a smile.

'What?'

'Well, you can give up smoking for a start.'

He stares at me, then starts to laugh, and I'm laughing too, even though we're half-coughing at the same time. Then suddenly, I don't quite know how, I'm in his arms and we're kissing as though our lives depended on it.

CHAPTER SIXTEEN

In the quietness of the plane cabin, Freya holds Miles's hand in hers under the blanket she's wrapped in. She can't shake the cold, shaky feeling that's filled her from the moment she heard the news about Summer. Miles hasn't left her alone since Flora's message arrived.

'I'm coming with you,' he had said shortly as soon as she told him.

She blinked at him in surprise. 'But ... you can't! The course ... the clients are arriving the day after tomorrow. It's your first major event and you've put so much time and effort into it. You can't leave it all, Miles. I mean it. I won't let you.'

Miles looked stubborn. 'You're not going alone, Freya. Chris has worked with me on the preparations and he knows exactly what needs to be done. I trust him to cover for me.'

'But those clients are expecting *you* to be here.'

'If they don't understand that family emergencies happen no matter how inconvenient, then they can piss off.' He wrapped her in his arms. 'I can't leave you. Not now.'

She'd relaxed into the warmth of his embrace, overcome with relief. He was right – she didn't think she could face this alone.

Now, as they fly out of their day and chase the sun round the earth to the brightness of California, she grasps his hand tightly.

'Are you all right?' he asks quietly. Their voices are masked by the deep thrum of the plane's engines but it doesn't matter much. Their nearest neighbours are wearing headphones and watching their in-flight entertainment. 'I guess this must be bringing it all back.'

Freya nods. Her stomach is knotted with a fear she hasn't felt since childhood and the terrible summer when she and her mother were taken from their villa and spirited away in the night to dank caves up in the mountains. She remembers the shock and bewilderment of being ripped away from the safety of her bed, and clinging to her mother, who was outwardly calm and strong but whose shaking hands showed the extent of her terror. How many days did she spend there, still in her pyjamas and dressing gown, until they were rescued? It felt like for ever, trapped in the damp coldness, allowed out only to relieve herself in a nearby pit, always with a guard observing, always the glint of metal on a gun barrel to remind her not to attempt to escape. As if she would run off and leave her mother. Not when her mother was growing weaker day by day . . .

She says, 'I can't stop seeing it all. The images . . . they're flashing back into my mind. But now I'm seeing Summer, all alone, a prisoner.' Her hand tightens around Miles's. 'What might he do to her? She's a beautiful girl, she's so young and innocent.' Horror sparks in her chest, making her feel like she can't breathe. 'We've got to find her, Miles.'

'We will,' he says firmly. 'Don't worry. He won't hurt her. A kidnap is for a reason and that reason is usually money. She'll be protected for as long as they want that money and think they might get it.'

Freya turns her face to him, her eyes wide. She knows

she's pale, her expression fearful. 'But what if they know that my father doesn't pay ransoms? He never did for me and Mama! And he's less likely to now than ever.'

'They won't know that, or they wouldn't have taken her in the first place.' Miles rubs his thumb over her palm to calm her down. 'Hey. I know it's frightening. But we're going to do everything it takes to get her back, don't worry about that. It won't be like it was for you. No one is going to die.'

Freya tries to smile but her lips won't obey. 'Promise?' she asks in a shaky whisper.

'I promise,' Miles says firmly. 'Try to rest, baby. You're going to need all your strength when we get there.'

She nods, a little comforted. But she doesn't know how she'll sleep until Summer is safely back.

Jane-Elizabeth rushes to the study, knocking and going in before her boss has barked out his customary 'Enter!'

Mr Hammond is sitting in the large leather armchair in front of his desk, and his girlfriend Estella is on his knee while they both gaze at the computer screen.

'Is this one big enough, Coochie?' he's saying and then looks up crossly as Jane-Elizabeth comes in, breathless, one hand pushing back the lock of hair that has escaped the clips. It's the white streak that makes her so distinctive, and which she tucks back into the rest of her dark hair.

Estella also looks up, her expression unreadable, her large brown Bambi eyes blinking slowly. She has always been careful not to offend Jane-Elizabeth, and has never attempted to come between her and Mr Hammond.

Because she's too clever for that, Jane-Elizabeth thinks, even though she is full of anxiety at Flora's message. She's always tried to keep her own feelings about Estella as well concealed as she can.

'What is it, Jane-Elizabeth?' her boss asks tersely. 'We're busy right now.'

'I think you'll want to hear this,' Jane-Elizabeth says, agitated and barely able to stay on one spot. 'I've just had a message from Flora. She and Freya think that Summer has been abducted in LA.'

'What?' He frowns, puzzled. Estella gets up off his knee without being asked and goes to sit on a nearby chair, evidently alert and listening. Mr Hammond picks up the phone and presses an extension. 'Pierre – get up here right now,' he barks and slams down the receiver. 'I don't understand. Why does Flora think this? Why has no one official been in touch?'

Jane-Elizabeth is about to stammer out everything she knows when Hammond holds up his hand, frowning. 'Wait for Pierre,' he says. 'We may as well hear everything at once.'

Pierre arrives in just a few minutes, his slight breathlessness showing that he has hurried as quickly as he can from the staff quarters up into the main house. He always jumps to it at the merest gesture from his boss. Jane-Elizabeth has never liked him. It's not just that he's physically unattractive, with his rough countenance and broken nose, but there's an aura around him that is off-putting. It's a high-testosterone toughness that seems to thrive on violence and aggression, and it's not tempered by any sense of honour or restraint. Jane-Elizabeth can't help comparing him to Miles Murray, who combines strength and courage with an ethical code that makes him completely trustworthy. Pierre, she thinks, isn't like that. She gets the impression that he would do anything Mr Hammond ordered without a moment's hesitation no matter what that entailed. Staying close to the source of money and power would be Pierre's priority.

'Sir?' he says in his heavy accent.

'Apparently my daughter Summer might have been kidnapped in Los Angeles.' Hammond looks at Jane-Elizabeth. 'You'd better tell us everything. Then we can decide our next step.'

In her chair, Estella crosses her long, tanned legs and listens carefully.

Flora is glad that Jimmy decided to stay with her. Charlie went home and Mac headed off to his office to start making enquiries into Jack Fuoco, while the two of them spent the rest of the day together until Flora had to crash out. As it is, she wakes fitfully through the night and is then wide awake when it's still dark outside.

She lies in her huge bed, wishing she had Andrei with her. They've barely been apart since their love affair began – not in a normal way, with dating and the slow burn towards falling in love, but with the agreement to find physical comfort with one another while they carried on yearning for their real loves – Flora for Jimmy (it seems so stupid now, when she thinks about it) and Andrei for Beth. It took some time – and some deliciously exciting encounters – before they realised that they had found love without even looking for it. For a while, Flora was troubled that Andrei had never shaken off his passion for Beth, but now she is sure that he no longer has feelings for her. The news from Freya has made her uneasy: it seems that Andrei is still bent on revenge on Dominic for winning Beth from him, and is going to take pleasure in bringing his business down. Even

181

though she's entirely focused on Summer and getting her back, she can't help wishing that it wasn't right now that she and Andrei had to be apart. It seems important that they're together, cementing their bond and building their still-young relationship.

Flora stares into the darkness, conjuring up Andrei in her mind. She remembers his large, muscled body, the strength in his arms and hands, the firmness of his buttocks and the iron hardness of his cock when they make love.

Which is often.

She sighs in the darkness, shifting between the cool sheets, feeling them slide over her skin. Just imagining Andrei's stiff cock makes her twitch and grow ready between her thighs. She slips a hand inside her silk pyjama top and runs it lightly over her breast. Her nipple is tight and stiff, ready to be kissed and sucked. Andrei loves to spend long minutes on her breasts, using his mouth and teeth on her nipples until she's almost ready to come just with the pleasure it gives her. While he sucks and nips, his long fingers play below, pushing into her with increasing fervour, sometimes coming out to stroke the hard bud above her entrance, making her jerk with the electric shocks of delight that he conjures up there.

She sighs. *Oh God, I can't stand it. I shouldn't think about it.*

But she can't stop the hunger growing in her body. She feels such a longing for Andrei she can hardly bear it. Her hand trails downwards and she wonders if bringing herself to a climax will help to damp down some of this burning desire she feels. Perhaps it will, but it will only work for a short while.

I need him.

Flora reaches out for her phone on the table beside the bed and brings the screen to life. She brings up Andrei's name and starts a video call to him. It rings for a while before he answers.

'Flora?' He sounds amused, happy to hear from her. 'I just had to get out of a meeting to answer.' She can see his face, craggy, smiling, his blue eyes a fierce aquamarine in the daylight. 'Where are you? I can't see you.'

'Oh yes, I forgot. It's still dark here.' She leans over and switches on the bedside light.

'Ah.' He smiles again. 'Now I can see you. You're in bed.'

'Yes. I can't sleep.' She gazes seductively at his face on the screen. 'I want you.'

His voice is husky. 'I want you too, my love. You can't think how much.'

'Don't you wish you were here with me?'

'Of course I do.'

'Look how much I want you.' She moves the phone down, and then pulls lightly at her silken pyjama top so that it falls open, revealing her breast. With her free hand, she rubs lightly at her nipple, tweaking it to even greater stiffness. She can hear his breathing thicken. She returns the phone to her face. 'See?'

'Yes . . . I can see.' His voice is low and intense.

'Would you like to see more?' she teases. 'Watch my fingers . . .' She positions the screen so that her fingertips are in view, resting lightly on the swell of her breast. Then she drags them downwards very gently, playing them over the softness of her flesh, across her belly and downwards to the waist of her silk pyjamas. 'Would you like to follow them . . . down here?' She slips two fingers under the waistband, and hears the sound of a low murmur from the phone. She brings the phone back to her face and smiles at Andrei. His eyes are hooded in a way she well knows. He's in the stir of lust now, thinking about the way she feels, the smell of her, the taste of her hidden delights. 'My fingers are still there,' she whispers. 'I'm thinking about you while I touch . . . and rub . . . and stroke . . .'

He seems still as stone but she can hear his breathing quicken. He is with her.

'Oh . . . Andrei . . .' she says, and plays across the hot, swollen bud of her clit with her fingertips. She moans lightly. 'Oh God. I wish you were here.'

'My dearest, you don't know what you're doing to me,' he says roughly. 'You're driving me mad.'

'Come and join me,' she says. 'I want you so much. I need you here with me.' Her tongue comes out to wet her lips, her eyes half close. She is thinking of the delicious feelings that her fingers are producing, and thinking of Andrei, the swelling of his cock that will now be so hungry for her even though she's thousands of miles away.

'Flora . . .' His voice is deep with longing. 'I have one meeting I must attend. You know which one. The one I've been waiting for all this time, with the man who will allow me to crush Dominic Stone once and for all.'

'What does he matter?' she asks. 'Does he matter more than me?'

'Of course not.'

'Then leave it. Forget him. Prove to me that you care more about us than about getting back at him.' Her tongue darts out to touch her lips again and she gasps a tiny gasp of arousal. 'I need you here,' she says again. 'Please, Andrei. Please . . .'

She can tell that he is struggling with his choice. She's

asking him to prove that he has relinquished all his feelings for Beth, even the last few pangs of jealousy towards the man Beth chose over him. More than that, she's asking him to leave the battlefield when he can see victory is in his grasp. Should she ask that of him? Is it really her right to force him to make that choice?

But I need him – and I need to know that I'm more important than crushing Dominic.

Andrei still says nothing, looking intently at her through the screen.

'So . . .' she says softly, 'will you come?'

CHAPTER SEVENTEEN

This could be the craziest thing that's ever happened to me.

Here, among the last acrid fumes of smoke, in the sudden chill of the night now that the fire is out, the two of us wet, sweaty and smeared in ash and soot, I'm kissing someone more wildly than I've ever kissed anyone in my life. All the intensity of the last few hours is in our kiss. The adrenalin of danger, the charge of the physical exertion, the relief and exhilaration at putting out the fire and escaping a terrible fate has keyed us both up to the point where we're seized with heightened passion.

But there's more than that. The moment he pulled me into his arms and pressed his lips on mine, his tongue taking possession of me with a kind of desperate hunger, I knew that this was what I'd wanted to happen since I met him. I know that it had to happen and that whatever is propelling us together is bigger and stronger than us both.

My arms are round his neck, my fingers deep in his dark hair, as we kiss madly, unable to get enough of each other. He tastes of smoke and sweetness and the delicious essence of himself. His skin is divine where my lips brush it, the warm scent of it tingling my senses. His tongue probes my mouth, his lips devour mine, and his hands run along my spine and over my bottom.

We don't bother to attempt to speak. We don't need to. This is our communication: every moment that we kiss we're showing our growing desire for one another. The kiss is more intense than any I've ever known or imagined. All I know is that it can't come to an end, not yet. Not before . . .

Before what?

He's your kidnapper, says a small voice in my mind. *This isn't supposed to happen.*

But I don't care about that. I can't do anything but obey my body and what it wants, and it wants Jack so badly there's nothing I can do about it.

Jack is breathing hard, a growling in his throat as he touches me. Then he moves suddenly and the next moment, I realise he's lifted me off my feet, literally. I'm in his arms, still kissing him, my hand caressing his neck, and the softness where his hair turns to light fuzz at the back of his skull. He walks towards my little room and opens the door. The air is relatively fresh in here; it escaped the thickest smoke. For a moment I wonder if he's going to deposit me there and lock me in again.

Have I been a complete fool? Have I walked back into a trap when I could have got free?

But then I'm on the bed and Jack is with me. He isn't going to leave me here and imprison me. We're here together, pressed close together on the single bed, our bodies writhing against each other as we cope with the incredible sensations our closeness is creating.

We're both moaning and gasping, our hands stroking and caressing as we explore one another, glorying in the feel of each other. My hand reaches under his T-shirt and touches the smoothness of his skin. His muscles are hard beneath its surface and they ripple as he moves too. Now I'm smoothing my palm along his back, enjoying its broadness. His hand is on my bare leg, beneath the frayed denim of my shorts, stroking the expanse of skin, and then he's lifted my leg to wrap it over his hip.

God . . . we're close to each other now.

I can feel the heat emanating from the groin of his jeans and wonder if he can feel the answering heat in mine. Arousal is burning hard through me.

I want him. I want his cock in me.

The thought startles me. I remember how often I've been on the brink of giving up my virginity and pulled back because it wasn't right: I wasn't with a guy I truly loved, or I didn't want to lose it in a casual way, in a situation that wasn't as romantic as I dreamed of.

Yeah – I guess I was saving it until I was in a half-burned-down shack with a guy who's kidnapped me.

The thought makes me want to laugh but it turns into a more fevered desire. I kiss Jack even more passionately, pulling his head to mine as hard as I can.

Maybe it's because tonight has made me realise there isn't any time to waste. Not any more. What am I waiting for? Some magic day when I'm given permission to live my life? My life is now. I've let too much slip by already.

I reach my hand down to Jack's jeans and start to unbuckle his belt, my fingers eager.

'Wait, Summer,' he says, pulling away from me and gently taking my hand in his. His brown eyes, so heartbreakingly beautiful, look anxious even while they burn with desire. 'Summer – this is what you want, right?'

'Of course,' I say breathlessly. 'More than anything.'

'I mean, *really* want it. I don't want you to do this because you think I want it and you're afraid to say no. I don't want to think that this is the way you can get yourself out of here. Only because you feel the way I do . . .'

'I do,' I say, panting. 'Can't you tell?'

'Oh God, you're beautiful,' he says, his voice cracking as he speaks. 'I'm so fucking mixed up.'

'Don't think about it,' I beg. 'Don't think at all right now – let's just feel and be.' I press my lips on to his and slide my tongue into his mouth, and he responds with fierce intensity, his fingers on my head, his other hand on my thigh, pulling me to him. I can't get enough of the taste of him, and I'm ravenous for him now, mad with longing and not caring a bit for anything but this.

My fingers are at his belt again, and I quickly finish unbuckling it. Now I flip the button out through the hole, and the waistband loosens. He's breathing hard, his fingers pressing into my skin, his tongue feverish in my mouth. I pull down the zip, my fingers already sensing the heat radiating out from within his pants. I brush the back of my hand over the solidness there, and my insides clench with excitement. Jack gasps as I touch him even through the soft cotton of his jockey shorts.

'Oh Christ,' he moans against my mouth.

As we kiss again, I rub my hand over the hardness again, fascinated by it, longing for it, then I slip my fingers inside the slit at the front and feel the hard, slightly ridged surface of his erection and its velvet softness. It's hot and stiff and as I go to grasp it, I realise that my fingers can hardly meet around it. He pulls away from my mouth so that he can look at my face as my hand caresses his cock. His dark-brown eyes are like liquid, but burn with an intensity I've never seen before. I sense his desire and it fills me with butterfly excitement, and a quivering need of my own. I know I'm damp with longing for him, already desperate to possess him. I've never felt like this before; in the past, when

I've got near to this, I've been apprehensive, afraid even. I haven't trusted that it will be all right, and that I will like whatever is coming my way. Now, I feel in control, as though I'm taking the lead here and Jack is helpless in the face of what we are both feeling. I know for sure that his cock will make me happy. It will give me pleasure. It will fill an emptiness I never even knew I had until this very moment. I have the feeling that Jack will complete me.

'I want to touch you,' Jack says in a low, intense whisper. 'Can I touch you?'

His shyness moves me. 'Of course,' I say. 'I want you to.'

We stare into one another's eyes as our hands roam over each other's bodies. His hand smooths down the skin over my hip, leaving a burning trail where his fingertips touch me. I gasp as he lightly drags it down over my belly to where my shorts are fastened just below my navel. He undoes the button quickly and, our gazes still locked, slides his fingers inside the cotton of my panties and over my mound. I can hardly breathe, the dizziness of the delight he's setting off inside me making me feel faint. I stroke the hardness beneath my fingers, moving the skin under my palm, taking my hand up and over the smooth top of his cock. As his fingers slip downwards in my smooth wetness, I can't help clutching him harder.

'You feel so gorgeous,' he says in a low rasp. 'So beautiful.'

'So do you.' I smile at him.

Then a fresh wave of hot desire overtakes us, and we're both filled with a fevered need. I lift up my T-shirt, tearing it up over my head and discarding it. At once, he moans at the sight of my breasts rising from my white lace bra. He dips his head to kiss the soft mounds and then puts his mouth over the lace itself to kiss my nipples, his tongue wet and soft through the scratchy material. It makes me shiver and groan, electric impulses connecting my nipple right to my groin, where my sex contracts and swells in response. He undoes my bra and sets my breasts free, caressing one with one hand while he kisses the other. The feeling is deliciously unbearable. Then our urgency steps up a gear. He lifts his dark head, his mouth lands on mine and I open to him at once, wanting only to sink into him and have him become part of me. I don't care about anything but having him right now. I pull him closer to me, pressing myself up against the rock-hard rod of his cock. We're possessed now, breathing hard, too eager to stop. He's pushing down my shorts and panties and I'm helping him by wriggling out of them while I push his jeans down to free him completely too. Now he's climbing on top of me while I open my thighs to let him lie between them. I'm breathless and needy, not wanting to stop but only to act on the instinct that's driving me on. I've never felt so alive. Nothing has ever felt so completely right before.

His mouth is at my ear. 'I'm gonna use something – okay?'

For a moment I don't know what he means, then he slides out of my grasp and is off me, scooping up his jeans and grabbing a small packet from the pocket. I guess at once.

'We have to be safe,' I say breathlessly.

'Always.' He grins at me, a lopsided smile that makes my stomach clench with the bliss of it. The next moment, he's torn open the little packet and is back with me, his body hot against mine. 'You want to help?'

'Yes, please.'

He guides my hand to his cock and puts my fingers to

where the small dome of slippery rubber sits on the huge hot head. 'That's right. I love the way you touch me.'

Our fingers move together, sliding the thin skin down over his shaft until it reaches the very root. His cock feels different now: cooler, more lubricated,

Maybe it will be easier for me this way, if he's slippery.

Jack is back now, where I need him, his hard body between my open thighs. He kisses me and I feel his erection at my entrance. I know that this is the moment I've wondered about, and waited for, for so long. A rush of happiness fills me at the same time as wild desire makes me urge him on, my arms round him now, my hands roaming down his back, over his buttocks, up to his neck. I can feel the smooth top of his erection pressing at me, and then it's inside, just a centimetre or two.

I gasp. It's so thick, I feel like I'm stretching wider than I can manage. Then, after a moment I begin to be accustomed to it, just as he pushes forward again, expanding me even more, and I cry out.

'Are you okay?' he pants.

'Yes, yes, don't stop,' I beg. I've never felt anything like this before, as though he's filling me up to a point I can barely stand. 'Please . . .'

'Oh my God,' he gasps, as he presses in again another few centimetres. 'You're so tight, so gorgeous . . .' He thrusts with his hips and moves forward again. This is such sweet agony, as I open gradually to receive him, taking him in deeper and deeper. I keep waiting for the real pain to begin, or for him to hit an insuperable barrier, but it doesn't seem to come. He just goes deeper and deeper into me until I feel as though he's filling my belly with his huge, thick cock. When I think that surely he can't go any deeper, he stops, resting inside me. I curl my legs round his to keep him as deep as he can go, breathing hard, arching my back and reaching for his lips with my mouth.

'Summer,' he says almost wonderingly.

'Jack.' I kiss him deeply. I've never felt so connected to another person. We're like one body now and the feeling is so deliciously ecstatic, I feel I could pass out from it. As we kiss, he starts to move, pulling back and thrusting forward with his hips. He's on his elbows now so that he can push forward as hard as possible. I lift my hips to meet him as he comes forward, unable to stop myself crying out as his cock goes even deeper into the heart of me. The friction inside me is the most amazing thing I've ever experienced, beyond anything I ever imagined. I can think of nothing but the way he's driving me onwards with that extraordinary girth of his, the way I'm stretched around him but still able to take him deeper and harder as he picks up pace. His body rubs against my clitoris as he goes up to the root of his cock, sending yet more pleasure racing to every nerve end. I don't know how long I can stand this but I also don't want it to end.

I feel like I'm part of the ancient human story of men and women fucking; as though I'm obeying the oldest instinct there is, as my hips drive up to meet Jack's, as I welcome him into my depths. But I also feel as though there has never been anything like this before. We are unique. This is unique. Our chemistry is so perfectly matched that only we can feel this beautiful, magical feeling of intense pleasure.

I can't help gasping out loud every time he rams home inside me. We're both moaning, shouting almost, as we move in time. Jack picks up the pace, fucking harder and faster now. I keep up with him, feeling a great stir deep within me that I know is the answer to this desperate need for him. My body has a way to make this need go away, or at least bring it to a resolution. I understand that now.

The pleasure begins to build in me, augmented by the relentless movement of that thick cock inside me. It swirls up from deep inside, prickling in my nipples and in my groin, making my heart race and my sex swell with the rush of blood going through me. I'm going to come, to orgasm, at last. It's going to be the first time this has happened to me. Jack's body batters against my longing clitoris, making it throb delightfully and send a buzz of pleasure through me that's building and building. He's gasping as he thrusts into me and I can feel his cock swelling up to become even thicker; the sensation is blissful.

The knowledge that he's on the brink of explosion is all I need: a fierce wave crashes over me and then lifts me up and out on the crest of pleasure. I shake all over, my limbs stiffening with the tremors possessing me, as ripples of electricity possess me. As I experience the great wonder of my climax, I feel him stroke deeper and slower inside me. His eyes are closed, every muscle tense, and then as the force of my orgasm starts to subside, he stiffens and I feel him swell inside me as his climax possesses him. I can even feel the pumping as it gushes out of him and into the rubber tip of the condom. When he has no more, he sinks down on to the bed beside me, panting and spent.

I hold him in my arms, a little shy now that it's over. I wonder if I should help take the condom off. *I guess I don't know the etiquette. Putting it on might be okay, but taking it off might be rude. And messy. I'll leave it to him, I guess.*

Jack is quiet now, watching me with that dark-brown

gaze of his. He's looking at me, tender but agonised. 'Summer, was that your first time?'

I nod, smiling happily. 'Yes. And it was beautiful. Thank you.'

'Thank *you*,' he says sincerely. 'It was an honour.' He lies back and looks up at the ceiling. With a deft movement, he rolls off the condom, ties a knot in the end and tosses it into the bin with a dead-sure aim. 'Kind of crazy. But an honour.'

'Now I know why everyone makes such a fuss about sex,' I say, and sigh contentedly. 'I really didn't get it before. But now I do.'

He laughs lightly. 'It's not always that good.' He turns back to look at me again, almost surprised. 'That was like nothing I've ever had before.'

'Good,' I say, and smile. 'So it was your first time too. In a way.'

He smiles back. 'In a way.'

We lie there for a moment in the half-light from the lamp. Then a second later, we're both fast asleep.

CHAPTER EIGHTEEN

Flora and Jimmy have a room service breakfast together, eating fresh fruit salad and yoghurt, though Flora can barely get that down with the anxiety churning inside, and sipping on strong coffee. Charlie arrives while they're still eating and sits down to join them for coffee. He goes straight into the developments he's made.

'I went to Jack's workplace – the place he told me he worked, anyway,' Charlie says. 'And I made sure they'd never heard of him. No one knows of any Jack Fuoco. Definitely not. I asked to see a staff list.' He pulls a sheet of paper out of his bag. 'The receptionist wasn't that keen to hand over the staff list to a complete stranger, but when I spun a story about a surprise birthday party and a lost friend, she kind of melted and got me a photocopy.'

'Well done, Charlie!' Jimmy says, and clinks a coffee cup against Charlie's.

'I suppose so,' Flora says slowly. 'But what good will it do if no one there has heard of him?'

'Well . . .' Charlie takes a sip of his coffee. 'Jack does live in Los Angeles – or at least he does at the moment. He told me that his sister works in a hospital downtown. That seems to me to indicate that he is based here.'

'Unless that was a lie too,' Jimmy puts in.

'Yeah – but it was said in the kind of way that seemed

more like throwaway information. As though he wasn't really thinking when he said it. I don't think it was something he said to mislead me, that's all.' Charlie sighs. 'So my train of thought is that he picked this car design company because he has some kind of connection there. A friend or something. That's why he uses it for his cover story.'

'Risky?' asks Jimmy.

'Maybe less risky than picking somewhere he's completely unconnected to. At least this way he can walk into the building if he has to.'

'Good point,' concedes Jimmy.

Flora picks up the staff list. 'So we work our way through this, and call them all? Ask if they know Jack Fuoco? As it's not his real name, as far as we can work out, I don't see how that will help.'

Charlie takes another sip of his coffee and says, 'Have you ever heard of the fifteen-inch rule?'

Flora shakes her head, and Jimmy says playfully, 'It sounds like a good one!'

Charlie shoots him a look and says, 'There's a saying that if you've mislaid something, the chances are that it's probably within fifteen inches of where you think you left it. I've tried it, and it works nine times out of ten. I think there's a similar kind of thing we can apply here. When Jack made his cover story, he probably created a life that was not that far removed from his actual one. It's easier to remember that way. So what do we know about Jack?'

Flora picks up a piece of paper and says, 'Let's write down everything you can think of.'

Charlie and Jimmy rack their brains for everything they

197

can recall about Jack, and at the end, they have a decent list of facts they absorbed over their friendship with him.

'How will this help us?' Flora says, scanning the list. 'Number one – he's Italian.' She looks over at the other two. 'Do you think that's true?'

'I do,' Jimmy says, 'if his looks are anything to go by. Classic olive skin, dark-brown eyes, dark hair. Very Mediterranean.'

'I agree,' Charlie says and looks at the staff list again. 'He might not be Jack Fuoco but he's definitely Italian. So let's look and see if there are any Italians working at the car company. Maybe that's a link we can identify.'

'Maybe,' Flora says, looking worried, 'but it's tenuous.'

'Here,' Jimmy says, pointing at a name on the list. 'Alvaro da Silva. Is that Italian?'

Charlie says, 'I don't think so – more Spanish, I think.'

'Yes, I agree,' says Flora, craning to see the list. 'But this one, Mark Belluccio. That's Italian, I'm sure.'

'And this one – Antony D'Angeli. That's definitely another.'

They find four in total that look as though they are Italian.

'I think this is hopeless,' Flora says, sitting back on the sofa and looking disheartened. 'We have no idea what might link these names to Jack. One could be his real name but how will we find out?'

'We'll think of something,' Jimmy says consolingly. 'And it's all we've got right now.'

They're still mulling over plans when the phone rings. It's the front desk, letting them know that a visitor is on the way up.

'A Mr McManus, Miss Hammond.'

'Thank you.' Flora puts the phone down and turns to the others. 'Mac's on his way up. Maybe he's got something to tell us. I'm desperate to have some information for Freya when she gets here.'

When Mac arrives at the suite, still dapper in his cowboy boots, jeans and a linen jacket, Flora tells him what they've been up to.

'That's a good start,' he says. 'I have to say that I've done some extensive searches and I haven't turned up anyone by the name of Jack Fuoco. Anyone with a name even vaguely similar checks out, I'm afraid. I was gonna ask you for exactly this – a resumé of everything you know about him. May I see, please?' He examines the piece of paper, pursing his lips and making little whistle noises through them as he does so. 'His sister is a nurse, is she? Any idea which hospital?'

Charlie shakes his head. 'I can't remember if he said. I did get the impression it's somewhere central though. And not so famous that I'd heard of it.'

'Yeah – nothing so easy as that.' Mac shakes his head. 'It never is. And maybe the sister is an invention anyway.'

'Charlie doesn't think so,' Jimmy puts in.

Mac pushes the fact sheet away from him and sits back on the sofa. 'What's puzzling me right now is that we still haven't heard anything from him. I expected some kind of communication last night. That would work with the kind of timeline these people usually have. They leave it long enough for fear and panic to set in, but they also want to come in before the police have got involved. They usually don't want to keep the victim for any longer than necessary, so find it hard not to make their demands within a day or two of the kidnap.' He frowns and his jaws move up and down as he chews his gum. 'Yeah, that really is strange. I'd have put good money on the fact that he was gonna call us last night. And then he didn't.'

'Maybe he called someone else – like my father,' suggests Flora.

'Does Summer know that number off by heart?' Mac asks.

Flora shakes her head. 'I don't think so. He changes phones and numbers all the time. We've never been able to learn them all. But she has the number stored on her phone.'

Mac says, 'I don't think he'll want to turn on that phone if he can avoid it. He'll know that it can be traced easily once it's turned on its location services. My guess is that he'll call from another phone and he'll want to use a number without accessing Summer's contact list inside her phone.'

'She knows my number off by heart,' Flora says quickly.

'I guessed as much. And that's why I thought I might get a call from you in the night or first thing this morning saying that contact had been made.' Mac ponders for a moment, staring at the remains of the breakfast. 'Say – can you think of any reason apart from money why your sister might be taken? Does she have any enemies?'

Flora shakes her head again, her expression bewildered. 'No! That's the crazy thing. It's got to be about money, there is literally no other reason. Summer doesn't have any bitter ex-boyfriends or anything like that.'

Mac stares at her thoughtfully. 'Okay. But I'm gonna make a copy of this list of yours, all right? Then I'm going to take it away and study it properly.'

Jimmy explains about their idea of finding a link at the car design company.

'That's not a bad avenue of enquiry at all,' Mac says encouragingly. 'You guys should carry on with that. Something might come of it, you never know.' He picks up a pen. 'I'll do the copy of this list and you can start making me a list of things I ought to know about Summer as well.'

'Okay,' Flora says. 'I can ask Freya when she gets here too.'

'Freya?'

'My older sister,' she explains. 'She's arriving from Scotland to help look for Summer.' Her phone beeps and she takes it out to look at it. Then she frowns. 'Goodness. My father is coming as well. Jane-Elizabeth says they're on the way to the airport now. They'll be here this evening.'

'Quite the gathering of the clan,' remarks Mac with a smile. 'Well, that's nice. I'm a pushover for a family reunion.'

'Somehow,' Flora says, rereading the message, 'I don't think that's quite what will happen here.' She looks over at Jimmy. 'This should be interesting.'

Freya finally manages to get to sleep not long before they come in to land at LAX. Miles doesn't wake her until the last possible moment, and she comes to properly when the plane hits the ground with a light bump and then the braking begins, the vast power of the plane's acceleration tamed and drained as they travel along the runway.

'We're here,' Miles says, with a smile. 'Do you feel all right?'

She blinks. 'I feel groggy.' A huge yawn overtakes her. 'How long did I sleep?'

'You got about two hours, I'd say,' Miles says. He rubs her hand. 'This is going to be a tough couple of days. I want you to know that I'm right here for you.'

'I know.' She leans over and kisses him. 'Thank you. I can't believe what you've given up for me.'

'Not as much as you've given up for me,' he says, and stares intently into her eyes. 'You know why.'

'Yes,' she whispers back, a dark excitement turning over in her stomach. He still has the power to turn her liquid with a look.

'Come on. Let's get ready to disembark,' he says. 'It's a bit sunnier here than Scotland, I'll give it that!'

Fifteen minutes later, they're off the plane and through passport control. Miles collects their luggage while Freya goes to the ladies' room. When they meet again, she's freshened up and is smiling.

'I'm ready for action,' she announces. 'Let's do this.'

'Great,' Miles says. Their cases are loaded on to a trolley and waiting. 'Let's go and find your sister.'

In the arrivals hall, they see Flora and Jimmy at once, even though Flora's partially hidden under a large floppy hat and shades. Flora waves hard and is dashing towards her sister in an instant and the next moment they are hugging fiercely. When they pull apart, Flora has tears falling down her cheeks.

'Hey!' Freya regards the tears with a worried expression. 'What's this? Is there news?'

'No – nothing,' sniffs Flora. 'I'm just so happy to see you. And I'm so worried about Summer. It's all getting on top of me.' She turns to Miles with a smile. 'Hi, Miles. Thanks for coming with Freya. I can't tell you how grateful we are.'

'You're welcome. I'm fond of Summer. I want her home safe and sound as much as anyone.' Miles looks at Freya with tenderness. 'And I wasn't going to let Freya go through this alone.'

Flora smiles at them both, but it's a little faltering. Freya wonders if something is wrong but before she can ask, Flora says brightly, 'And it's going to be quite a gathering before too long. Dad is on his way.'

'Oh God.' Freya shuts her eyes and feels faint for a second. 'It must be bad. Is there something you're not telling me?'

'No, no,' Flora says hastily. 'But I had to tell Jane-Elizabeth to alert him. You know that.'

Freya nods. 'Yes, I suppose so.'

'Jane-Elizabeth emailed me to say that they've booked an entire floor of the Ritz-Carlton. She wanted to know if I would like to move suites and join them.'

'Not surprisingly, Flora wants to stay exactly where she is!' pipes up Jimmy. 'Hi, Freya. Great to see you. I'm just sorry it's in these circumstances.'

'Hi Jimmy.' Freya kisses him hello. 'Lovely to see you too. Now – much as I love the airport, do you think we can head off now? I'm dying for a good cup of coffee.'

'I booked you on the same floor as us,' Flora says as they head for the exit.

'So it really is going to be all of us together,' Freya says, shaking her head. 'I thought we might never be together again, after the last time.'

'We don't have Summer,' Flora reminds her.

'Not yet,' Miles puts in firmly. 'But we will.'

Flora smiles at him gratefully. 'Yes, we will. And I'll tell you all about our private investigator in the car. He's on the case.'

Miles raises his eyebrows. 'A gumshoe, eh? Interesting.'

Freya is struck by a cold thought. 'We won't just have Dad, though, will we? We'll have Estella as well.'

'I suppose so,' Flora says. 'I don't think she'd tolerate being left behind.'

They emerge into the warm sunshine from the air-conditioned chill of the airport.

Freya says, 'I just hope she doesn't make things more difficult than they need to be. Surely even Estella has enough compassion to stay in the background at a time like this.'

Flora gestures to the sleek SUV that the hotel has sent to pick them up. 'There's our ride. And as far as Estella is concerned, I wouldn't bank on any kind of compassion, no matter what the circumstances. If I know her, she'll be looking for opportunities to further her own cause – and nothing else.'

'She sounds like a real charmer,' Jimmy says cheerfully.

Freya shoots him a meaningful look. 'You'd better believe it. And then some.'

'I can't wait to meet her,' Jimmy says, almost gleeful.

Flora laughs. 'You'll probably love her,' she says, 'and the two of you will end up best of friends.'

'Are you kidding?' Jimmy opens the door of the SUV as the driver loads the luggage into the back. 'You girls are my number one stars, and always will be. Now let's go and take over the Ritz.'

CHAPTER NINETEEN

When I wake, Jack and I are lying in each other's arms, covered by the homespun quilt that gave my little cell its only touch of comfort when I arrived. I did not expect that it would one day be covering my naked body as I lay pressed against the warmth of Jack's bare skin.

I hear the soft rhythm of his breathing and remember with a fizzing somersault in my stomach what happened between us last night. There was the fire . . . I got out of my room . . . we doused the flames . . . then fell into one another's arms and . . . I pull in a sharp breath as I recall what Jack did to me last night, and the intensity of the pleasure we experienced. Images play back through my mind: the sight of his dark head against my chest as his mouth fastens on my breast; the look on his face as he enters me, and the gasp as he came hard. I remember the stream of kisses over my neck and cheeks as he made love to me, and when I came. *I had an orgasm! It was amazing!* I feel stupidly proud of myself, and as though I've passed an important milestone in my life. So I'm normal. Secretly I'd been afraid I'd never know what it was like. I recall the soft caressing and murmuring as he told me what a beautiful experience that had been. And then, exhausted, we fell deeply asleep. It must be quite late in the day already, judging by the bright daylight coming in through the window.

Oh my God. Now what? I stare at his face, the long dark

lashes curled on his cheek, the dark stubble prickling across his jaw and chin, the curve of his beautiful lips. *He's my kidnapper. But here he is, naked, asleep, and the door is open. I can just go if I want.*

But what do I want? I could have gone last night.

He would have died without my help. I didn't have a choice.

So I could get up right now, and be dressed and out of here in two minutes. I could find my phone. I could call someone and then take the car and drive away.

I'd be safe. But I'd never see Jack again.

I imagine how Jack would react to finding me gone, and the police turning up to arrest him. I feel suddenly sure that if I go now, it would mean that nothing really has changed. He would still be filled with anger and resentment towards me and my family. He would still want vindication.

I would live the rest of my life in fear that he was coming to get me. Or Flora. Or Freya. We'd never be safe. Even if he went to prison, one day he'd be out. Or he could arrange something at a distance. No. Leaving and turning him in is not an option.

And even if I just got up and left, and never told anyone what had happened, it would be the same. I would still wonder if he was out there, waiting, cooking up another plan, working out how to get revenge for the death of his father.

I can't go until this is settled between us. I beat down the voice that tells me I'm being foolish, and this is the most dangerous path of all. I'm choosing to remain in Jack's power, after everything that he's done. Am I just a fool?

You'd better think hard about why you're doing this. Is it because of what's happened? Are you under his spell, is that it? You just want more of his glorious body and his beautiful cock and his amazing mouth and all the pleasure he can give you?

I sigh at the thought. Perhaps I am just erotically obsessed now, and that's why I can't walk out of the door.

Jack shifts beside me, and opens his eyes slowly, blinking in the morning sunshine. 'Hi,' he says and yawns. 'How are you?'

'Good.' I smile at his sleepy face. 'You?'

'Pretty good, considering.' He moves to kiss me on the lips. 'Boy, you sure brighten up a morning, Summer. Look at you. Mmm.' He kisses me again, his warm tongue probing softly between my lips. I open my mouth under his, my insides turning liquid with his touch. I press my body against him, revelling in the feeling of my breasts on his hard chest, the smattering of dark hair rough on my soft skin.

We kiss long and soft, our hands playing across each other. I feel the hard bullets of his nipples within the small circle of dark hair that surrounds them and the superb hardness of his abdominals. Whatever he's been doing at the gym has paid off. My hands caress the firmness of his buttocks and the dip at either side that shows how muscled he is. I think of the way he used those muscles last night, thrusting into me, and sigh as my sex shimmers and swells again.

I want more. I want more and more.

Jack must feel the same, as he kisses my neck with a sweet tickling and then dips his head to my breasts, kissing and nibbling at each nipple in turn, gently licking the under-curve of my breasts, glorying in them. He makes me feel beautiful and desirable, I love the way he's so turned on.

Then suddenly, he's kissing downwards, his lips burning a trail over my stomach and down towards my mound.

I gasp and my eyes fly open. *Is he going to . . . is he going to do . . . that?* Seized by sudden embarrassment, I reach down to put my hands round his head. He looks up at me, his dark eyes intense with desire.

'What is it?' he asks in a low rasp. 'Are you okay?'

'What are you doing?' I ask, as though I can't guess.

'I want to kiss you and taste you. You're so beautiful to me, Summer, it's almost unbearable. Do you want me to?'

I do. But I feel awkward. I don't know if I am pretty down there. I know that I'm tingling with excitement at the thought of his mouth against me, but . . .

'Don't think about it, just lie back and enjoy,' he murmurs. 'You don't need to worry. I love it, I'm in heaven being here with you.'

'Okay,' I say, and lie back on the pillows, gazing up at the ceiling without seeing it, my hands still buried in his dark hair. He is lying between my legs now, pressing my thighs gently apart, a hand resting on each as he brings his mouth to me. He's so gentle at first, so tantalising, his breath playing over my skin, that I can hardly bear it. I tense, every muscle stiff with anticipation.

'Relax,' he murmurs gently. 'Relax.'

I try to do as he says, but my sex is alive with need, melting with juice. My body delights in his nearness, and then I feel it: the merest stroke of his tongue over my swollen bud. I jerk as though I've been attached to an electrical socket, and gasp. He licks again, and then again, and I twist and writhe as he stimulates me. My hands leave his head and clutch at the sheets instead. He begins to lap softly at me, stroking upwards through the soft lips to the hard bud of my clit and, despite the pounding of my heart and the twitching of my limbs, I begin to relax into what he's doing. The pleasure is extreme, delicious, incredible. His tongue slips downwards to my entrance and I realise he's pushing it inside me. The thought is so exciting, I reach another level of arousal. I can sense that dark whirlpool rising inside me, ready to take me into its swirling heart and drown me in ecstasy. He returns to my clit, licking harder now, nipping it with his teeth, increasing the pressure. Now his fingers are at my slit, pushing in, thrusting in like his cock did last night. My hands clench on the sheets, pulling and twisting under the impact of what I'm feeling. I feel like I'm gushing honeydew over him as his mouth pays homage to my sex, his tongue stroking harder and more rhythmically at my bud, his fingers driving in and out. I can't resist it. It's too much. It's more than I can stand. I feel like I can't bear it and yet I need him to keep on going and going and going.

'Oh my God,' I shout, my hips rising to meet him. 'Holy . . . shit! Oh, oh . . .!' This orgasm is like an intense explosion of fireworks going off in my head and through my body, shaking me with its force. I can't help shouting, my eyes squeezed shut as the intensity of the exquisite agony hits me, radiating out in swarms of quakes. It seems to go on for ever until suddenly it's over and his tongue is licking my clit even though it really can't take another moment of stimulation. I sit up, panting and gasping, and lift his head from my sex. He grins at me.

'I guess you liked that,' he murmurs.

I can't speak, just nod breathlessly. I look down as he gets to his knees and see that monster thick cock of his rearing up towards me. I pull him towards me and on to my chest, while with one hand I guide his hot erection towards my dripping sex.

'Wait,' he says, holding back despite the longing in his eyes. 'I need a condom. We can't risk it, Summer . . .'

'But I've never had anyone except you,' I whisper. 'What about you?'

He bites his lip, his gaze intense. 'I had some tests when I renewed my insurance a coupla months ago. I haven't been with anyone since then. But it's not just that – what about pregnancy?'

'I've got an implant. Because of stuff to do with my period. Flora and I are both the same, we got them together. I can't get pregnant.' I grasp him a little firmer, glorying in his cock. 'Please, Jack, I need you . . .' I'm ready for him, so oiled and ready, that the great girth slips easily inside, stretching me out deliciously as he goes in.

'Fuck,' he says in a strained whisper. 'Oh fuck . . .' He stares down at my body beneath him, my breasts topped with rosy nipples as hard as pebbles, and bites his lip, his expression close to a wince as he experiences the sensations of being inside me. 'You just came all over my face,' he murmurs. 'It was gorgeous, baby. I'm so hot for you, so turned on . . . Oh God, you feel amazing.'

He's tense with lust as he pushes deep into me. I reach up for his mouth, pulling his head to mine and we kiss as he thrusts up into my very depths.

'I want you to come,' I say against his lips. 'I want you to have what I had.'

'I won't be long,' he says, his eyes shutting under the force of what he's feeling. 'I can't hold it even if I wanted.'

He starts to move hard inside me, thrusting forward, each stroke of his cock sending a gasp from my lips as he hits my core. He gathers speed, thrusting harder and harder, and I glory in the pleasure he's giving me and taking for himself. Then, he tenses, gasps and pulls his cock out again so that I can see it pumping out his orgasm. I thrill to the sight and the knowledge that I was the cause of it.

He falls back beside me.

'That was beautiful,' I say, unable to stop the huge smile all over my face. 'Like nothing I've ever known. Thank you. Really. Thank you.'

Jack smiles back. 'It was my pleasure. Literally.'

I laugh and sigh luxuriously. 'Oh God, I could do that all day.'

'You're incredible,' he says. 'I can't get enough of you.' He stares at me for a moment and then suddenly his expression changes. The laughter drains away and he looks stormy as he says, 'Shit. Shit!' He lies back beside me and stares at the ceiling. 'What a fucking mess.'

'Why?' I ask, my own happiness vanishing in an instant. 'What is it? We need to work this out.'

He doesn't answer for a minute and then turns to look at me. To my astonishment, his eyes are full of anger. 'Why the fuck didn't you leave last night?' he demands in a harsh voice.

I blink with surprise. Hurt washes over me and I flinch from him. 'You'd be dead if I had!' I retort.

'Ah – fuck it. Maybe. We'll never know.'

'I saved your life!' I say hotly. 'Doesn't that count for anything? Doesn't it mean that we're even now? You think my father was responsible for your father's death. Well, haven't I done something to erase that by making sure you survived the fire?'

Jack's lips tighten and he stares angrily at the ceiling. I

211

can't work him out. I thought he would be pleased that he now had a way out of a situation that I truly believe he doesn't want to be in. But now he's acting like I messed up by doing the right thing. 'You don't understand,' he mutters.

'So help me to understand,' I say, more softly now. I run my fingers over his shoulder. 'Why doesn't this make things better, not worse?'

'Because it doesn't change the promise I made,' he says quietly. 'Nothing can change that, except doing what I said I would.'

A cold shiver shakes me suddenly. 'What promise, Jack? What are you talking about?'

'I promised my brother. He wanted me to do this. We planned it together. He explained to me how it was the right thing to do, for our father, for his memory, for our grand-parents and our mother. He told me that I had it in my power to make life right for our sister – all I had to do was sacrifice myself for that cause.'

'Sacrifice yourself?' I echo, a clammy feeling of fear rising in me. 'What do you mean?'

'I'd have to be prepared to give up my own future for the family,' Jack says in a low voice. 'I might have to go to prison.'

'Your brother shouldn't ask that of you,' I say firmly. 'It wouldn't make things right for your family if you ruin your life for some point of honour that won't make any differ-ence to anything. It would only make things worse for them, I swear. You've already lost your father and your brother is in prison. Why would your mother want to lose you too? She wants the best for you and your sister, you know that. That's why she brought you two here, am I right?'

The look on his face tells me I've hit a nerve and I go on.

'Your mother wanted to get you away from your brother, didn't she? You said she needed to get away from your grandparents because they couldn't forget the past, and couldn't stop mourning it. Right? Was it also because she knew your brother felt the same way and that he would use you for his plans of revenge?'

Jack turns so that I can't see his face but I know I'm on the right lines. When I speak again, I try to sound persuasive, gentle, like I imagine a seasoned negotiator might speak when he's talking someone out of jumping off a roof.

'Your mother doesn't want you to do this, does she? And what does your sister want with ransom money – if that's what you mean by changing her life – if it means she can never see you again? My guess is that she would rather have her big brother. She'd rather have a family – a parcel of nephews and nieces to fuss over, cousins for her own kids. Don't take all that real happiness from her, Jack. Not when she never asked for it. She doesn't want any amount of money in exchange.'

I stop. I know it's time to let my words sink in, or they will lose their impact. There's a long silence.

What's he thinking? Have I struck a chord with him?

I can hardly bear the waiting but I force myself to be patient and not to speak. Then, suddenly, he turns, his eyes flashing.

'Why don't you just go?' he demands. 'Go! The door is open. Take your things and go back to your family. I'm not going to stop you. This is fucking over now.' He turns away again, clutching his pillow to his chest as though for comfort. He buries his face in it. My heart fills with sympathy for him, though I don't know why.

'I'm not going, Jack. Not without you.' I can hardly believe I'm saying it. But I mean it. I'm astonished at myself but I also know every word is true.

'Why the fuck not?' he says, his voice muffled by his pillow.

'Because you're not free of your promise. If I go now, maybe you'll come and get me, or my sisters, some other day, when your brother talks you into it. Or maybe you'll decide you're not fit to live after you've broken your vow and you'll do something stupid. I didn't go through what we went through last night to have you do that. Besides. You've got to get home too, right? We both have families who miss us. Let's go back together.'

'Nuh uh,' he says. 'No way.'

'Then I'm staying right here with you,' I say with determination. 'Sorry if you don't like it, Jack. But that's the way it is.'

CHAPTER TWENTY

Flora doesn't have a chance to speak privately to her sister before they get back into the city. Then there's the bustle of checking into the hotel and getting up to Freya's suite, which is just down the corridor from Flora's.

'We weren't going to stay in a place as expensive as this,' Freya says as they ride up in the lift. 'Not now that Dad's cut off my money.' She glances at Miles and smiles. 'We're supporting ourselves now.'

'Don't worry,' Flora says, without thinking. 'Andrei is paying for everything.'

Freya's expression changes immediately. 'What? You can stop the lift right now. We're going somewhere else. Right, Miles?'

Miles looks at her thoughtfully but before he can say anything, Flora hurries in to correct her mistake, annoyed at herself for being so tactless. 'Wait, Freya, I'm sorry, I shouldn't have come out with it just like that.' She puts her hand on her sister's arm. 'I should have explained first—'

'There's nothing to explain,' Freya says frostily. 'You know how I feel about him. After what he's done to Beth and Dominic, I don't want to accept his hospitality.'

'That's what I'm trying to tell you. Andrei is on his way here right now.'

Freya looks even more annoyed. 'I don't see why you think that makes it any better. I've just said I don't want to

215

accept his hospitality – and I don't want to be all friendly with him either! I know where my loyalties lie.' She shoots a cold look at her sister. 'So I'll make arrangements for us to stay somewhere else.'

Just then the lift pings to announce they've reached their floor. As the doors slide open, Freya goes to press the button for the ground floor, but Miles holds her back.

'Wait,' he says. 'Let's hear what Flora has to say before we do anything hasty.'

'Thanks, Miles,' Flora says gratefully, as they all step out of the lift and follow the impassive-faced bellboy down the carpeted corridor to the suite. When he has opened the door and ushered them in, pointing out the complimentary champagne and fruit basket, and gratefully taken his twenty-dollar tip, they are finally left in peace.

'Hey – I love this champagne,' Jimmy says, going over to inspect it. 'Let's open it now. We can drink it while you make up your minds about whether you're staying.'

'Don't, Jimmy,' Freya says warningly. 'And don't get too comfortable because we're not staying, and that's that.'

Flora looks over at her sister, exasperated. 'You're not prepared to give Andrei a chance, Freya. I wish you'd listen to me before you make up your mind.'

'You know how I feel,' Freya says firmly. 'I asked you to intervene with Andrei and you made it clear that you weren't going to do any such thing. Beth called me two days ago in tears because she knows that Andrei is meeting with Dom's prime investor with the express intention of fucking up the whole thing. Andrei can't wait to see Dom's company collapse and fail, and he's going to do all he can to make it happen. So excuse me if I don't welcome him with open arms – or take his money.'

'But Freya – that's just the point. The meeting with Dominic's investor was set for today. It's the only time the meeting can be held. After that, the investor will be committed to his deal with Dominic.'

'So?' Freya's expression is stony. Miles watches her, concerned, but he obviously isn't going to intervene between the sisters. It looks like he's already worked out what Flora is trying to say.

'So,' Flora says patiently, 'Andrei isn't going to be at the meeting. He's decided to drop his vendetta against Dominic.' She quietly crosses her fingers behind her back. 'We talked it through and he agreed it wasn't the right course of action, for him or for Dominic. He's prepared to let bygones be bygones.'

Freya looks sceptical. 'Really?'

Flora nods. 'Really. Like I said, he's on his way here. The meeting can't happen.'

Her sister frowns, clearly nonplussed. 'Oh. I see.'

Flora senses a wavering and rushes in to make the most of it. 'He's desperately concerned about Summer. That's why he's insisted on providing these hotel suites – because he thinks it's important we're all together, working together to get Summer back. He'll do anything to help and he has the money . . .' She spreads her hands, her fingers now uncrossed. 'Please, will you give him a chance? He wants to help.'

Freya says nothing for a moment, but looks over at Miles, an unspoken communication going between them. Then she says slowly, 'I suppose he's right. It's better for us all to be in the same place.'

'Then you'll stay?' Flora asks.

'I . . . I guess so. Though I'm not entirely happy. But if

what you say is true, and Andrei's decided to leave Dom and Beth in peace, then . . . all right.'

'Goodie!' Jimmy declares. 'Well, well, Daddy Hammond, Andrei and Estella, all in one place. This is getting intriguing. Now – shall we open the champagne?'

Freya gives him a look. 'We're hardly in the mood for celebrating, Jimmy,' she says sternly.

Jimmy looks suitably abashed. 'Okay. I get that. Sorry. I was just trying to lighten the mood. Maybe it was inappropriate.'

'Maybe for now,' Flora says gently. 'We'll open a bottle when Summer is safely back.'

'One?' Jimmy says fervently. 'Fuck it, we'll have a dozen!'

'So.' Miles speaks up, throwing his coat down on the nearest chair. 'Let's get to work. Tell us everything you have so far.'

While Jimmy explains to Freya and Miles exactly what they know, Flora excuses herself and goes to the bathroom. It's a vast marble-clad room, with an enormous bath and a walk-in shower with two shower heads side by side. She goes over and sits down on the lavatory, her head in her hands. The strain of not knowing the whereabouts of her twin sister is beginning to tell on her, and she feels a constant sense of loss and pain. Earlier, Mac was careful to stress to her that he believed Summer was alive and not likely to be harmed. Even so, Flora is close to being overwhelmed with the emotional turmoil she's experiencing.

She pulls out her mobile phone and stares at the screen background photo: it's her and Summer, their arms round each other, just a few months ago in Paris. They're standing outside the Louvre, their heads close together so that it's possible to see their similarities despite Summer's blonde, wholesome prettiness and Flora's pale skin and tumbling russet curls. Their eyes are the same shape, and their noses too. They are exactly the same size, and their smiles curl in just the same way.

Flora's eyes fill with tears at the sight. Jimmy took the photograph. That night, she and Andrei made very hot love in a hotel room. It all seems so long ago. She speed dials Summer's number, as she has so often in the last few days, each time hoping desperately that Summer will pick up, and her heart plummeting each time the voicemail kicks in. It's the same this time. The recorded message starts, each time making her think that Summer has answered as the breezy 'Hi! comes down the line, then it continues and she knows that it's just the usual message.

When the tone sounds, Flora speaks into her phone. It's useless, she knows, but at least it gives her the sense of being connected to her sister. She's never felt so far from her before, and this is one scrap of comfort. 'Hi, darling. You're still nowhere to be found. We're so worried, I can't tell you. Freya is here with Miles. Dad is on his way. We're all determined to find you, honey, so hang on in there. I miss you. I love you. I need you. Come back to me, okay? I can't stand waiting for much longer! Stay safe. Bye.'

Her voice cracks on the last word and she ends the call, before dropping her hand back into her hands and sobbing.

Summer, where are you? I'm so frightened! Please be okay. Please come home. I can't go on without you.

The release of the hot stream of tears helps a little, and after a while, she wipes her eyes, sniffs, goes to the marble basin and washes her face. Her eyes are a little red but she thinks she looks okay. Then she straightens her shoulders and takes a deep breath.

It's time to go back and be as strong as she can manage. *Andrei will be here later. All I can do is hang on till then.*

Mac calls to say he is on his way back to join them for the afternoon, and they order tea and sandwiches while they wait for him.

Miles looks over the list of facts they've assembled about Jack, frowning as he scans it. 'So you're pretty sure he's Italian and lives here in LA. And it says here his sister is a nurse and works at a hospital.' He looks over at Jimmy. 'That's a lead, isn't it? Can we start looking for an Italian nurse? How many hospitals are there in LA?'

'Oooh – about a hundred and thirty-nine.' Jimmy sips his tea from his position on the sofa. 'I had the same idea, so I checked. We're going to find it hard to track down one nurse when we know nothing about her, not even her name, except that she's Italian. I mean, it could take months.'

'Okay, I see. That's not going to happen.' Miles sighs and bites his lip thoughtfully as he scans the paper again. 'And it says you think his father died when he was young.'

Jimmy nods again. 'That's what Summer told us. She said that Jack's father died when he was a boy and he came over here as a teenager. And he told Charlie that his mother worked really hard to support him and his sister, and his sister is now a nurse.'

'That's all you've got?' Freya says disbelievingly. She looks pale and tired, her brown bob dishevelled, but she can't sit down. She keeps pacing about the suite, picking things up and putting them down, unable to relax. Flora watches her but stays curled up in an armchair, as though trying to find some warmth and comfort by turning in on herself and staying very still.

'There's a bit more,' Jimmy says, taking the list from Miles and having a look. 'Charlie can't remember everything Jack said word for word but he got a general impression of his life. He knew there was no girlfriend, but not much more. Charlie liked him. I never could warm to him.'

'Jesus, Jimmy!' Freya's sudden shout makes everyone jump. She stalks over and stands in front of him, her hands on her hips and her eyes blazing. 'Why the fuck did you let Summer go out with this guy? You knew nothing about him! Nothing at all! I mean, of all the crazy things to do! You were responsible for her!'

Flora watches as Jimmy, usually so unflappable, reddens beneath his tan. He stands up. 'Hold on a minute, Freya. You know what? Summer wanted to go! She is a grown woman and she'd met Jack on at least three occasions. Charlie introduced him as a friend. She trusted him and so did Charlie! Maybe they were wrong in that, but I was really happy to see her open up to someone. You know what it's been like for her and how much she struggled over the years. It was amazing that for once she met someone who made her feel good.'

'And look where it's got her!' jeers Freya. 'Well fucking done on that one! Maybe you skip the therapy next time and just concentrate on being a good friend.'

Jimmy looks outraged and clearly hardly knows where to start rebutting this. As he's stuttering over his reply, Freya continues. 'I expect you and Charlie were showing off about how you're friends with the Hammond sisters. I bet Jack knew all about us and that if he hung out with you, he was likely to meet one of the geese who could lay the golden eggs. Is that how it happened, Jimmy? I bet it was!'

'Freya, you are so wrong!' shouts Jimmy, his eyes blazing. 'That is not true, not at all.'

'Well, well . . .' The voice, drawling and easy-going, comes from the doorway. Flora turns to see Mac standing there, leaning against the doorframe with one cowboy boot crossed over the other, his thumbs pushed through his belt loops. He's smiling, showing all those broad white teeth. 'That's interesting, Jimmy, I was about to ask you that very question.'

Freya and Miles are looking at Mac with bewilderment.

'Who are you?' demands Freya.

Flora uncurls herself and gets up off her chair. 'It's okay. This is Mac, the private investigator who's working on the case. Come in, Mac. Have some tea.'

'How very kind.' Mac comes sauntering in, eyeing up the spread on the table. Then he tips his hat to Freya. 'Afternoon, ma'am. No need to tell me who you are, I recognise you from your pictures.' He nods to Miles. 'And you too, Mr Murray. I'm only sorry to meet you under these inauspicious circumstances. Nevertheless, it's an honour. I'm aware of your work.'

'Really?' Miles smiles but looks surprised.

'That's right. I used to be in the protection business myself, but it was a while ago. I still have my contacts though, and I've heard you're well regarded. Now, I'll have a cup of this tea, if that's all right with you all.' He picks up an empty cup and pours in some tea from the pot.

'I'll order some fresh tea,' Flora says, going to the phone.

Jimmy says defensively, 'I already told you that Jack didn't know that Summer was a Hammond sister. We never told him who she was.'

'Okay, okay.' Mac stirs milk into his tea thoughtfully. He looks up at Jimmy with a friendly smile. 'How's about you give your boyfriend a call and ask him to join us? I think we ought to have him here as well.'

'He's working at the Hall this afternoon, but I'll ask if he can get away,' Jimmy says, pulling out his cellphone. 'He's not far from here.'

Freya seems a little calmer now that Mac is here, and she sinks down on to the sofa opposite him and next to Miles. 'Do you have any leads, Mac? Anything to go on?'

'I'm making some progress, Miss Hammond, but I'll say that I've got more questions than answers right now. I'd be lying if I said anything else.' He sips loudly at his tea and makes a face. He says to Flora, 'Ordering some fresh tea was a good call, ma'am. This is a little over-brewed.' He puts his cup back down on the table. 'Now, what I'd like to do is run through Miss Summer's movements when she got here from wherever she flew in from, and all the encounters she had with Mr Fuoco, but I would really like Charlie here for this bit.'

'He's on his way,' Jimmy says, holding up his phone. 'He just texted. I guess he'll be ten minutes or so.'

'Good, good.' Mac looks pleased. 'Just in time to join us for some fresh tea.'

While they wait for Charlie and the tea, Mac asks Freya and Flora to fill him in on the background to the trip to the States. Freya starts off explaining that their father summoned them all to the Alpine house to explain that the girls were now on their own financially.

'And this came as a shock to you?' Mac asks. 'You weren't expecting it at all?'

'Well, things have been coming to a head,' Freya says

carefully. She glances at Miles. 'He wasn't happy when I got together with Miles.'

'I think I saw the news stories.' Mac nods. 'The heiress and the bodyguard. The papers just loved it, didn't they?'

Freya nods. She looks over at Miles again and says carefully, 'It led to some trouble, if I'm being completely honest.'

'Really? What kind of trouble?' Mac looks interested.

Miles says, 'I'd be very surprised if it had anything to do with this case.'

'That doesn't rule anything out, I'm afraid,' Mac replies calmly. 'So why don't you explain?'

Freya tells Mac about the mysterious way her liaisons with Miles kept being reported in the press, even though they were a complete secret, and that details of her break-up with her previous boyfriend Jacob also made the front pages. 'It was terrible,' she says. 'I suspected everyone, even Jane-Elizabeth, our father's assistant. But it wasn't her. It was our father's girlfriend, Estella. She's been trying to drive a wedge between our father and us since they got together.'

'She tried the same trick on me,' Flora puts in. 'She managed to get compromising photographs of me with Andrei and threatened to give them to my father. Luckily, Andrei had his men sort the situation out and get the photos back.'

'This is Andrei Dubrovski, I believe?' Mac nods. 'Yes, I read that you two are together when I did my research last night. Interesting. And Miss Estella was behind this too. Did she have anything on your sister, Summer? Is it possible she has something to do with this? She seems to want to harm you girls.'

Flora exchanges a look with Freya, and then says doubtfully, 'I suppose it's possible – but up until now she's tried to separate us from our father by poisoning our relationship with him. This is different, isn't it? Summer disappearing has had the opposite effect. Dad is on his way here now, and I'm sure Estella would prefer it if he saw us as little as possible.'

'All right,' Mac says, appearing to accept their explanation. 'You've no reason to protect her so if you think she's not likely to be involved, I figure your instincts are right. What about this Jane lady you mentioned?'

'Jane-Elizabeth?' Freya looks horrified and shakes her head. 'Absolutely not.'

Flora joins in. 'No, not Jane-Elizabeth. She's like a mother to us.'

'Hmm. Okay. Well, this is all very interesting, ladies. So after your father told you that you were no longer supported by him, you all went your separate ways. And I imagine you were extremely upset.'

'Of course. But not because of the money. It was because of the problems with our father,' Flora says and then remembers how alone Summer seemed when they parted at the airport. 'But I think Summer took it hardest. With Freya and me in new relationships, she seemed to feel very isolated.'

'And ripe, perhaps, for a man to play a little with her heart.' Mac looks over at Jimmy. 'What does he look like, this Jack fella?'

Jimmy says, 'Oh – gorgeous. Very good-looking. And he has that moodiness that plays very well.'

'Uh huh. Handsome and moody, huh.' Mac grins. 'Much like myself as a younger man.'

At that moment there's a knock on the door. 'Room service!'

Flora goes to answer it and as the bellboy brings in the

tray of tea things and a plate of fresh sandwiches, Charlie comes panting in behind.

'Hi!' he says. 'I'm here.' He sees Freya. 'Hi! Lovely to see you.' He goes over for hello kisses on both cheeks and then shakes hands with Miles.

'Just in time for some tea,' Mac drawls. He watches the bellboy place the tea things down and leave. 'I'm a little picky about these things. It comes from the fact that the first Mrs Mac was an English lady and she gave me a proper appreciation of tea.'

'Oh my God!' Charlie exclaims and sits down suddenly.

'Oh?' Mac raises his eyebrows. 'Is that very shocking?'

'No, of course not, not about Mrs Mac – it's just that when you said that, I remembered something Summer told me about Jack.'

Everyone turns to look at him expectantly.

'Please go on,' Mac says.

Charlie is frowning, trying to remember. 'We were working at the Hall, making sandwiches together, and Summer wanted to know how much I'd told Jack about her. She was worried that I might have told him about her family background and I told her that of course I hadn't breathed a word. We never did talk about her like that to our friends. And she said that Jack had known she had an English mother. I said I definitely hadn't told him that. And then I forgot about it.'

Mac whistles lightly. 'Well, well. Now that is interesting. I guess you could call it evidence that he had already found out all he needed to know about her beforehand.'

'It looks like that,' Miles says, grim-faced. 'But how does it help us trace him?'

'Well, that's the next question, isn't it?' Mac turns to Flora. 'I understand your mother died when you were very young.'

'That's right,' Flora says softly. 'Summer and I were nine.' She looks over at Freya, who has gone dead white and looks stricken. 'Freya was a little older.'

'I'm sorry for your loss,' Mac says respectfully. 'I know that time never does heal a grief like that.'

Freya makes a choking sound and hides her face in her hands. Miles is with her in an instant, wrapping his arms round her and soothing her.

'This is very hard for her,' Miles explains to Mac, who's watching carefully as Freya sobs, her head on Miles's shoulder. 'It's bringing it all back to her.'

'Bringing what back?' enquires Mac, frowning.

'Well . . . the kidnap. The original kidnap.' Miles looks over at Flora. 'Have you said?'

'No . . .' Flora falters. 'No. I . . . I haven't.'

'What kidnap is this?' Mac says, going very still. Freya is sobbing quietly, her face still hidden.

Miles hesitates, then says, 'Years ago, Freya and her mother were kidnapped in Italy by local hoodlums. They were kept for about a fortnight in some hillside caves before they were rescued. Sadly, Mrs Hammond died soon after-wards, from lack of treatment for her medical condition. I believe it was a form of diabetes.'

Flora feels amazed to hear it said so simply and clearly. It's been the family's deepest, darkest secret for so long, its hidden guilt, that she never thought it could be spoken of aloud. She's trained herself almost never to think of it.

Mac is on his feet, his face a picture of outrage and indignation. 'What? Are you kidding me?' He strides around the suite. 'Let me get this right – Freya and Mrs Hammond were kidnapped years ago, in *Italy*? How could I not know this already?'

'There was a news blackout,' Miles says. 'It never made the papers.'

Freya has stopped weeping and is sniffing gently, looking up with damp eyes. 'It was so long ago. And it was in Italy! We're in America now. It's completely different.'

'But one of you was abducted before, and no one thought to tell me?' Mac looks incredulous.

'It was years ago,' Flora says faintly. 'Years and years ago. It can't possibly be connected to what's happening now. Can it?'

Freya's expression is frightened. 'Is it connected? Is it?' She looks sick now.

Mac stares at them all and says loudly, 'Ladies and gentlemen, it changes everything. Completely. You must all see that – don't you?'

PART THREE

PART THREE

CHAPTER TWENTY-ONE

Jack looks moodier than ever but I try to ignore it. I'm like the girl at school who doesn't realise how unpopular she is, but acts like she's everyone's best friend. In other words, I don't let him get to me.

There's no more talk of shutting me in the little bedroom – the door is left unlocked and I'm free to go where I like. If anything, I get the impression that he wishes I would do as he asked and just take myself off. It's a turnaround to say the least.

I laugh wryly to myself. *Uh uh, Jacky boy. I'm not letting you get out of it that easily. I'm not going to leave you alone with your guilt and your honour and all the shit your brother has infected you with.*

It's amazing to think how much our relationship has changed in the short time we've been here. When I arrived at this place, I was deathly afraid and unsure of what Jack had in mind. Now I know that he won't hurt me. He can't. I don't believe he ever really could have, even without what's happened between us.

And that is something pretty incredible.

I gaze over at him as he prepares the coffee in the little kitchen area, his movements graceful as he spoons the grounds into the pot, and my stomach does one of those hard, painful flips it likes to perform when I look at Jack, or even think about him. Just a flash of memory – the sight

231

of his face set hard with desire, the recollection of his mouth on my nipples or his dark head buried in the apex of my thighs – and I'm throbbing with need for him.

I stifle a little sigh as I think wistfully of how easy this might have been if we'd just been two people who met, liked each other, dated and then fell in love. Instead, we're each twisted up by the conflict inside us: we're both falling for people we ought to hate. No wonder Jack is retreating inside himself, trying to cut himself off from me. After all, he's had years of mulling over what my family did to his, and goodness knows how many hours of listening to his brother convince him that it's his job to put it all right with this crazy, hare-brained scheme that can only end in tears.

I wish I could have five minutes with that brother of his, that's all.

A gentle breeze is coming off the sea where the balcony doors are open, and I turn my face to the fresh air. It's wafting away the bitterness left by last night's smoke, but outside is a mess. The balcony is a charred trellis of planks, the middle section vanished entirely where it burned right through and dropped to the sand beneath. I wonder if the loss of the balcony will affect the stability of the shack but it seems pretty firm and the supports are still there, if a little blackened by the fire. I remember the astonishing heat that last night's blaze created and feel a rush of gratitude that we're both all right. The loss of the balcony isn't so bad. It can be rebuilt.

'Is this your place?' I ask Jack as he brings two cups of coffee over to where I'm sitting at the small pine table.

He shakes his head and sits down. Staring into his coffee, he mumbles, 'It belongs to a friend.'

'Oh dear. Then I guess you're going to have some explaining to do.'

He looks up at me with an intense gaze.

I look at him helplessly. 'I just don't understand, Jack. You were going to repay your friend for lending you his beach house by using it to lock someone up? What did you hope to get out of all of this?

'You don't need to make it worse,' he replies curtly. 'I'm fully aware that this was going to have ramifications for everyone involved. But that was the price to pay for ... satisfying the honour of our family.'

I bite back the words that spring to my tongue to tell him what I think of *that*. What's the point in making it worse by hectoring him? I can tell that Jack is completely mixed up by everything that's happened. He's been brainwashed by his brother and now he's realising that the world is far more complicated than he's assumed. No one is all good or all bad. The rich bitch he couldn't wait to punish for her father's crimes turns out to be me: an ordinary girl who isn't to blame for the past, who can be hurt. Who can be loved.

'Jack, what are we going to do?' I ask him, my voice suddenly urgent. 'There's still time for me to spin a story to my family, about how we ran off for a few crazy days, lost our phones or couldn't get reception ... we can still go back and make it all fine again. Maybe we could even have a chance of getting to know each other in a more ... normal way ...'

He looks up at me, his expression agonised. 'Summer – can't you see? It's over for me either way. Do you really think we could go back and be boyfriend and girlfriend after this? And besides, I've got to face the fact that I've let

233

my family down. I wanted security for my sister, I wanted to show my brother that I don't chicken out of stuff.'

'And your mother?' I ask quietly. 'Don't you owe her something? Like trying to live the decent life she's worked so hard to make possible?'

Jack shakes his head, his face contorting. He stands up. 'Just *don't*. Don't try and make me feel bad. Don't you understand that I feel like shit already? This whole thing is a disaster. My brother was right. I'm not up to it. I'm always gonna disappoint him.'

'What?' I stand up too, and we face one another, our eyes blazing. 'This is the craziest horseshit I ever heard! Don't you see that it's stronger and braver to do what you're doing and put an end to whatever your brother has convinced you is the answer to all your problems? You must be able to see that he's all wrong!'

There's a long pause and Jack's jaw clenches, his lips tightening with the pressure of his emotions. Then he says quietly in a tense voice, 'I promised. That's the problem. I've promised and it's killing me that I can't keep my word.' Then he pushes his chair back forcefully and strides out across the room to stare over the blackened remains of the balcony and out to the sea beyond.

I watch him for a while, not sure of what to do. I'm only making things worse. He's tormented by duty to his brother and to the promise he's made and he needs to make his own peace with it. My heart goes out to him as he stands there, one arm up against the door frame, his head low as he stares out. He's struggling with so much. I just want to make it easier, to help him somehow.

I get up and go quietly to him, putting my hand gently on his back. It's warm and firm beneath my touch. 'Jack?'

He doesn't respond.

'Please. Let me help you. I want to help make things right.'

He bites his lip, his eyes closing. 'I know,' he says at last. 'But what can you do?'

'I can comfort you.'

'How?'

'Like this.'

I move round in front of him and tip his face down to mine, touching my lips on to his. He moves to meet me but pulls away. I persist, brushing my mouth against his with increasing pressure until he can't fight it any more. He begins to kiss me back properly, opening his mouth, darting out his tongue to meet mine. We play with each other, our tongues entwining, touching, licking and exploring. My hand slides down to the hardness in his pants, the other running up and down his back and over the firmness of his bottom. I'm breathing faster and the rush of arousal gushes through me like a torrent of spring water. I want him to possess me completely, but first I want to pay homage to him, show him how much I adore what he does to me and give him the pleasure he has given me. I sink downwards, lifting his shirt so I can kiss his belly. The skin there is smooth and tanned, warm under my lips. I can hear his breathing quicken as I let my breath play over his skin and then let my tongue lick a soft trail downwards towards the waistband of his jeans.

I'm on my knees now, unbuckling his belt, slowly letting down the zipper of his jeans. My insides clench with pleasure as I see the hard column beneath the shorts he's wearing. Jack moans lightly as I bring my face close to where his erection is straining against the soft cotton. I press my mouth to it, feeling its iron-hard heat through the material, and breathe a long hot breath on to it. He twitches under the sensation and I hear him gasp a little. Taking my time, I move my mouth up and down the shaft, still with his pants between me and it, warming it with my breath and tantalising him with the closeness of my mouth.

'Summer,' he says, his voice hoarse.

'Shh.' I run my fingertip along the hardness and he moves his hips. 'You don't need to talk.' I slip my hand inside the opening of his shorts and there it is, the source of so much of the delight Jack has given me. His beautiful cock, rearing up, hard and thick, throbbing with the nearness of my mouth to him. I have no idea what I'm doing but I follow my instinct and pull it out. I start to kiss it, pressing my lips against the smooth skin and then pushing out the tip of my tongue to tickle him with it. My hand wraps around his girth and squeezes him gently, and I lick upwards towards the top where he is even smoother and softer. His erection is solid against his stomach as he watches me move my mouth along him, his breathing deeper and more intense now. I reach the dome, and run my tongue along its rim, savouring him and the beauty of his swollen cock. I take him into my mouth, as much as I can fit, sucking him and rolling him in and out of my mouth, while my hand works further down, rubbing and squeezing until he seems to grow even longer. I seem to know what to do even though this is all new to me. My desire for him is teaching me all I need to know.

'Oh, that's so good,' he murmurs. 'You're driving me wild.'

I can tell that whatever I'm doing is having the effect I want. I long to give him the pleasure he's given me, and I love it too, relishing the deliciously erotic experience of having his hard cock in my mouth, wet with my saliva and anointed by my tongue.

He is moving now, responding to the rhythm of my sucking, pushing forward into my mouth. I wonder how much I can take but I know I want as much as I can get. He moves faster in and out of my mouth, getting harder every second. His eyes are closed now as he gives himself over to the delicious sensations I'm creating for him, and I move my hands and mouth faster, responding to his need.

The pleasure I'm giving him is making me damp with desire as well. I'm filled with voluptuous need as I tend to his huge cock, worshipping it with my mouth, working him towards his climax. He is throbbing now, the head of his cock shiny and smooth as it pokes hard into my mouth; he can't resist pressing it forward with his hips.

'Oh, that's too much,' he groans, 'it's too good, don't stop, I'm going to come.'

Jack opens his eyes to watch me and the sight is too much for him; his features convulse and he moans, as his cock stiffens even more and a flood of hot liquid enters my mouth in strong, spurting jets. I swallow as much as I can, the burning saltiness running a trail down my throat, and I suck until his cock stops throbbing and his breathing calms down.

He's kneeling next to me in a second, kissing me again with a kind of rapture. 'That was beautiful, Summer. You sent me to heaven.' He pulls away and looks at me with a kind of wonderment. 'I want to do the same for you.'

'You already did.' I smile at him. 'Remember?'

'I'm not leaving you without the kind of bliss you give me.' He kisses me gently again.

I look down towards his erection, which is already subsiding into soft limpness. 'But . . .'

'There're plenty of other ways,' he murmurs, 'if you want to come.'

He pushes me down gently so that I'm lying on the floor. I'm glad he's going to satisfy me, I'm tingling so much and so full of desire after the pleasure of sucking him off. He kisses me as he unbuttons my shorts and slips his hand inside my pants. I'm slick and ready down there already, my button swollen and alive to his touch. He tickles it lightly with his fingertip and then slides his fingers down to play at my slit. I'm making little noises in my throat as he moves and strokes, and my thighs fall apart to give him more access. My shorts and panties are tight and his hand is pressed hard against me in the small space allowed to him but that just increases my pleasure. He pushes one finger inside me, and then another, then another. He's deep inside, moving in and out and making the pleasure travel up within me and radiate out down every limb. I'm moaning softly as he runs his thumb over my bud. He kisses me, stifling my moans with the delightful invasion of his tongue, and I relax into the exquisite sensations he's provoking in me. My mind reels with delight as his fingers thrust in and out, and he carries on rubbing with his thumb in that hotly pleasing way. I can feel pleasure growing in my belly and in the excited depths where his fingers are working hard. I'm shuddering with the almost unbearable delight as he works harder, bringing me to a fever pitch, turning me into liquid ecstasy inside. Then, I feel the sensations of climax approaching, the waves of pleasure beginning to grow and spread inside.

'Oh, it's coming,' I gasp. 'Don't stop.'

He fucks me harder with his fingers, rubs me more firmly, my clit now alive to his touch and ready to send me over the edge. 'Come, baby, do it,' he murmurs.

Then I tumble over the brink, and my orgasm explodes, more intense than anything I've ever experienced, making me stiffen, arch my back and cry out in shouts that match the waves of pleasure his fingers are sending through me. Wave after wave crashes over me until I'm left gasping, breathless, staring at him with satisfied wonder as he smiles.

'That was amazing,' I say. Then I sigh with the luxurious feeling of satiety. 'Oh. Oh, oh oh.'

'Oh indeed.' He kisses me softly. 'You were so beautiful when you came.'

'I feel better,' I say with a smile. 'Do you?'

He laughs. 'You certainly took my mind off things, if that's what you mean.'

I feel a sudden rush of guilt as I lie there on the floor with him, still recovering from the ferocity of my climax. My family must be worried sick and here I am, losing myself in ecstasy.

Somehow I have to reach them. I have to let Flora know I'm safe.

But evening is already drawing on and I don't think Jack will let me send a message. How can I do it without him knowing?

CHAPTER TWENTY-TWO

Freya's suite has been transformed into an operations room now, with both Mac and Miles working on computers set up on various tables. She is being carefully and thoroughly questioned about everything she can remember about the original kidnap, and now sits curled up on the sofa, wrapped in a blanket. It's getting late in the day but no one is talking about dinner. There is an urgency now, to make some real progress on finding Summer. Mac seems to think that the kidnap that took place years ago is the key and he wants Freya to tell them everything.

Remembering is an ordeal. She's spent so long forgetting, only going back to those dark, dank hillside caves in her nightmares and now it's hard to distinguish between the reality and the awful flashes of terror that come in her sleep – less now, though, since she's been with Miles. He's beside her, her hand in his, while she racks her memory and goes back through the years. Flora is there listening too, paler than ever, as Freya recounts the ordeal, from the moment she and her mother were snatched from the villa outside Naples. She recalls how it was one of the guards supposed to protect them who allowed the gang access.

'That was why you found it so hard to trust me at first,' Miles says quietly. 'I couldn't understand why you had such hostility towards the security staff.'

'I guess I never forgot seeing that guy who was supposed

to protect us taking his wad of cash while we were being thrown in the back of a truck just in our pyjamas, Mama trying to keep me calm even though she was terrified herself.'

Flora looks scared too, as though she's living every moment with Freya's recollection.

Mac is listening very carefully from his place leaning on one side of the sofa. 'And did you get to know any of the kidnappers at all?'

Freya thinks back, remembering the way that over the days she learned to know the men who had charge of them. 'There were about six of them, I think, but they came and went. There were never fewer than three. Mostly they ignored us. I don't think they spoke English and when we spoke to them, they would say just "yes" or "no" – if they even understood what we were saying. They gave us food, showed us where to sleep, took us outside if we needed the bathroom. But they acted almost as if we weren't there most of the time.' She wrinkles her brow, remembering. 'It was weird, but sometimes I wondered if they even realised that we were there, but I knew we had to be the reason that they were in the caves. I found that really confusing.'

'Classic dissociation,' Miles says. 'To cope with what they were doing. They had to blank you out somehow and not admit that you were just a helpless woman and her daughter – otherwise you'd be like their wives and children, and they wouldn't have been able to do it.'

Mac nods. 'Makes sense. But I'm surprised they kept it up for longer than a few days. How long were you there?'

'Nearly two weeks.' Half of Freya's mind is back there, in the twilit cave, watching men sitting at the entrance, moon-light glinting off the steel of their weapons, their profiles. 'I lost track of time.' She is shaking now, her skin prickling as she remembers the cool dankness of the cave, the lack of daylight and the meagre rations that always left her hungry and dreaming of chocolate cake and ice cream. But the thing that rocks her most is the way her imagination conjures up her mother's presence, and the comfort that it brought her until she realised that her mother was growing weaker and sicker by the hour. She hears her own voice, piping and young, begging for help and remembers the shrugs and frowns of their captors, the muttered Italian conferences, their immovability. And then . . . Her face contorts.

'What is it?' Mac asks quickly. He is watching her closely and must be reading her expressions, ready to pounce when something comes back to her.

She has just remembered a time when the cave was full of angry voices.

The captors are arguing and she knows that it's about them, the prisoners. One of the men is furious, trying to make the others understand something, do something. He gestures at Freya's mother, then back to the men, and she knows that he is saying they must do something about the woman. Her heart is filled with hope that something will happen to bring help and to set them free . . . but as the argument goes on, it's clear that the one man is losing his side of it. There are shaking heads, clear refusals. She doesn't know their language but she understands when they are saying no. Panic and despair flood through her in equal measure.

'Freya?' Flora is there, kneeling on the floor, looking up at her. 'Are you all right?'

Miles's hand tightens around hers. 'You're doing so well, darling.'

Freya says weakly, 'There was one of them who wanted to help us, I remember that now. But the others wouldn't let him. He was kind to us. He tried to look after us in lots of little ways so the others didn't notice. One day . . . there was a boy . . . I think it was his son. He had big brown eyes and dark hair and he stared and stared at me until the other men saw him and shouted at him to go away. The kind man had an argument with the others to make them let us go, I think. Then . . . I think it was the following night that we were rescued.'

Mac is listening intently. Miles looks over at him. Mac says to Freya, 'Can you remember any names at all?'

She closes her eyes. 'When they shouted at the boy, they said, "*Vai, Fredo, vai*!" I remember it so clearly. And the kind man was called . . . Paolo. Yes, that was it. Paolo. They said, "*Non è possibile, Paolo*" and I knew what that meant. Not possible. I felt so awful when I heard it.'

Mac is up and striding over to his computer in a moment. 'Paolo and Fredo. That gives us something to go on.'

Flora looks over at him and says, 'My father is arriving here later. He'll be able to help you with more details than we can.' She glances at her sister. 'He's never spoken to us about what happened.'

Miles says grimly, 'Well, now he'll have to.' He kisses Freya's cheek softly. 'What do you remember about the rescue?'

'Not much,' Freya says in a small voice. 'Just that it was terrifying. I hid under a blanket and saw nothing. Then I was being lifted into a car, but I screamed and screamed, because that was when they took Mama away. I couldn't bear to be parted from her.' She blinks quickly to clear the mist in her eyes. 'And she was never well again.'

Miles rubs her hand gently. 'You've been so brave.' He smiles at her, touches her face with his hand. 'You're wonderful.'

She smiles back at him, taking comfort from his closeness and his concern for her. She longs for them to be alone – but the time isn't right yet.

Jimmy is sitting with them, though Charlie has gone back home. He's been very quiet while Freya went through the ordeal of remembering. Now he says, 'I still can't work out why we haven't heard anything from Summer or Jack. Why hasn't he given some kind of demand for ransom?'

'Because,' Mac says from his place at his computer, 'it may not be money he's after at all. Not if the kidnaps are connected – and I'm beginning to think that way, I have to say.'

Miles's phone beeps with an incoming text and he inspects it, then stands up quickly. 'That's a message from a friend of mine who works in the security service. He's come up trumps with something that might just help us locate Summer.' He turns to Flora. 'I'll need you to give me some details, though.'

Flora nods. 'Fine.'

Just then Freya's phone chimes as well, and she quickly picks it up from where it's lying on the sofa. She reads the text, then looks over at her sister. 'It's from Jane-Elizabeth. She's on her way with Dad and Estella from the airport right now.'

'Oh, great,' Flora says faintly.

They exchange looks, and each can read the apprehension in the other's eyes.

'We need your father here, ladies,' Mac says, picking up on their anxiety. 'It's really a very good thing that he's coming.'

Freya nods. She's exhausted, having barely slept for hours.

Miles is working away at his computer now and he calls Flora over. 'Okay, I need you to give me Summer's cellphone number.'

'Sure.' Flora goes over and watches as he types in the number she gives him. 'What are you doing?'

'I'm sending an app to Summer's phone. I take it she's got a smartphone that's 4G enabled?'

'She's got the very latest of whatever the best is,' Flora says, 'so you don't have to worry about that.'

'Good.' Miles is working quickly now.

'So what is this app?' Freya asks from the sofa, looking over at where Miles is working.

'It's something that's been developed by the security services, although there are commercial versions of it available too. I've called in a favour from my old friend and he's agreed to let me have a copy of it. As soon as Summer's phone is switched on, as long as she can access the data network, this app will download itself to her phone. It's designed for secret service agents and it appears as a game on the home screen. The agents can access it, but it looks pretty innocent just in case the phone gets into the wrong hands. And once it's installed, it can start sending us information about her whereabouts.'

'Really?' Flora looks excited. 'That's brilliant! You mean, as soon as you enable that app, we might find out where she is?'

'Well . . . that would be the ideal scenario.' Miles continues tapping away at his keyboard, setting his plan in motion. 'But it depends on her accessing the network. If the phone is out of range, the app won't download. And – of course – it has to be switched on.'

Mac says laconically, 'My theory is that Jack won't switch that phone on at all. Sorry to rain on your parade and all.'

Freya is frowning, anxiety still churning inside her. She's not so easily convinced as Flora that they've just found the answer to all her problems. 'Summer's been gone for days. What if her phone is out of juice? I bet she didn't take a charger with her.'

Miles nods slowly. 'That is another issue. Her phone may be dead by now if she hasn't charged it, but there's a chance that if it's been kept off most of the time, it might have sufficient battery life in it.' He turns to look at Freya and shrugs. 'It's the best I can do, honey. Right now.'

'I know.' Freya droops her head on the sofa back and closes her eyes. She is dead tired. 'I know. I just feel so hopeless, that's all.'

The hotel phone rings suddenly, startling everyone. Flora goes to the side table and picks up the receiver. 'Hello?' She listens for a moment and then says, 'Thank you.' Putting the receiver back on its cradle, she turns to look at them all. 'Dad is on his way up right now. He'll be here any second.'

CHAPTER TWENTY-THREE

Jack and I lie on the floor of the shack on the shaggy white rug and watch the sun going down. It sinks gently into the ocean, setting the sky afire with pink and gold.

We're lying in a kind of companionable silence, comfortable with one another. Jack is playing with a lock of my hair, twisting it round and round his finger, then uncoiling it and twisting it up again. I wonder what he's thinking and then I find my thoughts trailing off on their own way. This place, this beach house, feels so familiar now.

'How long have we been here?' I ask Jack. 'I mean, in this house, together?'

'I guess . . .' He thinks. 'This is the fourth day.'

'Four days.' I wonder what is happening in the outside world. I can guess that by now, everyone has realised that something has happened to me. Even if Jimmy and Charlie were being very open to the idea that I might have dashed off on some romantic escapade, by now they would be worrying. I went on a date five days ago and they've heard nothing at all. Perhaps by now my sisters know that I've not appeared. Maybe they're beginning to get anxious. I think of Flora, lost in her relationship with Andrei. Has she given me a thought in the last few days? The last time we spoke, she was going to call me back when it wasn't going to disturb Andrei – and then I heard nothing from her. I feel a pang of hurt at the thought that maybe she hasn't missed me yet.

But Jimmy will have told her. He must be worried by now, surely. He knows that I would never go off without telling him.

I know Flora well enough to be sure that once the alarm was raised, she'd be in full panic mode. I can't bear to think of what kind of state she'll be in if she thinks something terrible has happened. I can see her now, pale and desperate, unable to do anything but worry.

I've got to let her know that I'm safe. But what am I going to say? I was kidnapped by Jack, but don't worry, I'm very happy fucking him now. I'll be back soon! Bye!

I realise as that thought crosses my mind how mixed up everything is. Right from the moment I set eyes on Jack, I felt incredibly drawn to him, with a deep physical attraction I found irresistible. It seems that it doesn't matter what he planned to do with me, nothing can override the way I feel about him. And I'm sure he feels the same, much as he may hate himself for it. The passion between us is not neediness or desperation or the weirdness that can develop between a prisoner and captor. It was there when we met. It's still there. It's the reason Jack can't do whatever it is he promised he would do.

I run my fingertips over the skin of his collarbone. 'How long were you planning to hold out? I mean . . . do you have enough supplies?'

His dark-brown velvety gaze slides to me. I can tell he hates talking like this about the plans he laid that haven't worked out. But he says slowly, 'I planned on anything up to two weeks. I've got supplies in the freezer. Everything I thought we might need.'

'And if it wasn't resolved by then? Like, if my father didn't pay the ransom?'

He shrugs. 'I guess I thought that one way or another the game would be up. If there was no ransom, then I thought maybe I would take the car and drive us both off a cliff somewhere.' He sighs. 'That was partly why I did that crazy thing on the way here – you know, taking us out into the road. I was thinking about what it would be like if I had to drive us off the cliff and I got lost in my imagination. I honestly didn't see that truck. I was just wondering if I'd ever be brave enough to finish the job.'

A nasty chill seizes me and I give a little shudder. For a moment I imagine what it must be like to sail over a cliff and plummet to the ground. A dizzying wave of horror passes over me, and then another thought pops into my mind: *maybe it wouldn't be the worst way to go. It would be quick, at least.* Then I remember that I don't want to die, and I don't want Jack to either.

Then another thought occurs to me and I say slowly, 'You're not planning to do that any more though – are you?'

He looks away, gazing down instead at the lock of my hair as he twists it up and then lets it uncurl again.

'Jack? I don't think you're going to hurt me. I don't think you ever really wanted to. Maybe, in a way, you're relieved that the fire came and changed everything between us. But I'm worried about you, the way you're beating yourself up. Are you still thinking about taking the car over a cliff – but on your own?'

Jack closes his eyes and an expression crosses his face that makes him look as though he's in pain. 'Christ,' he mutters. 'You have the craziest way . . .'

'What do you mean?' I prop myself up on one elbow.

'How do you know so much about me?' He opens his

eyes and looks at me in a kind of bewildered astonishment. 'It's like you can read my mind. And some of the stuff you say, it's like you're my conscience or something, coming to life and telling me the things I don't want to hear.'

'I'm not psychic,' I say gently. 'I'm just a normal person. I'm just telling you things that normal people think: like, it's not a good idea to kidnap someone. And blood feuds and family vendettas are stupid and pointless and a waste of time and life. And that you've got too much to live for to throw it away because of a promise you should never have been made to swear. You think all this yourself somewhere inside, it's what you call your conscience. You know I'm right.'

He won't look at me but gazes moodily away into the distance. After a while he speaks in a low voice. 'Maybe. Maybe you're right.'

'You know I am.' I'm overcome with emotion suddenly, wrapping my arms round him and dropping kisses all over his face and neck, savouring the touch of his warm sweet skin under my lips. 'Jack, I don't want you to do something stupid. I don't want you to die! I need you too much.'

Jack turns to me with an expression of such longing in his eyes that I feel like my breath has been knocked out of me. 'You need me?' he says wonderingly. 'After all of this? You really need me?'

I nod. My eyes sting suddenly and I realise there are tears there. 'I don't know why. But I do.' I grab him by both arms and say fiercely, 'You'd better not let me down after this, Mr Jack Kidnapper! I've waited my whole life for someone to come along who makes me feel the way you do. I tried to fight it and I can't. So you'd better get a grip and not do the wrong thing. We can get through this together, if you want to. Because I do. I need you, do you hear me? Do you hear me?' I start to sob even as I smile, and then I've let go of his arms and I'm hitting his chest, thumping him ineffectually with my fists, full of frustration that it's all turned out this way and that I don't know, even now, if I can stop him from doing something reckless.

He seizes my wrists to stop the thumping on his chest. 'Hey, Summer, stop it! Calm down, calm down, baby! It's okay, really!'

Then he's kissing me, his lips on me, his tongue pressing into my mouth to taste me and set me on fire for him again. I'm filled with wild desire for him, and I know he feels the same from the hungry way he touches me. This time I want him inside me, to fill that desperate need he inspires in me. I feel myself swell and grow wet with need. My shorts are already undone from the last time, and I wriggle out of them, and then slide off my T-shirt between fervent kisses. He drops his head to my chest and kisses the globes of my breasts, murmuring with pleasure as he does so. My bra is off in a second and he fastens his mouth to my breast, sucking hard on the nipple of first one and then the other. I want him so fiercely that I pull him between my open legs, reaching for his cock which is rock-hard inside his jeans.

'You're so large and stiff,' I say, and his face darkens with desire to push himself in me, just as I hoped it would.

He takes it to the entrance to my slit, which is now open and ready for him, and runs the smooth head over my lips, playing it in the wetness there, rolling its head over my bud and setting flames of delight shooting out all over me. I yearn for him to enter me and in a moment, he's returned to the place, pressing forward, stretching me out to take him in. We look into one another's eyes, reading the excitement there and feeding off each other's desire to become even more lustful. I lie back and press my hips up to force him deeper inside me, almost sobbing with the rapture he inspires in me. He is wild with lust as well, thrusting as hard and deep as he can, his chest heavy on mine, his lips pressing against mine as his tongue darts into my mouth. I rake at his buttocks with my nails, making him reach deeper inside me as he slides in and out right to the root of his cock.

The pleasure mounts in both of us in rapid waves of excitement. I'm already convulsing around his thick shaft as he moves against all the most fevered places, meeting each lunge with a loud cry until the spasms burst over me and I'm coming hard in a turmoil of delight. Jack is only moments behind me, exploding hard inside and flooding me with his orgasm.

We slow our movements as our climaxes leave us breathless and spent. It's darkening outside and we lie there on the floor for a few more minutes until Jack says, 'We'd better get up or we'll be here all night.' He kisses me gently. 'Are you hungry? I'll make us some dinner.'

I sigh happily. 'I'm ravenous.'

He smiles. 'I noticed.' And kisses me again.

Later, when we're in bed and Jack is asleep, I get up and go out into the sitting room again, searching quietly until I find what I'm looking for. Then I find it, slid under a book on the shelves. My phone. It's off, the screen dead black. I hold it in my hands, turning it over and over. Shall I switch it on? I'm desperate to let Flora know that I'm alive and unharmed. But I don't want to bring whoever might be looking for me – *the police?* – to find me here with Jack before I'm ready for it.

I never want them to find out what's happened. I don't want anyone to know.

I want to save Jack before the world discovers what he's done and he's taken away from me to face justice from people who will never be able to understand that he never truly wanted to hurt me and that he felt he had no choice in all of this.

But I have to tell Flora that I'm okay.

I stare at my phone for a long time. And then I decide.

I switch the button to on.

CHAPTER TWENTY-FOUR

Despite his small stature, Mr Hammond seems to fill the doorway of the suite.

'Where is my baby?' he shouts, staring at them all as though they have the answer. Flora stares at him, suddenly frightened now that her father is actually there. *Why am I afraid?* Then she realises. *It's because I don't know where I stand with him any more. I'm not sure he loves me the way he used to.* She doesn't feel touched by his demand for his 'baby'. After all, just over a week ago, he threw out all his babies and told them to get on with it without him. She looks over at Freya, who seems more drained than Flora has ever seen her, and also unable to find anything to say to their father.

Miles steps forward. 'Mr Hammond, we're very glad you're here. And you can rest assured that we're doing everything we can to find Summer.'

Hammond advances into the room, followed by his small entourage: Pierre and another bodyguard, massive and meaty in a dark suit, Jane-Elizabeth and then Estella, wriggling along behind him in tight jeans, high boots and a vast hairy coat that makes her look like a species of bear. She also has dark glasses on so that her eyes remain hidden.

'Where are the police?' he asks, looking around as though there might be cops concealed all over the room. 'Are they here?'

'We haven't involved the police yet, sir. I'm sure you understand why we've waited.' Miles is smooth and confident and sounds completely in control. 'We're making enormous progress on finding Summer.'

Hammond harrumphs and turns to Pierre. 'You'd better start taking over.' Then he turns to Miles. 'You've probably done the right thing, Murray. I hoped I would never have to lay eyes on you again, but considering the circumstances, I'm glad to see you. You were a good bodyguard – until you ran off with my daughter.' He looks over to Flora and then Freya. 'Are you going to say hello, girls?'

Flora goes over obediently and kisses her father's cheek. 'Hi, Dad. I'm glad to see you.' To her surprise, she means it. His presence has made her feel safer almost instantly. Even the sight of Pierre is somehow comforting. But most of all she's delighted to see Jane-Elizabeth, whose face is etched with worry but who still radiates the warmth and affection she always has. Her arms are open to engulf Flora in a hug as she moves away from her father to let Freya greet him.

'Darling!' Jane-Elizabeth holds her tight and Flora inhales the familiar smell of her perfume and feels relief deep inside. 'You must be suffering so terribly. We're all frantic. But I know she's going to be all right.' Flora nods, unable to speak.

Freya gives their father a brief hug. 'Hello,' she says, her voice tight.

'You look awful,' says her father, regarding her with a frown.

'I'm worried about Summer,' Freya replies faintly.

Miles steps forward protectively and puts an arm round her. 'She's had a difficult day, sir. She's had to go through

255

all the details of her own kidnap this evening, and it's not been easy for her to remember it all.'

Freya seems to shrink into his arms and away from her father. Flora realises suddenly that her sister has a genuine problem with their father, not just from recent events but from the after-effects of her dreadful experience all those years ago.

'What?' Their father looks surprised and then almost cross. 'What on earth does that have to do with this? That . . . event . . . was a very long time ago.'

Mac is standing quietly at the back of the room next to his computer but now he steps forward and says very politely, 'We believe it may have some connection with what's happened to your daughter, sir. It's important we go through everything that happened then in order to find the link, if there is one.'

'Who are you?' demands Hammond, looking him up and down.

Mac holds out his hand. 'Calvin McManus. Pleased to meet you, sir. I'm a private investigator and I can assure you that I am very hard at work on this case.'

Hammond takes Mac's hand warily and releases it almost at once. 'Who hired you?'

'An interested party, sir.'

Flora breaks in. 'It was Andrei, Dad. He's paid for Mac's services. He knows we want to keep the police out of it for as long as possible.'

'Dubrovski?' Hammond says disbelievingly, then his expression changes to one of disgust. 'I don't think so. Mr McManus, thank you for your efforts so far. My man Pierre here will be in charge of the investigation from now on. Please pass him all the information you've accumulated.

But I have to say, you're wasting your time with the Italian connection.'

'Dad, no, you can't sack Mac!' Flora says, grabbing her father's arm. 'He's so far into the case! We need him!'

'I'm not having Dubrovski's man find my daughter!' snaps their father.

Flora looks at him helplessly. *Who cares who finds her as long as she's found?*

Mac says, 'Sir, I'm no one's man. I'm my own man. Mr Dubrovski is paying my fee thus far, but if you'd like to take over that aspect, then I'd be glad to continue working on the case.'

'Hmm.' Hammond eyes him again, appraising him. 'Very generous of you to offer me the opportunity to pay your wages.'

'Dad, please!' Flora says beseechingly. 'Mac is good, I trust him. He's making progress. What harm can there be in letting him carry on?'

'I need someone interested in the here and now, working on finding Summer as soon as possible. Not looking into what happened over a decade ago. Pierre will take over.' Hammond nods at his chief of security.

Mac picks up his jacket. 'All right then, sir. I understand.' He closes his computer and slips it into its case. 'You're the boss.' He turns and gives a little bow to Flora. 'Good luck with finding your sister. I'm sure Pierre here will do a good job.' He turns and gives Pierre a long stare. 'Isn't that right, Pierre?'

Pierre stares back at him and says nothing but Flora is sure she picks up on something between the two men. *Do they know each other?*

Jane-Elizabeth has led Freya back to the sofa and is

sitting down with her, her arms round Freya's shoulders. She speaks up suddenly. 'Whatever is going to happen will have to happen somewhere else. This poor child is in a bad way. She's exhausted. I'm going to order her some dinner and then put her to bed at once. So out you all go.'

'I should like some dinner as well,' rings out a clear voice. It's Estella, who's been standing quietly observing the proceedings. 'I didn't eat a thing on the plane.'

Hammond turns to her at once, his face a picture of concern. 'Coochie, I'm so sorry. Of course we must have dinner. Would you like to dine in the restaurant here, or go out?'

Flora is full of cold hatred in an instant. Why should Estella's needs be put before everything else? Did their father not hear what Jane-Elizabeth said about Freya? What about giving her some comfort and proving that he cares for her?

'I don't care,' Estella says with a sigh. 'To be honest, I would like to get to our suite and unpack.' She turns to Jane-Elizabeth. 'We're in the penthouse, aren't we?'

Jane-Elizabeth nods.

'Good.' Estella goes to Mr Hammond and slips her arm through his. 'Then I think you should escort me there at once. If it's pleasant, we will order dinner there. I don't really feel like dressing up after that flight. A bath and an early night will do wonders for me.'

Flora wonders if her father is aware of the brittle tension in the air after Estella's little speech. Miles is gaping at her and so is Jimmy, who has been sitting very quietly and observing. He stood up when his erstwhile employer came in but since then, he's melted into the background.

His eyes flash a little now at this display of selfishness from Estella.

'Let's go up then, Coochie, and get settled. And perhaps Pierre can start work in his own room.' Hammond speaks to Mac. 'Please send him everything of interest you've discovered so far.'

'Glad to.' Mac smiles at him, flashing the big white teeth.

Then Hammond and Estella are gone, the muscly bodyguard following after them as they head for the elevators and the penthouse suite. Pierre hands his card to Mac with a rough instruction to email him everything, and then goes as well.

There's a moment's silence when they've gone, and then Jimmy lets out a low whistle. 'Goddamn it,' he says. 'She is something else. She really is something else.'

Flora shoots him a look. 'What did I tell you?'

'I thought you might be exaggerating. But you weren't.' He shakes his head. 'I sure hope she enjoys her bath and her dinner and her early night. I bet she'll sleep like a baby.'

Jane-Elizabeth is clucking over Freya, clearly concerned and probably also enjoying being able to mother someone. 'Come on, all the rest of you. Out. Freya needs to rest.'

Flora turns to Mac. 'You're not really giving up the case, are you, Mac?'

'Not until Mr Dubrovski dispenses with my services,' Mac said comfortingly. 'Your father can't actually fire me without hiring me. It's one of those little rules in life. I'll just carry on and tomorrow I'll come back to your room, if that's all right, Miss Flora, and continue there.'

'Oh yes,' she says, relieved. 'Of course. My room is at your disposal. There's plenty of space for you to work there. But . . .' She frowns. 'You have to pass everything to Pierre.'

'He can have a copy of whatever I've got,' Mac replies. 'I don't think he'll make much of it.'

'Do you know Pierre?' asks Flora quizzically. 'I got the impression you do.'

'Let's just say our paths have crossed once or twice, and neither of us much enjoyed the experience.' Mac slips his computer under his arm. 'But I'm going to head off now myself. I'll carry on working tonight and let you know if I discover anything.'

After Mac has gone, Flora says, 'I'll leave you in peace too.' She gives Jimmy a meaningful look and he gets up to go as well.

'Yes,' he says. 'I'd better get home. Charlie will be wondering what's become of me. Goodnight, Freya. I hope you get some rest. Everything will seem better in the morning.'

Out in the corridor, Jimmy kisses Flora goodnight. 'I'll see you tomorrow.' He stands back to look at her. 'And how about you? Are you all right?'

She nods. 'Yes.' The tension in her has eased today, though she isn't quite sure why. She's still thinking about Summer every minute and still feeling as though a part of herself is missing but the awful fear-filled pressure has lifted. 'I'm all right. I feel like things are moving forward. I don't know why I trust Mac – but I do.'

Jimmy smiles. 'He seems like a good guy. A smart one too. And that's what counts.'

'Yes.' She hugs him quickly. 'Goodnight, Jimmy. Sleep well.'

In her suite, she breathes a deep sigh. She's exhausted too after the long and intense day. She's also wrung out by the emotions she's experienced listening to Freya tell her story of what it was like to be kidnapped. Her sister, always so much older and wiser and stronger, suddenly seems frail and damaged.

I just hope that this whole thing isn't awakening some-thing in Freya that was better off left dormant. But she has Miles now. He is her rock. He'll make sure she's all right.

Flora sighs again, yearning for her own comfort. She looks at her watch. Surely ... surely it's almost time. She goes to the bathroom and runs a deep bath foaming up with bubbles. When she's slipped into the hot water and closed her eyes, she starts to dream of where Andrei might be and whether he's close to her now or not, and drifts off into a half-doze.

A pounding on the door of her suite brings her back with a bump.

'Who is it?' she shouts, her shoulders rising dripping from the water.

'Room service!' comes the reply.

Flora gets up out of the hot water, leaving it with regret, and wraps a large fluffy towel around herself. Then she pads out to the door and opens it, saying crossly, 'I didn't order any room service! Did the lady in suite 770 order something to be delivered to me?'

But before there's an answer, she's engulfed in a huge hug, lifted off her feet, and eager lips are on hers, kissing her wildly.

'Andrei!' she cries as soon as she can speak. He carries her into the room, pushing the door shut behind them with a kick. 'You're here!'

'I'm here,' he says jubilantly, his bright blue eyes alight with pleasure at seeing her. 'And you are spectacularly delicious, my darling. Come, and let me see what treasures you have hidden under that towel . . .'

Giggling, she's carried to the bed and the next moment she's losing herself in the delight of his kiss while his hands take possession of her soft, damp flesh and she surrenders to the pleasure of his touch.

CHAPTER TWENTY-FIVE

My telephone screen doesn't respond at the first touch of the button, or so it seems. The screen is blank for a long time and then the icon appears, rising out of the blackness like a petal floating up to the surface of a pond. Then suddenly, the screen is back with the familiar photo of Flora and me as its screen saver, and all the usual icons glowing there. I have dozens of texts and voice messages. But the battery life is in the red zone. It's critical.

I call up the messaging function and quickly tap out a message to Flora.

I'm all right. Don't worry about me. I'll be back as soon as I can.

I want to say more but I don't know how to begin to explain what's happening, and besides, I have to get this sent before the small amount of power left in the battery dies altogether. So I hesitate only for a moment, before I press send. Then, thinking fast, I switch off the location services. As soon as I've done that, I turn the phone off again, only moments, I'm certain, before it would have died in my hand anyway. I wish there was time to read some of the texts, but I've done what I needed to.

Knowing that the message has gone fills me with a sense of calm. I don't have to worry that Flora is in a state now. She'll get my message and know that everything's all right. And she'll wait for me to get in touch with her again.

I replace the phone quietly where it was before and tiptoe back to bed. Jack is still soundly asleep and I slip beside him under the covers. I close my eyes, wondering if I'll be able to get to sleep, but within a short time I've sunk into unconsciousness.

When I wake in the morning, Jack is already up and about. I head out of the bedroom and find him in the kitchen getting some breakfast ready.

'Hi,' he says with a smile. 'I was going to surprise you and bring it through.'

'That's so sweet,' I say, smiling back. 'We could go back to bed together maybe?'

'Maybe. But shall we eat first, seeing as you're here?'

'Yes, of course. I'll help set up.'

A few minutes later, we're eating muesli and drinking coffee while bread toasts, creating the perfect melange of breakfast smells. I can't help thinking about my text and wondering how Flora felt when she read it. I don't know if I'll be able to send another. There was not enough power left in the phone for that, I suspect. I don't think the phone will even turn on now without some juice. I resolve to look out for a charger. After all, Jack must have one.

'Is anyone wondering where you are, Jack?' I say suddenly. 'What about your mother and sister? Will they be worried about you?'

He shakes his head. 'I told them I was going away for a while. They won't worry. They know what I'm like.'

'What are you like?' I ask teasingly. 'Tell me.'

Jack shrugs, looking a little sheepish. I love his morning look so much, before he's shaved and when the stubble is all over his face like a dark cloud. His maleness excites me when I can see it like that. 'Well, I go off on expeditions on my own. I like to walk in the hills – you know, to hike and camp and stuff. I've always done it, maybe because my dad used to take me up into the hills around Naples and we'd camp there together. It was the best fun. I loved it. Because it was just me and him, you know? Fredo never came with us, my dad took him on his own trips. It was a chance to be alone with Dad and get to know him. And he showed me how to make a campfire, and pitch a tent and skin a rabbit, and all the stuff dads teach their sons.'

'Maybe you'll teach your own son something like that one day,' I say softly.

Jack's smile fades and he toys with his muesli. 'Maybe,' he says gruffly. 'Who knows.'

'Jack . . .' I put down my spoon. 'We have to face this. Soon we'll have been here nearly a week. What are we going to do?'

'I told you – you're free to go.' Jack puts his spoon down too and looks at me. 'In fact, I think I should take you home.'

'Really?' My face lights up with pleasure. 'We're going to go home? The two of us?'

'Yes. Why not?'

He says it so easily, I'm instantly suspicious. 'And then what you are going to do?'

'I'll go and hand myself in. I've been thinking about it, and it's the only way.'

'But . . .' I gape at him, horrified. If Jack hands himself in, he'll be arrested. There'll be some kind of trial . . . he

265

might go to prison. 'Okay,' I say, determined. 'If you do that, I'll tell them it isn't true.'

'What isn't true?'

'The kidnap. I'll say I came here of my own accord and that we've been having a lovely romantic time by the sea.'

Jack frowns. 'What? You'd do that?'

'Yes. So you see, you can't hand yourself in.'

Jack stares at the table, biting his lip again, his eyes intense. 'I know you're trying to help,' he says at last. 'But you're really not. You're making this harder for me.'

'How?'

He sighs. 'If I'm arrested for this, at least Fredo will know I did what I promised. If you pretend it never happened . . .' He sighs. 'I won't be able to convince him that I tried to keep my word.'

'Okay.' I'm so angry with his brother and the stupid promise he extracted from Jack, but I'm not going to show it. 'So handing yourself in is no good. Then . . .' I think fast. 'Here's what we do. We ask for a ransom. My father pays it. You keep the money and I turn up back at home safe and well, and we never see you again. You prove to Fredo that you've got the money so the kidnap must have been a success. And then everything is okay!' I smile and hold out my hands as if to say 'job done!' But then I remember that part of the plan is never seeing Jack again, and my face falls.

Jack looks away. 'Fredo will only be satisfied when he gets what he wants. What he thinks we're owed.'

'Money?' I say, thinking fast. Money should be one of the least of our problems, if I can talk my father round. 'You're right, you should be compensated for the loss of your father. When I get home, I'm going to do everything I can to make that happen. You and your family should get something for that.'

Jack shakes his head. 'No. He wants more than that.'

I go cold and my skin crawls with something unpleasant. 'What does he want?' I whisper.

'He wants me to . . . make honours even. An eye for an eye. A tooth for a tooth.'

'A death for a death,' I say shakily. 'Fredo wants you to kill me.'

He is very still, then he nods and fixes me with a steely look. 'I'm not going to do it.'

'I'm glad to hear it!' I say, filled with relief, but also with sadness. I can't wipe myself out, erase myself from the world's notice. Fredo is going to know I'm not dead. And that leaves us almost back where we started. 'But what are we going to do?'

He shrugs. 'I'm sorry,' he says. 'I've made this into a really terrible mess. I thought I could do it – but I can't.'

'I'm glad you can't – not just because I don't want to die, but because I don't want you to be the kind of man who could do something like that.' I reach out and take his hand. 'You're a good guy, Jack. I know it. We'll work something out. We just need to keep thinking.'

He doesn't speak but tightens his grip on mine, and we sit there for a long time without speaking. The mood has changed and there's no talk of going back to bed.

Later, I tidy up the cabin, glad to have something to do. It also gives me the chance to look for a charger. Jack goes out to examine the state of the balcony, breaking off the really dead wood and tossing it on to the sand below, where it looks like a pile of driftwood or the remains of a summer bonfire. I can't imagine what he's going to say to the owner of the hut but maybe he intends to get it fixed somehow.

Now that I'm free, I feel as though I have a vested interest in our welfare, and I check the fridge and freezer for food. Jack's right – he's well stocked, with plenty of stores tucked away. There's certainly enough here for a few weeks before we'd need to venture out.

But a few weeks? Can we stay here that long?

I look down at my shorts and T-shirt. I'm beginning to wish seriously that I could have a change of clothing. I've been washing out my underwear so I have something clean to put on every day but it's not easy coping with only two pairs of panties and virtually nothing else.

I go into Jack's room and look through the drawers in there. They have some clothing in them that doesn't look as though it belongs to Jack – the kind of stuff that gets left in a holiday house. His things are in a soft bag tucked between the chest of drawers and the wall, but there's not much beyond the basics: another pair of jeans, some T-shirts and a jumper. The suit he was wearing on our date – *my goodness, that seems like a long time ago now, like another lifetime* – is hanging on the back of the door. There's another bag too, hidden under the bed. I pull it out and open it up. Inside are some women's things – underwear, a pair of jeans, some tops and jumpers and a pair of sneakers.

He was obviously prepared for a long stay here. But he hasn't given me any of these things until now.

I hold up the jeans. They look about my size and I'm longing to change my clothes. A few moments later, I'm enjoying the sensation of fresh, clean fabric against my skin, wearing the jeans, a stripy Breton top and the sneakers.

A thought occurs to me and I go back to Jack's bag,

looking quickly through the mess of clothing inside. Then I look in the side pouch.

'Bingo,' I breathe to myself as I pull out a phone charger. But my excitement is short-lived. It's not the right kind for my cellphone. I examine it and don't recognise the kind of model it would suit.

'Shit,' I say, throwing it back into the bag. Once the option of charging my phone is gone, I'm frightened again. I wonder what has happened with the text I've sent through and what it has created with my family. Perhaps they're imagining me in the hands of a brutal gang, tied up and gagged in a basement. They'd be surprised if they could see me doing some housework while my kidnapper lover does some mending. It's the kind of cosy picture that doesn't spring to mind when the word abduction is mentioned.

I sit on the bed and sigh heavily. I can't see how all this can end well. I want to be with Jack and I want these stolen hours for us together, before the world has to intrude. If only we could have the time we need to get to know one another properly, and if only being together here didn't mean that my family has to be frightened on my behalf. I see very clearly all of a sudden that the longer we are here, the harder it will be for anything to be normal again afterwards.

The sound of Jack's voice floats up from below, and I realise he's talking to someone. *Oh my God, is someone there?* Instantly I freeze as I sit on the bed, listening. He has left the balcony and is walking around the side of the shack, probably for privacy. But he's now standing right outside the open window of his room, though it's far too high up for him to see through it. As he stands below on the sandy stretch of ground, the sound of his conversation rises easily to me. Then I realise I can only hear one voice. *He's on the phone! He must have a cell with him. Well, of course. He must have hidden it.*

But I don't understand a word. He's talking very fast Italian. I know enough to catch odd words, but not to get a firm grasp of what's going on. He seems to be explaining himself to whoever is on the other end, at times sounding exasperated and at others persuasive. At last he says, '*Si, si, ciao. Ciao, Adriana.*'

I swallow, my hands clutching at the bedcover. *Who is Adriana?* A nasty chill convulses me as I imagine that Jack has a girlfriend he hasn't mentioned to me. Maybe all of this is some kind of clever act to make me stay with him. How brilliant it would be to turn your kidnapping on its head and get the victim to stay with you of their own accord?

I look around the room that I've been tidying.

And even do the fucking housework!

But my mind keeps working. It doesn't make sense. Jack might be a cool customer sometimes but there's no way he's pretending when we make love, or when I see the agony that crosses his face. He's in a mess, I can see that clearly. He's not faking anything, I'm sure of it.

So who is Adriana?

There are only two candidates from what I know of Jack. One is his mother and the other his sister. And a good Italian boy does not call his mother by her name. No way. So maybe Adriana is his sister. I tuck this thought away. There's nothing I can do now, just wait and see what happens next, and think of how this knowledge can come in useful when the opportunity arises. *Maybe I can find that phone.*

And anyway, there's another and bigger problem facing me, and I have no idea how I'm going to solve it.

How the hell am I going to free Jack from the promise he's made to Fredo?

CHAPTER TWENTY-SIX

Flora wakes in her hotel bed, feeling calmer and happier than she has in days. Then she remembers why. Beside her, Andrei is asleep, his body close to hers. He's big and radiating heat and she feels as though something vital has been restored to her.

Sighing happily, she runs her hand across his chest and drops kisses on his shoulder, inhaling the scent of his skin. Then she lets her hand trail lightly down over his stomach and to where his cock is standing hard against his belly.

Morning glory, she thinks, with an internal laugh. *He shouldn't put such temptation in my way.* She runs her hand over the hard length, moving the skin softly under her fingertips. The way Andrei took her so hard last night was renewing; she needed to take all the tension and emotion of the last few days and expend it in the frenzy of making love to him. He pushed into her very depths and she wanted him there, as much as she could take. She recalls how he turned her round so that she could grasp the headboard, her knees wide so that he could see her, the round globes of her buttocks and the welcoming lips of her sex, glistening with readiness. The thrust of his cock inside her made her gasp and moan, throwing back her head, her back arching, as he hit her core. It was delicious, hovering on that intense border between pleasure and pain. As he thrust hard, he slapped her buttocks so that they juddered under his palm, and sank his face on to her neck, biting at her skin in a way that stimulated her almost unbearably. She wanted to feel everything she could, and Andrei knew how to do that. He understood that she loved the sweet softness of tender kisses, but sometimes she yearned for the twist of his fingers on her nipples firing up her nerve endings to something beyond gentle pleasure, and the graze of his teeth on her skin, nipping hard where she was most sensitive, and the feel of his palm against her bottom and thighs. She wanted and needed to feel, and when she was with Andrei, she felt that there was nothing she wouldn't do. She wanted to go on that journey with him, wherever it took her.

She sighs luxuriously thinking of it, her clitoris twitching and swelling at the thought. She wants him now, right now, and she rubs a little harder along the hot shaft of his cock. He murmurs and opens his eyes sleepily.

'Oh, my angel,' he says in a voice thick with sleep. 'This is the best way to wake up.'

She smiles and kisses him softly. Then she moves down the bed to where his hardness is rearing up, and kisses its smooth soft cap as well. 'I haven't said a proper hello,' she whispers and takes the head of his cock into her mouth, her hand working on the shaft with regular strokes. He fills her mouth, hot and hard, and she works her tongue around him, tickling, sucking and licking, relishing the feel of him and the evident pleasure she is giving him. Andrei's hands are in her hair, his hips lifting to thrust a little into her mouth with every stroke of her hand along his cock, and he pushes her lightly down to take more of him inside, while he moans gently. She shifts so that, with her other hand, she can cradle his balls, rubbing them gently with her thumb, tickling down beneath them, using her fingertips to stimulate the skin around them. Andrei begins to thrust harder now, and she holds his shaft tighter, partly to increase the pleasure she's giving him and partly to hold him back from thrusting too far down her throat and making her gag. But she can tell he is entering a place where the pleasure she is giving him is overcoming him, and that knowledge heightens her own desire. She wriggles against him, unable to stop herself moving under the clamouring need growing between her thighs.

Suddenly Andrei pulls himself out of her mouth. His cock is huge now, even more swollen, and red with the surge of blood within it. His eyes are dark with lust as he pulls her up to him and kisses her fiercely, swirling his tongue around her mouth as his fingers reach hungrily for her. He's buried inside her in an instant, as though he can't resist the soft sweet oil there, then he brings his fingertips up to play on the hard bud at the top of her sex. She shivers with delight as he touches her, gasping with every tingling impulse that springs from his touch. Then she opens her thighs wide and they roll over so that he's on top of her, his cock hard at her entrance and in a vigorous thrust, he's inside her. She sighs and moans as he goes deep inside her, wrapping her legs over the back of his to pull him in as far as he will go, and then he starts the course, pushing with his mighty strength as hard as he can, fired up with the desire she fuels in him. She answers every thrust with her own, lifting her hips to meet him, glorying in the way he fills her and the pressure of his pubic bone grinding down on her most sensitive place.

'Andrei,' she gasps, her eyes wide, searching his face, finding even more excitement in the intensity of his expression. 'Oh Andrei.'

'Come for me,' he commands. 'I want to see you do it.'

She surrenders to him, giving herself up to the sensation, the erotic delight of his fucking. As he swells even bigger within her, she lets herself yield to the ecstasy building inside, and as he begins to hit the moment when he cannot hold back any longer, his buttocks tightening, his pace slowing but growing in intensity, she can't help but let herself be carried away on the great wave of her climax, shuddering and shouting with its force until her cry is smothered by Andrei's kiss and her body is filled up with his orgasm too.

They collapse, panting together, as the force of it all drains away.

Flora sighs happily. 'I needed that.'

'I'm glad.' Andrei lifts her hand to his lips and kisses it gently. 'I can't imagine a life without this pleasure in it. Can you?'

She shakes her head. Life before Andrei seems a bleak place now and she has no desire to return to it.

'Thank you,' he says, 'for everything you have given me, and continue to give me.'

They kiss tenderly and when they pull apart, she feels deeply and intimately connected to him in a way she has with no other person. *Not in this way. Not with my body as well as my soul.*

She leans over to pick up her phone, which has been sitting on the bedside table, and check the time. As soon as she sees the screen light up, she gasps and sits bolt upright.

'Oh my God!' she shouts.

'What is it?' Andrei asks at once.

'It's Summer.' She holds out the phone, her eyes wide with astonishment. 'She's texted me!'

*   *   *

The emergency conference is held in her suite twenty minutes later. She alerted Miles and Freya and Mac at once, but something made her hold back from telling her father and Pierre. It seemed important to confer with the others first.

Mac made it to the hotel so quickly that Flora couldn't help suspecting that he might actually be staying there. Now he holds Flora's phone, staring at the text with a frown.

'"I'm all right. Don't worry about me. I'll be back as soon as I can",' he reads. Then he looks around at the others. 'And this arrived late last night, right?'

Flora reddens. 'Yes – but I didn't see it until this morning.'

No one looks at Andrei but there is a general sense that his presence explains why that was.

'I feel awful,' Flora says guiltily. 'I just didn't hear it arrive. But it's good news isn't it?' She's felt elated since she saw the message, as though her darkest fear can be put away and forgotten about. Summer is all right. She has made contact. The worst part of this nightmare is surely over. 'Summer is alive, we know that.'

Freya looks much better after her night's sleep, but even so she's still a little pale. 'I'm so happy,' she says quietly. 'Maybe she hasn't been kidnapped after all.'

Mac hums for a moment, and then says, 'I don't want to depress you all, but anyone could have sent this text.'

'But Summer knows my number,' Flora says quickly.

'Yes. But that still doesn't mean she wrote this actual text. It came from her phone, though, didn't it?'

Flora nods. Then she gazes hopefully at Miles. 'So this means your app must have downloaded on to her phone, and now we can find her. Right?'

Miles has brought his computer with him and is already tapping away, a frown on his face. Now he looks up, shaking his head. 'I'm afraid not. It looks as though the system attempted to download but it simply didn't have enough time. By the time the phone had located a network and joined it, and begun to trigger the download, it was switched off. And I don't think it's been on again since.' He sighs with frustration. 'The phone needs to be on for a few minutes at least. It would have sent a ping to a satellite as soon as it was switched on, but we'll need the phone company to release that information, which they won't do without official authorisation.'

Freya says quietly, 'So we still have no idea where she is.'

Mac is pacing around the suite, still staring at Flora's phone. 'Where is the ransom demand? That's what's bothering me. No demand. No reason for this disappearance. A text that could have been sent by anyone with access to Summer's phone and a knowledge of Flora's phone number, which Summer could have given at any time in the last few days.' He stops pacing and turns to Miles. 'Have you ever heard of an abduction like this?'

Miles shakes his head slowly. 'It's outside the range of my experience, or anything I've heard of. But I'm beginning to get anxious now. The longer we have no contact with the captor, the worse it generally is.'

Flora sinks down in her seat, all the happiness draining out of her. 'So this text means nothing after all!'

'Oh, it means something,' Mac says grimly. 'We just don't know what.' He sits down and opens up his own computer. 'But I've made a little progress of my own. I've been doing some in-depth research and pulling a few strings here and there, and I'm glad to say that there might be a breakthrough. I've traced an Italian family who happen to have a father by the name of Paolo and a son by the name of Alfredo. Their surname is Guidotti. And the reason I found them is because they featured in their local newspaper not long after the successful rescue of Freya and her mother. No more than a matter of a couple of weeks. And they are from the very same area outside Naples we're interested in.'

The tension in the room is at once electric.

'That's got to be them,' Miles says, turning to Freya, who is wide-eyed. 'Fredo must be short for Alfredo, right? Were there any pictures in the article?'

Mac nods slowly, taps on his keyboard, then turns the screen so that they can see the blow-up of the photograph inside the picture of the newspaper article. It's a handsome Italian man smiling into the camera, his dark eyes creased at the edges as he grins, his dark hair thinning a little on top. Next to him is a boy, a smaller, sweeter-faced version of his handsome father. Everyone turns to look at Freya, who seems stunned, her hands clenched into fists.

'That's him,' she says in a strained whisper. 'That's the guard. That's Paolo.'

Mac turns the screen back round and reads the Italian out loud without any attempt at an accent and sounding it out just as it looks. '*Paolo Guidotti con suo figlio Giacomo.*' He looks up at them all. 'I think we can guess what that means. This is Paolo with his son Giacomo.'

'Not Fredo?' Miles says. 'I thought you said that there was a Fredo?'

'There is,' Mac replies. 'I've got a translation of the article here. Alfredo is mentioned in the text but he's not in the picture.'

Flora rises to her feet, her hands trembling. She hasn't

277

seen the name written down but only heard how Mac has pronounced it. 'What was the boy's name?'

'It's a strange one,' Mac says, 'I apologise for my Italian, I don't speak the language.' He says it again slowly. 'Ghee-a-como.'

'Let me see it.' Flora hurries over and looks at the screen. When she stands up, her eyes are bright and her colour high. 'It looks like Ghee-a-como. But in Italian, the "i" after the letter "g" makes a sound like our letter j. It's pronounced *Jackomo*.' She stares round at them all in excitement. 'Don't you see? That must be Jack!'

There's an intake of breath and then everyone speaks at once, each wanting to look at the photograph and see the image of the boy. Flora texts Jimmy to get over fast so that he can look at the picture and confirm Jack's identity. Mac frowns and nods and looks a little as though he'd like to pretend that he knew from the start he'd found Jack, but in the end, he says, 'I thought Fredo was our boy. I thought he'd changed his name to Jack. Never occurred to me that it might be the younger brother.'

Then Freya says suddenly, 'But why were they in the paper at all? What's the news story about anyway?'

Mac goes quiet, looking over at her with something like concern. 'I guess you've got to know this, Freya. But I'm sorry to put you through even more.'

Freya stiffens. 'Know what? What is it, Mac?'

'Paolo Guidotti was in the news because his body was discovered in the woods outside the town. He'd been murdered and there were signs of torture carried out on him in the favoured way of the local Mafia – the Camorra, as it's known around Naples. It looks as though he was killed by organised criminals although the article doesn't speculate very much on it. No doubt everyone knew exactly who committed crimes like that, and no one wanted to ask too many questions.'

'He was murdered?' Freya looks stunned. 'But why?'

Mac shrugs. 'I don't have any evidence yet, but I could make some educated guesses. Why would they turn on one of their own? Only if they thought he was a traitor, I'd say.' Mac fixes her with a look. 'Someone suspected that Paolo Guidotti was responsible for the rescue. And he paid a very high price for that indeed.'

Freya looks sick. Miles puts out his hand to comfort her, his eyes full of sympathy for her.

Flora feels a prickle of horror spreading out over her body. 'And now his son's got Summer. Jack has Summer.'

She and Freya stare at each other with growing terror as they start to realise what this means.

Flora says quietly, 'He doesn't want money. He must blame us somehow for his father's death.' She puts her hand to her face. 'Oh my God. He wants revenge.'

Mac snaps shut the lid of his computer. 'Ladies,' he says, 'I think it's time we spoke to your father.'

CHAPTER TWENTY-SEVEN

When Jack comes in after a few hours of clearing the damage, I seem cheerful and normal. I've prepared us a lunch. Now that I've seen the stores of food, I have a good idea of what we can eat. I don't think I'll be seeing a salad any time soon, but there are frozen vegetables and I've managed to rustle up something that's healthy and fairly tasty, even with my limited range of cooking skills.

'What's this?' Jack says suspiciously, eyeing up the dish of food as he comes to the table.

'Pasta!' I say proudly.

'What kind?'

'Oh . . . you know, just a throw-together, potluck kind of meal. Bits of this, bits of that. I found sweetcorn.'

He looks vaguely appalled, and then says firmly, 'I'll do the cooking from now on, okay?'

As we eat, I have to admit that my pasta is not up to the standards of what Jack's been serving – which has been some tasty Italian food, now I think of it – but I don't think it's too bad considering my experience in a kitchen is practically nil. I chat happily to him, asking him about the state of the balcony and what he plans to do to it. I don't tell him that I know he's been on the phone to Adriana, whoever she is, or that I tried to turn on my phone again, only to find that the battery was definitely flat. Until I can find a charger, it's useless to me. The knowledge depressed me more than I expected. I'd been clinging to the idea of Jack and me against the world and hadn't realised how much I craved contact with Flora. Not knowing whether she's received the text causes physical pain, and not being able to know what she might have replied in return is torture. But I have to subdue that need for now. The main thing is that I will be going back to her soon – I just don't know exactly when.

When lunch is over, Jack and I clear away together. He frowns as he watches me washing up our plates.

'Hey – you're wearing something different.'

I look down at my new outfit. I'd forgotten that I got changed. 'Oh yeah,' I say. 'I found a bag in your room and I really needed some fresh clothes.'

He stiffens and I see a cloud of suspicion in his eyes. Then he relaxes. I get the feeling he was mentally checking what I might have found in his room, and then coming to the conclusion that there was nothing dangerous there. He smiles. 'You look nice. I guess they fit then?'

'I guess they do,' I say slowly. This situation will always come between us until we can resolve it. Until then, there will always be secrets hidden away. Mine from Jack – the searches, the phone, the text – and his from me: Adriana and whatever else he's hiding.

I know more clearly than ever that we have to get out of this. I have to get word to Flora somehow, ask her help.

But how am I going to do that, with no phone?

Then I remember that there is a phone. Jack's.

The afternoon passes harmoniously enough on the surface but underneath we are wary of each other. My new clothes seem to remind us both constantly of not only why I am here, but of the fact that I found the bag hidden in Jack's room. In other words, I'd clearly been looking for something, or at least snooping about. Jack's eyes are on me for the rest of the day, constantly watching me. I feel cross with myself. Just when I want to locate his phone and use it, he's on guard. I prickle with annoyance, thinking that as I'm here of my own volition now, I don't need to be watched like a prisoner. Jack has more or less indicated that he doesn't care what happens to him. So why all this wariness?

I consider just getting into the car and driving off, leaving him here. *But that's when he's liable to do something stupid. As long as I'm with him, we can save this situation. I just have to figure out a way to get him to forget that promise he made.*

Later in the afternoon we walk up the beach, not far as I can tell Jack doesn't want to stray into the path of any other visitors, and then back down in the other direction past the shack. We walk up and down a couple of times in a friendly silence, enjoying the fresh air and the sense of relative freedom. Every now and then I steal a glance at him as he walks along, his hands thrust into his pockets, his head downturned as he watches the sand disappearing under his steps. The wind ruffles his dark hair and I draw my breath in again at the sight of his handsomeness. He has a face I don't think I could ever tire of marvelling at. The curve of his lips makes my stomach swoop and my breathing quicken. Just the merest recollection of what it's like when we make love sets my heart pounding and a thousand nerve endings quivering. It's the intensity in his nature that draws me to him. Everything means so much to him – and that's why he's locked into the promise he made his brother.

As we walk, he puts out his hand to me and takes mine. Then, when I least expect it, he turns to me and says in that rasping voice of his, 'Summer. I've been thinking.'

'Yes?' I feel a mixture of excitement and trepidation. This could be good or it could be bad. With Jack, I never know what's coming.

'I have to tell you something. I know it sounds weird considering how long we've known each other, but I guess we've been through a lot since we met.' He gives me one of those half smiles of his, a little bit shamefaced.

'You could say that,' I answer drily.

'The way you are . . . it blows me away. I never thought anyone could be as generous and forgiving and kind as you, after what I've done.' He stops and takes my other hand, turning to face me so that we're gazing into one another's faces. Behind him is the ocean stretching away into the distance. He's staring at my mouth and then into my eyes. He says softly, 'I want to say something but I don't know how. I don't think you'll believe me.'

My heart speeds up. 'What is it?' I ask.

'I love you, Summer. It's the craziest thing in the world. I never thought this would happen, but it has. I love you, and I love life.' He looks so crazily mixed up but somehow I know that he's sincere. Then his eyes fill with sadness. 'But I don't see how I can have either. Not any more.'

His words frighten me at the very moment that I'm full of joy at what he's said. He loves me . . . but he doesn't even know how he'll carry on living . . . *Holy shit. How do I deal with this?* 'Jack,' I say desperately.

'Please, don't talk,' he says. 'There are no words.' Then he pulls me to him and kisses me with all his strength. I sink into the warmth of his body and of his mouth, clutching

283

him to me as though someone is about to march him away.
I need him so much. I can't believe life could be this unfair.
I want to laugh and cry at the same time, but instead all I
do is glory in the salty, tangy taste of his lips and the deli-
ciousness of his mouth.

After dinner that night, we go to bed and make soft, sweet
love to one another, our arms wrapped round each other,
whispering the whole time. He tells me he loves me and
needs me, and I tell him that I only want him to be happy
and that we can make this right. After our climaxes have
shaken us into calm again, he buries his head in my neck
and when he finally emerges, I feel wetness where he's been
weeping. The realisation makes my heart want to break. I
lie awake until he's sleeping peacefully and then I slip out
of bed and pull on a robe. It's dark in the room but there's
some glimmering from the moon that's out overhead and
shining down. I pick up Jack's discarded clothes and check
the pockets of his jeans but there's no phone there. Then I
go into the sitting room, turning on a lamp so that I can
see clearly.

Now, where would I hide a phone?

I check the obvious places first: drawers, shelves, behind
books, but it's nowhere as simple as that.

*Okay, he doesn't know I know about the phone so I
don't think the hiding place is going to be super clever. It's
just to keep it concealed, not to stop me when I'm hunting
for it. So . . .* I look around. Somewhere easy to hide, and
easy to remember. My eyes fall on the couch and I go
straight to it, lifting all the cushions off the surface, but
there's nothing there. I take off the seat cushions, and see
that there's a gap between the arm of the couch and the

seat. I realise that this is a sofa bed, that folds out. I reach down and slip my fingers under the seat and into the folds of the foam mattress beneath. Nothing. But that's only one side. I go to the other side where, now I think of it, I most often see Jack sit. I slide my fingers into the depths of the mattress and immediately hit something smooth and hard. I grapple for it and then have it. I pull it out. It's Jack's phone.

I feel a rush of triumph. I looked for it and I found it. Turning it over, I guess that it's just a pay-as-you-go type of phone, not smart or network-enabled. It won't be registered or traceable. The perfect phone for a kidnapper. But it still has a few features that can help me.

I fumble with the buttons. It's been so long since I've used a phone like this, I can't remember how they work, but I switch it on and it lights up, then I navigate my way through the menu to find the last number dialled. It's a cellphone number and the name it's recorded under is Adriana.

That's no surprise, I guess.

I slip the phone into my pocket and replace all the couch cushions. Then, as quietly as I can, I let myself out of the shack and go down on to the beach. Taking the phone out where I'm sure my voice won't carry, I carefully press in Flora's number and send the call. Then I wait, my hands trembling and my heart racing.

Flora answers in a tremulous voice. 'Hello? Who is this?'

The sound sends judders all through me and tears rush to my eyes. I've missed her so much. Hearing her voice is the sweetest sound I can think of right now. I'm so overcome, I can't speak.

'Hello? Hello?' She sounds frightened now. 'Who's there?'

I find my voice at last. 'Flora, it's me.' It comes out

croaky and not like my normal voice, but she seems to recognise me without any difficulty because she shouts in response.

'Summer! Oh my God, Summer, I can't believe it! Are you okay? Where are you, where are you? We're coming to get you, wherever you are.'

'Flora, listen to me, please . . .' But she's talking louder and faster now, and I can sense there are other people with her.

'We know who he is, Summer, we know who Jack is! We're in the process of tracking him down and we're going to get you away from him, don't you worry. Jack is the son of a man who was murdered after he helped Freya and Mama escape. He's taken you for revenge.'

'I know!' I say. 'I know all that!'

That stops her and then she says, 'What? You know?'

'Yes. Jack told me.'

Now she's lost for words. I can hear her breathing as she takes it in.

I say patiently, 'I need your help, Flora. I need to find a way to get out of this.'

'I know.' She's recovered now and is talking urgently again. 'We want to get you out of there. So where are you? Whose phone are you on?'

'Jack's. He doesn't know I've taken it. Mine is out of power.'

'Okay, that's a shame but we can still find you if you have a rough idea of your whereabouts.'

'I'm not going to tell you,' I say more loudly, feeling steamrollered. She won't listen. She has one idea of how this is, and can't take in any other.

'What? Why not?' She sounds surprised.

'Because I'm not coming back. Not until I've sorted out this situation.'

'Have you gone *insane*? What are you talking about?'

'I can't explain everything right now, but you have to trust me. Jack isn't a bad guy, he's under the influence of someone else. I want you to listen really carefully. You need to find his sister – I think she's called Adriana. She's in the city somewhere, she's a nurse. Ask her how to get Fredo to let Jack free from his promise. Do you understand?'

'Adriana? Was that the name?'

'Yes. Do you think you can find her?'

'We can try but—'

'Just find her and ask her, it's really important. Fredo needs to let Jack free of his promise. I'll call again tomorrow if I can, all right?'

'But Summer, this is madness! We think Jack wants to kill you!' Her voice is high with fear. 'We've got to get you out of there! Please, don't go without telling us where you are.'

I pause. I can't bear to hear the suffering in her voice. Perhaps I should give them the information they need to close in on me. I look up to see a light flicking on in the shack. It's in Jack's bedroom.

'I have to go, I'll call later,' I say quickly into the phone, and click off the connection. When Jack comes out, I'm sitting on the sand, gazing out to the moonlit water.

'Hey,' he says, coming down the wooden steps.

'Hey.' I smile up at him, my heart pounding from almost being discovered. 'I couldn't sleep. I'm just getting some air. It's so peaceful out here.'

'Yeah.' He looks out to the grandeur of the ocean. 'Are you coming back to bed now?'

'Sure.' I stand up, aware of the phone in my pocket. I'm going to have to slip it back into its hiding place when Jack isn't watching and hope he doesn't need it until then.

I follow him back to bed, wondering what kind of bomb I've just set off in the middle of my family.

CHAPTER TWENTY-EIGHT

Flora puts down her cellphone, her face a picture of amazement, elation and fright. 'Oh my God,' she says. 'Did you hear that?'

They are all gathered in Freya's suite, eating a room-service dinner while research continues into the Guidotti family. Mac and Miles are searching the Internet and making calls all over the world, pulling whatever strings they can to open up the secrets of what happened to the Guidottis in the years since Paolo's brutal murder. The facts are creating a picture that will lead them, eventually, to Jack – at least, that's what they all hope. Andrei is there too, eating chicken sandwiches and listening intently to what's going on, ready to offer whatever help he can when it's needed. His plane is at their disposal.

Now Flora is faced with six anxious faces, all of them having heard only her end of the conversation. Mac has scrawled the name Adriana in big letters over a paper napkin, the closest thing at hand.

Freya stares at her, a feeling that is equal measures of excitement and horror swirling around in her stomach. 'She wouldn't say where she is?'

Flora shakes her head, stunned, and looks at her phone as if it might hold the secrets of how to find her sister. Then she says in a dazed voice, 'No. She said she wasn't going to tell me. She said she needs help getting out of the situation she's in.' She looks over at Mac almost helplessly. 'I'm sorry, I tried to make her tell me but she just wouldn't.'

Mac is clearly thinking hard and he says brusquely, 'But she knew all about Jack, did she? She knew what you told her about him being Paolo's son?'

'Yes. She didn't seem very interested in that, or in the fact that he might want to kill her.'

'That's a good sign, isn't it?' Freya says, hopeful. She looks at Miles for reassurance and he smiles back and nods.

'I think so,' Miles says. 'What do you think, Mac?'

'It sure shows that the two of them are on a different footing to the one we feared. He's confided in her. That's good.' Mac frowns at the napkin where the name is written down. 'But I'm also worried because she's putting his welfare above her own, and that's not so good. It seems to show she's under his influence to a very large degree.' He looks straight at Flora as he taps the napkin. 'So what about this name?'

Miles is already tapping it into his keyboard ready to run an Internet search.

Flora sinks down on to the sofa, next to Jane-Elizabeth, who puts a hand on hers and grips it tightly. 'She said we should find Adriana, Jack's sister, and give her a message. She said "ask her how to get Fredo to let Jack free of his promise". And she said Jack wasn't a bad guy.'

Mac nods. 'So we're looking for Adriana Guidotti, a nurse, as far as we know, and one who hasn't got married and changed her name. We hope.' He shoots a look at Miles. 'Let me know when you've got it.' Then he smiles. 'Well, ladies and gentlemen, it looks like this case is nearly sewn up.'

Freya looks at him in astonishment. 'How can you say

that?' she demands. 'We still don't know where Summer is! As far as we know, she could be killed at any time!'

'I don't think so.' Mac sits back on his chair and stretches out his legs, crossing his cowboy boots slowly. 'If we're going to find a body any time soon, my money would be on Jack's. I think the guy is probably suicidal. He's not going to hurt Summer and my theory is that he was never going to. But he's in the grip of a promise to his brother and Summer wants him out of it.' He looks around and smiles. 'So it's good news, people. Summer will be back here whenever she wants.'

Freya leaps to her feet, anger rushing through her. 'I've never heard anything so stupid in my life! How can you assume that? As far as we know, my sister is still in the power of a man who is very likely to hurt her in retaliation – who seems to have sworn an oath that he will! There's no way I'm about to whoop and cheer and start relaxing. No way!'

Flora nods vigorously. 'You're right, Freya! I'm not going to stop any of our efforts until we have Summer safely back and this Jack is arrested and thrown in jail.'

Just then, Miles says, 'Bingo.' He looks up at Freya with a smile. 'I've traced Adriana Guidotti. It helps when you have a name. I know where she works and in a few minutes, I'll know where she lives too.'

'I'm going to see her the minute you do,' Freya says with determination.

Mac sighs and says, 'Ladies, I apologise if I gave you the impression that I intend to slack on this case. That is not correct. I'm just glad that if my hunch is right, then your sister is not in the kind of danger I've been afraid of. That's a good thing. But we still need to find her.' He nods slowly. 'And you're right – there's still a chance Jack could lose his head and hurt her, if he decides he's going to keep this promise of his.' He looks directly at the sisters. 'Now, might I suggest that you let me do the interview with Miss Guidotti? I'm worried that things may become too heated.'

'No,' Freya says firmly. 'I need to see her. I have to. And so do you, Flora.'

Flora nods slowly.

'Why?' Andrei asks, leaning forward in his seat. 'Why is it so important?'

Freya looks back at him. 'Because we need to apologise. Both of us.'

The car glides through the city, its powerful engine a barely audible hum. At red lights, its advanced engine cuts out altogether but comes smoothly back on when the driver presses the accelerator.

Miles is in the front seat beside the driver, helping navigate to the apartment building where Adriana Guidotti lives with her mother. In the back Andrei sits with the sisters, listening as they talk quietly about what they are going to say to Adriana.

'I want you to let me do the talking,' Freya says firmly. 'I was there. I knew her father. It's right that I make the apology. But we should both be present. I just hope she wants to help us, that's all.'

'I can't believe what Dad did,' Flora says quietly, looking at the city as it slides past the window. They feel disconnected behind the bulletproof frame and thick, darkened glass of the car.

'It was not your father,' Andrei says in a neutral voice.

'It was his security who cocked it up. His men should have ensured that any promise given was kept.'

Freya turns to look at him. She can't quite hide her hostility to Andrei, although she is finding it less terrible to be around him than she'd expected. She respects the way he is keeping in the background of this situation and not trying to take over as she'd imagined he would. She can also see that he treats Miles as an equal, which pleases her. 'My father was partly to blame. He knew about the deal that was struck with Paolo Guidotti. It should have been a point of honour to make sure it was kept. He should have put the kids through school and on to college. They could have had a bright future. Now look – one boy's in prison and the other has turned into a kidnapper.'

Andrei nods. 'Yes. The wrong thing was done.'

'Easy to say,' returns Freya. 'Not so easy if you're the one whose father was brutally murdered for helping get some rich guy's family released.' She sighs. 'If only we could go back and change things.'

'If only,' echoes Flora. 'The saddest words there are.'

Freya thinks back to the interview earlier that day between Mac and her father. They were all there, except Estella who had gone to the hotel spa, and Pierre who was working on the case from the penthouse suite. At first Mr Hammond blustered and told Mac he wasn't answering any questions, and that his own security would find Summer in no time. It was Jane-Elizabeth who stepped in, to everyone's surprise. She stood up, her eyes blazing, and said, 'I've bitten my tongue more times than I can count, but, so help me, I'm not going to now. Your daughter's life is at stake! Summer is in danger and you are damn well going to tell Mac everything he wants to know, or . . . or . . . I'll quit!'

Her face was bright red and her fists were clenched. 'Do you hear me? I've had all I can take over this, and everything else! To be honest, I wanted to hand in my notice over the way you've treated the girls. From the day Freya and Miles got together, you haven't thought of anyone but yourself. Their happiness! Doesn't that matter? Perhaps it was right to ask them to stand on their own two feet for a while, but the manner of doing it left a lot to be desired. You need to show love and kindness, not the kind of harshness and rejection you've been handing out! I only stayed to look after them, so there was someone on hand to make sure you weren't turned into a complete fool by that . . . bimbo!' She ran out of breath and came to a halt, redder than ever and panting with the effort of her speech. She looked mortified almost immediately, but no less defiant.

Hammond gaped at her, and then said, 'Jane-Elizabeth!' in tones of hurt rather than anger.

'I'm sorry but you had to hear it,' she said more quietly. 'And you need to help Mac, right now.'

And their father had obeyed, sitting down and answering all of Mac's questions with the docile air of someone well chastened. Freya had listened, amazed and appalled, as her father had recounted his reactions to the kidnap of his wife and daughter. Yes, he had been frightened and concerned for their welfare. Yes, he had wanted to free them. But he was damned if anyone was going to hold him to ransom to get his family back. And anyway, his head of security had advised him that paying was as potentially risky as not paying.

'Then you had a lucky break,' prompted Mac.

'Yes.' Hammond thought back, frowning. 'I was told that we had infiltrated the gang and managed to get in contact with someone who had access to my wife and Freya. He was willing to give us the information we needed in return for money.'

'And that was a deal you were willing to accept,' Mac says, doodling on his yellow notepad.

'Of course,' Hammond says. 'They were rescued successfully not long afterwards.'

'You do know,' Mac says slowly, 'that the promised money was never handed over.'

Hammond shrugged. 'That was not my remit. I left that matter in the hands of my head of security.'

'Do you know that the gang member who helped you needed that money to relocate away from the criminals who took your wife and daughter? So that he could escape any reprisals?'

Hammond was silent and then said, 'No.'

'And he was tortured and murdered shortly afterwards. Probably as a result of the information he passed to you.'

Hammond blinked three times very fast. 'I see.'

Freya couldn't hold her tongue any longer, and she said in a trembling voice, 'Dad – did you know how sick Mama was? Didn't you think that she would suffer in captivity? It was because Paolo Guidotti saw her condition that he helped us – I know that's what it was, I remember how he looked at her, with pity in his eyes.'

Her father couldn't look at her. For a long time he didn't speak and then he said in a low voice, 'I forgot. I forgot she needed her medication.' When he looked up at his daughter, his eyes were full of remorse, something she'd never seen in them before. Then he said, 'I'm sorry, Freya. Sorry for all of it. Sorry it happened to you, and for what we all lost.' He looked over to Flora too. 'And I'm sorry for you, darling.

And for Summer. You didn't deserve what happened either. If I can put it right, I will.'

But what can he do? Freya thinks now, as Miles directs the driver the last few miles to the apartment block they're heading for. *It's too late to bring Mama back.* The knowledge that her father had forgotten her mother's condition has chilled her to the bone. She looks at Miles, following the satellite navigation on his phone and talking to the driver in a low voice. *Miles would never do that. He'll never leave me alone like that.* A feeling of safety and well-being floods through her suddenly, with a golden skein of happiness at the knowledge that he loves her.

Flora is evidently thinking back to their talk with their father too, as she leans over and says, 'Wasn't Jane-Elizabeth amazing this afternoon?'

Freya nods and smiles. 'Amazing. Dad couldn't believe it.'

'He did what she said!' Flora grins. 'Don't you think it would have been marvellous if he'd married her instead of falling for Estella? But he could never see what was right in front of his face – how much she adores him, and how much he needs and trusts her.'

Freya sighs. 'It would be perfect. But don't hold your breath. Estella doesn't intend to let Dad out of her grasp anytime soon.'

They are coming to a halt now, turning into the parking lot of a tall apartment building, lights shining from its many windows. Freya wonders how many lives are being lived in there right now, and whether the occupants of Apartment 6019 have any idea of what is about to happen.

'Is Mac still following?' she asks Miles, and he nods.

'Yup,' he says. 'He's just a little bit behind. He said he had some work to do before he could leave the hotel but he's just a few minutes away now.' He twists in his seat so that he can look at Freya, and says gently, 'Are you ready, baby?'

She nods. 'Ready as I'll ever be.'

It's just Freya and Flora who knock on the door of Apartment 6019 and when it's answered by a grey-haired woman in an apron, she gasps and steps back. It's clear that she knows exactly who they are, even though she's stunned to see them on her doorstep.

'Good evening, Mrs Guidotti,' Freya says politely. 'I know it's late. I hope we're not disturbing you?'

'Who is it, Mama?' comes a sweet, clear voice from inside the apartment, and the next minute a pretty girl appears in the doorway beside her mother. She stares at the women, bewildered. 'Who are you?'

'Hammond!' says the older woman in a strong Italian accent. She looks terrified now, and appalled.

'What?' The girl looks at them quizzically, frowning. Freya thinks that if looks run in the family, it's easy to see why Jack is so handsome. The girl is beautiful, with clear olive skin, dark velvety-brown eyes and a rich river of almost black hair that falls over her shoulder in a thick ponytail. Then realisation comes to her and she says quickly, 'Oh no. No, no. Go away. We don't want to see you. My mother does not need to see you.'

She goes to shut the door but Freya is too quick for her, holding it open and talking fast. 'Please, Miss Guidotti – please talk to us. I promise you, this is vitally important for all of us.'

The girl is saying no over and over, and trying to shut the door on them.

Freya says, 'Please, Adriana, please! This is about Jack! And Fredo. You have to listen to me.'

The girl is quiet suddenly, and stops trying to push the door shut. Then she says from behind it, 'What about Jack? Is something wrong?'

'He's done something very stupid. Really stupid and dangerous. There's still time to save the situation and save him too. But we'll need your help. Just listen, that's all we ask.'

Flora is gazing up at her with wide, anxious eyes, her lip between her teeth. Freya hopes she's said enough to convince the Guidottis to let them in. There's a conversation in muttered Italian behind the door and Freya picks up a few words – *Jack. Hammond. Fredo.*

After a moment, the door opens slowly and reveals Adriana standing there, her mother just behind her. 'All right,' she says, her eyes still hostile. 'You can come in and talk to us. But we've taken shit from your family and I'm warning you, we don't want any more.'

Flora's phone chirps with an incoming text and she quickly looks at it, gasps and shows it to Freya, saying quietly, 'It's from Summer.'

Freya looks. It reads:

Tell Adriana we will give them the money we owe.

She exchanges looks with Flora. 'She's right. And it's the least we can do.' Then they both follow the Guidotti women into the apartment.

298

CHAPTER TWENTY-NINE

I slide the phone back into the folds of the mattress and turn to tiptoe back to bed, where Jack is sleeping. I've been lying awake, waiting for him to slip into unconsciousness so that I can return the phone to its hiding place before he decides to use it again. I lay there, blinking in the darkness and thinking about what to do, and once I was sure that Jack was asleep, I slid out of bed and headed to the sitting room. Before I returned the phone, I tapped out a quick text and sent it through to Flora's phone. I don't know if money will help the situation but whether or not it does, I want the family to be compensated. We owe them that much after what Jack's father did for us.

As I start to return to the bedroom, it suddenly occurs to me that Jack will be able to see my outgoing text and the call I made on the phone's log if he looks. I need to delete it.

'Shit,' I curse under my breath. Hurrying back, I get the phone and turn it on. I'm not familiar with the make and the buttons are confusing me. I want to swipe the screen like I do on my cell, but that achieves precisely nothing. At last I navigate to the texts and press delete on my outgoing message. It vanishes from the outbox. Success.

I turn off the phone and press it back under the sofa cushion, making sure it's gone to the same place I first found it. That's when the light switches on and I hear Jack say: 'Summer, what the hell are you doing?'

My heart swoops downwards and my palms prickle unpleasantly as I turn to face him. He looks furious but also sad, as though he hates the sight of me doing this secretive thing.

'What are you doing?' he asks again. He's so handsome with his bare chest, wearing only his pyjama bottoms.

'I . . .I . . .' Colour is flooding my face and my heart is pounding. 'I found your phone.'

'I guess I can see that,' he says, and he just sounds tired, as though he can't really cope with all of this any more. 'What did you do with it?'

I think of what to say. Do I lie? Pretend? Ask him how the hell he has the cheek to be angry with me, when he's the one hiding phones and making secret calls and all the rest of it? But I'm tired too. I'm tired of the lies and the secrets. I'm not going to do it any more. 'I sent a text to my sister. And I called her as well. I told her I'm safe.'

'Uh huh.' Jack nods. 'So can I expect the cops anytime now? You really should have told me. I'd like to get dressed. Maybe get some coffee on. They'll need some after the journey.'

He looks disgusted and I feel rotten. *How does he do that? He's very good at turning the tables on me.*

'I wouldn't tell her where I am. But she has to know I'm safe, Jack. She's suffering. My whole family is suffering.'

'Well, excuse me, I'll just get a handkerchief cos I need to mop up my tears. The Hammonds are suffering?' His voice is dripping with sarcasm. 'Someone should hold a fucking benefit!'

'My sister doesn't deserve it,' I say quietly. 'She's no more guilty for what happened than I am, or Freya come to that. And we did suffer. I know you lost your father. I lost my mother. We ought to be quits on the suffering front.'

'Maybe. But you didn't lose your future. We did. If you knew what it's been like for my mother . . .' His voice breaks and he winces, biting his lip and unable to talk.

'I know, baby. That's why I'm doing everything I can to make it better.' I go towards him, my arms out. 'Please, baby. Please let me help you.'

'No one can make it right again,' he says sadly, looking away and ignoring my embrace.

'No one can bring back our parents, that's for sure,' I say, 'but we don't have to make it a million times worse. And we can do our best to make peace with it, and with each other. Can't we?'

'Why didn't you tell me you'd found the phone?' he asks, still avoiding my eye.

'I needed to process everything,' I say truthfully. 'I want this sorted out. We can't go on like this for ever. Eventually, we'll have to go back to the real world and I want that to be as easy as possible. As simple as it can be.'

'Yeah.' He nods his head slowly. 'I know you're right. We can't stay hidden out here for ever, much as I would like that.' He looks at me at last, a slow smile forming on his lips. 'You know you're one unpredictable girl. I thought you would go crazy out here. I didn't think you'd save my life and then end up staying when I virtually order you to leave.'

'I'm kind of obstinate I guess,' I say with a smile.

'You could say that.' His eyes soften as he looks at me. Now his gaze is on my lips. I love the way he looks at my mouth like that, as though he can't stop desiring it. He looks like he wants to kiss me. Then he says, 'I get the feeling our time here is coming to an end.'

'It has to. But that doesn't mean it's the end of everything we've had here.'

He laughs ironically. 'I find that hard to believe. I think we'll probably never see each other again.'

'Don't say that!' A stab of pain hits me at the very thought. 'Neither of us wants it, so why should it be?'

'It's impossible,' he says softly, his gaze travelling back to my eyes. 'You know that. I know that.'

'I won't give up,' I whisper. Now I'm looking at his mouth, the curve of his lips, the brooding turn to it. 'I can't.'

'I love that about you.' We're getting closer to one another, standing as near as we can without touching. His breath is gentle on my skin, and I can feel the heat coming from him. I'm full of longing, desperate to touch him and feel his fingers on me.

'What if we could be together?' I ask, my heart fluttering with nerves. I can't believe how much this means to me. 'Would you want that?'

Now he reaches out and takes my hand, swinging it gently. 'Hey,' he says. 'It would be my dream come true. But it's impossible.'

'I just need to know that you would want it, that's all.'

'You . . .' He looks lost for words for a moment, overcome. Then he says simply, 'You would make my life complete. But I don't deserve you.'

Our mouths are close now, and then we start to kiss: soft fluttering kisses that set every nerve tingling as we brush lips, stealing tender touches from each other.

'You do,' I murmur. 'And I need you, Jack. I don't want to lose you.'

'Let's just enjoy the time we have,' he murmurs back. 'I don't want to think about the future . . . not tonight.'

He takes me in his arms and kisses me long and passionately, his desire growing with every swirl of our tongues. I want him in an elemental way that I never thought possible, with my whole being. I want us to be joined together and be one. He drops his head to my chest, pushing aside my robe so that he can see my breasts and glue his lips to my rosy nipples and suck them hard. I'm panting almost at once, revelling in the excitement his sucking is causing me. My sex is hot and wet and I drop my hands to undo his pyjama bottoms and let him spring free. He's already stiff but as I touch him, his cock grows harder in quick, muscular jerks in my hand. I pull free from his mouth and drop to my knees, taking him in my mouth and sucking him hard, savouring his taste and the feel of him sliding hot and hard between my lips. I slide one hand underneath to feel the root and balls and tickle him gently. He responds, pressing his shaft into me with thrusts of his hips, and I spend as long as I can taking him in and out of my mouth, before he slides down and comes to join me on the floor. He pulls open my robe to reveal my full nakedness, his dark eyes glassy at the sight.

'You're beautiful, my gorgeous girl.'

'It's all for you,' I say, and open my thighs so he can feast his eyes on my open, wet slit.

He groans as I reach for him, guiding his shaft to my entrance, and then he's possessed by the frenzy that has me in its grip. He thrusts hard inside me, stretching me around him as he goes halfway up in one push. Then, with delicious slowness, he rams further in, filling me deliciously.

'Harder,' I beg. 'Don't hold back, I need you so much. I want to feel you inside me.'

He obeys with vigour, pressing his buttocks back and forth, sending his cock as far as he can. 'You're so tight,' he mutters. 'God, you feel so amazing.'

I tighten my muscles to hold him all the better and he moans appreciatively. Wrapping my legs round him, I try to make him go in to the greatest extent he can. My lust for him is fuelled by the heightened emotions of our situation; how many more times will we be together like this? I'm filled with reckless abandon, a desperate desire to live this moment as acutely as I can. I rise to meet him as he fucks hard, giving back everything I get from him. I sense that this is intense for him as well; we both read the craziness of all of this in each other's eyes, and want to take it to another level of depth and passion. I don't know how long we are joined together, moving in delicious time, pushing each other towards the heights of ecstasy that we engender in one another. My lips are parted, I gasp for air, I stiffen and arch with the sensation of Jack inside me, and we grow more fevered, more rapid, more desperate to reach the climax we need so much. Jack groans as we writhe together, thrusting deep with his teeth set and his face contorted by what he is feeling. I love to watch him losing himself in me and riding to the peak of his pleasure. He makes me thrill all over to the tips of my fingers and in the burning heat that's possessing my clitoris and making it throb, swell and tingle convulsively. I rise to meet him again, my thighs hard against his hips, and the blissful rapture comes to possess me, making me shake with a kind of volcanic eruption. He comes too at the same moment, and we cling together in the great shuddering that possesses us as Jack pours out his orgasm in torrents inside me.

'Summer,' he groans as his climax leaves him in great jets.

When the fierce convulsions have passed, I say softly, 'I love you, Jack. You know that, don't you?'

'Yes,' he says softly. 'And I love you too.'

We lie for a while in each other's arms, not knowing what to say. It feels as though this moment could be one of the last we ever have.

We're both exhausted and we go through to the bedroom. After we've showered, I climb into bed and wait for Jack to join me, but before he does, he goes back to the sitting room. A moment later, he's back. He gets into bed and puts something down on the cover in front of me. 'Your phone. You should have it back. I forgot I had it.'

I pick it up and try to switch it on. Nothing happens. 'I think it's out of power,' I say. 'And I didn't bring a charger.' I shrug lightly. 'Oh well. They know I'm safe. It's fine.'

'You never know when you might need it,' he says, taking the phone and looking at the charger inlet. 'I think I've got one for this in the car. I'll go and have a look.'

I open my mouth to stop him but I can't think of a good reason, and he's gone before I get my act together enough to speak. When he comes back a few minutes later with a charger in his hand, I say casually, 'Oh, I can't be bothered to charge it now. I'll do it in the morning.'

'No problem, I'll do it,' he says, leans over and takes my phone almost before I've realised what he's doing. He plugs in the charger and connects my phone to it. I watch him.

I guess it can't do any harm. The location services are switched off.

Jack leaves my phone on the bedside cabinet and climbs back in beside me. He's chilled from his trip outside.

305

'Mmm, come here,' I say and he wraps his arms round me, nuzzling into my neck. 'Let's get warm together.'

'I can't think of anything nicer,' he murmurs.

When we switch off the lamp, the phone sends up a small beam of light into the room until it shuts off and sleeps.

CHAPTER THIRTY

Freya and Flora face the Guidotti women over the small table in their kitchen.

'Okay. So what do you want to tell us about Jack?' asks Adriana, her expression cool.

'He's in trouble. Big trouble,' Freya says firmly. 'Do you know where he is?'

'Sure I do,' returns Adriana. 'And he's not in trouble. I spoke to him this morning and he was fine. He's fishing with friends, the place he usually goes. I think he's heading back in a week or so.'

'Right.' Freya looks at Flora, who looks back with wide eyes, then turns back to Adriana. 'I don't think so. If that's what he's told you, I think it's a lie.'

Adriana's eyes flash. 'Are you really accusing my brother of lying to me?'

'I'm afraid so. I don't know where he is, and maybe he is fishing. Maybe he even has a friend or two with him, but they'd have to be pretty good friends.' Freya takes a deep breath and says, 'Jack has kidnapped our sister. He is keeping her somewhere. We don't know where.'

Adriana stares at them disbelievingly. Her mother tugs at her sleeve and says something in Italian, which Adriana answers quickly before saying, 'This is nonsense. Jack wouldn't do something like that.'

Freya fixes her with a look. 'Really?'

Adriana drops her gaze for a second and then looks back again defiantly. 'Yes. He wouldn't do it. Not Jack.'

'Is it something Fredo would do?'

Adriana gasps and her mother says, 'What do you know about Fredo?' Her voice is strongly accented but there is no hiding her anxiety at hearing her other son's name mentioned.

Flora can't restrain herself any longer. They agreed that Freya would do the talking but she's desperate to find out what they need to know. 'You've got to believe us!' she says urgently. 'He has Summer. She sent us a message telling us we had to find you because you're the only one who will know what to do.'

Adriana's dark-brown gaze slides over to her and then returns to Freya. 'Jack is fishing,' she says obstinately. 'He hasn't taken your sister.'

Freya leans towards her over the small table. 'Adriana, she was last seen going to meet him. She told us that we had to find you because you're the only one who will know how to get Fredo to let Jack free of his promise! You know we're telling the truth. You know Jack has done this. We have to get Summer back before he does something stupid.'

Adriana stares at her, obviously stunned by what she's heard.

'What promise?' demands her mother. She is looking between Freya and Adriana, asking them both the question. 'What promise is this? Adriana, tell me! What has Fredo done now?' Then she looks frightened. 'Not my Jack. Not my good boy! No, no.'

'Shhh, Mama,' Adriana chides. She looks scared now. 'Oh my God.'

'What is it, Adriana?' Flora says quickly. 'Do you know

what this promise is? Please tell us – and let us know how to make Fredo break it.'

Adriana looks down at the table, knitting her fingers together, biting her lip anxiously. Her mother mutters in Italian and Adriana brushes her away impatiently.

Freya says, 'You know this is serious. I understand that it goes against everything in you to cooperate with us, when you've always blamed us for what happened to your family. But we want to make it right. We want to pay you the compensation you deserve for what happened to you and to your father. What was done was wrong and ended tragically. We want to put it right.'

Adriana jumps to her feet, her expression furious. 'You want to buy us? Buy us with your filthy money? I don't think so!'

Flora stands up too, leaning on the table towards Adriana. 'We're not buying you!' she cries. 'But you need to know that we're serious about this. Don't do this for Summer – do this for Jack. It's the only way to save him too. If we don't find Summer soon, we'll have to go to the police and once that happens, it will be out of our hands. Jack could go to prison. He could do something stupid.' She remembers Mac's verdict earlier. 'He could even kill himself.'

Adriana looks frightened again now. She sinks back into her chair.

Her mother puts a hand on her arm. 'Adriana, we must help Jack. I can't lose my son, not another son! What has Fredo done? Tell us!'

Adriana says, 'All right.' Then she flicks an angry glance at the sisters. 'But this is for Jack! And not for any money, is that clear?'

'It's clear. I shouldn't have mentioned it,' Freya says calmly. 'Of course you're doing this to help your brother. How will you make Fredo release him from his promise – and what is this promise anyway?'

'I don't know exactly. It's to do with what happened to our father. Fredo has always been mad for revenge, that's why he's in prison. He was in a fight with the son of one of the men we think killed our father. When he went to prison, he couldn't fight for justice any more, so he worked on Jack, through letters and calls and any other way he could think of to reach him. He sent video messages, I think. He wanted Jack to carry on the fight, but Jack never seemed that serious about it. Not serious enough to do this.'

'Well, he was,' Freya says. 'Can you tell Fredo to send Jack a message to stop this all right now?'

'I can try,' Adriana says doubtfully. 'But it could take a while.'

'We don't have long,' Freya says, urgent now. 'It has to be quick.'

'There's a problem,' Adriana says. 'I don't think Fredo will do it.' She stares at the sisters with sad eyes. 'I think he would rather see Jack dead. That is the honest truth. I'm sorry.'

'Jack? *È morto*?' The old woman looks grief-stricken. 'No, not my precious boy!'

Freya looks at her with pity in her eyes. 'He's not dead, Mrs Guidotti. I promise.' Then, as she watches the tears spring to the other woman's eyes, she says slowly, 'Perhaps there's another way after all.'

Back at the hotel, now quiet as the guests begin turning in for the night, Pierre is in Freya and Miles's suite, taking a quick look at Miles's computer. It was easy enough to bribe one of the hotel staff to give him a card key for the room and he has connected his own laptop to allow him to hack in and take a look. Miles has put in some effective firewalls and protective measures but Pierre is good too, and he manages to get in without too much trouble. He is scrolling down the email folder when a pop-up comes up on to the screen. 'Download on remote phone complete,' it reads. 'Location available.'

Pierre blinks at it in surprise, and then recalls that he's seen something like this before. It only takes him an instant to make the link. This is important.

He clicks on the pop-up and it takes him to a screen; a map where a small red pip is flashing. On the menu he selects 'Location name' and then 'Satellite image'. When he's examined both for as long as he needs, he sees another option – remote device name – and he clicks on that too. The name comes up. *Summer's phone.*

Pierre chuckles to himself. This is working out very well. He's found out the girl's location and now he'll be able to take the credit for it with his boss. Excellent.

He closes the page and sends the computer to sleep, then hurries out to the penthouse.

When the door opens, it is Estella who's there, slinky in white satin pyjamas. When she sees that it's Pierre, she bats her lashes at him seductively and says, 'Hello there. How nice to see you here.'

Pierre goes past her, looking for his boss. 'Is he here?'

'No.' She follows him into the room. 'He's gone downstairs for a massage. He says he needs to relax. He has to pay triple at this time of night. They had to call the masseur

311

back specially.' Going up behind Pierre, she rubs his back. 'There's time for you to fuck me, baby, if you want to.'

Pierre turns round and looks at her appreciatively. His lip curls in a kind of sneer but there's lust in his eyes. 'You want me to fuck you? Here?'

'You know I do.' She runs her hand over his chest. 'Good and hard, the way I like it.'

He laughs throatily. 'I know exactly how you like it. I don't know why you stay with that old man when he doesn't give you what you want.'

'But I have you for that,' she says smoothly. 'You give me what I want.'

'Yes.' His gaze drops to her chest where large breasts are just contained by the white satin and then to her bottom. She sees his glance and wriggles it suggestively. 'I can fuck you very well.'

Estella licks her lips. 'My pussy wants you,' she says, pouting. 'Really badly.'

His gaze darkens as he looks at her body. The lust growing in him is apparent and Estella slips her hand on to the hardness in his trousers and says, 'Mmm.'

'You like your dangerous games,' he mutters. 'We can't do this now. Here. It would be madness. But when we're home, I'm going to give you exactly what you want – until you scream.'

She closes her eyes and sighs happily at the thought. 'I can't wait that long.'

'Where's the old bitch?' Pierre says abruptly, looking around for Jane-Elizabeth.

'She's not here of course. Do you think I'd be touching your cock if she was?' Estella looks sulky. 'She's in her room. She's said something to the old man, I don't know what. But he was shaken up and said she'd delivered quite a speech. That's why he needs a massage, apparently.' Then she looks keenly at Pierre. 'What is it? You know something don't you?'

'I've got the girl's location. Murray sent a tracer to her phone and it's just downloaded. I can get her any time I want.'

Estella looks interested now. 'Really? But that's great. You should get her right now.'

Pierre frowns. 'I ought to get Mr Hammond's permission first.'

'Don't be silly.' Estella gives him a persuasive look. 'If you go and get her, imagine – you'll be quite the hero. I think it would do your cause a lot of good. And mine too, if I tell him that I ordered you to get her right away. It will blow Murray out of the water, no one will remember that it was his tracer that found her. You don't want Murray back on the staff, do you?'

Pierre shakes his head. 'Maybe you're right. I'll find Georg and we'll go off now.' He pats his jacket and feels the hardness of steel tucked under his arm. 'I'm prepared.'

'You certainly are.' Estella strokes the erection in his pants a little harder. 'Are you sure there isn't time for a little relaxation before you go?'

'When I get back,' Pierre promises. 'If you can get away for a while.'

'I'll manage it somehow,' Estella says, smiling. 'I can always give him one of my sleepy drinks. They knock him out for hours. Handy when I can't get horny for his tiny cock.' She presses up against him and murmurs, 'Not like I can for yours. Any time.'

'Business first.' He pushes her away gently. 'Pleasure later. I have to find Georg and get on the road.'

An hour later, Freya and Flora arrive back at the hotel with Andrei and Miles. Mac is behind them, following along in his battered old car. Freya is holding her phone as though it's as precious and vulnerable as a newborn. In it there is what she hopes is the key to getting Summer out.

Flora is alternately elated and despairing. 'We still don't know where she is!' she cries as they head up to Freya's suite.

'It won't take long now,' Miles says firmly. 'Adriana has given us every location she can think of that Jack might have gone to. We can track all of those very quickly. And we have his phone number, right? We could call him. Tell him what we've got.'

'I'm not sure about that,' Freya says, worried. 'What if he doesn't know that Summer's used his phone and that makes him angry? Or if he won't listen to us and we lose our chance?'

They reach the suite and Freya swipes the card down to open the door. As they go in, Miles stiffens at once.

'Someone's been here,' he says and frowns. He strides over to the computer and opens it. It pops into life. 'It's been looked at.' He goes to the launchpad screen and finds the tracer app. 'This has been opened.' He grimaces. 'Shit. I'm an idiot. I'm a fucking idiot.'

'What is it?' Freya asks. 'Who's looked?'

'I'd put money on Pierre. And look. Summer's phone has downloaded the tracer. We can see exactly where she is.' He gestures at the screen. The girls crowd round to look, Andrei coming up behind them.

'Oh my God!' Flora cries, grabbing his arm. 'We've found her!'

Andrei smiles down at her, his blue eyes happy. 'This is wonderful news. Well done, Miles. Your tracer has worked.'

'Yes – but Pierre has found her too. And he doesn't have what we have.' Miles is grim-faced now. 'That makes him dangerous.'

There's a knock at the door and Flora hurries to open it. Mac comes in, whistling cheerily until he sees Miles's face. 'Uh oh. What's up?'

Miles explains quickly.

'We have to get there. Fast.' Mac looks as serious as Miles. 'We don't need Pierre going in and messing this up.'

'When do you think he left?' Andrei says. 'I can arrange a helicopter.'

'How long will that take?' asks Miles.

Andrei shrugs. 'Not long. There will be a heliport very close. But it may take a short while to arrange the charter. The company I use here is very good, but it's late.'

'And to drive to the location?' asks Mac.

'The map suggests it's two and a half hours out of Los Angeles.'

'Let's say Pierre left an hour ago,' Mac says, looking at his watch. 'If we can get a copter within an hour . . . what's the flying time?'

'I'd say around thirty minutes. But we have no idea of where we can land when we get there,' Miles says.

'That still gets us there before Pierre,' Mac points out.

'If he left an hour ago. It could be longer.'

'Boy, you sure like to look on the bright side. Listen, we'll do both. I'll go in the car. You guys go by helicopter. Then both bases are covered.'

315

'I'm going in the helicopter,' Freya says. 'It'll be faster.'

'Me too,' Flora says quickly.

Andrei pulls out his mobile phone to start making the arrangements.

'We'd better get on with it then,' says Mac. 'I'll start right away. Miles, I'll see you there.'

'Should we tell Dad?' Flora asks. 'He ought to know.'

'I think Pierre will have told him,' Miles says abruptly as he goes back to his screen. 'He's probably obeying orders to go and get Summer.'

'Then we should tell him we're going too.'

'If you want,' Miles says. 'But we could leave at any moment. We need to get this girl home as soon as possible.'

CHAPTER THIRTY-ONE

I'm fast asleep, deep in slumber, and dreaming about Jack. The shack is on fire again, and I know we can do the same as we did before and put it out. But I can't find him, no matter how hard I look. I know he's here, but I can't see him and every moment that goes by the shack is filling with thick, black smoke.

I wake feeling choked. I reach for him and the bed is empty. He's gone. I feel a rush of panic. *Has he left me here alone? Am I going to lose him after all?*

'Jack?' I sit bolt upright, trying to accustom my eyes to the gloom. 'Where are you?'

My phone is on the bedside table where he left it charging last night, and a white beam of light shines up from the screen, enough to show me that Jack is nowhere about. But why is the phone awake anyway? I lean over and pick it up. The screen is bright, with the time and above it the icon showing the battery fully charged. Four little boxes request my code. Jack doesn't know it, so he can't have looked on the phone. There's nothing here that could have made him leave.

Then I see it. The little arrow by the battery icon that indicates location services are switched on.

I gasp. *How is that possible? I switched them off myself!*

As quickly as I can with trembling fingers, I enter my passcode and the screen takes me to the home page, where

I can see my inbox is now crammed with emails and my voicemail bulging with messages. I have over a hundred texts waiting for me to read. I ignore them, instead going to my settings so that I can check that the location services are off, as I left them last time. They are on.

What? How? I know I turned them off. I swipe through the screens showing all my apps, and there, on the last screen, is something I've never seen before. It looks innocuous, with a cute cartoon bird on the front, but I know I haven't ever seen it. I tap on it and it opens. Now it seems to be some kind of game, where the tiles are shuffled and a picture emerges – a picture of this bird, as far as I can see. This is weird. I never downloaded a game like this, and here it is. I start to move the tiles around to complete the picture of the bird.

Great move, Summer. Let's just stop for a nice little game before we get on with the serious business of finding Jack!

But something compels me to carry on. The game isn't that taxing; it just takes patience to get the tiles moving around in the right way so that they can meet each other in the right formation. When I get a wing completed, I have to break it up again to get the beak through from the bottom and that messes up the chest area I'd nearly finished. But then, suddenly, the pieces fall into place and the bird is complete. As soon as the last tile goes in, the tile lines vanish and the bird comes to life, flapping its wings and squawking silently, before rising up and flying out of the frame and away as though it's disappearing into the heart of the phone itself, and the animation changes so that I'm following it into wherever it's going: a new page opens up. It's a map, and the bird – now a tiny red dot – comes down to roost, a menu bar appearing at the side. Now I understand. This app is a locating device that's hidden itself on my phone in the form of a game. I've been taken into it but when I try to use the menu, a request for a password pops up and I don't know it. I can't go any further. That means I can't switch it off. That's when I know.

They're coming. They're on their way.

The realisation sends a mixture of horror and excitement coursing through me. I want to see them, I'm desperate to be with Flora again. But I'm afraid too, because I don't know what this means for Jack. Have they found Adriana and passed on my message? Or are they coming convinced that Jack is intent on killing me? I won't know until they get here. And I don't know when that will be but I have to assume it won't be long now.

Shit. I have to find Jack.

Then something occurs to me. I go to my text screen and write out a message to Flora as fast as I can. I press send and it pops to show it's been sent. Then I switch on the light, scramble out of bed and pull on my clothes.

Jack's not in the shack. I go down the rickety stairs to the beach, calling for him.

'Jack! Where are you? Are you there?'

He's sitting where I sat the other night, after I found his phone, and he's gazing out to the blackness of the sea. The only light is from the lamp I switched on in the shack, a golden shaft falling down through the dark and touching his black hair.

'Jack! There you are. Can't you sleep?' I go and sit beside him, putting my arms round him.

He shakes his head. 'No. I guess I'd rather be awake when it happens.'

319

'When what happens?'

'When they get here.'

I look at him. He's staring outwards, not looking at me. 'How do you know that?'

'I knew that if we switched your phone on, they'd be able to trace us.'

'So why did you turn it on?' I say.

He turns to look at me, his eyes glimmering in the light so it looks like they're filled with tears. 'Because we had to bring this to an end somehow. I can't take you back. I promised . . . well, you know what I promised. The only way is if they come for you.'

'What about you?' I say desperately.

He looks away again. 'We'll see. Whatever happens, that's the way it's meant to be.'

'Jack . . .' My heart swells with everything I feel for him. I can't help the overflow of compassion that makes me hurt inside. I know how he got into this mess, and that he can see no way out that doesn't destroy him in his own eyes. I also know that he's a good man and that he loves me. I know he'd never hurt me. 'I love you, Jack. I don't want to lose you. Not now.' Tears spring to my eyes. 'These days with you have been the most amazing time of my life. I've learned a lot, about myself and who I am. All these years, I've been a playgirl on the run, always moving, always partying, filling my days with endless activity. I thought I was living life to the full, but in reality I was skating over the surface, feeling nothing but fear and mistrust. Then you came along, and you made my worst nightmare into a reality. All my life I've been afraid of someone taking me – because of what happened to my sister, and because of my father's paranoia, and the way we were surrounded by guards. I couldn't trust anyone, and the one time I did . . .' I laugh ironically. 'Well, you know the rest. But now I've come alive. You've made me feel things I've never felt. You've become my friend and my lover – my amazing, beautiful lover.'

'Summer, please.' His voice is low, rasping. 'This is killing me. Do you think I don't feel the same?'

'The things that are trapping you are not real! You don't owe anyone your happiness and your life. What would your father want for you? This? He'd want you to be happy and live without fear. He had to do what he did, he didn't have a choice. When he could, he did the right thing and tried to get you away from everything that blighted his life. Don't go back there. Don't let the men who killed him ruin your life too.'

There's silence. I know this has touched him in the way I'd hoped it would. I wait, almost holding my breath, hoping that at last I'll hear what I'm so desperate to have him say – that all this is over, and he intends to walk away from the past.

Then at last he says, 'I can't break my word. I'm sorry, Summer. That's the way it is.'

The pain in my heart is overwhelming. I can't bear this. It's so wrong. I get up.

'Where are you going?' he asks.

'I can't watch you destroy yourself,' I say in a broken voice. 'I'm sorry but I can't do that.'

'Then you'd better go, because that's what going to happen.'

A sob catches in my throat and I start to walk away, not towards the shack but down the beach. As I go, I feel a vibration in my pocket, and I pull out my phone. There's a new text for me, but not from Flora. It's from Freya.

*Summer, I don't know if you'll get this but your phone
is switched on so I hope you will. It's a video attachment.
You have to show it to Jack. Then get to some place safe
away from where you are now. Pierre is coming.*

My heart races and dampness springs to my palms. I hate
Pierre. We all do. He's a thug but one my father trusts
completely. Pierre is brutal and unthinking and will do anything to stay in my father's good books. I understand why
Freya is telling me this. Jack is in serious danger if Pierre
gets here.

I shoot back a message.

Okay. When will he arrive?

Then I turn around and head back across the sand to Jack.

'Jack, we've got to get out of here. A man is on his way
who will hurt you if he gets the least opportunity.'

'That's the idea.' His voice is low and the tone bleak.

I sit down beside him. 'There's something you have to
see. Freya sent it.' I hold my phone out to him. 'Tap on the
attachment.'

He stares at it for a moment, then takes it and, shrugging,
he taps on the arrow to play the video Freya has sent.

The screen turns to a scene in a kitchen, with an old
grey-haired woman staring into the camera, her eyes
appealing, her expression desperate. She speaks, the sound
quality not great but clear enough. I can't make out what
she's saying as it's in rapid Italian, but I know what her first
words are. *Giacomo, listen to your mother . . .*

As soon as he sees her image, Jack gasps and I feel him
tense all over. The phone shakes slightly in his hand until

he grips it with both, staring intently at the woman on the screen and listening to her. Now my ear is tuning in. I've studied a little Italian, enough to follow roughly what she's saying. She calls him her darling son and begs him, begs him to . . . forget the past, let the girl go. Come home, please Giacomo, don't break my heart when I've lost so much already. We love you and need you. The old woman sobs and twists her hands. I've got tears in my eyes listening to her heart-wrenching plea. She can't continue. The focus moves to a girl sitting beside her, who looks so like Jack I know it can only be his sister. She gazes straight into the camera and says:

'Jack, you can't do this. I know what Fredo has said to you and I know what he made you promise. But Fredo is sick, very sick. The prison doctors have evaluated him and he has been classified as mentally ill with psychosis and psychopathic tendencies. He will probably not be released, not ever, Jack. You can't keep your word to him, Jack, because he's insane and what he asked of you is insane.' She leans into the camera, her face filling the screen. 'Don't be like him, Jack. Don't do this mad thing. Mama and I need you. Come home. Look – the Hammond sisters are here. We're united. We all want the same – for you and Summer to come back safe. We want to live in peace now. Okay?'

She stares into the camera for a second longer, and then I hear Freya's voice. 'Thank you, Adriana. Thank you.'

I hear the word 'Summer' from Flora's lips though I don't see her, and then the film clicks off. The screen is dark. Our loved ones have vanished, and we are alone again.

'Jack?' I whisper.

He's hunched over, his arms round his legs, rocking. I put

323

my arm round his shoulders. Then he looks up and his face is wet with tears.

'Are you okay?'

'I don't know.' He wipes quickly at his eyes. 'Fuck. I mean . . .' He frowns as though in pain. 'This changes it. I didn't think anything could. But this does.'

Overwhelming relief washes over me, and I let out a long breath. 'Really?' Hope flickers up in my heart. 'Does it really?'

He nods, the flicker of a smile showing through his pain. 'Yeah. It does.'

CHAPTER THIRTY-TWO

Summer's text arrives while Andrei is arranging the private helicopter to pick them up. Flora opens it and reads it out.

I know you're coming. Please don't hurt Jack. I love him. He's a good man.

She looks up, frightened. 'We have to get there before Pierre.'

Miles says grimly, 'I can't guarantee it. He could have quite a head start on us.'

'There must be some way of reaching him! He'll have a phone with him. Miles, do you have his number?'

Miles shakes his head. 'Not any more. It will have changed since I last had it, it's staff policy to update every few months.'

'Then Dad will have it.' Flora looks over to Freya and says, 'Come on. We'll go up and find him. He ought to know what we're doing anyway.'

A minute later, the sisters are on their way to the penthouse, leaving the men in the suite preparing for the trip. Flora is buzzing with fear, excitement and adrenalin. Summer could be back with them within a couple of hours, and it's something she longs for with all her heart. If only all the dangers and unknowns were over and they were all home safely! Freya is pale and thoughtful, still reeling from her encounter with the Guidottis. Flora saw how deeply it affected her to meet the wife of the man who effectively gave his life to save hers. As they went to leave, Freya hugged the old woman tightly and thanked her quietly. Then she said, 'I'm so sorry. We will do what we can to make it right. I promise. We will keep Jack safe.'

Now there's another promise to contend with, Flora thinks as the lift heads upwards. *We've given our word to bring Jack home. All the more reason to stop Pierre.*

The door to the suite is answered by Estella, looking vampy in white satin pyjamas. 'Evening, girls,' she says. 'What do you want?'

'Is our father there?' Freya asks coolly.

Estella stands back to reveal their father sitting on the couch in a white robe, watching the television. He turns as Freya and Flora come in.

'Dad, we need to contact Pierre right away,' Freya says, advancing into the room, her phone in her hand. 'What's his number? None of us have it.'

'Why do you want it?' their father says, frowning. 'Why not go to his room and talk to him?'

'Because he's gone,' Flora bursts out. 'He's gone to get Summer! He found Miles's tracer and it had her location on it. He's already on his way.'

Their father looks astonished. He flicks off the television with the remote, and turns to face them. 'That's why I pay him. Because he's someone I can rely on. If Murray knew Summer's location, why wasn't he going to get her? Pierre is a man of action.' He looks satisfied. 'I'm glad I've managed to get this situation sorted out.'

'You don't understand!' Flora cries passionately. 'He could hurt Jack!'

'The kidnapper?' His lip curls in a sneer. 'So what? I hope he does. And why should you care if he hurts him or not?'

Freya and Flora gape at him, both with too much to say to know where to start. Their father still feels no personal responsibility for this, when it was his actions years ago that set it all in motion. At last Freya finds her tongue. 'You owe it to the Guidotti family, Dad. Can't you see? They lost Paolo because of you. They can't lose Jack too. And Summer loves him.'

'This is sentimental rubbish,' their father says impatiently. 'I did nothing wrong. And the man took my daughter. He won't walk away without paying for it.'

'He paid all his damn life for what you did!' Freya shouts. 'The time for vengeance and bloodletting is over now. We've got to let go of all that, can't you see?' She marches up to her father. 'You're hiding behind that thug you hired. You always let everyone do your dirty work for you! Can't you see that you put your trust in the wrong people?' She looks very quickly at Estella and then away. 'You don't listen to the people who really love you. Your children. Jane-Elizabeth. We don't want anything from you, like those others. That's why we say things you don't want to hear.'

Her father goes very still. Something she says has struck home.

'Please, Dad.' Flora goes to him and takes his hand as he sits there. 'Please give us Pierre's number. Tell him that you don't want Jack hurt. We would never ask this if it weren't important.'

'Does Jane-Elizabeth want this too?' he asks quietly.

'She's a hundred per cent behind us,' Freya says firmly, sure that Jane-Elizabeth would support them.

Estella watches quietly from the sidelines and says nothing.

Slowly, their father gets up. He looks suddenly very sad and old. Going to the console table by the door, he picks up his cellphone, which is charging there. 'All right,' he says. 'I'll send him a message. Tell me what you want me to say.'

When it's time to get to the heliport, Andrei's car comes to collect them. The four of them go together. Mac has already set off in his car and is about an hour along the road. It was hoped that the late hour would mean the traffic would be lighter and the journey faster.

Flora can hardly speak. She's glad Andrei is there with her, holding her small hand tightly in his large one. He doesn't say very much but she knows he's there for her and whatever happens tonight, he'll be at her side. The helicopter is waiting for them at the top of a tower building, a large dark-green aircraft with lights flashing on the hull. When they've climbed abroad and taken their seats, strapping the four-piece belt into place in the centre of their chests and putting on the headsets, Flora notices that this is a six-seater helicopter. There is only one spare place. She hopes that is not a bad omen. Almost before they are aboard, the pilot sets the rotor blades moving and soon they are spinning overhead with a heavy thrum and the engine is roaring into life. The internal lights are switched off and the pilot radios air traffic control to alert them to his flight path. Then, with a surge of power, the craft lifts off, straight up into the air with a slight rocking motion until Flora can see the city spread out below them, a mass of roads and buildings, lights twinkling everywhere, and then with a swoop they head over the city and up towards the coast road. Now there's nothing to do but wait as they travel ever closer to Summer.

Flora wonders what her sister is doing right now. The text floats before her mind's eye. So her sister has fallen in love with Jack. According to Jimmy, Summer was bowled over by Jack right from the start. It was because of that she went on a date with him in the first place. *What happened between them? How did they change the course of their relationship?*

For a while now, Flora has had the strongest sensation that Summer is out of danger and that whatever she's doing is of her own free will. The sense of terror and helplessness that plagued her when Summer first disappeared has vanished. That can be no coincidence, she's sure of it.

As the city vanishes behind them, she thinks about her sister, so often the one left behind, the least considered. It looks as though Summer has done what so many other people couldn't do and mended the breach between the Hammond family and the Guidottis. For so long, the pain and resentment caused by what happened years ago festered and grew until it exploded into this act of madness by Jack. But something has come along to stop the cycle.

Love. What a crazy thing.

As long as they can reach Summer before Pierre does something stupid. As long as Pierre gets the message from their father and obeys him.

There's still so much that can go wrong. Flora closes her eyes and sighs. *Please let us arrive in time.*

Pierre has his foot down hard, and the car – a top-of-the-range Mercedes, which Mr Hammond buys in bulk for his staff – flies along the coast road. Georg is in the passenger seat, enjoying the ride, whooping when they take a sharp bend or when they pass another slower car, Pierre usually pounding on the horn as they zoom past.

'Cool, man!' Georg says in his Estonian accent. 'This is great!'

'I've been getting tired of that fucking hotel life and all the hysterical fucking women,' Pierre rasps. 'I needed some goddamned air, and a little action.'

Georg laughs. 'You get plenty of action, man!'

'What do you mean?'

'With that sexy piece of the boss! You fucky fucky her all the time.'

Pierre's expression freezes. 'What the hell are you talking about?' His voice is ice cold.

'C'mon. I'm not going to tell! You're a lucky guy. So, what's she like?' Georg grins conspiratorially. 'She's got a nice ass. I'm so hard for her.'

'Shut up,' Pierre commands. 'How many people are talking about this . . . fucking crap?'

'Ah!' Georg shrugs his shoulders. 'I know. I haven't told anyone. It's your business man! Anyway, she's not the type to want only the boss, is she? She's soooo sexy.'

'What made you think this?' Pierre says.

'I saw you. Back at the house one time. I was in the surveillance room and you forgot the camera, or you thought it wasn't on you, I guess. You fucked real hard, right in the garage, on the top of that car. Remember?' Georg grins again at the memory. 'Real nice. I thought about that a lot afterwards.'

'So it was on film,' Pierre says quietly, his eyes on the road.

'Maybe. I don't know. I didn't watch the tape, if that's

what you think! But listen, don't worry. Your secret is safe with me. I'm not gonna tell no one.'

'Glad to hear it.' Pierre keeps his eyes on the road, his fists tightly clenched round the steering wheel and his mouth in a firm line. 'We're nearly there. Just about twenty minutes to go.'

'What shall we do, Jack?' I ask, my arms round him as we stand on the beach.

He gazes down at me. He's at peace – really at peace – for the first time since I've known him. I can feel that the tension has seeped out of him. He looks happy too. 'We'll wait until we hear them arrive. Then I'll go out to meet them.'

'No, no . . .' I look up at him anxiously. 'I'll go out. They won't do anything to me. I'll go first and protect you.'

'Summer.' He laughs and his voice is full of love. 'You're my Joan of Arc, aren't you? Riding into battle for me, protecting me. You don't need to. I can protect myself and you. We can go out together if you want, but I'm not going to cower behind the couch until you tell me it's safe to come out, okay?' He drops a kiss on each cheek and then on the end of my nose. 'Okay?'

'Yes,' I say, filled with happiness. *Everything is going to be all right. I'm not afraid any more. I hope they hurry up.*

In the helicopter, the noise of the engines is so loud that the only way to communicate is through the headsets, with their little microphones. They are wired so that everyone can hear everyone else. There is no chance of a private conversation. So Flora hears easily enough when Andrei leans forward towards Miles and says, 'Hey, Miles – are you armed? Just in case there's trouble.'

331

Miles nods and his voice comes tinnily over the system. 'Yes. I hope it won't be necessary. But if it is, I'm ready.'

The two girls exchange frightened looks. Freya puts out her hand and Flora takes it. They squeeze a message of comfort to one another and smile in the darkness, both praying that Miles will have no need to use the gun he is most certainly carrying.

'How long now?' Freya asks.

'Just over twenty minutes,' Miles says into his microphone. 'Not long.'

Flora closes her eyes. *Twenty more minutes and this will all be over.*

Pierre stops the car before the end of the track so that they can make the last part of the journey on foot. Georg is not exactly nimble and he makes plenty of noise getting out of the car, shutting his door and following Pierre down the track.

'For fuck's sake,' hisses Pierre, 'keep quiet.'

'I can't see in the dark!' moans Georg. 'It's not easy.'

'Here.' Pierre activates the flashlight on his phone and directs the beam to the rugged track. 'Use this to see where you're going. Come on.'

They haven't gone far when they see a light through the trees, and soon Pierre can make out a clapboard beach hut, a modest holiday home built on the edge of the woods and just on to the beach that stretches out beyond. It's a good hiding place – isolated, with no neighbours for miles. Pierre pulls out his gun, glad to feel its cool, heavy weight in his hand. He always feels safer when he has it, knowing the bullets stowed in its chamber are ready to protect him at any time.

'What are we going to do?' Georg asks. 'Surprise them?'

'Drive them out of the hut and into range,' Pierre says. 'Here's what we'll do. You go around the hut over that way to the beach. Then come back round behind the hut and scout out where they are. Once you have them in sight, attack from the rear and he'll move out from the front of the house, taking the girl. I'll be waiting for them and then we'll have them both.'

'Good plan.' Georg nods enthusiastically. 'I know exactly what to do.'

'Off you go then. I'll be here waiting.'

Excited, Georg heads in the direction Pierre indicated, his heavy frame moving audibly through the trees. Pierre sighs. It's too late to worry about that now. There's only one way this can end.

We're in the sitting room when we hear it. We're so used to the silence that surrounds us, only the rhythmic pattern of the waves providing a constant low backdrop, that a new sound alerts us at once.

'Are they here?' I ask, turning my head to locate the sound. 'Where's the car?'

Jack frowns, still and listening. Then he says, 'I don't know. There was no car I heard. They would come by car, right?'

'Yes.' Then I remember the message from Freya. With the impact of the video she sent, I've forgotten the rest of it. I pull out my phone and read it. Then I look up at Jack with frightened eyes. 'Pierre is coming. Freya said we have to get somewhere safe.'

'Who's Pierre?'

'He's my father's head of security. He's like a gangster

and he's likely to be in the mood for a fight if he gets here first. He's a macho idiot and my father is impressed by that kind of thing, unfortunately.' I stand up hurriedly. 'Come on. We've got to leave here.'

Jack stands up too. 'Okay. Let me think.'

'Should we hide in the woods?' I look out through the kitchen window at the dark mass beyond. I don't like it. The woods have never frightened me before, but right now I'm feeling creeped out by them.

Jack looks down at me, his expression grave. 'I think it may be too late for that.'

'What?' My heart starts to beat faster and a nasty weakness invades my knees. 'What do you mean?'

'Listen – I'm sure I just heard someone moving around in the trees off to the right.'

We both stand very still and listen hard. There it is – the sound of twigs and branches breaking and the rustle of leaves.

'Oh shit,' I say. 'It must be Pierre. My sisters would come to the front and tell us they're there.'

'Okay.' Jack is very calm but suddenly alert. 'Let's get down to the beach. We can head up towards the cliffs.'

He goes to the balcony door in a few strides, opens it and steps out, navigating the burnt section carefully, and checks there is no one below on the sand. Then he beckons me down to follow him, moving very quietly, and starts down the wooden steps to the beach. I go after him, staying as close as I can and moving with as little sound as possible. We reach the sand, and stop. There is someone close by now, in the trees above the grassy dune between us and the woods. My stomach swoops over with fright. *What the hell is going on? What is Pierre thinking of?*

Jack pulls me very close and puts his mouth right on my ear so that he can whisper into it with no sound escaping. 'He's coming down on to the beach. If we head up it, we'll be easy targets. Let's go back up through the house and out to the car.'

I nod and we turn back towards the wooden steps we've just descended. Just as we reach them, there's a loud crashing, a yell and a man breaks out of the wood and comes running down the dune, a big black shape in the darkness. He's yelling in some language I don't understand but it sounds extremely threatening. I scream as I jump, and then dash for the stairs, Jack close behind.

'Get out the front!' he yells. 'Get the car!'

'What will you do?' I'm clattering up the stairs, my heart thudding so hard I can hardly speak.

'I'll be right behind you.'

Our pursuer has thumped across the sand and is now coming up to the stairs behind us, still shouting. I run faster, my legs feeling like lead, and reach the balcony. The door is still open and I dash inside, stopping to scrabble for the car key, before I get to the front door. I turn to see what Jack is doing and realise he's still outside.

'C'mon,' he shouts from the top of the stairs. 'Come and get me!'

'Jack!' I shout, terrified. I can hear the pounding footsteps getting closer and closer, the mad shouting louder. 'Jack!'

But it's too late. The big black shape is up on the balcony, next to Jack now, still bellowing like a bull. Jack dashes forward and gives him a mighty shove. The great shape totters backwards and out on to the balcony, where the yawning hole left by the fire waits for him. With a cry of surprise, he drops through it, plummeting down to the sand below, where he moans.

I rush to join Jack at the edge of the hole. 'Is he dead?'

Jack shakes his head. 'Dazed. He might have broken something though, or the sand might have cushioned the fall. But he won't be getting up quickly.' He turns to me, and grabs my hand. 'Let's get to the car. We've got to get away from here.'

We run to the front door and wrench it open, but we've only gone a few steps towards the car when another shape emerges from the shadows and shouts, 'Stop right there!'

We halt, staring out, and I see the rugged features and grizzled face of Pierre coming out of the darkness. He has a gun pointed right at Jack. 'Stay where you are,' he orders, advancing.

Jack and I are perfectly still for a second, and then I leap in front of him. 'Don't hurt him, Pierre!' I command. I try to sound as though I have a full expectation that Pierre will do whatever I say, even though I'm terrified. 'Jack hasn't hurt me. There's no call for any violence.'

Pierre ignores me, keeping the steel barrel of the gun pointed right at me now that I'm obscuring Jack. He gets closer and raps out, 'Go back into the house.'

'We'd better do as he says,' mutters Jack, and we both back away the way we came, through the front door. Pierre moves forward.

I feel incredibly tense, hardly able to breathe, but I try to hide it. 'Let's put the gun away, shall we, Pierre? It's just us here. There's no need for it. Jack won't try anything stupid and he's not armed. You've found me! Congratulations. I'm sure my father will be extremely grateful to you – all the

more so if this is done without any unnecessary unpleas-
antness. Okay?'

'Shut up,' he says, and waves the barrel at us again. 'Back.
Into the house.'

When we're all standing in the kitchen, he looks around.
'Where's Georg?' he says, frowning. 'I heard him come
down here.'

'Oh, I see,' Jack says, 'he was flushing us out to you. Well
– he's out there, having a little lie-down on the sand.' He
gestures to the outside. 'I told him it wasn't really the time
of day for sunbathing but he wouldn't listen.'

Pierre takes this in, and then indicates we're to keep
going backwards, to the balcony. When we're at the door,
Pierre skirts around us and sees from the light of the sitting
room that the balcony is missing at the centre. He goes
carefully to the hole and peers down. We can hear Georg
moaning now as he tries to get up. It sounds like he's in
pain.

'We should call for help,' I say brightly. 'I think he needs
a doctor.' I pull out my phone. 'I'll call someone.'

Instantly Pierre leans forward and hits my hand hard
with the gun. I scream with pain as the phone flies out of
my hand and crashes downwards, through the balcony to
the beach below.

'Hey, what the fuck are you doing!' yells Jack furiously
and he launches himself at Pierre. Pierre grapples with him
and they start to struggle, Jack trying to land punches on
the bigger man, but he's no real match for Pierre with the
older man's training in combat. In just a few moments, Jack
is overpowered. He fights back hard, hitting Pierre a right
hook that seems to stun him and following it up with a
sharp knee in the stomach. It looks for a second as though

he might be gaining an advantage, but Pierre pulls himself together and uses the handle of his gun to beat Jack about the head. Jack throws himself closer to Pierre to reduce the momentum of the blows and they wrestle together on the brink of the hole. He's trying to force Pierre out over the gap so that he'll follow Georg to the bottom, but Pierre is too strong. They waver together and I can't tell who is going to fall and then, before I can do anything at all, Pierre draws on a huge reserve of strength and forces Jack out into the gap and pushes him loose. Jack scrabbles and then is gone. I hear the thump as he hits the ground.

'Jack!' I scream and rush forward but Pierre puts out a hand and holds me back. He's standing on the edge now, looking down to the beach below where the two men lie. Then, to my horror, he points the gun downwards and fires two shots in quick succession. Georg's moaning is instantly cut off and there is no more sound from below at all.

'No!' I shout. 'No! What have you done? Jack, Jack! Oh my God, what have you done? You've killed them!'

Pierre turns to face me. His eyes are like nothing I've ever seen: black pits of expressionless evil. Real fear grips me, a curdling deep inside, a dark panic climbing my spine and numbing my brain at the same time as every nerve seems to come alive. I want to run but I'm frozen.

'I'm sorry you saw that, Summer,' he says. 'But you did. Your father wants you back alive but it's more important that he never knows about this.'

'What do you mean?' My lips are dry and can barely move. Dizzy horror is growing in my head. I know what he means. 'I won't tell.'

'Oh yes you will. I know you will. And I can't risk it anyway. I'm sorry because I always liked you best out of all of you. The oldest one is such a stroppy cow. It would be easier to shoot her. I wished they'd finished her off in Italy. But you were sweet.'

'Don't do this.' I shake my head. I can't believe I've come through so much for it to end like this. 'Don't do it, Pierre. You're making a big mistake.'

'You'll not be around to find out,' he says, with something almost like regret in his voice. He lifts the gun so the round black mouth of the barrel is pointing right at me. 'Like I said, I wish it didn't have to be like this.'

I know this must be the end. I think about Flora, and then Freya, and my father. I think of how stupid he's been to trust this man and if he'll ever know the truth. I say goodbye to my life and everyone I've known, and I think suddenly that maybe, in a second or two, I'll be with Jack again. That thought almost makes me happy. It comforts me a little anyway. I shut my eyes. I don't want my last sight to be Pierre's horrible face and that nasty, evil gun. I conjure up Jack in my mind's eye. He's smiling. Then Flora is there too. I see stars in a huge velvet sky, thousands and thousands, twinkling and glittering and filling the universe with beauty. I'm on my way to join them in eternity now.

Then I hear it. The crack of a gun, the zing of a bullet, its flight ending abruptly when it meets its target, the smell of cordite.

It's happened. My time is up.

CHAPTER THIRTY-THREE

Flora runs into the beach shack just in time to see the bullet hit Pierre right in the forehead. He stiffens, dropping his gun, and falls like a stone to the balcony, his body slumping into the stairway.

Miles relaxes, bringing down his weapon, quietly pleased with the shot that bypassed Summer and still got Pierre dead on.

Flora races past him to where Summer is standing, her eyes still closed, her body tense and waiting for the bullet she's expecting.

'Summer! Summer!' Flora's sobbing now as she embraces her sister. Summer opens her eyes, dazed and uncomprehending. 'It's okay, we're here, we're here.'

Freya is close behind her, with Andrei following. He stops to say to Miles, 'What the fuck happened?' while the sisters hug together on the balcony.

'Pierre was about to kill her.' Miles puts away his gun.

'What?' Andrei looks astonished. 'Why would he do that?'

Miles shrugs. 'Who knows? But I had to stop him.'

'Of course.' Andrei whistles lightly. 'Crazy night.'

On the balcony, Summer is regaining herself. She clutches her sisters and then says, 'Jack! He's down there! Pierre shot him.' At once she's at the hole, peering down to see him, and then she tries to climb over Pierre's body

340

so she can reach the stairs. Miles is with her in a moment, and he then races down the steps and under the balcony to where the two bodies lie on the sand. He turns the larger one over, then looks up to the anxious faces bent over the hole.

'It's Georg,' he says. 'He's been shot clean through the head.'

Summer has scrambled over Pierre and is half-falling down the stairs in her hurry to get to the beach. 'Jack!' she calls. When she reaches him, Miles is already checking his vital signs. He looks up at Summer.

'He's unconscious. I think he hit his head when he landed. He's out cold.'

'But has he been shot?' Summer is sobbing now, reaching out to him, touching his hair and holding his hand. 'Jack, oh Jack . . .'

'He seems stable. I can't see where he's been shot – if he's been shot. We'll strap him up and airlift him straight to hospital. He'll get the best possible care. Where's the gun?'

Summer looks up confused. 'What gun?'

'The gun Jack used to shoot Georg.'

'He didn't. Pierre did.'

Miles is shocked. 'Pierre did?'

Summer nods. 'Just like that. Without any warning. I got the feeling that was why he was going to kill me. Because I'd seen it.'

Miles looks thoughtful. Just then Jack moans and shifts. All attention is on him again. Andrei is on the phone to the pilot, to alert him to the return flight with the extra passenger, and the girls join Summer on the beach, unable to be far away from her for long.

Summer can't answer their questions. She's too dazed and too concerned with Jack. When Mac arrives, walking through the door in a casual manner but taking everything in at once, she is just beginning to regain her self-possession but still too worried about Jack to concentrate on much else. Mac wanders out to the balcony and looks around.

'Well, someone had quite a barbecue out here!' he remarks, and takes in the bodies, Pierre's on the balcony and Georg's down on the sand. 'Oh dear. This is a fine mess, isn't it? Who knows why Pierre would do something like that . . . I have no idea.' He shakes his head and clicks his tongue. Then he sighs. 'Still. We've got Summer back and it looks like Jack will be in the doctors' hands in a very short time. It's a good outcome.' No one appears to be looking at him or paying any attention and he says again, 'Yes, sirree. A very good outcome.'

The pilot takes Summer, Flora, Andrei and Jack back to the city in the helicopter. Andrei has already made arrangements for them to land on the roof of the best private hospital he can find. Mac makes the calls to the police and waits for them to arrive so that he can fill them in on what's happened. Miles will have to be there too, to explain how Pierre came to be shot.

'Mr Hammond hates publicity,' he says to Mac. Freya is curled up on the sofa, recovering from the night's events, while the two men stand on the balcony, regarding the two bodies with solemnity.

'Well he might,' Mac replies. 'But he's got to learn that his money doesn't put him above the law. If he'd realised that a while ago, this might never have happened.'

Miles looks at him oddly. 'Do you know why this happened, Mac? Pierre shooting Georg?'

'I have my suspicions,' Mac says knowingly. 'I think Georg stumbled on a little secret that Pierre would have liked kept concealed.'

'What secret is that?' Miles says, his eyebrows raised.

'Well, I had a hunch and let's just say that I discovered it to be true. Pierre was engaging in a little hanky-panky with Mr Hammond's girlfriend. Georg found out and must have made the mistake of telling Pierre he knew. He didn't realise, I think, quite how fanatical Pierre was about keeping on Mr Hammond's good side.'

'How did you find out it was true?'

'A little light bugging of the penthouse can reveal many things,' Mac says with a smile. 'It's as well to be prepared.'

Miles shakes his head. 'Well, it certainly explains a few things. Like how Estella was able to infiltrate private email in the house, and access secret family files, so she could disclose whatever she wanted to the press. And how she got security staff to carry out her dirty work, like the time Flora got photographed with Andrei.' He laughs lightly then stops. 'It's not funny. It's awful. Poor Georg. But I did wonder how Hammond managed to keep a girl like Estella satisfied. Obviously he doesn't.'

Mac nods slowly and says, 'I'm going to make a little call later. Let's just say, I don't think Miss Estella will be slow in packing her suitcase.'

Miles slaps him on the back. 'You are going to be popular around here.'

'Oh I don't want thanks,' Mac says quickly. 'I'm a modest fellow. I don't even want anyone to know so I'd be grateful if you kept it to yourself. But I don't like rudeness, you see. And that lady was downright rude. There's just no need for it.'

Miles laughs properly now. 'This is a lesson in manners she'll never forget.'

EPILOGUE

Freya feels as though she can breathe again. The bright, fresh, cool air of Scotland tingles her nostrils and brings her back to life.

'Glad to be home?' Miles asks, coming up behind her as she stands at the window of their cottage and nuzzling into her neck.

'Very glad.' She turns to him. 'I feel like I've walked through fire.'

'But you've come out the other side,' he reminds her. 'And don't forget our lesson about the elements – fire is purifying.'

She gives him a smile. 'How could I forget?' She sighs. 'I feel as though I went through it all again. The kidnap. The loss. The shock and the fear.'

'You did. But this time, with a happy ending. Your sister is alive. The Guidottis still have their son, and the compensation your father has agreed. He's even taken you all back to his bosom.'

Freya frowns, wrapping her hands over his where they clasp her. 'I know. That was so weird. I mean, I never imagined Estella would just get up and go like that. Without any real explanation. After everything she's done.'

'It's strange,' Miles agrees. 'But for the best, don't you think?'

'Oh yes. Really . . . for the best. I'm happy here though.

Maybe Dad will come out and visit us instead of making us go to him all the time. I'd really like that.'

'I'm sure he will.' Miles kisses her again. 'You seem happier. Calmer.'

'I am.' She sighs again, but with content. 'Life is good now. Those ghosts have been laid to rest. I want to look forward.' She turns and he takes her into his strong embrace. They kiss deeply and then she says, 'My future is with you.'

He strokes her face and says, 'I know. I wouldn't have it any other way.'

On the Hammond private plane, Mr Hammond is staring out at the blanket of clouds stretching away as far as the eye can see.

'Are you all right?' Jane-Elizabeth ventures. She's in the large leather seat opposite his, reading a book but, as always, with one eye on her boss.

Hammond sighs. 'I'm fine, thank you, Jane-Elizabeth. It's been a very odd time.'

'It certainly has,' she agrees. 'It's going to take a little while to adjust.'

'My girls are good girls, aren't they?' he asks suddenly.

'Oh, yes. The best. Wonderful girls,' she says fondly. Then adds, 'Like their mother. And a credit to you.'

Hammond nods and looks out of the window again. At last he says, 'I've been a fool, haven't I, Jane-Elizabeth? I let them all take me in. First Pierre, then Estella. I trusted them over my own daughters, and look where it got me. If I hadn't let her persuade me to send the girls away like that, Summer would never have been in danger. I don't know what got into me.' He stares at the table, his expression remorseful, his face suddenly older-looking. 'I'd deserve it if they never spoke to me again.'

'Of course they will. They love you,' Jane-Elizabeth says. 'You're their father and you always will be, no matter what. They'd stand by you through thick and thin.'

Tears fill his eyes. 'You're right. I can't believe I didn't see it.' Then he says vehemently, 'I'm going to restore their allowances and everything they had before I took it away!'

Jane-Elizabeth raises her eyebrows almost imperceptibly. 'You could . . . but I think they will turn you down. All three of them. From what I understand they want the chance to work. Summer told me she wanted to make something of her role at the Foundation. I wouldn't be surprised if that's what she chooses to do. Flora wants to make acting her life. Freya is determined to help Miles set up his business in the Highlands. I have a feeling they might raise a family out there, where it's so peaceful and beautiful.'

Hammond stares at her, astonished. Then he says in a tone that's almost frightened, 'Have I lost them?'

'No.' She smiles back. 'Not at all. By setting them free, you'll only make it more certain they always come back. As long as you love them.'

'You're right. I need to be a proper father to them. I haven't been that for a while, even though I thought I was doing my best.' He thinks for a moment, frowning. 'Is it true that Summer really has fallen in love with that man? The villain who kidnapped her?'

'That's what she told me,' Jane-Elizabeth says simply. 'And I believe her. She was in pieces when he was taken to the hospital. From what she said to me, they went through a lot together.'

'But she can't!' he exclaims. 'She can't really want to be with him . . . after all that . . . can she?'

Jane-Elizabeth gives him a stern look. 'Now – I thought we decided that you weren't going to dictate the girls' love lives to them any more? Let them make their own choices. Besides, I think we all know that the story is more complicated than that. Don't we?'

Hammond looks shamefaced, remembering his own part in the motives for Summer's abduction. At last he says, 'You're a wise woman, Jane-Elizabeth. I think I'm learning my lesson. You'll have to pull me up if I ever forget it. Tell me – that girl, Estella – she was never going to stay with me, was she? Not really. Not for good.'

'I don't know. Perhaps she was.' Jane-Elizabeth speaks carefully but it's clear that she wouldn't have bet on it.

He shrugs. 'Ah well. No use thinking about it. She's gone and I wish her well. She's got enough from me to keep her comfortable.' He looks over to Jane-Elizabeth with a wan smile. 'So it's just you and me. For now.'

'Yes,' she says comfortably. 'Just us. Shall we have some tea?'

Flora pulls away from Andrei, her body damp with sweat, feeling replete.

'Oh,' she sighs. 'That was beautiful.'

'Mmm.' Andrei rolls on to his back and stretches. 'I can't believe that however much I make love to you, it's never enough.'

'Good.' She rolls on to her front and drops little kisses on his chest. 'I want to thank you.'

'You're welcome.' He grins raffishly, his blue eyes sparkling.

'No . . . for doing this. For staying in LA for as long as Summer needs us.'

Andrei shrugs. 'It's fine. I can work here. I'm even looking into some investments here. And I like to acquire new properties.'

She laughs. 'Only you could get a fully furnished luxury apartment in the best part of town within days.'

'Only me, or anyone else with the money to do it.' He chuckles. 'That makes things easier.'

'Yes. But you understand that I need to be with Summer right now. And that means everything.'

'I will be where you are,' Andrei says simply. 'We have tried to be apart and we both hate it. So. We'll be together. That's the end of it.'

'Life according to Andrei,' Flora says, laughing. 'Very straightforward.' She kisses him again. 'I adore you.'

'I worship you.' His mouth finds hers and they kiss again, ready to fire up their passion once more.

I'm not the only one at Jack's bedside. His mother, Monica, is often here too, and Adriana. All of us keeping a vigil on the man we love. Jack is going to be okay, they tell us. He took a bullet to the shoulder, not where Miles could see it when he first examined him. It left a tiny entry wound and a huge exit, spilling dark blood into the sand that we only saw when we moved him. Fortunately it missed his spine and vital organs but he lost a lot of blood. We bound him tightly with ripped-up sheets before he was taken on board the helicopter and flown back to the hospital where he is now recovering. Besides the bullet wound he has a nasty crack on his head where he hit the ground.

'Not the ground,' Jack puts in when I say this. 'I hit that man.'

'Georg.'

'Yeah – Georg. He must have been built of brick. I knocked myself out on him.'

'Or the rock that was lying next to him,' I suggest.

'Maybe that. It doesn't really matter now.' Jack smiles at me.

Monica and Adriana are getting lunch, and I'm here on my own with him, my hand in his.

'I want to get out of here,' he says tetchily. 'I'm going crazy in this place.'

'You need to get better.' I smile at him. 'Do you know how lucky you are to be alive?'

He's a different Jack now. Still the same in all the important ways, but without the brooding despair I sensed when I first met him. He's more gorgeous than ever, even with a bandage round his head. Despite his wound, he's crackling with energy, eager to get on with life. 'I knew I was doing a crazy thing when I decided to take on Pierre,' he grins.

'He almost killed you.'

'He tried to hurt you,' Jack says, his eyes flashing at the memory. 'That wasn't going to happen.'

I've seen this man in so many guises: broken and despairing, as well as fierce and protective. I've seen him angry and cold, and I've seen his eyes dark with lust and his face full of tenderness and love. Now he's happy, even though he's in hospital and too weak to walk, and I can't wait until he can take me in his arms and show me how much he loves me.

Sometimes he pretends to grumble and kids me around. 'I am never kidnapping anyone again!' he complains, as he opens his eyes from a sleep to see me at his bedside. 'Honestly, one little kidnapping and I'm never going to get rid of you!'

'Exactly,' I say, kissing him. 'You took the wrong girl, mister. You can't pick me up and put me down according to your moods.'

'Ah,' he says, unable to hide his smile. 'I'll just have to put up with you then.'

Not long after that strange final night, after Andrei had set his people to work clearing everything up and sorting things out with the authorities, I finally saw Jimmy and Charlie again.

'How was the date?' Jimmy said, smiling all over his face as he rushed up to hug me. 'Did you have fun?'

'Sure – I didn't want to leave!' I joked back and hugged him in return. Despite the banter, I could feel the emotion in the way he hugged me tight and the tears in his eyes when he looked at me.

'I'm so happy you're home, baby,' he whispered every now and then, grabbing my hand and clasping it in his as though he never wanted to let it go.

Charlie burst right out into tears when he saw me and wouldn't stop apologising until I told him firmly to stop.

'But I feel so responsible!' he wailed, until I pointed out that now it was all over, I had no regrets.

'The only thing that scares me is that I might not have met Jack,' I insisted. When he finally believed me and calmed down, we talked about the whole episode from every angle over spritzers and potato chips. They were a great audience, gasping at the tense moments, melting almost visibly at the tender ones.

'You mean you nearly died in a *fire*?' shrieked Jimmy, clutching his armchair. 'On top of everything else that happened? My God, you are a drama magnet!'

'So . . . you and Jack . . .' Charlie leaned forward, his eyes misty. 'Was he . . . good?'

I blushed violently, then said frankly, 'Very good.'

'I'm not surprised,' he murmured and sighed.

Jimmy looked at me with the kind of expression a protective older brother might have. 'I hope this isn't some kind of Stockholm syndrome,' he said almost sternly. 'He better have your best interests at heart.'

'He does. I really believe that,' I said. 'I hope you'll give him a chance.'

Jimmy considered for a moment. 'I guess I will,' he said finally. 'Though it's re-established my faith in my gut instinct. I knew there was something odd about him.'

Charlie leaned forward and put a hand on my arm. 'But what are you going to do now, Summer?'

'I'm going to stick around,' I said slowly. 'Flora's going to stay out here for a while too. I'm going to rent a house – something simple, maybe near you guys. Flora's going to share with me for a while.'

'And Andrei?' said Charlie, his eyes wide. 'That won't be exactly cosy, will it? Imagine sharing a bathroom with a tough-as-nails Russian billionaire! I mean, you wouldn't want to complain when he hogged the shower!'

Jimmy grinned. 'I don't know. At least you won't run out of vodka.'

I said laughing, 'No, not sharing with Andrei. He's getting his own apartment and Flora will move in with him when Jack gets out of hospital. And then I'm going to work.'

'Really?' Jimmy looked pleased. 'So you might stay for a while? What will you do for a job?'

'I'm going to develop my role in the Hammond Foundation. Help underprivileged kids. See what I can offer at the Hall, maybe.' I smiled at Charlie. 'I want to make a difference if I can.'

'That's great,' Jimmy said, as Charlie clapped his hands and whooped with pleasure. 'Really great.' Then, after a moment, he asked, 'Does this mean your dad is reinstating you all? Now that the bitch queen is off the scene?'

'It's his aim, I think. But I don't know if that's what we want. Not yet, anyway. We need to earn our stripes.'

Jimmy raised his glass. 'Wow – here's to the Hammond sisters! I call that ballsy. And here's to you. And the gorgeous Jack. Maybe something good can come out of all of this.'

Happiness filled my chest until it almost cracked under my ribs. 'I hope so, Jimmy. I want that more than anything.'

I love being with Jack every minute I can. At first it was awkward being around his mother and sister. I found it hard to forget that our family had caused theirs so much pain. But we soon got used to it, united in our concern for Jack. Then one day, Monica stopped me in the corridor outside Jack's room. She had tears in her eyes.

'I want to say . . . this is good. It is healing. It unites our families in happiness. Not sadness any more.'

I know what she means. Jack and I are the triumph of love over hate. All three of us sisters have fallen for men that my father had problems accepting, leading me to wonder who exactly would have been his ideal candidate, if one ever existed, but Jack is the one who poses the most challenges. His presence is going to remind my father of what happened all those years ago. I only hope that he will be able to see it for the good thing it is.

When we are alone late at night, in the hospital room with its view of the sparkling city, Jack tells me what I mean to him and how I've changed his life.

'I was longing for you, though I never knew it. I thought I hated you and that was what drew me to you.' He gazes at me intensely, making my stomach twist and swoop with pleasure when I see that look in his eyes.

'I was longing for you too.' I tighten my grip on his hand.

'You'll always have me. You have my word. And I love you.'

I kiss him softly, slowly, deliciously. He's a man of his word. I know that for sure. My sweet, brave, faithful Jack.

ACKNOWLEDGEMENTS

With all my grateful thanks to everyone at Hodder, particularly to the ever patient and understanding Francesca Best. With special thanks to Justine, my copyeditor, and Jacqui, my proofreader. Thanks to the friends at Fischer Verlag, Cordelia and Tatjana. And to all the readers who've shared the adventures of Freya, Flora and Summer through their seasons. Your encouragement has been amazing.

SM

Have you read the first novels in Sadie Matthews's exhilarating, intoxicating Seasons trilogy?

Season of Desire
Seasons Trilogy: Book One

Freya Hammond is used to people fulfilling her every whim. Wealthy and spoiled, she lives a butterfly existence of fashion and parties and is accustomed to getting her own way. Which is why the new bodyguard is riling her. Miles Murray is ex-SAS and obeys her instructions with barely repressed scorn. She can sense that he doesn't think much of her.

The Hammonds have been staying at their luxurious retreat high in the Alps. Now Miles is driving Freya to the airport but the rapidly worsening weather and a near-miss with a dangerously driven jeep causes him to lose control, and sends the car plummeting off the side of the mountain.

When Freya comes to, she is lying on the freezing ground, Miles beside her. The car is a mangled mess far below them. Now Freya needs Miles to save her life. Using all his survival skills, Miles manages to locate an old shepherd's hut and get them both there despite Freya's twisted ankle. Rescue will surely come before too long . . . but until then Freya is no longer in control. The tension between them is soon at fever pitch as she tries to dominate a man who no longer obeys her orders.

And when rescue does come, how will they return to their old life of mistress and bodyguard after what has happened between them?

Out now in paperback and ebook

HODDER

SADIE MATTHEWS

Season of Passion
Seasons Trilogy: Book Two

Flora Hammond is trying to make her dream of being an actress come true by studying her craft in Paris. But she cannot escape her privileged background and the paranoia of her wealthy father who is obsessive about his daughters' safety. The situation is not helped by the fact that Flora's older sister, Freya, has just run off with her bodyguard.

Drawn into the family scandal, Flora tries to make peace between the warring factions. In the meantime, her path crosses with that of a mysterious businessman, Andrei Dubrovski, and there is an instant attraction between them. Even though Flora is warned off getting involved with him, she doesn't think she can resist.

Is Freya right when she claims that their father's girlfriend Estella is engaged in a campaign against the sisters? And where has Freya disappeared to? Does Estella have the power to split the family apart, even to the point of breaking the bond between Flora and her twin sister, Summer?

As Flora's obsession with Andrei grows, it's clear that where passion is concerned, the heart has its reasons . . .

Out now in paperback and ebook

HODDER

Have you read the *After Dark* series by Sadie Matthews?
Deeply intense and romantic, provocative and sensual,
it will take you to a place where love and sex are liberated
from their limits. It begins with:

Fire After Dark

It started with a spark . . .

Everything changed when I met Dominic. My heart had just been
broken, split into jagged fragments that can jigsaw together to
make me look enough like a normal, happy person.

Dominic has shown me a kind of abandonment I've never known
before. He takes me down a path of pure pleasure, but of pain,
too – his love offers me both lightness and dark. And where he
leads me, I have no choice but to follow.

Out now in ebook, paperback and audio

HODDER

Find your next delicious read at

THE
Book
BAKERY

The place to come for cherry-picked monthly reading recommendations, competitions, reading group guides, author interviews and more.

Visit our website to see which great books we're serving up this month.

www.TheBookBakery.co.uk

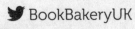